Peter Burton was born in 1945. He has written for a wide range of newspapers and magazines – including the *Independent*, *The Times*, *Disc*, *Melody Maker*, *New Musical Express*, *Sounds*, *The Stage*, *After Dark*, *Adam International Review*, *Books & Bookmen*, the *Literary Review*, *Gay News* and *Gay Times* (he is Literary Editor). His work has appeared in America, Australia, France, Germany and Italy. He has written, co-authored or contributed to more than thirty books, including *Parallel Lives, Amongst the Aliens: Some aspects of a gay life*, *The Art of Gay Love* and *The Boy from Beirut and Other Stories* (with Robin Maugham). He is commissioning editor for Millivres Books, specialists in contemporary gay fiction.

The Mammoth Book of

GAY SHORT STORIES

Edited by

Peter Burton

Carroll & Graf Publishers, Inc.
NEW YORK

Carroll & Graf Publishers, Inc.
260 Fifth Avenue
New York
NY 10001

Selection, introduction and editorial
matter copyright © Peter Burton 1997

First published in the UK by Robinson Publishing 1997

First Carroll & Graf edition 1997

The moral right of the editor has been asserted.

ISBN 0–7867–0430–6

Printed and bound in the EC

10 9 8 7 6 5 4 3 2 1

CONTENTS

ACKNOWLEDGEMENTS

Thanks to Sebastian Beaumont and Simon Lovat who (as usual) put the entire manuscript onto disk; John Budden for supplying a copy of Simon Raven's "The Amateur"; Timothy d'Arch Smith for so willingly dealing with queries – not least about print runs of obscure texts; and Luke Stoneham – whose assistance with the more mundane aspects of my life makes the professional side run all the more smoothly.

Individual stories remain the copyright of their respective authors.

Previous publishing details for the following stories are listed below:

THIS IS SERIOUS by James Robert Baker is taken from *Testosterone*, a novel-in-progress.

THE VOYEUR by Peter Baker first appeared in *Gay Times*, April 1985.

MINERVA'S RING by Diesel Balaam first appeared in *Him*, August 1984.

RIVER by Peter Burton first appeared in *Jeremy*, Vol 1, Number 9, London, 1970.

WHATEVER HAPPENED TO THE GIRL NEXT DOOR? by Matthew Butler first appeared in *Spartacus*, No 9, Brighton, 1969.

YOUNG HUNKS ON COKE by Toni Davidson first appeared in *Queer Words*, No 4, Aberystwyth, 1995.

PURPLE PROSE IN SOHO by Paul de Havilland first appeared in *Queer Words*, No 3, Aberystwyth, 1995.

A DAY IN THE COUNTRY by Gary Dunne is taken from *Shadows on the Dance Floor*, published by Blackwattle Press, NSW, Australia, 1992.

KISSING IN THE WHEAT by Richard K. Edwards first appeared in *Queer Words*, No 1, Aberystwyth, 1995.

SHADOWS by Damon Galgut was first published in *Small Circles of Beings*, published by Constable & Co, 1988.

SNOWFALL by Joseph Hansen was first published over the pseudonym James Colton in the magazine *Tangents*. It was reprinted in *The Corrupter*, still over the name James Colton, Greenleaf Classics, San Francisco, 1968. It first appeared over the name Joseph Hansen in *Different: An anthology of homosexual short stories*, Bantam Books, New York, 1974.

DIRTY STORIES by Tim Herbert is taken from *Angel Tails*, published by Blackwattle Press, NSW, Australia, 1992.

SOMEONE IS CRYING IN THE CHATEAU DE BERNE by Andrew Holleran was first published in *Christopher Street*, New York, USA, 1980.

THE STEAM PARLOUR by Witi Ihimaera is taken from *Nights in the Gardens of Spain*, published by Secker & Warburg/Reed Publishing, Auckland, New Zealand, 1995.

A VISIT TO THE GENERAL by Francis King is taken from *So Hurt and Humiliated*, published by Longmans, 1949.

BILLY & BUD by Michael Leech first appeared in *Gay Times*, March 1989.

GINGER ROGERS'S PRIVATE COLLECTION by Robert Leek is taken from *Sweet and Sour Cocktails*, published by Reed Publishing, Auckland, New Zealand, 1993.

THE LAST PIECE OF TRADE IN AMERICA by John Mitzel is taken from *On the Line: New gay fiction*, published by The Crossing Press, Trumansburg, NY, USA, 1981.

THE WAR OVER JANE FONDA by Robert Patrick is a revised version of previously published story.

A SON'S STORY by Tony Peake first appeared in *Winter's Tales*, Constable & Co, 1993.

HUNTER by Felice Picano is taken from *On the Line: New gay fiction*, published by The Crossing Press, Trumansburg, NY, USA, 1981.

THE AMATEUR by Simon Raven first appeared in *Turf Accounts: A connoisseur's racing anthology*, published by Gollancz/Witherby, 1994.

EMBRACING VERDI by Philip Ridley is taken from *Flamingoes in Orbit*, published by Hamish Hamilton, 1990.

THREE FRIENDS by Jerry Rosco first appeared in *On the Line: New gay fiction*, published by The Crossing Press, Trumansburg, NY, USA, 1981.

PROSTITUTION by Aiden Shaw is a revised version of a previously published story.

NYMPH AND SHEPHERD by Colin Spencer was first published in the *London Magazine*, Vol 6, Number 8, August 1959.

THE GREEK AMBASSADOR by John Stapleton was first published in *Gay News*, Number 248, 1982.

THE MAN IN THE DARK by Mansel Stimpson was first published in *Gay News*, number 247, 1982.

OUTING by Peter Wells is taken from *Dangerous Desires*, published by Reed Publishing, Auckland, New Zealand, 1991.

Unless otherwise stated, stories were originally published in London. All other stories were specially written for this collection.

The Editor dedicates this book to
the memory of
Jeremy J. Beadle, Steven Corbin,
Dave Royle and Tom Wakefield
who, had they not died untimely,
would have been contributors.

ESCAPE FROM THE SHADOWS

An introductory note of explanation

From the moment of inception, it was my intention that *The Mammoth Book of Gay Short Stories* should encompass only work published since the end of the Second World War in 1945 as, for me at least, the conclusion of that conflict marks a watershed after which the precarious pre-war *status quo* could not be regained.

The liberty and licence which had prevailed in and perhaps because of impossible circumstances could not be entirely banished with the cessation of hostilities and although the heightened sexuality which appeared to be a direct consequence of the imminence of death could be restrained – those restraints were destined for demise in the not too distant future.

"For most of 1940 London by night was like one of those dimly lit parties that their hosts hope are slightly wicked," Quentin Crisp wrote in *The Naked Civil Servant*. "In a cosy gloom young men and women strolled arm in arm along Picadilly murmuring, 'It's not as bad tonight as last night, is it?' Policemen allowed themselves a certain skittishness. 'Don't care, huh?' they cried as I passed them sheltering in doorways. Taxi-drivers unbent so far as to take one part of the way home free of charge. As soon as bombs started to fall, the city became like a paved double bed. Voices whispered suggestively to you as you walked along; hands reached out if you stood still and in dimly lit trains people carried on as they once behaved in taxis . . ." Once forbidden fruit had been tasted it became familiar and there was no returning it to the realms of out-of-reach.

Working to a self-imposed brief which spanned but fifty years of gay writing would have allowed me to trawl through the work of some great late twentieth century writers. But that brief was refined even further by my decision to restrict the anthology to writers whose first language was English. And even that refinement was further honed. This final constriction was brought about by the deaths of the co-dedicatees of this book.

It had been my intention to ask Jeremy J. Beadle, Steven Corbin, Dave Royle and Tom Wakefield to contribute to this book – indeed Jeremy J. Beadle and Tom Wakefield had already promised a story apiece. Suddenly this quartet of deaths provoked me to want to produce an anthology which at once spanned the past fifty years of gay experience as written by writers in English and which utilized contributors who were alive at the time of the completion of the book.

This final narrowing of choice of contents for *The Mammoth Book of Gay Short Stories* meant that it became impossible to avail myself of stories by such Americans as James Baldwin, John Horne Burns, Truman Capote, John Cheever, Christopher Isherwood (British-born, long-since become an American citizen) or Tennessee Williams; it precluded the use of stories by such brilliant Australians as Martin Boyd, Sumner Locke Elliott, Hal Porter and Patrick White; it removed from my area of choice work by such British writers as Noël Coward, Rhys Davies, E. M. Forster, L. P. Hartley, C. H. B. Kitchin, Robin Maugham, W. Somerset Maugham, David Rees and Angus Wilson.

Ultimately of course this did not worry me. We have long since escaped from the shadows of our past (to borrow the telling but not entirely honest title of Robin Maugham's autobiography *Escape From the Shadows*). Classic stories by distinguished authors – Christopher Isherwood's "On Reugen

Island", Henry James' "The Pupil" and D. H. Lawrence's "The Prussian Officer" – are easily found. Even the more arcane – John Francis Bloxam's "The Priest and the Acolyte" or Eric, Count Stenbock's "The True Story of a Vampire" for example – have now been so frequently reprinted as to make them almost commonplace. Certainly these two stories both dating from 1894 have more latterly received readerships far, far larger than those for which they were originally written. "The Priest and the Acolyte" first appeared in the single issue of the Oxford undergraduate magazine *The Chameleon*, published in an edition limited to one hundred copies; "The True Story of a Vampire" was originally published in Stenbock's *Studies of Death*, of which only a small edition was ever printed.

Of course the archaeology of writing about men-loving-men (such terms as "urning", "uranian" and "homosexual" are nineteenth century; terms such as "gay" and "queer" were coined in the twentieth century and are thus rather anomalous when used in connection with earlier historical periods) has long established it as an integral part of literary tradition – tracing manifestations back as far as the relationship between Gilgamesh and Enkidu in the Mesopotamian *The Epic of Gilgamesh* (*c*. 2000 BC); visual texts from Ancient Egypt, in the Homeric epics, *The Satyricon* of Petronius (perhaps the first "gay" novel) and a whole library of writing from the ancient world. "We know that homosexuality flourished," Colin Spencer wrote in his exhaustive and individual *Homosexuality: A history*. "However, with archaic societies, as in the ancient world, there was simply sexuality. The only disgrace connected with sexual expression concerned the type of act and the status, not the sex, of your partner . . ."

Thus not only have men-loving-men always been *there*, they have equally been *there* in world literature. There can be no mistaking the sentiments expressed by the Elizabethan poet Richard Barnfield in "The Affectionate Shepheard":

Scarce had the morning starre hid from the light
Heavens crimson canopie with stars bespangled.

> But I began to rue th' unhappy sight
> Of that faire boy that had my hart intangled';
> Cursing the time, the place, the sense, the sin;
> I came, I saw, I viewed, I slipped in.

Barnfield's is an honest expression of simple lust most elegantly phrased. Unlike too many writers today, he is not attempting to disguise his feelings as something entirely cerebral. That directness has been replicated by a large number of stories in this collection – the writers whose work appears here are fully aware that the centres that make someone homosexual, gay, queer (to use the three most universal terms of the past fifty years) are located above the neck *and* below the waist.

By the late nineteenth century (in the years immediately before Oscar Wilde's arrest, trials and imprisonment for committing acts of "gross indecency with another male person"), Uranian literature was flourishing. The chronological organization of Brian Reade's *Sexual Heretic: Male homosexuality in English Literature from 1850 to 1900* gives a good indication of just how much was being published – a good deal of it still in circulation today. *The Sins of the Cities of the Plain or the Recollections of a Mary-Ann* had appeared in 1881 and may be the first known example of a still popular sub-genre: the autobiography of a male prostitute. The author was an Irish 'Mary-Ann' called John or Jack Saul whose career appears to have spanned several years. He appeared as a witness for the defence in the Cleveland Street libel case in 1890 when a British peer won an action against a newspaper editor who had published an article in which it was alleged that the peer frequented a by-then notorious male brothel. *Sins of the Cities of the Plain* is but one of several instances of Victorian homoerotica to have been reissued in recent years (*Teleny*, 1890, is another); both have been reworked, however, and issued in editions evidently particularly aimed at those wanting a "one-handed read".

Even Wilde's very public downfall didn't halt the flow of homosexual literature – though perhaps authors and publishers may have become a tad more circumspect.

If there had been no need for such circumspection, it is

interesting to speculate upon the directions the careers of such novelists as E. F. Benson, E. M. Forster, W. Somerset Maugham and Hugh Walpole *might* have taken. Whilst a young man, Maugham was an intimate of many survivors of the Wilde circle – Ada Leverson, Robert Ross and Reginald Turner, for example. It is pretty evident that he must have hovered at least at the periphery of that circle while Wilde was still alive. But the debacle of 1895 deeply scarred him and many others. Those homosexual characters who do appear in his novels are either excessively flamboyant (Elliot Templeton in *The Razor's Edge*) or covert (the opium-smoking Doctor in *The Narrow Corner*).

E. F. Benson, who spent time in Egypt and Greece with Lord Alfred Douglas, seems to have been a monument of respectability who yet managed to produce a series of novels which were at the very least intensely homoerotic – most famously in his public school novel *David Blaize* (1916), but also in his novels of the supernatural. Witness the following passage from *The Inheritor* (1930):

> Strolling along the shore towards them came a strange and beautiful figure, a boy of seventeen or eighteen, naked but for a pair of tattered breeches, with his skin tanned to iodine brown by the sun and the sea. A wreath of ivy and wild-vine was twined in his yellow hair, and to his mouth he held a reed-pipe on which he blew squealing sounds . . .

The social-climbing Walpole (famously lampooned by Maugham in *Cakes and Ale*) was altogether more cautious in his books. The two novels with the most claim to containing homosexual characters are *Fortitude* (1913) and *The Killer and the Slain* (1942) – though claim could be made for *The Old Ladies* (1924) as it is perfectly possible to "read" the three old women of the title as three feuding old queens.

And what would E. M. Forster have produced had he been able to write more honestly? Certainly *Where Angels Fear to Tread* could have posed some fascinating problems had Lilia Charles been *Len* Charles. Maybe he wouldn't have bothered with the naive and sentimental *Maurice*? Never satisfactorily concluded and published posthumously because (one suspects)

Forster knew the damage it would cause his reputation *as a novelist*.

On either side of the Atlantic in the years leading up to the Second World War there appeared any number of novels and short stories which had an especial appeal to homosexuals.

Blair Niles' *Strange Brother* was published in America in 1931 and in Britain in 1932. Reissued in Britain in 1991, my Introduction defines the book as "an invaluable Baedeker to the gay New York of more than half-a-century ago".

Amongst other titles of note are Sherwood Anderson's *Winesberg, Ohio* (1919), notably for the much anthologized story "Hands": Beverley Nichols' *Prelude* (but one in an ever growing shelf of novels based in public schools in various parts of the world) appeared in 1920; Carl Van Vechten's *The Blind Bow Boy* was published in 1923; Herman Melville's posthumously published *Billy Budd* in 1924; *The Strange Confession of Monsieur Mountcairn*, was published anonymously and privately printed in an edition of seven hundred and fifty copies in 1928; Andre Tellier's *Twilight Men* ("This edition is limited to one thousand privately printed for subscribers only by T. Werner Laurie Limited" reads a note on the title page) appeared in 1933 and Kenneth Matthews' *Aleko* was published in 1934.

Even during the Second World War (1939–1945) and despite paper restrictions, literature by men who were homosexual writing often startlingly explicit texts was published. An obvious example is the autobiographical fiction by Denton Welch (an important influence on William S. Burroughs), all of whose novels appeared between 1943 and 1950.

Also intensely important in promoting homosexual literature were a number of essentially literary magazines, including *Horizons, Penguin New Writing, The London Magazine* and the *Evergreen Review*. There were also a small number of gay publications which percolated through the world: *Der Kreis*, founded in 1932 and running until 1967, Swiss-based, published in English, French and German; *One*, the magazine of the American homosexual law reform group The Mattachine Society.

The period covered by this collection spans exactly fifty years; Francis King's "A Visit to the General" was written in 1946;

Neil Bartlett's "Caesar's Gallic Wars" was completed during the Christmas holidays, 1996. And although the bulk of the stories come from Britain and the United States, Australia, New Zealand and South Africa are represented by three stories apiece. Of the forty-seven stories in the book, almost half were specially commissioned. Those that have appeared elsewhere had a place in the scheme of things both because of *when* they were written and for *what* they had to say. As a general rule of thumb, most of the previously published work appeared in small magazines (some long-since defunct) or in a collection never widely available.

For various reasons, *The Mammoth Book of Gay Short Stories* has been arranged alphabetically by name of author. Had the book been organized by date of publication (or writing), it would have been extremely unbalanced – not least by a preponderance of stories in which HIV and/or Aids figured. This *might* have left the reader feeling at once depressed and certain that gay life = painful death. By organizing the contents so that – as it were – A follows B through to Z, my intention is that the book should function as a literary kaleidoscope so that a story on childhood experience may be followed by one about coming out or Aids, the inter-action between women and groups of gay men, football and revenge or prostitution and true love. Expressly, this book should represent some parts of the vast diversity of gay life.

There is perhaps a hint in the earliest stories that homosexuality was a problem; Colin Spencer's protagonist in the 1954 story "Nymph and Shepherd" is what today would be termed self-loathing – but self-loathing was not unique to the 1950s. Simon Lovat submitted a story written in 1996 which not only followed the theme of Spencer's story (which he'd never seen), but also followed the form. Yet even in the bleakest stories, there is still evidence that the unhappiest of characters is crying not because of his homosexuality but because of his lost homosexual love.

When campaigning novels with homosexual themes began to proliferate in the 1950s and 1960s (Gore Vidal's *The City and the Pillar* and *A Thirsty Evil*; James Baldwin's *Giovanni's Room* and *Another Country*; Kenneth Martin's *Aubade*; Rodney

Garland's *The Heart in Exile*; Mary Renault's *The Charioteer*; Angus Wilson's *Hemlock and After*) homosexuality *was* the theme. Since the Sexual Offences Act in 1967 which partly decriminalized homosexuality in England and Wales and the Stonewall riots in New York in 1969 – two vitally important dates – novelists and short story writers have been able to move away from fiction about homosexuality-as-a-problem to gay-(or queer)-as-a-way-of-life.

Even though these stories pan across a landscape marked by attitude and generation, it seems safe to say that all the writers present here are ultimately positive about a way of life that has been criminal, a medical condition, an object of religious condemnation but forever a huge and hugely creative part of the world.

Peter Burton
Brighton, 1997

THIS IS SERIOUS

James Robert Baker

[Excerpt from tape recordings made by Dean Seagrave in his car, as he hunts down his ex-boyfriend, Pablo Orega, in Los Angeles, on 24 June 1996.]

OK, I'M OUT of here. Oh, man, I think I blew it. Let me get out of here. Fuck. I don't think they'd dare call the cops though. I'm probably OK.

Hold on. Let me make sure I'm getting out of here. What the fuck street is this? Romaine? What's this up here? It must be Highland. Fuck. OK, I'm running the light. Fuck it.

That wasn't smart. But I guess I'm OK. Shit, I've still got a hard-on. I think I'm insane.

Man, I'm still shaken. I really thought it was him. That poor guy. I think I scared the fuck out of him.

So OK. So I go in the door and there's a window. I have to show ID and all that, which is fucked. Because of course they've got my name now. But I really can't see them calling the cops. They've already been hassled. I mean, these sex places are kind of controversial. Even though they've sprung up all over now. And gotten progressively bolder in their gay-rag ads. Instead of being the guilty secret they were a few years ago. Now they're almost proudly proclaiming: *Yes,*

*we spread HIV through multi-partner cocksucking and unprotected
buttfucking. Won't you please join us on our fabulous death boat,
the SS Jonestown. Special college boy discount rates. Just show us
your uninfected buns and student ID.*

Of course, if you say anything, if you point out that these
places are mass-suicide parlors, they call you sex-negative.
Which no self-respecting PC queer wants to be. And the
health department, the liberal supervisors who are all taking
fag money – nobody gives a shit or does anything. They're
probably thinking: Fuck, we give up. If those fags want to
kill themselves, why should we try and stop them? You know
what? They've got a point.

Anyway, I show the guy at the window my license. And
I can see him noting the birth date, then checking me out,
making this judgement call. That OK, I may be thirty-eight, but
I don't look *that* old. Or I won't anyway under a twenty-watt
red light bulb. Because it turns out that most of the guys inside
are young. In their twenties. The new sex-positive nineties
sero-conversion set.

So I get my card, all that, he buzzes me in. It's very dark,
of course. My geriatric eyes need time to adjust. So the first
thing I notice is the music and the smell. The music is the
U2 song, "One". Which I really like, but it's a strange kind
of moody, grief-riddled, heavily Aids-coded song, which seems
like a very bleak *comment* on this scene. Like this incredibly
moving, re-humanizing, de-objectifying *comment*. But I get the
feeling I'm the only one who's taking it that way.

It's this labyrinthine place. Guys wandering around through
the plywood cubicles and corridors. Glory holes everywhere.
Smell of piss and stale come. Some guy back in one urine-
scented booth, hunched in the shadows, squatting on a toilet
that doesn't work. He's emaciated, like he's got maybe three
T-cells left, and he sticks out his tongue. I don't think he
wants to blow me. I think he wants me to piss in his mouth.
Last call.

Another guy, with a honey-blond beard, is kind of listlessly
jerking off back in a barred, jail-like cubicle. Like Vincent Van
Gogh on crystal. So fried, he's kind of talking to himself. Like
muttering sex talk to himself. He worries me. Like I half-expect

him to flash a straight-razor or something. Cut off his ear. Or his dick or something. He looks just like Kirk Douglas in *Lust for Life*. Except the more fitting title is *Lust for Death*.

The whole place reminds me of the old Basic Plumbing. Which got to be so mean I quit going there way before Aids, just because of the attitudes, the evil, callous way guys treated each other. So I'm having all these flashbacks about things I haven't seen or felt since 1981.

I mean, it's crowded but nobody's really doing that much. Just walking around, like bored rats in a maze. Like the bigger the selection, the pickier people get. So there's this air of frustration. This sense of judgement, of tense restraint. It doesn't seem very warm-hearted. That's the term that *LA Weekly* moron used in his PC propaganda piece a while back. "Unlike the sex clubs of yesteryear, the new sexual anarchy is warm-hearted – " Something like that. Maybe I'm missing something, but it seems about as joyful as Buchenwald.

I see one guy with a goatee, which makes me quake for a second. Till I notice the hair on his forearms, which Pablo doesn't have. So I make the rounds a few times, feel a few looks of interest, which is cheaply reassuring. I finally see some action. Three or four guys around another guy, who's down on his knees. But it feels disembodied for some reason. Like the first time I ever went to a bath house, in the early seventies. Even though there were other times, later, when the same scene, say at the beach, might have turned me on. Like I'd get a hard-on and join the crowd. But this doesn't thrill me. It's like looking at a porno photo that no longer turns you on.

Speaking of porno, that's my next stop. The room that's like a lounge with a TV monitor showing a tape. But I don't stay there long. This tape's completely insane. It's like four or five guys in this intense frenetic scene. Like this rough sex scene where they're yelling abuse. "Suck his cock, you cock-hungry pig." But that's not what bothers me. It's the pitch the film's maintaining. The frantic, borderline hysteria. Like some abject fiend on the edge of coming. Except it never stops. There's just this sense of frantic violence that goes on and on. And the sound's also fucked up for some reason, distorting. So you hear these garbled yells of: "Suck on it! Choke on it, you pig!" And it seems very clear that sex is not enough, that they don't want to fuck, they want to fucking kill each other. So you're starting to feel: Why don't they just cut the shit and *do it*! Forget about their dicks, whip out a goddamn machete. Let's see some fucking *blood*! That's what you *want*!

So I have to get out of there. I feel like this tape is ridiculing me. Turning what I feel, what for me is very serious, into a cheap porno conceit. As if the culture, the gay consumerist culture, wants to defuse and neutralize me.

So I kind of stumble down the corridor, feeling panicked, even paranoid. Like everyone sees me as some floridly short-circuiting, pathetic loser who isn't cold enough to function in this scene. Like I should be stuck in the dumpster out back like a broken, discarded *replicant*. So I duck into one of the cubicles, just to get away from all the eyes.

It's like a stall with a door on a spring. So I hook the door and try to collect myself. And I can smell marijuana smoke in the air, which I've smelled since I came in and that reminds me of this joint I lifted at Reese's. Guess I haven't mentioned that until now. Not especially proud of it. But there was a box on the coffee table, filled with maybe two dozen joints. Didn't think Reese would miss one. I thought it might help bring me down from the speed, when I needed to do that. I stuck it in my pocket a second before Stan came in.

Now feels like the time to bring myself down some, so I fire up the joint in the cubicle. And it's odd. This other strange song starts to play. I mean, strange for the setting. That Frente! acoustic version of "Bizarre Love Triangle," which is one of my two favourite New Order songs. I mean, it was weird the first time I heard the Frente! version, since I've been singing that song to myself for years. My own acoustic version in the car, in the shower, idly walking around the house. I like the chorus especially. [sings] where you get down on your knees and pray . . .

Which is maybe what I should be doing now. Praying. If I knew who to pray to or what, but I don't anymore.

And so for a while I was gone. I mean, the dope was good, very good, and for a while I was lost in the sad lost world of that song. Like I could write a whole novel, a Proustian novel, about everything that went through my mind in those three minutes.

But then the song was over and there was nothing for a moment. And that's when I heard these two guys talking in the next cubicle. Like having this conversation after sex. And I reel because this one guy is saying, "So my friend John goes: 'I don't know why you keep attracting these guys who always get obsessed with you.' And I go, 'John, it's because I have a kind of sexual magnetism that I can't turn off - '"

So it's him. It has to be him. It's his voice, his phrasing, it's him.

Except I'm buzzed now, from the dope, so how can I be sure my mind isn't playing tricks? That's when I notice the peephole. I turn down the light in my cubicle, and crouch down and look through the peep hole. Meanwhile the other guy's talking, all very low-key, about his boring job as a claims adjuster or something. So I look through the peep hole and there they are on a small cot. I can't see a lot at first in the weak yellow light. Their crotches mostly. They've taken their clothes off. You can see their limp dicks, their hands holding cigarettes, as they go on talking. But I'm sure it's him.

"I'm working on this paper now. It's really been exhausting me," he says. Playing grad student on study break.

Then he reaches over to stub out his cigarette and I see his mustache and goatee. I see his Auschwitz buzz cut, as predicted. So I have no further doubt that it's him.

The other guy gets up, pulls on his pants, says he has to take a leak.

Pablo says, "So you're going back on Tuesday?" Like the guy's from out of town. Like Pablo wants to spend some more time with him. So I know I have to act now, before the guy comes back and they leave together.

I don't have time to think, or to savor the anticipation. Which is somewhat disappointing, that the moment is coming so fast. I take out the Glock, hold it under my T-shirt as I step out. I press the door to his cubicle. It's unlatched. I enter, pulling out the gun. He jumps as I say, "Don't make a fucking sound."

That's when I see all the hair on his chest and stomach and I know it's not Pablo. I still don't want to believe it though.

I was so sure. I keep looking at his face, as though his body could be lying. Like he's grown hair on his chest to fool me, to fuck with my head. Which is crazy, I know. But my mind really wants to be right.

Finally, I have to admit it though. It's not his face either. This guy's nose is too long, his cheeks too sunken. So I say, "Look, sorry. I thought you were someone else."

So that's when I leave. And then this strange thing happens. Except it's not so strange, which is why I'm very concerned now. But as I step outside, into the bracing night air, I suddenly get an erection. Like for no apparent reason. Except I think at first it's maybe some weird form of relief. Like I've been in this hellhole of death, this stinking, suffocating prison, and now I'm busting free, embracing the fresh night air and life or something. I don't want to admit yet what's really going on. It's too horrendous.

But I'm admitting it now. Because I've still got a hard-on. It's been a half hour now and it still hasn't gone down. I can't wait any longer. The stakes are too high. It's the hemp that did it. My doctor warns you about that. It can cause this kind of side-effect. Smoking dope when you're taking Desyrel. I thought about it at Reese's when I lifted the joint. I guess I just didn't believe it. Or maybe I was thinking, when I smoked in the sex club . . . Maybe I was thinking, if I'm really honest, that as foul as the place was, if I got a killer hard-on, I might just – who knows? – get all this sucked out of my system. But I'm in trouble now. I'm in deep shit, I can tell. It's a different kind of hard-on. I mean, it's a great hard-on. Like an *extra-hard* hard-on. But the problem is this. I'm not thinking about sex. And I can tell I could think about anything – Pat Boone, Rush Limbaugh naked, Nancy Reagan's twat – *and I would not lose this erection.*

Which may sound funny. Or like a highly desirable state. Boy, you could fuck all night, ha ha. But here's the thing. If I don't do something now, this could permanently damage me. Make me permanently impotent. Which is really no joke at all. That's why I'm closing in on Cedars [Sinai Hospital] right now.

*   *   *

OK, I'm back. It's about eleven. A lot's been going on. I'm moving, as you can tell. I feel OK now. Levelled out. Just did some more speed. I kind of had to. They hit me up with something at Cedars. Valium or something. They could tell I was tweaked. But right now I feel perfect. Wired out but not frantic. In control.

Which is good. I feel like this is it. I'm closing in. It's going to happen. I've never been more sure of anything in my life.

So I go into Emergency. Which for starters is painfully bright. And I've got my T-shirt out and all that. But it's not completely covering my crotch. So I'm very self-conscious. Like some teen-age kid with a boner who has to share in front of the class.

The waiting room's not crowded, fortunately. Just this elderly Jewish couple. I kind of walk to the window half-turned away from them. The guy at the window turns out to be the problem. This icky young queen who reminds me of Calvin. Calvin pre-Aids. So he asks me what the problem is and I tell him I've got an erection.

He says, "We should all be so lucky."

And I say, "No, look, this isn't a joke. I'm taking Desyrel, this anti-depressant, and this is one of the side-effects. It gives you a permanent erection and if you don't do something about it, it can physically damage your penis."

I realize this old Jewish couple can hear me. And this queen is kind of smiling. And I'm starting to feel like no one's going to believe me. Like no one here is going to know what I'm talking about.

"How long have you had it?" the guy asks.

"I don't know. Forty-five minutes."

"You mean, constantly?"

"Yes."

He's looking at me like he thinks I'm a nut case. Or like if the Jewish couple weren't there in the waiting room, he'd ask me to show him.

I say, "Look, this is serious. I need to see a doctor immediately."

So he finally takes my Blue Cross card and all that. Then he says, "Why don't you have a seat, Mr Seagrave? It'll be a few minutes."

So I say, "Look, man. You're not getting it. I know this sounds silly or something, compared to gun shot victims and people having heart attacks. But it's a very real thing! If I'm not treated, damage will result. I'll be impotent, man! Don't you get it? Maybe you don't give a shit, but it's my fucking life! I want to see a doctor and I want to see him now!"

So he goes and talks to someone, and this nurse comes and gets me. She leads me back into one of the examining places, and I have to tell her all over again what's going on. Then finally the doctor comes over, this young Jewish guy who I recognize immediately from a local news show. Like he's this doctor who always does the medical reports. So I explain for a third time what's going on and he wants to see. But this nurse is still there, and I know she's a nurse, but I say, "Do you think she could step out? I'm shy, OK?"

So she does, and I show the doctor my boner, which is totally huge and dark red. I mean, the color freaks me out, it's so dark, like all the blood in my dick is clotting or something.

And the doctor says: "Are you sure you weren't just stimulated?"

And I almost say: No I was just at this truly vile sex club that if anything had the opposite effect. But I decide not to mention that, in case he's homophobic or something. But I'm already getting terrified, since I can tell that he doesn't know anything about this. He's got this expression like he's thinking: This is a puzzler.

I say, "Look, I knew this could happen. If you smoke marijuana. My doctor gave me that warning. I just didn't take it that seriously. But I know there are drugs you can give me that will counteract the effect."

I didn't want to say anything more. Because I knew, I remembered this conversation with my doctor that seemed like a joke at the time, that if the drugs didn't work they had to do surgery. Cut the blood vessels or something. Which will also result in permanent impotence. That's part of why I don't want this guy to know I'm gay. He might say, "Sorry, Bud. Only one way to deal with *this*."

But this guy just looks baffled. Then he goes and uses the phone. Which seems to take forever. Getting through to some other doctor. I can see him from the examining room. At one point he laughs into the phone. And I'm thinking: Man, chat it up some other time, dude. This is fucking *serious*, you asshole!

Finally he comes and gives me a shot of something. As he does it, he says, "If this doesn't work, we may have to perform surgery. Which could leave you impotent."

I say, "Oh, man. My girlfriend will shit."

Not taking any chances, since I'm kind of at his mercy.

Then he says, "Your pupils are dilated. What else have you taken tonight?"

So I tell him I did a couple of lines of crank, since I was working on a project. That's when he calls for the Valium shot.

Then it's like this waiting game. This big suspense scene. Like if it's going to work, it should work within minutes. So the doctor's there and so is the nurse. And other people are kind of watching from further back. Like everyone in the ER knows what's going on.

I'm just sitting on the table at this point. My pants are up, my shirt's covering my crotch, so everybody's watching my face, like I'm supposed to tell them if there's any change.

I'm really thinking if this doesn't work, I'm going to kill myself. Since I can't see living if I can't fuck.

The tension gets unbelievable. Not that I care a lot, since I'm kind of peaking on Valium. But on another level, I still know what's at stake. The doctor keeps looking at his watch. I half expect him to say at any moment, "We tried. Call surgery."

But finally I say, "OK, I feel something. It's going down. Yeah, it is."

The doctor wants to see it again, so I make him draw the curtain. Like I don't need an audience watching me lose my erection.

And it's OK. It's going down. Way down. Until my dick's so shriveled up it looks like it was dipped in ice water. At which point I get panicked. I say, "Look, this isn't permanent – "

He says, "No, no. You'll be fine in a day or two. But you should definitely avoid re-stimulation."

Re-stimulation? Like he still thinks I was probably fucking.

Anyway, that was it. They wanted me to stay there and rest for an hour or so, just to be sure. They didn't try to have me admitted, like I thought they might. But I left after about forty minutes, because I suddenly realized where Pablo will be tonight, it suddenly hit me. I'm almost certain I'm right this time. And it's been a long day. I just want to find him and kill him and get it over with, so I can go somewhere and get a good night's sleep.

THE VOYEUR

Peter Baker

THE TWO THICK ladies were struggling with their cross, as they had done every day for the past twenty-two years, ever since Rafael was born with a sub-standard telephone exchange that failed to send the right signals to his muscles. The ginger-haired lady had been widowed a few months after Rafael's birth; and her unmarried sister had joined her from the north, so that Rafael might grow up in a home, and not an institution. He was overweight from being confined to the wheelchair; and every day the cross became heavier, more daunting, as it had to be negotiated down the treacherous flight of stairs from the old apartment opposite mine, to the street. Of course, there was always someone to help; but their independence was such that they always insisted on doing something just as burdensome in return, like repairing my torn sheets. And last night they had certainly got torn!

"I may see you later, Raf," I told him. "I'm watching the processions tonight. Maybe I'll get religion!"

"We have seats in the Alameda," the mother beamed. She tried lifting her son's head from where it lolled on his shoulders; but he'd been over-sedated, and the movement did little more than produce an outflowing of saliva from the parted lips.

The wet mouth indecently reminded me of the sixty-nining

that had gone on for the best part of five hours last night. Like it or not, my programme for Radio Andaluz had obliged me to participate in Malaga's Santa Semana; and a couple of nights previously I'd played tempter to a dishy RENFE platelayer I'd met in the crowd, touching him up in the very precincts of the cathedral. He had to return to the bosom of his family; but last night he had been processing with other railway workers – it never occurred to me before that the Compagnie International des Wagons Lits had catered for the Last Supper – and he didn't have to be home till morning. I'd given him my address and told him I'd leave the latch off the apartment door, so he could let himself in when the night's sackcloth and ashes were finally over. He'd woken me about two in the morning. I'd thought his penitent's candle was big, but—

"Virtue's only a lack of opportunity," my lover, Paul, used to say.

Paul had drifted into oblivion five years ago, a victim of leukaemia, after twenty-five wonderful years together. We had been inseparable. Our love had grown from the dunghill of lust and had perpetually blossomed because neither legal sanctions in our teens, nor the delights of gay-adultery in our maturity, had deflected us from a shared belief that total confidence in the loved one in all things, conquered all. One flesh, divided by death, I hadn't found it easy to adjust; but I knew it wouldn't be Paul's wish that I should cut myself off from the living world and take me to a monastery. So that, as I lay on my bed last night, sixty-nining this muscular young railwayman, I wasn't surprised to sense Paul enjoying it with me. We so often talked to each other when apart in life, it seemed illogical not to do so when apart in death. But what had surprised me were the eyes. As I looked over the landscape of the sex-partner's solid thighs, in the dim light at the far end of the room I was certain I saw a pair of eye watching. Wanting. But unable to make contact. "Paul? Is that you?" I'd whispered through a mouthful of pre-cum; but my vision was obscured by pubic hairs, and when I next came up for air, the eyes had gone.

I heard the solemn beat of muffled drums and smelt the incense before I'd walked to the other side of the park. Six *cofradias* were processing tonight, each starting from its holy shrine and returning to the shrine some five, or six, hours later, having taken in the four corners of the ancient city. The vast *tronos*, each weighing several tons and bearing either an effigy of the crucified Christ, or the mother, Mary, were encrusted with gold-leaf, gilt or silver paint, according to the affluence of its sponsors. They were carried from within by scores of men and boys, paid for their services – rough porters from the central market, students in their formal blue serge suits. The *nazarenos*, anyone who thought himself, or herself, important in this world, had paid for the privilege of processing with their particular *cofradia*, anonymous in hooded robes, theatrically spectacular in their colour and design, the whole scene lit by a thousand flickering candles.

"Mr Hardman's lot will be at the Puerto Nuevo about midnight," Mari Carmen said. "If you hold a little placard, he'll probably recognize you."

My producer had popped out, hot and sweaty, from a purple hood, taking me completely by surprise as I was being sent up by one of the Foreign Legion band boys. Douggie Hardman shipped a vast quantity of moscatel wine back to the UK and was the obvious angle for my programme, but I was damned if I was going to hold a placard, big or little.

"Can't I hold the drummer boy?" I asked.

"Oh, you *are* awful!" she said, quickly hiding her embarrassment under the hood.

High up on a balcony overlooking the Plaza de la Merced, a *flamenco* singer was penetrating the night air with his *saeta* for the Virgin. Nearer the cathedral, I saw a procession led by over-barbered Guardia Civil officers, their drawn swords painted a matt black. Every few minutes, a high pitched bell would signal a rest break and there would be a rush for the nearest bar, the penitents to down a little *copa*, the bearers to refill their *botas*, the leather wine skins they kept on hooks in the secret underbelly of the *trono*. Hucksters were selling popcorn, dips were picking pockets, and old ladies were shedding tears.

"If Jesus was alive today, no one would bother to crucify him," my lover, Paul, had said a few years before his death, when we had stood in this very place, watching the Easter processions together. "The gutter press of Fleet Street would find him at some nuclear protest, down a coal mine, or urging a grant to help teenage gays. Wouldn't that be torture enough?"

Paul was very close to me tonight. I saw his eyes watching me from the deep recesses of every penitental hood. Outside the law courts, a mob was shouting its praises of a petty robber released to join the procession, a modern day Barabbas. Black velvet robes. The gut-turning roll of a hundred drums. Bare flesh of the macho legionnaires. An unemployed youth shouts insults at the effigy of the crucified, throws a stone, chips a waxen cheek. Ungentle police drag protester from lamp-post and deliver eye-for-eye and tooth-for-tooth with loaded truncheons. A *nazareno* raises his hood to vomit from too much fear, or booze. Under his robe, a silk suit and handmade shoes, faint shadow of those penitents of yore with their bare feet and blooded backs. Hooded, so not to display their dark love, they had flagellated themselves to fulfilment, just as today some gay brothers can only express their love through pain.

I was wondering if there would be a market for a crown of thorns among the SM toys, when I found Rafael and the two thick ladies. "Are you enjoying it?" I asked him.

Only after I'd asked did I realize what a damned silly question it was. How could anyone enjoy an execution? Rafael's eyes were sparkling in a way I had never seen before, as his sub-standard telephone exchange struggled to tell me how he had been wheeled the length of the Alameda by the Real Hermandad de Nuestra Senora de la Piedad.

"We are thinking of taking him to Lourdes next year," the mother said.

Suddenly, I was aware that Rafael had reached out to hold my hand. It went through me like an electric shock and I blew a fuse. "I have work to do," I said. "We'll talk about Lourdes some other time."

Could it be the eyes of yet another plaster Jesus that penetrated the back of my head as I tried to lose myself in the milling crowd? I couldn't get away from eyes tonight, real, or imaginary, or glass. I was being forced to ask myself questions to which I had no answers. I hated these public celebrations of Easter for just this reason. Why did a man

called Jesus have no brothers or sisters? Was his carpenter
dad gay? Was Jesus gay? He was executed, aged thirty-two,
without having wife or children, surely a miracle the world
survived at all with men and women on it to form a church,
any church, if that was the example of procreation they were
supposed to follow. Did a Rafael hold his hand? Or his cock?
Did Jesus and his fishers of men express themselves with no
physical contact? Did not their love for each other grow, as
my dead lover's for me had grown and mine for him, from
our awareness that we were made in the image of God, that
our bodies, with which we expressed our universal love of life,
were truly the temporary habitats of our souls? Or did God
make only a plaster effigy of man, to be chipped by a yobbo's
thrown stone, so that for eternity man is left to make a god in
his own image? Or worship the sun, the phallus, or the golden
calf. The solemn brass of the Foreign Legion band pounded
my ears, my nostrils were afire with burning incense, my eyes
filled with the tears of doubt, as I allowed the swelling crowd
to carry me towards the Puerta Nuevo. Why was Jesus a he
and not a she? Was he a hermaphrodite, a true bi-sexual? Why
had no great artist portrayed a full frontal nude? What are the
sins of the flesh if they are not the Crusades, the Papal Wars,
the blessing of World War Two bombers, the daily bloodshed
on the streets of Northern Ireland in the name of – God?

"*Seco Montes grande, porfavor.*"

I had swung into the tiny *bodega* near the confluence of
narrow roads at the Puerta Nuevo, desperate for a drink. Outside, three *tronos* had arrived simultaneously, vying for position
to be first to head towards the snob stands in the Plaza de la
Constitucion. The black-and-purple *nazarenos* were elbowing
the white-and-gold *nazarenos*, while a couple of embarrassed
Municipal Policemen lurked in the background, hoping it
wasn't going to end in a punch-up. A candle inadvertently set
light to a penitent's robe. An onlooker obligingly extinguished
the flame with a can of beer. It was impossible to get out of the
bodega for the crush of multi-coloured *nazarenos* trying to get
in. Fortunately, plonk king Douggie Hardman was crushing
in with them. They stacked their hoods on the bar like sailors
stack their hats and bald-headed Douggie, voice louder than

any Spaniard, began ordering Scotch. It wasn't available, so he started to call down the wrath of the Deity for having to settle with brandy from the cask.

"Mr Hardman, will you say a few words for the Radio Andaluz English show, please?" I asked, edging my way along the bar with my recorder.

"There's no such thing as a bad Spanish wine," Douggie said, going into his sales spiel. "It's just that some are better than others."

I recalled Paul's favourite maxim. If you cannot comfort the afflicted, then at least afflict the comfortable. So I stuck the mike up Douggie's hairy nostrils and asked, "What does Jesus Christ mean to you? Sir?"

I knew from the instant hostility in his eyes that tomorrow he would complain about me to Tio Mac, the station manager: but tonight was tonight, and I stood my ground.

Douggie smiled uncomfortably and gulped his brandy. "He kept the wedding party going by turning water into wine," he said.

"You really believe that, sir? You believe in miracles?"

Fortunately for Douggie, he was saved by the bell. As soon as they heard the tinkling, the brotherhood of vintners grabbed their hoods and disappeared into the comforting anonymity of wealth. I suddenly felt alone in the crowd, in desperate need for someone to hold my hand. All my life I'd been asking the questions, the professional cynic. Was there nothing in which I believed? Yes, the sun would rise tomorrow. But could I be sure to wake to see it? And if I didn't wake . . . what? I stepped smartly aside to prevent walking on a printed cross on a Semana Santa poster that was blowing about on the pavement, and knocked into a dark-eyed young man. He smiled, that knowing smile of recognition. He would hold my hand. But for once my cock did not give a beat of anticipation. He asked me the time and I pointed callously to the cathedral clock, leaving him to find another's hand to hold. How many times throughout the world tonight was the cry of rejected love going up to the stars, "My God, my God, why hast thou forsaken me?"

I returned to my apartment just in time to see the two thick ladies struggling with their cross. Rafael was holding a parcel in his lap. I took the weight of the wheelchair at his feet, while the two women guided it backwards up the twisting staircase, one step at a time.

"Have you been buying *churros* for tomorrow's breakfast?" I asked him. "They'll make you fatter than you already are!"

He could usually take a ribbing from me. Like all invalids, he'd come to terms with his disability, or so I thought. But tonight there were tears in his eyes. It was a night for tears. In the far distance we could still hear the beat of muffled drums. I recalled too many occasions when I had given Paul cause for tears. His eyes had been like Rafael's eyes. Soft. Brown. Deep pools of desire.

"I'm afraid Rafael has been molesting you," the mother said, dragging the wheelchair up the next step.

Molestar. It was an odd choice of word. To annoy. To trouble. So often I'd been afraid of troubling them, with the hunky sex-partners I brought back nights. Tearing the sheets.

"We've bought Rafael a lock and chain for his chair," she went on. "I'm afraid he's started sleepwalking. He could distress us all . . . if anything happened."

Tears were streaming down Rafael's cheeks now. The apartment door I'd left off the latch! The big-pricked platelayer I'd been sixty-nining! The eyes watching us in the dark had been Rafael's eyes, yearning, longing for something beyond his reach. Crying out from the confines of his imprisoned body, "Am I, too, not made in his image?" And the hollow answer floating back on the muffled drums across the city. "God is love."

MINERVA'S RING

Diesel Balaam

"HOLD IT THERE!"

Clunk. The shutter on Darryl's camera snapped shut trapping Oliver's image inside the secrets of its dark interior. Darryl's love of photography was only surpassed by Oliver's even greater love of archaeology, an obsession that was a legacy from his university days.

"Take one of me standing against this section of wall!" Oliver shouted, "It'll give an idea of the scale!" The shutter snapped shut once more.

Neither shared an interest in the other's pastime, but after living together for three years Oliver had come to accept that the kitchen might at any time be plunged into darkness for the purpose of developing films. Likewise, Darryl had resigned himself to spending weekends like this one in muddy locations watching Oliver sifting through bucketfuls of dirt.

It was a hot summer's day and the dig had been abandoned due to the heat. Now they were alone. Darryl had agreed to come along as the site under excavation was on top of Solsbury Hill and afforded many photographic possibilities. However, he had spent most of the afternoon watching Oliver's bronzed muscular body, stripped to the waist, toiling over the dark ancient soil. His was an athletic torso gleaming with fresh perspiration that saturated his dark body hairs.

"Hurry up!" Darryl called over to Oliver, who was busy cataloguing his finds.

Darryl thought to himself how much happier Oliver had become since they had first met. It was about four years now since John, Oliver's former lover and flatmate, had been killed in a car accident whilst returning from a dig. Oliver had met John at university and it was he who had first interested Oliver in archaeology. After his death Oliver had sunk beneath layers of sadness and guilt until Darryl had rediscovered him and helped him to piece his life together again.

Only now, three years later, did Darryl feel entirely secure with Oliver. When he had first moved in with Oliver it seemed as though John still somehow possessed him. Darryl would find old photographs of John scattered around the flat, and even the mere mention of John's name was enough to precipitate an almost physical presence between them. Now at last, Darryl was sure that he had succeeded in relegating John from the status of a fond memory to a fading one. Well almost.

"I'll just have a wash and we'll call it a day!" Oliver cried. He began splashing water from a crude washstand over his face and arms.

Just before he was killed, John had given Oliver a ring. This was no ordinary ring, but a ring he had retrieved from a well on the site of a Roman temple dedicated to the goddess Minerva. Contrary to the strict rules governing archaeology he had kept the ring and didn't report the find, a crime he had never even contemplated before.

When he had discovered the ring he had been instantly spellbound by its striking design, incorporating three stones set in silver, in as good a condition as the day it had been tossed into the well as an offering to Minerva. The three-stone design symbolized a solar eclipse. A turquoise stone represented the Earth, an amber stone the Sun, and a small bead of jet wedged between them represented the Moon.

Oliver dried himself and pulled on his T-shirt. Darryl loved the way that the dark hairs on his chest cascaded over the neckline. Striding over to Darryl who was sitting on the outer rim of the excavations, Oliver took the ring from his pocket where he had put it for safe-keeping, and slipped it onto his finger.

"Sorry I took so long," he said and sat down.

Darryl smiled. Oliver put an arm around Darryl's shoulders and pulled him closer, his hand coming to rest in front of Darryl's face, the ring glinting in the sunlight. The smile fell from Darryl's face. How he hated that ring! To him it symbolized everything that was B.D. – before Darryl. It was certainly the last bond between Oliver and John.

"Are you OK?" Oliver asked.

"Sure," Darryl answered. "I was day-dreaming."

Playfully Oliver pushed Darryl over onto his back before quickly sitting astride his prostrate body. "Get off!" Darryl protested, but Oliver just laughed, teasing Darryl by gyrating his hips in front of his face, the tempting mound behind the zip dormant, yet so full of potential.

"Come on get off!" Darryl demanded, taking a swing at Oliver's jaw, but Oliver just grabbed hold of his wrist and grinned disarmingly.

Darryl looked up into Oliver's blue eyes and glimpsed the sparkle lurking there like a smuggler of pure mischief. Oliver laughed again and Darryl began to laugh too. In the course of this high-spiritedness Darryl rolled Oliver off his body and managed to sit astride him, but Oliver being the stronger of the two, soon managed to roll Darryl underneath him once more, before Darryl reversed their position yet again. In a moment, the two playful wrestlers had become locked in ceaseless combat as they rolled faster and faster down the hill.

Fortunately the slope was gentle and even, carpeted in short soft grass that swept down to the tree-lined river at the bottom of the hill. As they rolled on to the narrow floodplain and slowed to a halt, their dizzy horseplay evaporated along with their yells and curses. After a moment's hesitation, Oliver jumped up and ran towards the river.

"Wait for me!" Darryl yelled after him giving chase. Panting, he reached the riverbank just in time to see Oliver levering himself into the inviting fork in the trunk of a large ash. The river below was babbling like an expectant

audience as it flowed across the auditorium it had eroded
for itself.

Oliver stepped confidently on to the branches that curved in
arched ecstasy beneath him. "Watch me!" he shouted, pulling
off his shirt and throwing it on to the riverbank below. A mixture
of thrill and shock zipped through Darryl's body as the T-shirt
was joined by Oliver's jeans, plimsolls, and finally his briefs.

"Oliver! Someone might see!" Darryl hissed. He knew the
riverbank was a popular route for ramblers. "Come and get
me!" Olive teased, stepping along the sturdy bough until he
was standing directly above the sparkling waters.

Darryl admired Oliver's naked form, well camouflaged as
it was by the patterns of the leaves that etched their shadows
on to his skin, with the precision of marquetry. It was if he
belonged to nature. The leaves rustled excitedly, the babbling
river applauded and Darryl felt his cock rising to an eager
standing ovation.

Seconds later Darryl was clambering up into the tree,
stepping cautiously towards Oliver. Oliver edged further along
the branch until it became too narrow to support him, and then
jumped into the river with an almighty splash that startled a
nearby woodpigeon. This caused the whole bough to shake
sending Darryl plunging into the water behind him.

Wasting no time, Oliver grabbed Darryl's soaking shirt and
wrenched it from his body. The two of them thrashed about
wildly as Oliver struggled to unfasten Darryl's jeans that clung
stubbornly to his legs. he didn't have to struggle for long though;
Darryl soon decided to co-operate! His clothes joined Oliver's
on the bank with a heavy wet slap.

Momentarily exhausted by their water-borne antics they lay
in the shallows under the trees, the cool fresh water exploring
their bodies lending their skin a new alertness and texture
pulled taut across firm muscles. Nature's prime agent of
change seemed to be adding a new dimension to their
physical love, as Darryl's dark nipples rose like cairns from
the plateau of his chest, while small whirlpools in the water
teased Oliver's armpits and balls. They were always graceful
when having sex, but today they were exceptionally so. Slipping
over each other's aroused flesh they writhed, rolled and pushed,

the intense pleasure welling up inside each of them, until the fruit of their passion leapt like venom from their pricks, leaving them refreshed and relaxed.

For a short while afterwards they lay in each other's arms savouring the sensations of the chilled tongue-like rivulets that still poured over their fatigued young bodies.

Later that afternoon they returned to Oliver's car having collected their belongings together and dried Darryl's clothes. They climbed in and Oliver reached over to put the photographic equipment on the back seat. "Christ this stuff gets heavier every . . ."

He stopped, freezing momentarily before turning round slowly and placing both outstretched hands on the steering wheel.

Darryl stared at Oliver, for he too had noticed that the ring was missing from Oliver's finger. "It must have come off in the river!" he said, barely managing to conceal his delight. "Then I must go and find it!" declared Oliver, opened the car door. Darryl pulled him back, "You'll never find it! Look, I'm sorry Oliver but it's lost for good. There's nothing we can do about it." Reluctantly Oliver slammed the door shut and turned the ignition key. The wheels spun furiously on the unpaved road kicking up a cloud of dust that seemed to choke the rest of the journey home with silence.

That evening, Darryl shut himself in the kitchen and proceeded to make the room light-proof. Five minutes later there was a knock on the door and Darryl was surprised to find Oliver asking to be let in. Oliver usually found the processing of films absorbed too much of his time and patience. He stood next to the door while Darryl busied himself preparing the developing chemicals.

"You're right," Oliver began. "What do you mean?" interrupted Darryl. "About the ring. It's wrong to cling on to the past. That's history, and history should be buried and forgotten, I guess."

Darryl couldn't help laughing at this last remark, but he was also pleased by Oliver's philosophical attitudes towards the loss of the ring. "Good," he said, and gave Oliver a quick hug.

"OK, we're ready!" Darryl announced. "Switch off the light will you?"

Oliver turned off the light while Darryl released the film from its cannister. "Here, take this and don't drop it!" he instructed, handing the film to Oliver. "Are you ready yet?" Oliver whispered. The dark always made him whisper. "Right. Give me seven or eight inches of film!" said Darryl. He reached out into the blackness before him, but it was not seven or eight inches of film that Oliver thrust into his hand.

"Well I don't think this needs to go through the enlarger!" Darryl said coolly. He squeezed the hard flesh that pulsated gently in the cradle of his fingertips, before kneeling down to cocoon it in his mouth. After all the film could wait for a few minutes.

The following Saturday, Oliver's monthly archaeology magazine was delivered along with Darryl's Amateur Photographer. Oliver flicked through his magazine immediately, until a large colour spread caught his eye. "Tripontium Re-excavated" read the title of the article. Yes, Oliver remembered now! His heart leapt. This was the site where John had recovered the ring from the well, the same site he had been returning from the night he was killed. When the site was first excavated four years ago they had only had time to dig up a quarter of the site, before the land was to disappear beneath the path of a new motorway.

At the time, the lack of time granted by the Department of the Environment to complete the dig had caused a storm of protest, but with a change of government came a change in policy, and the new road was axed. Evidently, sufficient funds had now been raised for extensive excavations to be carried out. Spectacular finds had already been made. Oliver knew he must go to the re-opened dig straight away.

He ran into the kitchen where Darryl was sitting at the breakfast table listening to the radio. "Come on, we're off to this dig!" Oliver declared. "Oh, not another of your damned digs!" exclaimed Darryl. "Well, you don't have to come I suppose," said Oliver throwing down the opened page in front of Darryl.

The radio broke into the silence ". . . with me I have astronomist . . ." Darryl soon recognized the place described as the site where John had found the Roman ring. ". . . spectacular solar eclipse lasting approximately . . ." Darryl switched off the radio. "OK I'll come." He knew he must accompany Oliver to this re-excavation of Tripontium. He knew it held a special significance for Oliver, a significance that was too special.

Darryl was determined that John's memory wouldn't come between them again. He changed into his old clothes and packed his camera.

Later that morning, the car turned off the straight Roman road it had been travelling on, and swept along the network of lanes that led to the site. "There it is!" Oliver said as they sped over the brow of a hill. Darryl looked up from the map and saw the red plastic tapes that stretched around the site's perimeter. In a moment they had arrived. Oliver parked the car in a nearby lay-by before they made their way over to the dig.

The whole site appeared strangely deserted. "Must be a late start today!" said Oliver, not hesitating in ducking under the tape. "Oliver, do you think we should . . ." Darryl began, but Oliver was already walking purposefully towards the centre of the site.

Darryl followed him keeping to the pathways that passed through the remains of the villas and bath houses. Inside one closed-off area was a sign that read. 'Temple to Minerva'. Oliver looked back along the approach road. No one was coming. He pushed his way under the tapes and jumped down onto the floor below. Darryl looked behind uneasily, then handed Oliver his camera before joining him.

In front of them stretched a stone colonnade that had survived the ravages of time, now supported by a cage of scaffolding. They stepped through the columns and into the inner sanctum of the temple, the far end of which was protected by two large green tarpaulins.

"This must be one of the best preserved sites in Britain!" Oliver enthused. "Look at that mosaic!"

The floor was occupied by a giant mosaic depicting Minerva pouring water from a jug over the land below. The colours were still vivid and most of the mosaic had survived intact. As they walked around the edge of the mosaic, they couldn't help noticing the gaze of the sloe-eyed Minerva following them, no doubt a deliberate trick of the mosaic's designer.

Darryl began taking a few pictures. Oliver meanwhile, walked slowly up to the uneven stone steps at the far end of the sanctum, where two stone pillars stood guard over the well. There it was, set in the floor lined with marble. John had described it many times during the original excavations. The tarpaulins above kept this end of the temple veiled in a cool shade, so that the mouth of the well looked dark and ominous.

At the other end of the sanctum Darryl was adjusting the controls of the camera. He simply had to get a picture of that mosaic. Then looking through the lens to focus it, he caught a glimpse of something moving behind the columns at the far end of the temple.

He looked up and watched as a lone figure walked silently towards Oliver. Oliver did not look up straight away but stayed staring into the well before him. Only as the mysterious figure came within two or three paces did Oliver look up.

"John?" whispered Oliver incredulously, taking two involuntary steps backwards. Darryl gasped; it was John! He watched petrified, as John approached Oliver and embraced him.

The embrace seemed to drain all of Oliver's strength, and his legs began to give way under the weight of his body. He slumped onto his knees and tried to grasp John's legs but his hands refused to grip. Helplessly rooted to the spot, Darryl remembered the camera in his hands and shakily raised it to his eye before taking picture after picture. John turned and walked back into the gloom behind the columns, his face calm and expressionless.

"Oliver?" Darryl called out, stirring from the hypnotism of the moment. He ran across the mosaic to where Oliver lay. His eyes were closed, his body motionless and limp except for an outstretched fist that was firmly clenched. "Oliver!" cried Darryl, lifting his head from the stone steps.

"Hey! What are you doing?" shouted a man from the other end of the sanctum. He ran across to where Darryl was sitting holding Oliver. "Has there been an accident?" he asked, taking Oliver by the shoulders and scanning his body for injury. The man tried to take Oliver's pulse but then shook his head. "We're too late, he's gone," he said.

Darryl didn't need to be told; he already knew that Oliver had gone, gone to whatever lies beyond the threshold of death, with John. John had finally and totally eclipsed Oliver from his life, yet no tears came. They were locked inside by the suffocating embrace of shock; his mind and body suspended in the embryo of grief. He glanced down and saw that the back of the camera had opened, the exposed film now grey and opaque.

"What happened? What were you doing here?" shouted the man impatiently. "Why don't you answer me?" Darryl looked into the man's face, confused. Then everything grew suddenly dim, until the man's head was just a silhouette demanding answers to unheard questions. No, it was Oliver talking; but Oliver was lying in his arms. It was really John laughing at him. The skies gradually began to get lighter again. "I'll go and fetch help!" the man was saying. He had become a stranger again.

Darryl looked down and noticed Oliver's fist unclenching on the stone step where it had come to rest. The fingers slowly opened to reveal the ring that Darryl had so long despised sitting in the palm of Oliver's hand. He stared in numb disbelief, before a reflex action of the forearm sent it tumbling once more into Minerva's well.

CAESAR'S GALLIC WARS

Neil Bartlett

AT TEN PAST three on the afternoon of June the twenty-fourth, at the hottest hour of the hottest day of the long summer of nineteen hundred and seventy-four, a boy with glasses is sitting in a school gymnasium on the edge of an undistinguished small town in the south of England. He is not alone – but he might as well be, since all heads are bowed, no one whispers, no one looks up at anyone else. Only the movement of pen-nibs across paper scratches at the edges of the silence. The boy is absorbed in completing the peculiar task of transcribing, by hand and in ink, an English translation of an eight-hundred-word long passage taken from the ending of the seventh book of Julius Caesar's account of his conquest of Gaul in the first century before Christ. This is the book in which the last of the rebellious Gallic chieftains, Vercingetorix, is captured, humiliated and led in chains through Rome before his execution.

The doomed Vercingetorix and his captains are wild, bare-chested; they fight half-naked and screaming, painted, each of their necks clasped in a gleaming gold torque. All of these details are catalogued by Caesar – the boy has committed them to memory – but needlessly, as it turns out, for they do not feature in the particular passage which the examination board has chosen this summer. The passage which they have selected is easy to recognize, much to the boy's relief. It features a word which is memorable chiefly by virtue of the fact that it has no English synonym or translation; a word which the boy feels sure he will never have reason to write again once this exam is over. The word is *quincunx*, which, as the notes to the boy's edition of Caesar explain, with the aid of a simple diagram, is the alignment of five like objects so that four are set at the corners of a square and the fifth is at the exact intersection of the two diagonal lines bisecting the same square from corner to corner. The *quincunx* was the formation in which the despairing Vercingetorix and his captains, stealing a trick learnt from their attackers, drove sharpened wooden stakes into the earthen ramparts of their final citadel, the points facing out and down, aimed viciously at the chests of the first men in the inexorably advancing Roman cohorts. To no avail; the breast-plated cohorts trampled their pierced and fallen colleagues as they clambered upwards; the citadel was taken, the bare were vanquished by the armoured, and the wildness of Gaul was for ever over.

At ten past three, with twenty minutes to spare, the boy looks round, and is not a little satisfied to see that he is the first to have finished – and not a little relieved to see that no one has apparently noticed the unnatural swiftness with which he had completed his task. For two years he has clumsily but successfully concealed his inability to understand Latin grammar or to translate an unseen Latin text, blushing and bluffing his way through every lesson; every evening for the last four weeks of those two years he has devoted a whole, secret hour to memorizing from a paperback translation the entire seventh book of Caesar's *Gallic Wars*. His only fear (the palms of his hands are still sweating slightly; his index finger is calloused from holding the pen so tight) was that he might, flustered by the silence of the examination room, have transcribed with faultless accuracy but in complete error a passage other than the one set. That one ridiculous word, *quincunx*, the word on which Vercingetorix pinned his last hope, the word that betrayed him and all his captains, has saved the boy. It only occurs once in the book, unmistakably placed at the opening of the description of the very last battle between rebel and ruler, and it has enabled him to select the appropriate string of sentences from his memory and so execute his fraud to perfection.

At half-past three, when the two hours of the exam are over, the master who sits at the front desk will call out "*Put your pens down please*"; but the boy does not wait for this instruction; he lays down his pen early. This is no small gesture, for this is the very last afternoon that the boys will be assembled in the school gymnasium in this way. Once this paper is over, the summer will be over; his fourteenth year will be, almost, over.

He lays down his pen, and he looks out of the window. Sixty-two boys bend their white-collared necks over their exam papers; but the sixty-third lifts his head, turns it, and gazes.

The school gymnasium has tall, metal-framed windows which reach from floor to ceiling, four of them. Between them are the racks of wooden wall-bars on which this boy, together with all the others, has clambered every Tuesday afternoon of the summer term, when the gym has been used for its normal, noisy, masculine purpose. The bars are empty of bare arms and legs now, and quiet. The windows are all shut – despite the heat – to keep out the sound of any passing plane or traffic which might hum, however distantly, over or beyond the school grounds, distracting. Beyond them is a stretch of black tarmac, turning oily in this heat. Beyond that are the playing fields, kept empty on this particular afternoon, and the turf is brown and the earth cracking where the groundsman has shaved the pitch too close. There are no long grasses for the hot wind to move, no gulls even; the playing fields are as quiet as the ramparts before a final attack. Only one thing is moving. Coming slowly up the drive which bisects the playing fields and leads to the playground is a car: a big, dark, shining and silent car.

The boy is instantly and unreasonably sure that the car is coming for him. Quite sure. The car halts, engine running, in the middle of the playground, and there it waits – waits as a lion might wait. Oddly, none of the sixty-two boys raise their heads, which they might have been expected to do when they caught sight of it stopping – after all, no group of boys of that particular age could be expected to concentrate quite that hard on anything written in Latin. Then one smoked glass car window slides down. Not to reveal the interior, or the identity of the (surely uniformed) driver, but as if to issue an unspoken invitation. As this happens, the boy looks to see if the supervising master has noticed what is happening; but he has not. A rear door swings open, revealing a glimpse of a dark, expensively upholstered interior. And now comes what is perhaps the oddest detail in this admittedly odd story; earlier in the afternoon the master had been very strict about insisting that none of the boys move either to or from their desks before precisely the allotted time; but now neither he nor any of the boy's classmates attempt to stop the boy as he rises neatly from his desk, leaves his blazer hanging forgotten on the back of his chair, moves towards the second of the four windows, climbs the wall bars, levers open a panel in the metal window-frame, climbs through it, drops to his hands and knees so as to break his eight foot fall onto the baking tarmac, gets to his feet, walks across the empty playground and then gets into the empty back seat of the car. The entire action is as unhesitating, as easy and as private as if he had dreamt it.

In retrospect we can be sure that this boy had had, that summer, many imaginings far stranger than the unheralded arrival of such an unlikely means of transport – he was, after all, fourteen. Any boy capable of memorizing the translation of an entire book of obscure military Latin prose clearly had a capable and practised mind. He surely, once the car door had closed, would have recognized as familiar from his adolescent fantasies the dark eyes in the rear-view mirror, the elegantly powerful hands on the wheel (one gloved, one ungloved), the quiet surge of the engine, the unhurried smoothness of the ride, the smoothly obscene voice which began to tell him that no one could see him as he was driven through the streets of his home town behind smoked glass windows. That no teachers, no parents and no neighbours could see him. That no one but the man glancing up to watch him in the rear-view mirror could see the smile which broke slowly across his face when he felt the leather of the seat sticking slightly to his back once his white school shirt was unbuttoned and off.

And now, twenty-two years later, we may be sure that this same boy has now done all or almost all of the things that he ever imagined doing on those hot afternoons of his fourteenth year. He has doubtless seen many men bare-chested, jewelled, captured; humiliated; lead in triumph. On many nights in the course of those twenty-two years he has turned the bedroom lamp back on so that he can see the exact transition from defiance to surrender pass over a man's face. But still, even after all this, there is something about the memory of a June afternoon and of an unseen driver that catches in his mind like a fish hook – like a fish hook will in the fleshy part of the hand at the base of the thumb, if you're careless.

It's a fierce pain, shocking. Almost unbearable, should the fishing line suddenly pull tight. It can hurt so much that you want to get a knife and cut it out.

Slice yourself open.

The boy cannot quite account for the odd power of this memory of his past self, no matter how often he replays it. Sometimes he feels sure that the key to it lies in the untranslatable word, the Latin word that has no translation, which is explicable only by a diagram, the word he learnt at fourteen but has never used since. He feels sure, also, that the meaning of the memory is something to do with the fact that he was never caught, that no one ever knew that his perfect marks for that translation paper were earned by his memorizing a set of words which he never understood – no one, neither his parents nor his teachers nor any of the adults who had so eagerly assured their prize pupil that his future was bright. He recognizes now that it is a lesson which has stood him in good stead, this trick of remembering what you never understood, of reproducing with perfect conviction the meaning of words that are meaningless. He also knows now that the driver of that car, whoever he was, knew how to do something that he himself has since learnt, but which none of the other boys nor their teacher could or would ever know; how to pick the right boy. How to pull a fourteen-year-old out through a schoolroom window without a sound, without a word, without even a look. Just by waiting. Waiting, on the hottest afternoon of the year. Doing it so that no one in that small town suspects what is being noiselessly done under their noses. Doing it so that a fourteen-year-old boy helplessly arches his back, later that afternoon, or on another afternoon later that year, the last afternoon of his boyhood, arches his back and lets his head fall, then lifts his astonished face at the last moment and looks down at the other man and comes and comes and comes and comes and now, now, twenty-two years later, looks at the clock, sees that it is ten past three, looks out of his window, and lays his pen down.

THE GANG

Sebastian Beaumont

MY NAME IS David. I didn't get my first taste of the gay scene until 1985, when I was eighteen. I'd been yearning to see what it was like for a couple of years before that, but I happen to be blessed (or cursed, depending on how you look at it) with extremely youthful looks. My peers at school called me "Billy" (as in Billy the Kid), which I didn't really mind, or "baby face", which I did. In my last year I was still only five foot two and could easily pass for fourteen if I wore my old shorts.

On my eighteenth birthday, I ventured out to a bar – The Aquarium – down near Brighton seafront. I was supposed to be doing last minute revision for my A levels, but had taken an evening off one Wednesday to come down from Haywards Heath, on the pretext of seeing my older sister. She was working as a secretary at American Express at the time and was living in a flat up by that pub that used to be a morgue. I walked down from her place to The Aquarium and was nervous as hell, and felt as young as I looked.

I wandered round the block more times than I care to admit before I summoned the courage to open the door and go in. I had, however, rehearsed the moment well. There were to be no timid requests for lemonade from me. I walked straight up to the bar and, in my best "authoritative prefect" voice asked for a pint of lager.

The two other men at the bar turned to look at me. The barman smirked in disbelief and said, "Pardon?"

I pulled out my passport and slapped it on the bar and said, "I'm eighteen. A pint of lager, please."

The barman studied the passport for a while, then laughed. "Happy birthday," he said and pulled me a pint.

I took the beer and went to stand in a corner, where I kept sipping it in that neurotic way that people have when they are nervous and want something to do with their hands. I guess you can imagine that for someone of my stature (slim as well as short) a pint of lager is, proportionally, far more than it would be for most men, and by the time I'd finished it I was feeling halfway drunk. I leaned against the wall and watched the others in the bar as they chatted. There weren't many there – half a dozen or so. It was only eight o'clock, after all, and I hadn't yet understood that gay men go out later in the evening than straight people. All but one of the men I saw in that bar had moustaches. I didn't know at the time that I had stumbled across *that kind* of pub, and assumed that all gay men wore moustaches.

I left after only twenty minutes, without talking to anyone, and took the train home, feeling decidedly affected by the alcohol. But I was also affected by the atmosphere – by that intense *frisson* that accompanies our first experience of seeing men together like that; of seeing the casual way in which a man can lean towards another and say something quietly, with an utterly assured intimacy and carelessness – and I knew, then, I *knew* that I had experienced something that would change me forever.

The next few weeks were taken up with my exams, which went OK-*ish*. After they were over – on the day I left school, in fact – I stopped shaving my upper lip. It took about a week before anyone noticed. My mother leaned over, at breakfast one morning, and pointed at my lip and said, "What's *that*?" as though it might have been some strange fungal growth. I think I blushed. In fact, I'm sure I did. But I knew better than to say anything and remained silent. My brother, three years younger than me and already taller, grinned and said, "I think it's supposed to be a moustache, mum." My dad grunted and looked disdainful. My thirteen-year-old sister, both proud and self-conscious of her incipient breasts, seemed even more embarrassed than I was at the mention of a secondary sexual characteristic.

My moustache continued its imperceptible growth, and at the end of the following week we went away to East Anglia for our annual holiday – a fortnight of windy walks and home-cooking with my uncle and aunt at their cottage near Hunstanton. I got into that terrible cycle of looking at my lip every morning in the mirror and not seeing any difference. Still, by the time we got back my moustache was nearly four weeks old, and, with the aid of a little of my mother's mascara, looked almost passable.

I ventured out to The Aquarium once more, on a Friday evening at around nine-thirty – a much more sensible time. I'd arranged to stay the night with my sister and when I told her I wanted to go out on my own, she smiled conspiratorially and slipped a fiver into my pocket and said, "Have fun."

This time I walked straight into the bar and, not wanting to make the same mistake twice, ordered a half-pint of lager (I never drank whole pints after that). I was served by a different barman that evening and had to go through the whole passport business again before he would serve me. There were more people there that evening and I drew plenty of stares as I stood on my own, sipping my beer, catching my reflection every now and then in the metal edging of the cigarette machine. I thought I looked like some kind of preppy twelve-year-old wearing a stick-on moustache. But I was incredibly proud of it and so I didn't care.

After a while a man sauntered over to me and said hello.

"I saw that business with the passport," he said. "I expect it's a real pain sometimes – to look so young."

"Yes," I replied.

"I used to be like that, too," he told me. "I hated it. I never had the nous to use proper ID. When I was eighteen I was always getting chucked out of pubs for under-age drinking, whilst other boys who couldn't have been more than fifteen looked on. It *is* a pain, now, but you'll think of it as an advantage in a few years' time, believe me. I'm thirty-five, though under most circumstances I don't admit to more than twenty-seven."

I held out my hand.

"I'm David," I said.

"Please," the man smiled, "don't be so formal. I'm Mark. I'm waiting for The Gang. There's nothing quite so desolate as hanging around in a bar on your own when you want company, is there? I'll introduce you around when the boys turn up – if you want."

So that was how I met The Gang. They were loud, jokey, sexy and almost all moustached. I seemed to strike a chord somewhere, because they took to me immediately. They did all those things that I would have taken offence at if they had been done by other people – they patted me on the head, cuddled me as though I was a toy, teased me and joked about my height and my extreme youth. They got away with it because it was all done with affection. That was the great part of it. They teased me, but they teased each other, too, about everything – appearance, domestic habits, sexual tastes . . . No one was let off, and so we all laughed together.

They called me the Half-Pint Clone and I loved it. I loved it, but there was something sad about it all too, because one of the reasons I'd come out to this bar was so that I could find someone with whom to loose my virginity, and although they liked me, they didn't want to sleep with me. They stood around and laughed, and talked about the sex they'd been having, and I listened, and I longed.

I mentioned this to Mark, who seemed the most approachable member of The Gang, and I remember his sympathetic look as I stammered out my wistful yearning to him, and he said, "You should find someone your own age for that, David, or maybe someone older who's into younger guys. It's not really our scene. If you went to the right place, and met the right people, you'd have more offers than you could deal with. If this was five years ago, rather than now, I'd suggest you went down to the bushes for a hearty, breathless encounter in the moonlight. But you must have heard about this thing, this *disease*? It's changing everything.''

His words had a curious, echoing ring to them, and I later found out that that was the night that the first member of The Gang was diagnosed as unwell – his name was Joe and he was a travel agent from Hove who held the kind of parties that we'll never see again. I went to one or two, but latterly they became so tinged with absence that it was hard to dance with a smile.

I met The Gang down at The Aquarium every Friday night that first summer, and, when I started at Sussex University, even more often than that. They bought me my half-pints, took me to their parties, made me laugh. They lectured me on safe sex, too. In those days, everything was potentially unsafe – there was even a debate about kissing.

It was at around that time that I met Gareth. He was only five foot five and so I didn't feel quite so small when I was with him. He was dark, with plaintive dog-like eyes and a straight mouth that made him look as though he was permanently being taken aback. His swarthy looks complemented my paler complexion and together we were light and shade, somehow. He had sure hands, too, and a gestural openness that made me trust him. He was in his third year of a media course, whilst I was doing computer studies and playing around with early ideas of artificial intelligence. We met at a Gay Soc evening and went out for a drink afterwards, each admitting after our third beer that we were virgins and worried way beyond rational explanation about the potential deadliness of sex. We skirted the subject of doing it with each other for some time, and, after a month or two of scheduling and rescheduling the event, finally managed a hesitant mutual masturbation, after which we fastidiously and warily cleaned up our own – virginal and therefore untainted – bodily fluids.

We became boyfriends. I felt that I might be falling in love with him, though it was hard to tell. I had intense flashes of tenderness for him, and I enjoyed his company, so I *assumed* that it was love. We slept together most nights, and because I was so relieved to have lost my virginity, I didn't question the restricted nature of our super-safe sexual repertoire –

which in those first few months meant basically tossing each other off.

I removed my moustache, then, because I realized it made me appear ridiculous. Also, I'd found out that it wasn't the ubiquitous sign of homosexuality that I'd first imagined it to be. So I became clean shaven once more and went back to looking like a fourteen-year-old – well, perhaps fifteen by then. At the end of the year, Gareth graduated and found a job in a PR firm in Brighton. He took a mortgage out on a flat and persuaded me to move in with him. I grew another inch that year, which obscurely seemed to make all the difference.

Setting up home together seemed so adult and final. I loved feeling secure and wanted and *enveloped* by my new domestic life. Gareth turned out to be a habitual television watcher, which didn't bother me at first. Sitting watching TV with my lover had been one of my "what life will be like one day" fantasies that I'd had when I was a teenager. But I can only watch so much television and if it hadn't been for my regular socializing with The Gang I would have become bored. My life settled into a comfortable routine where Gareth fulfilled most of my needs and The Gang provided that all-important outside influence.

Gradually, more and more sexual acts became passed as safe by HIV experts, but Gareth remained steadfastly unversatile. He was the only lover I'd ever had, and vice versa, so you'd think that we'd have been happy doing *everything* to each other. But he didn't trust me, not deep down, which I found painful. He didn't trust me because of The Gang, with whom he refused to socialize. He avoided them as much as possible, though we often bumped into one or other of them in the street and I would talk to whoever it was, or go for coffee somewhere and sit around gossiping, whilst Gareth sat silently smiling one of his "I'm not really interested" smiles.

When I met The Gang for drinks, I went on my own. When I went to their parties (which I did less and less frequently), I also went alone. Later on, especially when I began to visit them in hospital, Gareth would treat me as though I was infected myself. I was always confused about this side of his personality because in other respects he was open, trusting, generous and affectionate. He clearly loved me, and was happy that I was with him, and pleased that my course was going well. But there was this one area in our lives that gave rise to conflict. Sex.

I had always wanted to take his penis into my mouth (I had always wanted to be fucked by him, if I'm honest, but *that* was out of the question). It was one of my fantasies, to give a really good blow job, but Gareth couldn't bring himself, even after we'd been together a couple of years, to let me do that. I once persuaded him to put a flavoured condom on, but at the approach of my lips, he sort of shuddered and pushed me away, his Adam's apple jittering up and down as though he was desperately trying to swallow a dry biscuit. I began to realize, belatedly, that he was suffering from a severe case of Aids panic. But I didn't press the point. At least we were having sex of a kind, and whatever else may have been true, I never had to bother about whether or not I was putting myself at risk.

I began to observe Gareth's responses around the whole area of sex and became aware that he was actually *unable* to make love to me on the days that I'd been to the hospital to visit a member of The Gang. This was crazy, but even a peripheral mention of the subject would send Gareth into a weird anxiety in which he would actually thrust out his hands as though warding off a physical presence. And so I decided to lie whenever I could, and go to the hospital on the sly.

At one point there were three members of The Gang in Ward 6 at the same time and it would sometimes get so that it was one big party, with all of us laughing and joking and making fun of the nurses and sneaking dirty videos in, and the odd beer, too. And one day, when I was sitting with Mark in the kitchen area and laughing so hard I thought I was going to be sick, I thought to myself, *they've had so much fun!*

Of course, laughter only took up a part of this time. There was all the other stuff that goes with illness, too. It was so hard to watch it happen, sometimes, especially when, in the middle of something hilarious, I would be hit by the thought that it was all so unfair.

I hated the funerals. Gareth never came with me to any of them. Not one. He was sympathetic in his way, I know, but just to think of that particular disease made him go into a still, silent area of dread, and there is no greater reminder of illness than death. So, he never saw the solidarity with which The Gang dwindled. He never saw the brave laughter, the sudden tears, the overwhelming sorrow of it all, and because he didn't see it, he didn't know how to give me the sympathy I needed.

I graduated from university in 1988 with a good degree. I could have chased money up to London, or abroad, but I chose instead to work with a small, personal company in Brighton that did not pay well, by industry standards, but which didn't demand long hours and which allowed me to stay on with Gareth. We sold the flat and bought a little house between Western Road and the sea, and moved in on November the fifth that year.

In almost all respects my life was going well. My family accepted us. My job was gay-friendly. The work I was doing was interesting. I had been with Gareth for nearly three years. I should have been content. But The Gang had decreased to only seven by then, and Gareth still treated my sperm as though it was radioactive.

I knew our relationship was dull, no matter how safe. But that was my fault, too. In saying that Gareth was the one who suffered from Aids panic, I'm not trying to imply that I was in some way nonchalant about it. I watched my friends succumb to this terrible illness and it made me shudder inside to realize that it was only a quirk of timing that was preventing me from following suit. It gave me a sense of responsibility for myself. If there was one thing I could learn from The Gang, it should be how to survive. That's why Gareth was, in many ways, the perfect haven. OK, so what if our life together was dull? Who said survival was going to be fun? Also, it was seductively easy to allow our life together to continue as it was, rather than make an effort to do anything about it. I was spending a lot of energy, that first winter in our house, just getting used to my new job. I kept looking on the plus side of things – I was in a town that I loved; Gareth and I were getting our home organized. And when I felt bored, or restricted, I could always go out with The Gang. It was all self-perpetuating and easy and managed to keep me going, without question, for a further two years.

Gareth came to accept, in his own limited way, my nights out without him. That is to say, we'd agreed not to talk about them, so I had to keep my wonderful times to myself, as well as my sad times, and gradually this came to seem to be for the best. Not sharing these things with Gareth made them seem precious to me, somehow, and I hoarded my happy memories, and nursed my sorrows as best I could. I would come in from the pub, or a party, or just a quiet night in watching a film and drinking tea, and he would be asleep in bed with the duvet pulled tightly to his cheek, and I would hug him briefly and he would smile and kiss me without really waking.

In January 1991, five and a half years after I met him, Mark went into hospital. He was the last member of The Gang alive by then and it was the most extraordinary experience for me. He was the first member of The Gang that I'd met, he was my closest friend, and even when the other members succumbed to illness, I still never expected Mark to get It. I can't think why, now.

When I visited him, there was no lively group to laugh with him, no one to make black jokes about his symptoms, no one to make the ward into one great house party. There was just me. He smiled often when I saw him, and held my hand, and, towards the end, he whispered to me, "You've grown up, you know. You look nearly adult now. Actually, I quite fancy you – at last."

I was twenty-three.

That night I cried in front of Gareth – for the first time, I am ashamed to say. He hugged me and told me that he loved me and he said what a relief it was that it would all be over soon.

I asked him what he meant.

"This blight," Gareth said, "this blight of illness that has affected you ever since we met. At last, it is almost finished."

I couldn't believe that he could say those words. As he continued to speak, I realized that all these years, all this time, he had seen The Gang as a terrible imposition on our life together, and somewhere in his mind – not consciously perhaps – he had been ticking them off as they died, making the assumption that when they were gone he would finally have me to himself.

This made me go into a kind of shock that I had never experienced before. It was a sort of calm numbness that allowed me to act as if nothing was wrong. I developed a habit of testing Gareth out, by talking about The Gang in the past tense, and I noticed a kind of smugness in him that I found hateful. He seemed to be saying "At last!" under his breath whenever my friends were mentioned, and I felt the great, smothering cloak of his dullness closing around me, getting more and more suffocating every day. It was only then that I fully realized what a compensation The Gang had been – how they'd made my life with Gareth bearable because they provided such vibrant relief from it. Gareth didn't notice this change in me, and nor did my work colleagues. Nor, it seemed, did Mark when I visited him in hospital. It seemed impossible that I could feel so changed inside without people noticing.

I managed to continue to make love to Gareth, in our half-hearted way; I managed to cook when it was my turn; to eat; to sleep. I also managed to hold Mark's hand when I sat beside him on his bed in Ward 6, and to smile and laugh with him.

The day before he died, he said, "At least you've survived, David. I'm so pleased you've been spared all of this. You have a lover. I so envy you your future."

And I looked at him and thought, *The only life I've EVER experienced, the only emotion that I have felt that has been truly worthwhile, has been experienced with YOU and with the rest of The Gang.*

"What am I going to do without you?" I mumbled, and he squeezed my hand, and cried when I cried, and managed to make me smile before I left. And when I went back to the hospital the next day, he had died.

The funeral was well-attended by family and friends. The only thing I could think of during the short service was that Mark had said he envied me. Me! I was the one who'd scuttled into a relationship out of fear of illness. I was the one who was so fettered by inhibition that I refused to let myself go in anything like the fearless way The Gang had – experiencing only through them, rather than with them. I was the one who'd never *lived*. I was too busy protecting this future of mine that Mark envied so much; too busy *not* doing things, so that I never really had a present, let alone a future. And the future was beginning to look frighteningly bleak and empty without The Gang around to give it emotional depth. OK, there had been too much sorrow along with the fun, but there had been love as well, in abundance. In everything The Gang did, and felt, and expressed, there was an intensity that gave it meaning.

I walked home from Mark's funeral that afternoon quiet inside, and calm. But no longer numb. Gareth was there when I got back. He was cooking dinner and he couldn't disguise the relief he felt that The Gang were gone. He hugged me briefly – a moment of dispassionate human contact.

"It's over," he sighed.

I stood in the doorway and watched him cooking, watched the calm sureness of his movements; the utter *separateness* of his being. And I thought of Mark, and the others, and how they would never have put up with the life I was leading for more than a weekend at the very most. Probably not more than an afternoon, and only then because it could be laughed about later. It suddenly astonished me that I had justified my inertia by blaming it on fear of illness. And as I stood, it struck me that the greatest lesson I could learn from The Gang was *not* survival, but the need to make the most of the life I had, however long or short. Perhaps I owed it to Mark to have a future that was worth envying . . .

I left Gareth to finish off dinner and slipped upstairs. I took my car keys from the bedside table and my wallet with its credit cards from the drawer. I looked down at the bed we had slept in for more nights than I care to remember, and I felt no emotion whatsoever – or rather, I realized that feeling nothing was a kind of dreadful emotion in itself. I crept down the stairs to the hall from where I could hear the sound of frying and the chink of cutlery, and let myself out onto the pavement.

Gently pulling the front door closed behind me for the last time, I whispered.

"Yes. It's over."

JONAH

David Patrick Beavers

SUNDAY. WITHOUT SUN. Rain. It slaps against the window. Much to do, yet nothing getting done. And Jonah watches me doing nothing. Jonah with his wild gray hair and furry brows.

"Quit staring," I said.

"I'll wait," he said. "Whenever you're ready."

The Sunday visitation. You weren't there. Just me. And him. Waiting. He stopped staring at me. Stared at the floor. Waiting. For me.

He looked sad. I wanted to care, but didn't. He'd said that I was born from a jackal's blood clot buried beneath the desert sand. He'd said that to you. You told him to be nice to me or never bother coming to our apartment again. He wasn't nice. He continued to come. For three years, seven months and three days, I'd left every Sunday when he rang the bell. We'd cross paths over the threshold. It made you crazy. You wanted me to get along with your father. Him to get along with me. He was part of the family and all that rot.

I pulled myself up from the chair. I resented him being here. He shifted his weight. Right foot to left. That's right. Step. Intrude further.

"No," I said. "I don't want to do this."

"You said you would. I'll wait."

I went to the bathroom. Shut him out. Your father, not mine. I collapsed on the bed. He won't wait forever, I thought. He *was* a part of the family. *Your* family. Now, the last of that line. Your mother – his wife – died some years back. Uterine cancer. And your brother not long after your mother. Three days out of This Man's Army and smashed between a Chevy pick-up and a '78 Mustang. You were your father's last. You were my only. You were dumb fuck dead, too. Maybe he'll tire of waiting.

You should have seen us at your funeral. Neither he nor I blinked a wet eye. The others did. Friends, a few scattered relatives belonging to your mother's gene pool. They clucked about hoping not to start a fight between Jonah and me. There was no cause for worry. We didn't talk. Not then.

It's strange how dead people's rooms are surreal, I thought. You'd lived here. With me. We fucked in this bed. Shaved and showered in there. I'd already distributed most of your belongings to friends and worthy charities. The kind of organizations your father called Communist Pig Farms. Jonah. Redder than a redneck's sunburned neck. He caught me off-guard when he asked me to do it. I'd said yes. He said that you'd told him I was a man of my word. I didn't know that you two had ever spoken about me. A man of my word. What the fuck does that mean? He asked me to prove that you were right about me. Why should I prove myself to him? He wasn't my blood. Wasn't anything to me, except an annoyance.

Do I keep you true to your word? Do as he asks? Make you out to be a liar and prove to him that his suspicions about my character were true? Why should I care? You were dead. I had no interest in maintaining a relationship with your Jonah. I should have just gone out there and tossed him out on his ass. But I couldn't. Because you were dead. You'd never lied while you were alive. I didn't want to make you a liar in death. Maybe, I thought, if I wait, he'll just give up and go away.

An hour slipped by. Another hour crawled almost at a standstill. I got up from the bed, cracked open the door and peered into the living room. There he still stood.

"Go home, Jonah!"

"You agreed to do it," he said.

"Not today."

"Then when?"

"I don't know that I can."

"A lie, then. You're no man of your word."

"What would be the point?"

"Everybody's dead! That's my point!"

"Your point's taken," I said. "Now get out."

"You're a liar. Should've figured . . ."

"I can't do it!"

"Then I'm not leaving."

"Do what you want," I said as I closed the door and went back to the bed. The rain continued to slap at my window like so much cat litter being scattered by a bladder-weak cat. Rain usually lulls me to sleep. Not that night. I lay waiting to hear him exit. Nothing. If I drifted into slumber, the slightest noise awoke me. Why doesn't he leave, I thought. Why don't I just give him what he wants? I couldn't. You would've thought this whole situation recondite, I know. Why weren't you there? I resented you for dying. Was angry with you for leaving me in this preposterous scenario. Fuck him. Fuck you. Sleep.

He was still there at dawn. Still standing. I was sure his legs had gone numb. Maybe he was paralyzed. But no. He'd learned to sleep standing on his feet. Something he'd mastered during a stint in the Marine Corps, you'd once said. He'd also pissed his pants. Wetted all down himself. He was pressing my limit, all right. He didn't say anything to me. I filled a bucket with scalding water and detergent and tossed it on him and the carpet. He flinched a bit.

"You're a pig," I said.

"I knew you were a fuckin' puss," he said.

"You won't get me to do it today, Jonah. I'm going out." And I did. Showered, shaved and went out into the world. Straight to the news-stand. I'd find a place to move to. A new place to live. Let Jonah stay and rot through the floorboards.

I found a new apartment. Smaller. Older than the one we'd lived in. Paid the deposit and went back to pack. Pack up my stuff and my few remnants of you.

Jonah hadn't moved. His pants had dried. He was determined not to give in. I worked round the clock boxing-up, tossing-out, and stacking-up my stuff for the movers. I called my landlord and tended notice, though I still had to pay a pro-rated rent charge for two weeks. Jonah said nothing through all this. Did nothing.

"The movers are coming," I said. He said nothing. I sighed and had the phone disconnected. Sent off change of address forms. Everything done that day.

The movers came. Loaded up their trucks. They rolled their eyes at the sight of Jonah standing in the middle of the floor. They had to maneuver around him. An annoyance. I pretended as if he wasn't there. With the last stick of furniture, the last suitcase, the last box out the door and the movers on their way to my new address, I turned to Jonah.

"I'm going."

"Do it," he said.

"Why should I?"

"Because . . . I'm asking."

"You've always hated me, Jonah. This would be like making amends. I can't do this for you."

"Then don't do it for me. Don't do it for yourself. Do it for my baby."

"*My* baby," I said. "My love."

"All right," he said. "For *your* love." He pulled it out from beneath his shirt and handed it to me. I took it. Stared at it.

"We loved each other," I said.

"I know," he said. "We both lost on this one. I know what you meant to each other. But, you're still young. I'm not. I'm tired. Help me find my family again."

Though I'd never done this before, I pulled the trigger. The bullet went straight through his chest. Then he lay still with a smile on his face. I'd never seen him smile. I hoped you were there to greet him.

RIVER

Peter Burton

THERE IS A feel of autumn in the air as I stand by the river in the early evening light. Brown leaves rustle on the slightly damp ground. It rained today, and the leaves of the plane tree above me rattle together. The globes of the lights along the Embankment bend away on either side in a slight half-circle. A bay in the very heart of London. A Chelsea bay. On one side is the bridge covered in lights and, near it, on the nether bank, the fun-fair, also a mass of coloured lights. It must be empty there tonight though, for although it is a still night no sounds are carried across the river on the occasional cool breezes. To the other side of me I can see towers and chimneys and feel the presence of industry. Smoke rises into the sky. And now an explosion of white steam or smoke, from the flour mill, white and straight against the purple blue sky.

Patches of light, upon the far bank. The squares of office and factory windows, lights where, probably, watchmen walk.

The river itself has no colour. It is an imitation. A copy of everything which surrounds it. A mirror which catches the lights from the fair, the factories and the other buildings. But, though it has no colour, it has a marvellous life and potency. The potency is so strong that it pulls me down here, to this unfeeling parapet, almost every night. To stand. Watching.

The life of the river moves so constantly. It laps and gnaws at the foundations of the wall I lean against, it ripples peacefully around the supporting colonnades of the bridges which span it. It carries, happily, the little river boats.

A police launch chugs downstream towards Greenwich. The river activates for a brief moment and then becomes calm and lapping still again. Moored on my side of the river are four small row-boats and one larger one, each tethered by an orange buoy. I wonder as I stare at them, how they got there. Who left them? How did they get away? Somehow I don't picture the boats being towed there, I imagine a man in each, rowing them, abandoning, and then swimming ashore.

There are very few people, though it is still early. An Indian woman walks carefully along, wrapped in a trailing sari. She is almost the only person to have passed in the hour I've stood here.

It is late. We have been sitting, talking. And drinking tea. These last weeks we haven't had enough money to afford both tea and coffee. We're bored with coffee anyway. Or so we say. But somehow tea does seem more soothing. More of a drink. Not sticky powder.

My three guests do not quite feel what I feel for the river, but they stand and gaze over it and make jokes and conjecture. It is late, it is cold, it is dark.

The two boys are dressed in thin summer clothes and they shiver. They are lovers and one is my friend. I want his lover. But he has said no to me. This refusal determines me to get him. He knows this and is playing a game with me. Leading me. Taunting me. It is impossible to tell what the outcome of the game will be. My friend knows of this game. Knows what I am after. I warned him before I started. I hate shifty, sly seductions. They are mean and uncomfortable. The game fascinates him. He hasn't, yet, slept with the boy, but they have a relationship.

They stand a little away from me and talk in hushed whispers. This frustrates me and makes me shrilly talkative, brittle, harsh and funny. The girl is amused by my antics and tales. She links her fantasies with mine. I don't know her well but she has a sense of fun and joins in. Does she feel anything about the situation which envelopes the three boys she stands by the river with?

We laugh. I've told her about my fantasy of filling, late one night, the Thames with crocodiles and savage tropical fish. We laugh as we imagine the faces of the river men the next morning. Steering their boats up and down stream in a cold London semblance of an African river.

There is a chill mist creeping over the river. We stand and watch it and watch the bridges slowly disappear. We call car headlights "dragon's-eyes", some in red and some in orange, and, as they accelerate, imagine the dragons chasing some delicious prey. The mist rises and whirls. We all shiver.

I boast that I am not feeling cold and force myself to laugh and say they "have no blood". The two boys want to return to my flat and further hot drinks. But I do not want to offer any further hospitality. I want to be alone to think about the boy . . .

How like a Whistler river it all is, in this chill mist.

We drift slowly back across the dead road and walk up the quiet side street. Even King's Road is without life. We stop and chatter outside my door. A boy, we know him, he does not acknowledge us, clatters by on the other side. We part and I climb the stairs to my flat.

It is hot. This August is not yet, then, truly autumn. The sun blazes mercilessly down upon me. The river stinks today. I gaze down at it, sniff disdainfully. It may have called me but it keeps me for only a short time. I turn sharply, dart between the cars, and hurry home. I think of him.

It is another night. I am alone again. This time I sit upon the parapet. My back rested against the curling Victorian lamp. I am slightly drunk. Wobbly. The evening has been spent with an old man of letters. A grand old man. He is sixty-odd years older than me and has seen everything from the invention of the telephone, through Casement and Oscar Wilde, to Moon landings. Which bore him. He is absorbing. Like a discursive book. He plucks names from the air and wraps a story around them. Then passes on. We supper together often, he and I, a simple meal, a glass of wine.

I had continued to drink in my own flat. Cans of iced beer. About six of them. They have mixed with the wine and now I sit wobbly on this river wall. The water is without colour, it is just blackness. It is so dark and unfeeling that it almost, this once, seems without life. I look down into it and wonder that anyone could drown themselves in it. And I tremble slightly because I remember the times I've stood and thought . . .

Sniff with irritation at my weaker self. And jump from the wall and hurry home.

Why do so few people use this peaceful part of London, one of the nicest river spots? I always wonder as I sit in the evening and see no one.

This evening I stand in a slightly different spot. Further along the Embankment. Near to the steps which lead up to the bridge. A bus stop is behind me and buses stop and spit out passengers. Traffic trickles across the bridge but the usual lateness of the hour sees an ever-diminishing flow of buses and cars. Though I am further from the pleasure gardens than usual I hear sounds from them. Wisps of shrill laughter, screams of fear and delight, and music. Whistling in the air. It is damp. Mist is coming up the river again tonight.

A man walks across the bridge and stops at mid-river. He looks down at the dark swirling waters. Is he going to jump? Is he thinking of jumping? Or is he just a romantic captured, as I am, by the magic of the river?

A girl and a boy hurry down the steps, off the bridge. I didn't see them on the bridge. They must have been walking on the far side. She is dressed in fringed jeans and a bright, clinging sweater. He wears motorcycle gear. They've probably come from one of the Battersea ton-up cafés. But they don't seem to have a motorcycle.

There are people about tonight. I have no peace. I want people and talk. I don't know what I want. The constant scurrying of people distracts me from thoughts of him. And boys seem to look like him. I wonder about the progress of the relationship. Have they had sex yet?

★   ★   ★

The kitchen of the flat. Bare. Uncovered boards. An armchair, a shelf for books and magazines. Pictures of pop stars pinned to one wall and a vast Madame Colette on another. Looking into the room. A pile of scrap paper on the floor and a mug with pencils in it standing near, where I jot down ideas, notes. Bits and pieces for stories or articles.

The window is open onto a wet night. I hear tugs hooting on the river and catch a glimmer of light from the illuminated bridge. The rain splashes in through the open window and I move to close it. But I don't. Instead I stand and stare out, over the garden at the back, and think of the river. The rain blows into my face and I let it trickle, like tears, down my face. Water.

A shrill whistling. I am absently aware of it. The kettle has boiled. Tea has to be made.

They are both here for the evening.

It is later. They have left. It still rains. Autumn is here. *He* must return, very soon to his far away university.

It rains all the time now. August is out. September is here and already I await winter. The river is furious. The rain lashes it. The wind whisks up little brisk waves. There are no people about at all and very little traffic. The rain even tries to hide the buildings on the other side of the river. Mournful river boats go occasionally by. They are the only life. I am soaking. Standing in a too small overcoat and summer shoes. My hair matted and heavy, slicked down to my head by the weight of the rain. Tears run down from it onto my eyes and tears from my eyes, hot and salty, run down my face. I lick them from my lips and swallow the salty water.

We met today, in the West End. He was buying clothes and books, preparing for his return to his studies. He looked as beautiful, as mournful, as ever. That lank hair, falling straight and smooth, like curtains, on either side of his face. The too big mouth. The knowing, mocking-me, eyes. Not at all beautiful. Hardly pretty. But exuding such a sexual power. We talked a while and then walked to a coffee bar and drank hot chocolate and ate Danish pastries. We both know that the game is almost over, in a kind of deadening emotional stalemate. It was quite dark by the time we left the coffee bar and walked together to Charing Cross underground station.

As we walked into the station we could see the river on the other side. Uncaring. Then we bought tickets and climbed on our District Line trains.

There is a feel of winter in the air as I stand by the river in the early-morning light. The brown leaves have all been blown away and soon, I feel, there will be frost on the ground. It has been a cold night and I have been unable to sleep. The empty branches shiver in the dawn and point their bony fingers accusingly at me. "What are you doing here?" they seem to ask. The lights on the bay, my Chelsea bay, have been put out and there is an absolute peace, calm and lack of humankind. No traffic disturbs me. No man walks near. No animal appears. Even the factories are still.

The sky is white. The river is a mirror. It is an imitation of the white sky and the grey and red buildings along its banks. The boats that float, moored but moving, are dead boats. The houseboats, which I passed as I walked to my favourite spot, appeared as gutted corpses.

In this cold early morning I can imagine I am the only person in the world. London belongs to me. But I feel no desire to run and claim, to take possession. I could not sleep so I came down here to calm myself and though I am not tired I have no energy. My limbs do not want to move.

The only part of me that is full of life, tumult, energy, is my mind. It will not cease from working, churning over. Last night I read four hundred pages, drank several cups of tea, talked. Endlessly and, in the end, to myself. But I could not tire myself.

The river flows down towards Greenwich. The boats move slowly towards the open sea, towards a certain kind of freedom away from the narrow London river. But the sea has boundaries too.

He went away today. Back to his Midland university. That is why I stand by the river thinking. That is why I cannot sleep. We didn't say goodbye. Why should we? We were hardly friends. We had just been playing a game. He has gone away and, when he returns, he will seem dull and I will not want to know him. If he asked me I should say no. NO.

River. River. You watch it all. You don't know, do you, what we up here on these banks, put ourselves through? You watch it all. But you have no feelings, you cannot care, concern yourself, hardly at all affect our lives. But you call to us and bring us down to your banks. In your mute way you try to calm us.

I still think of him. Think: No.

I never could bear to lose games.

WHATEVER HAPPENED TO THE GIRL NEXT DOOR?

Matthew Butler

GLORY, GLORY, GLORY, Gloria, but who'd admit to a name like Gloria Ramsbottom. Gloria Ramsbottom from one of those obscure, small villages "up North". Her parents were ordinary small-town folk, friendly, kind, narrow-minded, riddled with prejudice, and religious. They were staunch Catholics and as such almost everything Gloria did seemed that much worse to them. They disapproved utterly of London and of their daughter being there. They disapproved quite frankly of their daughter. She stood, for them, for all they disliked about modern society in general and modern youth in particular. Her manner of dress was too peculiar for them, period gowns were far from being Mrs Ramsbottom's idea of either "nice" or fashionable. To her they smacked of either penury or the brothel. Most of all the brothel, for that was how she visualized the whole of London. As Gloria wore dresses that were in vogue in the 1940s amongst the less well-off, and used make-up to excess, then the whorish associations came easily to her mother.

The very fact that she lived with two boys didn't look very good either. Her father, the gentler man, had fewer suspicions;

knowing and loving his daughter as he did he saw her as a person
and not as a symbol to be held up proudly to the neighbours or,
as his wife did, a disgrace to be forgotten. It would not have
helped Glory if she had told her parents that the two boys she
lived with were homophile. She had once tried, shortly after
moving into the flat with Peter and Paul, to tell her mother.

"Mother," she had begun, "I've moved."

"Aye, love, where are you living now? Still with Sue?"

"No mother, we weren't getting on that well."

"Who is it with then, girls I hope?"

"No mother, I'm living in Chelsea, with two boys."

Her mother jerked her head up and glared at Glory.

"Two boys in Chelsea? That's not very nice is it? What
would the family think if I told them about the way you live?
Two boys indeed. What are they like?"

"Oh it's all right mum, very respectable . . . they're," and
she lowered her voice, "both queer."

Her mother didn't hear her or, if she did, pretended not
to. The idea of homosexuality was something quite beyond
her range of comprehension. The nearest her mind went to
thinking about queers was with recollections of vague stories
about Oscar Wilde she had heard years ago. And all she'd heard
about him was that he was "dirty" and not to be mentioned
in polite company. Glory had watched her mother to see if she
had reacted in any way. Of course her mother had remained
impassive, showing no sign that she had heard her daughter.

"Peter's a writer, short stories and poems and bits of
journalism. Paul is a waiter."

"Hmm. Very nice for you dear, I'm sure," her mother had
replied but with no show of interest. She didn't really care what
Glory did now, she was in London, out of the way, and as long
as she didn't become involved in any real scandal there was no
fear of the neighbours finding out about her. She was looked
upon as the errant daughter.

That visit home had been as short as all the previous ones that
Gloria had made. She'd been so relieved to return to London,
to the flat, the surroundings and the people that she did feel
completely at home with.

"I may be a poove's moll," she thought, "but at least I get

some fun and have friends, a bloody sight more than if I'd not left home."

The Ramsbottoms wanted the best for their family without really wanting their family. The best to them was education, good clothing and plenty to eat. The best did not include love and generous helpings of affection. Mr Ramsbottom worked in an executive position in one of the large business concerns in the nearest major town. His wife had, therefore, no need to work. She occupied herself, however, with aiding the local poor and organizing jumble sales and children's outings – she forgot her husband and four children. Her Women's Institute-type work enabled her to feel martyred with the minimum amount of effort for she bypassed the nastier things, hospital visiting and assisting old and infirm people. She spent so much time on her charitable works that it was Glory who had to act as mother to the family. Her mother would appear at home to give orders, instructions and to allocate work, treating her children as if they were hired servants, and Glory had to keep an eye on everything from cooking and scrubbing to looking after the babies.

It was fortunate that she liked children and was able to contend with them. She quite enjoyed the responsibility of running the home, though she felt later that it had affected her outlook and made her turn slightly anti-feminist. It was not surprising to see Mr Ramsbottom pottering around the kitchen in an apron and clutching a cookery book as he tried to arrange some interesting meal for his brood.

"After all," Mrs Ramsbottom would say if he ever dared reproach her, "it's a good thing for a man to look after himself. Don't know how you would all manage without me."

"A bloody sight better," thought Gloria, though didn't say anything. She had once and caused the most almighty row. Her mother really believed, too, that she did work and slave for her family.

Glory had been sent to a convent school, which she'd hated but at which she had begun to develop so much into the girl she was today. It was here that all of her fears and neuroses had their roots. She had soon drifted away from the church and often found herself in violent disagreement with the harsh, unsympathetic nuns over many important matters. She found that by the time she came to leave she had, ironically, no belief in God at all and that all the years with the nuns had done had been to destroy every vestige of faith. From the convent school she had gone on to the local art college, where she did little, learned a lot and had a great deal of pleasure. She had only limited creative talents, though, and after a year she had left. She found that she thought more and more of leaving home, for the responsibilities now were much heavier, and of living in London. Eventually she and a girlfriend, equally a sufferer of parental dismissal, religious doubts and wanderlust, had left home and made their way to London. Neither had much money or a place to live. They quickly found a job, in one of London's large department stores, and soon after a double bedsitting room in Earls Court.

The sense of adventure fully compensated for the fact that the job was only paying starvation wages and that the room was little more than a glorified slum. They were free and that was what mattered most. Both girls worked steadily and tried hard to resist the many temptations that London had to offer. Then one of the boys in the store became friendly with Gloria, and when he suggested they see a film they both fancied, she accepted. Maybe he liked her, she thought. After the cinema he suggested they go to a club together. She had been thrilled. They went to a club he knew called "Pop" which was, as the name suggested, bright and very, very with-it. It was full of boys too, absolutely beautiful boys Gloria had thought.

She'd look around in amazement. None of the clubs she had frequented at home had been anything like this. They had all been much dingier and dirtier and the boys had not been anywhere near as good-looking. She turned to her friend from work and said, "But where do they all come from, so many lovely boys?"

He'd smiled slyly, a little secretively, and said, "Oh, they're about you know," and then, changing the direction of the conversation, "What do you think of it here then?"

"I like it, it seems very good." She'd been unsure how to phrase her reply as he so obviously had a kind of pride in the place. It was rather lavish for the sort of teenage club it was.

It had ample seating, a dance floor, soft drinks and a small restaurant on the floor above. And all the boys were dressed in the latest up-to-the-minute fashions – much in evidence were tapered shirts and flared trousers.

"Back home," she'd said, "the boys are still wearing winkle-pickers and jeans."

"Well as long as the jeans are Levi's they're OK. Otherwise they're pretty . . ." And then he'd used that odd word that started it all off, "Naf."

She remembered that very well, and asking him what this word *naf* meant.

"Naf? Well . . ." and he'd thought for a moment and looked at her as if sizing her up, "it's slang, it means something like not up to much, naf, boring, see?"

And during the course of the evening he had used other odd words and had to explain them to her. She realized quickly that he and the boys he spoke to seemed to use a language of their own. At first it struck her as odd but lots of the boys at home used words and expressions that she didn't understand and which appeared to possess special meanings for them, so why shouldn't these London boys have their own way of speaking? She listened interestedly to the conversations but noticed that they all seemed very general when she was listening, and that as soon as they moved away they livened the talk up. After a while she noticed that there were very few girls and that they were extravagantly dressed, with high *coiffures* and expensive-looking dresses.

"There don't seem to be many girls down here."

He looked about, "No, it's nearly all boys here, not many girls get on this scene."

"Oh." Pause. "Why not?"

"Well luv, have a look around you, why do you think?"

She had stared about her, trying hard to find a reason. The way the boys behaved made her feel, however, that the girls there didn't really seem to be *with* any of the boys, they were treated more as friends, or better still as other boys. She had given up. He had been silent for a little while, as if deciding, as if preparing to make some momentous, world-shattering explanation.

"Well Glory," it had been he who had changed her name for her. "You see, well it's a bit difficult, do you think you can understand?"

"Understand what?"

"That they're all homosexual."

So that was it. The whole club suddenly changed for her. She had to readjust her picture of the entire club. Her impressions of the people there. But it had been very easy. In fact, somehow, it had all seemed absolutely right to her and, rather surprisingly, it had made her feel completely at home, safe and comfortable. For the first time in her life she felt like a girl and a person and not just a girl or, as she thought all girls were thought of by normal men and boys, a hole to be filled. Normal boys she had always thought dull, unfun, frequently rude and often aggressive and, unless freakishly boring, only after one thing, "fuck and forget". Even the boring boys were after sex – it was just that they were dull enough not to mind prolonging the wait. Glory actually found them the more objectionable. All the little kindnesses, the paying court, were so unmeaning. They were trimmings which tried to disguise the inevitable and the obvious.

These gay boys she had already found companionable, friendly and amusing. They seemed to be able to talk about the things she was interested in and with them she didn't have to worry about any of them trying to lay her. What a relief. Her sense of enjoyment of the club was considerably heightened by her knowledge that she was "safe".

On that first night at "Pop" she had said to the pretty boy from work, "Yes, I can understand it. It doesn't bother me, and luv," she had quickly fallen into their mock affectionate way of speaking, "I adore it here."

The boys in the club came to accept her for she frequented it most weekends now and even some evenings in the week. She learned their dances, adopted a lot of their mannerisms and eccentricities of speech and slowly felt herself coming to life.

One weekend at the club, and "Pop" always seemed to be spoken of as "The Club", as if it were the only one of its kind, she had seen a particularly beautiful boy standing alone in the corner. Most of the boys had cast admiring glances at him but his air of aloofness kept people at a distance. There was something almost awe-inspiring about him, certainly something slightly forbidding. He knew he was beautiful, knew he was much desired, felt, too, stirring desires but felt that if he were too obviously sexually generous it might harm him, the reputation he probably had. His sleeping partners were carefully chosen and lured into his bed by some magical process of his of which they were almost unaware. His aloneness and quiet made him more attractive and it was these two factors which drew people to him and which enabled him to rebuff those that he did not like without appearing too unpleasant.

Glory had stared across the dance floor at him and thought, in her sexually detached way, that he was rather fanciable. He looked so willowy, so interesting. He was a little over average height, beautifully thin, had marvellous high cheek bones, and casually erotic heavy-lidded eyes. His hair was long and black and perfectly kept and he was dressed in a black T-shirt and white jeans. He wore white tennis shoes on his feet and no socks. She could see that he wore no jewellery, neither rings nor watch, and that the only piece of decoration was a pair of metal-rimmed dark glasses pushed back up on the top of his head. She stared at him and willed him to turn and see her. For Glory he was the epitome of a beautiful man, the type of male she found sexually attractive, thought of as probably artistic, and would love to mother. It was a strange physical lust she felt for him, completely without sex, a lust, maybe, of possession. She wanted to be able to talk to him, and to be able to touch him, stroke his thin, bony face and feel his eyes staring into hers. She wanted to feel him touch her, to be able to hold on to him. She did not think of sex. Then he turned and seemed to be looking her way. But the movement was so laconic that she couldn't be sure whether he were noticing her or one of the many boys around her. She continued to look his way in the hope that she would be more successful with her quest. A casual friend, Georgie, came up and spoke to her.

"Who're you looking at with so much interest, luv?"

She nodded towards the corner.

"That one. He's really divine."

"Paul, mmm. Want me to introduce him to you, I kind of know him."

She looked questioningly at him.

"Oh, no. Nothing like that, worse luck. He's a friend of friends."

She smiled at herself and at Georgie's reply to her unspoken question. It always surprised her just how much this whole world hinged on sex and how almost every little look could be so easily read. They drifted on the crowd over in the general direction of Paul. Georgie stopped to chat to various groups of friends as they made their way through the crush until eventually they were within greeting distance of him. Georgie waved and pretended he had only just noticed him.

"Hi, what are you doing over here in this nasty corner? It's so far out of the way. And you're all on your own, come trogging round with us?"

"Thanks but I'm quite happy here, can see everything I want to."

"Meet Glory anyway, Glory this is Paul, Paul this is Gloria Ramsbottom but Glory to everyone."

"Hello, weren't you staring at me from over there?"

Glory was taken aback by the directness of the question and the hint of rudeness in it. Georgie giggled. She rather felt like saying something very bitchy and leaving but, well, he was beautiful and she had, after all, been staring.

"Yes, I was, but then," and she'd grinned playfully, "a cat may look at a queen."

He smiled down at her.

"I stand corrected, sorry I sounded rude, I didn't mean to."

"That's OK. And I was staring at you, I wanted to talk to you, you look sort of interesting."

Paul's ego had puffed up visibly and the flattery made him generous – "Let me get you a coke or something."

Paul bought Georgie and Glory Coca-Colas and they found seats and settled into them. As soon as it became obvious to Georgie that he wasn't going to get off with Paul he left them, wandered into the dancers in search of some lover for the night. Paul and Glory were left alone to talk. And talk they did until the club closed and when she was asked if she wanted to go back to Paul's King's Road flat Glory had said yes.

They had walked from the club, through the seamy Soho veil – dank wet streets, reeking of stale pee, beer and decadence, a three o'clock tired blaze of light – and along Green Park a scratch of freshness on the stale London surface. At St George's Hospital they picked up a cab and rolled off down Knightsbridge, Sloane Street and into the King's Road. As they walked and as they sat in the back of the taxi they twined themselves together for warmth, company, out of sheer friendliness. They looked like lovers but weren't, would never be.

He knew and she knew the value of closeness of mind and body. Both felt the desire for physical contact. And the contact had absolutely no need for sex. It was the body to hold that was important, not the body to love and explore. She was emotionally underdeveloped and ill-fed and both Peter and Paul and their many friends would shake her and wake her. They would install her on the gay scene so firmly that she would never want to leave. So much so that she would undergo a mental sex change. After years with gay boys Glory was a homosexual boy.

YOUNG HUNKS ON COKE

Toni Davidson

PEACE IN OUR time, heroes, peace in our grime. Taking you on a climb, an up and up through your senses. A mountain climbing story see, no base camp, straight to the pinnacle. A mountain climbing story with grip, a snowed up and under tale with crampons and style. Straight to the summit, but wait for the plummet with brothers Lynch and Leer.

Fine fettled men, fine indeed, stringy legs, wasted muscles and nose tendons finely toned to the snow. Snowed up. What beauty past compare to these giggling wrecks. Taking a joy-ride into the mountains, ramraiding the peaks, boyo, Welsh valleys, singing choirs and fuckers in waxed jackets. Cheerio, cheerio, cheerio. Ooh ahh hezbollah! Taking it in their stride man, the wide and open gait of two men higher than the mountains. A tale then of two mild mannered boys taking a leaf out of the old Muriel Grays, taking a gung hung at the old Munro. One and counting.

Day trip from the city. Up and away on the old choo choo. Scenic route and all with gangs of hardnosed crampons filling flasks with style, strapping on gaiters with assurance, writing wills on Kendal mint cake and prayers for rescuers everywhere. Lynch and Leer, young hunks on coke heading for the big snow in the sky, mean little snowboarding ride to the ultimate. Munro

Gungho and a'that. And it's *ooh ahh Cantona* from the crampons with flasks of hot steaming coffee as they cream themselves over the scenery man, with lips curled around knots to tie on the worn rucksacks. Making it like one merry train all the way to mountains.

Not so for Lynch and Leer, not so at all for our two intrepid hikers but once butch bikers in less technoed days. Not so for them at all. In the stink they were, in the shoogling gyrating can, leading the merry coke dance on the mountain shuttle. There they were with not a gaiter to their name, not a crampon in their throat, not a Kendal mint bloc tucked into high booted socks. No such sensible trappings. These were joy-riders in the mountains. Lynch and Leer. Can't keep their balance on the pan snorting the snow never mind on a striding edge with clouds below cushioning the yodelheyhos of the crampons with style, their Munro Count getting higher. No psyching up for the adventure ahead for these two, no way José, not a chance Lance. In the BR can Lynch bent over the pan with Leer getting the foil delivered to the nose.

"Whisk out the pound. Sound."

"Take it easy." Leer said, "It's coming, the little white choo choo's a'comin, open wide for your pal Lynch, open wide. The nostrils that is you fuck."

"A hole's a hole for a'that."

"Gird your nostrils man, here it is. Whoooosh."

At the foot of the mountains. Lynch and Leer look up full of awe and snow, their trainers iced in a thrice.

"Check out the crampons, sleekit of foot and determined of jaw. It's fucking amazing innit? Makes you proud tho dunnit, Leer, makes you proud to be braving the elements, away from the sewers and bar room brawls, makes it good to be in the world."

"Getting Cosmic on me Lynch, must be the altitude I guess. Yeah man, it must be the snow."

They watched the crampons levitate up in the ski lifts, skis and poles spare Kendal mint cake jutting out at all angles. Our intrepid heroes, our loin stirring Shakespearos watched them go and looked up at the mountains.

"Check out the size of that thing man, check out the size of that *thing*."

"It's the snow Leer, don't get enthralled, it's the snow. Always does that."

Lynch and Leer brave heroes all, fresh from a TV course on mountaineering hitch a ride on the lift and set off for the distant hills.

"I'm getting high Leer."

"Good stuff innit?"

"No, the mountains, the great big fucking mountains with huffy clouds and a sparkling sun creeping through the summits. Tis beautiful to be alive in this world, so it is, so it is."

"Check out the crampon in front. You got a stone?"

"Man, I haven't been this stoned since that brave in Shakespeare Street."

"No man not a stone, a *stone*."

"What for?"

"For the crampon, to dislodge a piece of Kendal mint cake, to take a slice from the wax jacket. You know."

"A bit of the old ooh ahh."

"Some say broohahah."

"Hah hah."

"A couple of thugs in the mountains."

"Take the home to Rome. When it's raining it pours."

"Take aim then."

With unsteady hand, Leer lobs a pebble towards the two mountain travellers ahead of them, taking in the sights, minding nobody's business it has to be said. But the stone cracks off the ice axe hanging from one of the rucksacks and pings to the ground. The crampons look around in puzzlement and get their gobs smacked not with another pebble but with Lynch and Leer getting it on big style getting all snowed under halfway up their first Munro, licking each others tonsils with mild abandon.

Filthy.

"Snow ain't what it used to be is it," Leer shouts to their disgruntled backs.

"Turn it down eh, Leer. I didn't come all this way to look up your rotting nose. Take in the sights and sounds man.

Enough time for love frenzy back home in the old four-poster."

"Indeedy. I'll sit back and Frankie."

"Two Tribes?"

"No, Relax."

"Ah!"

Our intrepid pair reach the top of the mountain and take a giant leap off the ski lift and tumble into the soft snow grappling with each other amongst the feet of the serious mountaineers and professional crampons who walk off in distaste towards the piste.

"Oh no, oh no, don't say it, don't you fucking dare say it."

Lynch shouted to Leer as he grappled with his button fly.

"Oh yes, oh yes. They've piste off ain't they, they've gawn and piste off and left us."

"It's the snow talking man, its the snow making you crack the cornies out."

"Yeah, the snow's talking. THE SNOW'S TALKING. Hey man you took a mite more than me so you did, an extra half nostril just to get the old cold stuff gabbing with you eh?"

"Yeah, yeah. Where we going then?"

The likely lads surveyed the scene. All around them, the serious assemblage girded themselves for descent, the Munro counters logged into their personal organizers and the Muriel Grays got down to the rhythm method, the time honoured chug of the amateur.

"This way."

"What way?"

"This way. Follow me."

"That slope's going up the way Leer, we're meant to be going down."

"Hey man, I've told you, I ain't never going down. You hear me. I'm going to stay up for th rest of my life. My ears full of the muse, my blood stream full of the MDMA of old. I ain't never coming down. I've got it in my blood man. You hear – in my blood. My dad was Leary, my mum Nico. I'm the hybrid son of generations of substance abuse."

"Downhill I mean, Leer, downhill so shut the fuck up, we're meant to be going downhill."

"Yeah well, I want to go this way."

And off they went. While the others glided down the slopes with the greatest of tease our heroic pair stumbled and tumbled; dived and tripped in the fluffy snow. They jested with each other in true spirit. Lynch taking a lump of snow and pushing it down the front of Leer's baggies.

"Snow on your cock, man. Keepin' it hard."

"Hey, you're shrinking it man, I've got my reputation to keep, you know what I mean?"

They grappled with each other once more, their thin legs chopping at each other like the blades of a mountain rescue helicopter, their tongues lashing the cold lips of the other.

But now readers, while our fine fettle lads make off across the white peninsula of snow, we'll jump ahead of them, round the corner as it were and wait for them to pass by. Their cries and shouts, farts and burps pepper the air as the woosh of expensive skis and the whoops of frantic climbers getting their Munros become ever distant. Clouds gather overhead rolling over the once blue sky with ever increasing speed. The wind picks up and the first flurry of snow since the last dances through the thin mountain air. By the time the pair reach our location a strong wind has brewed and fermented with a haste that experienced folk will tell you can happen in a moment in the hills. The expert crampons know what to do. They can dig a snow hole within five minutes and wrap themselves in Bacofoil in less than two. Emergency rations, homing beacons, giant flashing bars of chocolate Kendal mint cake suddenly come into play and within minutes the mountain cavalry whisks them off back to comfy hotels to try again the next day.

Not so Lynch and Leer. By the time they come round the corners, their pipe-cleaner legs have been gaitered with thick snow and their baseball caps have two inches quivering on their peaks.

They turn the corner and are met by a relentless unbridled wind.

"Jesus Lynch, we better find shelter."

"Oh aye trust you Leer, trust you. The first sign of trouble you want to turn off the decks, turf everybody into the bathroom, burn the incense and put on the telly. *What party officer? I'm just watching the telly. I love the quiz shows don't you?* Yeah, you and playing it safe man, it makes me sick."

"No, no don't go off half-cocked, ya skinny bumbagger, I mean we should take shelter so the snow doesn't go flying out the old nostrils."

"Another toot? What a hoot. You're a devil and no mistake Lynch."

"Open your shirt man, let's chase the chest."

"In this weather, you're out your farter."

"Hey, who's playing it safe now then? Come on. This is our first outing, out the old grime, away from the endless nights of monotonous hedonism and you don't want to open your shirt for fear of the odd goosebump. Don't worry, I can snort round the bumps man."

"Yeah, OK but make it quick."

"You're a sport."

Lynch bent over Leer and unzipped the bomber jacket, then the shirt, then the T-shirt which he pulled over Leer's face. He opened the wrap and diced a little on Leer's pale quivering chest.

"'Tis a beautiful sight so it is."

"Get on with it."

Lynch took the note and ploughed across the sunken chest, gabbing Leer's cock at the same time and squeezing harder and harder until he ran out of breath.

"My turn, my turn before you get all whimsical on me."

"On my cheeks, baby on my cheeks."

"Hey, it'll fall into the crevasse man and I don't mean a snow one."

"Get it done. And fast. My head's wanting to fly."

Leer yanked down Lynch's fading jeans and took the undies from them.

He grabbed the wrap from Lynch and diced swiftly on the quivering cheeks.

"Hey, you got the wobblies. I never want to see you again. I like my cheeks firm."

"GET ON WITH IT."

The weather was deteriorating. Flurries of snow had turned to a rage and visibility was edging towards zilch. But our intrepid travellers, hoisting up their trousers and buttoning up their jackets had not a care for the elements. This was what they had come for.

"This way."

"We've just come that way."

"No we haven't."

"Yes we have."

"No we haven't."

"Ah fuck it I'm going this way."

"Don't leave me. This snow hitting me real hard, it's *getting* me real hard. I want to fuck up a storm."

"Catch me if you can."

"Tig in the snow on snow. Whopping."

They raced as well as they could. Through three-foot drifts, limb after limb, Lynch just ahead of Leer, racing and shouting and showing two fingers to avalanche speculators. On and on they went leaving the ski lift and recommended routes far behind.

"Hey Lynch, what if we see the yeti?"

"We'll fuck him."

"What if we see the Abominable Snowman?"

"We'll blow him."

"Run Lynch, I'm coming to get you. And I'm going to bag myself a Munro. Your Munro. I'm coming, I'm coming."

Stop. Sudden stop. Everything brought to a grinding halt. Ahead of the fine fettled lads, just a few feet away was the shadow of something.

"What the fuck's that?"

"I'm scared Leer."

"What the fuck is it tho?"

"Its too big to be a yeti, or the abominable snowman."

"Well it sure as fuck isn't Muriel Gray. What is it?"

"A house man, a fucking house."

"A house party up here. Alright. Fucking techno, ooh aah Cantona and gellie pies man."

"Burning . . ."

"A fucking house, Leer, not a fucking house party. But what's it doing up here?"

"Waiting for a party of course, let's rush on in. I'm just in the mood."

Lynch sensing something was wrong, held back but Leer grabbed and pulled him.

"Its a boothy."

"That's bothy, crackhead."

"A bothy then."

"Sound. Let's hope no one's at home."

"Hey the more the merrier, man. We could organize ourselves an illegal gathering and some repetitive beats in no time. We'll bring the house down man, we'll bop the bothy. Eh Lynch, eh? Lynch? Lynch? Lynch, this ain't the time to play funny buggers. Not in the snow, not *on* the snow. We're in this together. Together forever. Brotherhood man, loverhood baby. Lynch? Where the fuck are you? I ain't laughing, I ain't chortlin'. Come on. You're spoiling the snow. Get your hand in mine girl and stop this messin'."

Leer panicked and ran towards the shadowy wall of the bothy. Then he saw Lynch glued to a window, his blue hands on the pane.

"Lynch what the fuck . . . ?"

But Lunch dragged him to his chest and held his face next to his and pressed them both to the window.

"What is this, what the fuck is this?"

Inside the bothy was a sight impossible to take in. A man – tall, bearded and naked was whirling around the four walls, throwing himself in the way of tables, chairs and a burning stove; he spun like a top, arms and legs akimbo, his long hair rushing through the air spattering sweaty fibre into the smokey cloud. He didn't stop. He had no sight, no sound of Lynch and Leer watching him agape; he didn't seem to be aware of anything not even the object that bruised and tore at his skin, not the hot fat oil that spat at him from the stove. He spun ever faster, a devilish whirling that would not cease. But that was not all. He wasn't just revolving, his hands would sometimes reach for and claw at his back, as though desperately trying to grab ahold of something, something painful, something so indescribably sore to make him dance this mad jig. When the bearded man couldn't reach the part on his back he grabbed his flaccid cock and pulled it with such force both Lynch and Leer winced in unison. He tugged and pulled at that pulp of flesh and began to wail, a low unnatural chant.

"What the fuck is this, Lynch?"

"What was in that coke, Leer?"

"Is this real?"

"Is this *for* real?"

"That sound man, what the fuck is that sound he's making?"

"This is shamanistic man, thats what this is. We've stumbled on something you know. This is fucking ritual. Stonehenge and a'that."

The bearded man's hands moved faster than his legs now. One second they were tearing and grazing a patch of dark skin revealed on his back and the next they grabbed his now erect cock, all the while the broken chairs and tables were further scattered around the small interior of the bothy.

"Fucking hell, my eyes are hurting."

"This is freaking me out Leer."

Smack. The boys jumped back. And the bearded man launched himself at the window, his head ramming the thick glass and denting the pane but not breaking it. Lynch and Leer took a step further back just to be sure and watched the whirl of the naked bearded man, his clawing hands leaving vapour trails in the yellow light of the bothy.

Smack. The bearded man's head came through the glass, his lacerated skin dripping from the shards. He said nothing, did nothing apart from withdraw his head and spin back into the room. But it was enough for Lynch and Leer.

Our intrepid heroes took flight, running as fast as they could.

"Keep going Leer."

"Where are we going to go?"

"Does it matter eh, does it fucking matter? I don't want to hang around there do you?"

"No man, you're absolutely right. Flight is the best thing."

"Well fucking move then."

The wind battered them back, the squalls of snow filled their eyes and ears and soon their motion became a blur not a speed but of confusion. Leer followed Lynch and Lynch just kept going. Leer grabbed a hold of Lynch's jacket as he began to lose sight of him. He just wanted to hang on until Lynch had run out of steam.

Then it came. Maybe it was their shouts and screams, maybe it was just nature on the old Munros laying a dirty on them; maybe it was meant just for them and not the crampons going downhill miles back. But it came all the same. Lynch stopped and Leer bumped into him and held on to his waist tighter than tight.

"A fucking avalanche, Leer."

"What we going to do?"

Lynch looked at Leer. Love and incredulity in his eyes. "What do you mean what we going to do?"

"Well, we could take a step to the right and it might miss us; or we could huff and puff it back up the mountain."

"You mean we're just going to stand here and let the snow take us out?"

They both stopped their next sentence mid breath, they locked on to each other's eyes.

"You got the wrap?"

"Yeah."

"Quick get it now."

"Stomach or arse."

"Arse."

"I'll take it on my stomach."

"Quick."

"I want to get snowed Lynch. I want to take the biggest gulp of my life and dance my way through the pearly gates."

"Kiss me, Leer, kiss me."

Within a minute, just before the wall of snow covered them, Lynch and Leer were dancing hand in hand, giving it Can Can leg kicks, singing:

I've got Cocaine running round my brain.

Then the snow came.

PURPLE PROSE IN SOHO

Paul de Havilland

I WALKED OUT of the Soho bar to the shock of still-bright sunshine, leaving my empty beer bottle on a side table. I had the impression that none of the other lone drinkers would especially regret my departure. The lure of sex had led to my refusal of an invitation to a convivial dinner, a decision I now bitterly regretted as I faced the long evening flitting from bar to bar to club in search of that elusive held moment of eye contact. Still it was too late to turn back now. Affecting what I hoped was a nonchalant saunter, I made my way towards the next bar-full of men.

I happened on a cinema, and the poster caught my eye. *South Pacific* was showing, and the advert made much of its full restoration with digitally enhanced sound. My attention, though, was on the stills, familiar since childhood, when I would look at them on the cover of my mother's soundtrack LP as the music played on her radiogram. I knew every song in that film, but realized with a start that I knew nothing of how they were pieced together to form the film's story. On a whim, I bought a ticket, and found myself sitting in the nearly empty, tiny "Screen 3".

I watched, fascinated, as figures freeze-framed in my mind for decades started into animation, until the novelty wore off and my mind wandered, unheld by the shallow dialogue. I found my attention drawn to one or two of the extras, shirtless sailors with their round sailor's caps at jaunty angles, swaggering in the background. As the characters gathered for "Bloody Mary" I began to imagine how life would be, with sex-starved men on every hand in this tropical wartime fantasy. One of the sailor extras suddenly seemed to meet my lascivious stare, and he waved as if to beckon me to him. I dismissed the coincidence, but as the song got into full swing, he did it again – this time mouthing the words, "Yes, you."

The man sitting two rows in front turned towards me. "I think he means you," he said.

Bewildered and disbelieving, I nevertheless climbed up onto the platform under the screen, and my white T-shirt became a jigsaw piece of the projected image, so that my head and limbs appeared disconnected. The picture was just a dancing Technicolor abstract as I walked into it, only to find I had badly misjudged the camera angle. I fell heavily two or three feet onto the islands's ground, stumbling headlong into Bloody Mary herself, knocking her over and getting a close-up of ample breast.

The entire cast dissolved into laughter. The song had ended abruptly as I had fallen forward, and everyone now slowly dispersed. Some walked away into the Cinemascope perspective, others abruptly winked out of existence as they reached the edges of the screen. Bloody Mary coughed.

"Excuse me," she said.

Recollecting myself, I mumbled an apology and climbed off her. I stood up, and looked around in wonder at my new, literally fantastic world. There was the familiar ocean, but now I could see the waves break, and hear them crash into shore in digital surrounded sound. The sand, the sea, the sky, the tropical trees, all in filtered, enriched preternatural colour.

I started to try to explore, but as I walked forward the world receded. As I walked to the left or right, everything remained in fixed perspective. I could move across my new domain, but the effect was two-dimensional, like walking along the Bayeux Tapestry. If I turned to look behind me the world turned with me.

I began to get a feel for this new existence, and as soon as I did to wonder how on earth I was to get out of it.

"That's what they all wonder at first."

I looked towards the voice, precisely located by the stereo sound. One of my horny sailors had spoken. The other stood beside him, languidly chewing gum. My heart sank a little; gum-chewing is a major turn-off for me. As I had this thought, he pushed the gum to the front of his mouth, and picked it out between two fingers. He raised a foot, and bent slightly sideways to stick the gum on the sole of his shoe. I watched, transfixed, as the muscles in his stomach and down his sides flexed and unflexed. I felt I wanted a closer look, and they both walked slowly up to me. We three were by now alone on the beach – none of the others had stayed. Searching for something to open a conversation, I asked about this.

"Sure, it was us on your mind, so we're all you get."

"Where are the others then?"

"We don't know."

I suppose they must still be in the film, or in someone else's fantasy.

"We're not in the film any more, are we?"

"No. When you jumped over, we span off into a new storyline."

"So, what's the plot?"

"Can't help you there buddy, that's up to you."

"You mean, I can make it up?"

"Yeah."

I instantly conjured up an image.

"Uh, no buddy, you can't do that."

Disappointment. "Why?"

"You can't actually interact with us. We're only characters, you know."

"But, Bloody Mary, I knocked her over."

"Sure. You have a physical presence here, you can touch us, but you can't feel us. Not in any real sense."

I reached out and touched him, and saw what he meant. It was like touching the film, not him. Like stroking a glossy paper arse in a porn mag.

"If I can't interact with you, how are we having this conversation?"

"You can't talk to us as characters. This is like stage directions, notes in the margin, that kind of thing."

"So I can make you do whatever I want?" Certain possibilities were entering my head. As they did so, my two characters looked at each other, and gave each other that indefinable stare I had been in search of in Soho.

"You can kind of make us do anything," the gum-chewer was speaking, "but it has to be in character. You have to re-invent us first."

I thought about this. Suddenly my excitement grew. Before then I had never found much vicarious pleasure in voyeurism of any kind. Porn mags, films, strippers – all these were completely dispensable to me. But here, I was not simply a beggar at the feast. This was a conscious, waking dream I could control. A fantasy to end all fantasies, with only characters, no living person, to be manipulated. Guilt-free, bespoke porn.

I began to think about who my sailors were. I wanted real passion, not just rough coupling or anonymous gratification. I thought about two men thrust by events into a bloody war. Men to whom the threat of sudden death had given an unaccustomed honesty, and mutual discovery. These were not two passing bodies in simple carnal coupling, but two people who would come together again and again, taking shelter from the war in embraces, caresses and kisses; and in licking, biting, sucking, grabbing, pushing, pushing, pushing, pushing, squirting, squirting.

I looked towards my two lovers. Gum-chewer had his hand on the other's cheek. They were talking quietly between smiles and kisses. It seemed I had succeeded in drawing my characters.

I watched them, feeling ever touch, every breath on the neck, every kiss with the intensity of a drugged hallucination. Each of their actions was the fulfilment of my momentary precognition, repeated gratification of each subtle shift in my fantasy. The memory is so intense it seems to be happening again.

They kiss more fully. I feel the roughness of their faces as they touch, each magnifying the other's maleness. A hand cups a muscular, bulging chest. Finger and thumb gently squeeze a nipple into pleasure-pain. Fingers, knuckle deep in belts, pull groins together. Arms enfold. Kisses are now fierce, hurting Hands grip powerful sides, bodies clamp together ever tighter, never tight enough. Always more urgency. Teeth and nipples meet, tongues languidly lick the squeezed points, then move, but slowly, slowly, down and down. At last nuzzling the white trousers, noses gain the distant musky smell of filling balls.

Buckles rattle as belts are ripped from loops. Pants unfold like paper napkins to reveal abundant, furry darkness. The nuzzling noses drink the richer odour.

Suddenly, by some mutual signal they slow, slow. Eyes meet eyes at eye level. Mouths gently, gently now caress. Hands enfold bodies in rice-paper touch. Delay becomes intense, then unbearable. Holding their stares, they step back, step out of their clothes, step forward. Their shared sexes now meet in a rush of adrenaline, they groan in introduction to a rough guttural fugue. What noses have smelled, tongues now taste, then mouths contain. Heads nod in ludicrously intense agreement, hands viciously grip arses. As the fugue builds, the lurid surroundings fade and these two bodies are all that exist. They plunge deeper and deeper into each other, onto each other, pounding desperately on that gate which finally bursts open in a flood of relief, filling mouths with sticky sugar, sticky salt.

They roll back from each other, move face to face, and roll together, warm and happy. There are a few precious moments of profound quiet.

"Thanks," I remember saying.

They looked at me, blankly. Then I realized they had no memory, as characters they existed only in the moment. I vaguely envied them this state, as reality returned to haunt my thoughts.

I began to reflect again on my surroundings. I wondered how I could escape back to the Soho fleapit.

"Can you tell me how to get back?"

"No. You have to work it out. We can answer questions, though."

I tried stepping backwards. The world followed me.

"Why didn't that work?"

"Because you can't abandon us."

I thought about this. We were now in some non-existent movie, two of us created for the purpose. There was no interface between us and reality. I had to re-create *South Pacific* in my mind, and return my characters to the plot.

"Do you appear in another scene?"

"Yes – but only one."

My mind ran over my scant knowledge of the film, then it came to me. "Honey Bun". A concert for the troops. Officers patronizing the men's perceived tastes with a Vaudeville performance.

"I bet you're in the audience for that."

"Try it and find out."

I re-created the familiar still in my mind. Ranks of sitting sailors, a makeshift stage, a drag-king singing about his-her ". . . cutey pie, only sixty inches high, every inch is packed with dynamite."

Nothing happened.

"What's wrong?"

"It's not us who were there."

Then I had it. I remembered the extras in the "Bloody Mary" scene. As I thought about them, and saw them as they were, I pictured them rhubarbing their way into my "Honey Bun" scene.

The sudden blast of the orchestra yanked me back into the film with a start. Quickly, I stepped back, and was now a new piece in a different jigsaw.

"Right you, out!"

An angry man in a lounge suit stood in the aisle of the cinema. The manager. I didn't bother to try to explain, but allowed myself to be bundled outside.

I stood there, stunned, at a loss as to what to do next.

"You missed the end."

It was the man from two rows in front. I hadn't realized in the dark of the cinema how good-looking he was.

"It was worth it," I told him.

"I know. If you're interested, I've got the video back at my flat."

I returned his smile.

A DAY IN THE COUNTRY

Gary Dunne

"I'M TURNING HOUSE-BOUND or something," grumbled Mr Pointy Head. "Everything bores me."

"What you need is a hobby," I said. "God knows what but I can't imagine you collecting stamps."

"I've got a hobby. I sit here all day and watch the cute mechanical-engineering students go by. They all wear tight King Gee shorts you know."

"That's not enough. You need something more social. It's a shame they won't have you back on the Aids hotline."

"Don't bring all that up again. It wasn't my fault. He started talking dirty first. I just got a bit over-involved in the conversation."

"The point is you don't get out enough."

"Nowhere around here is worth the effort it takes to walk to," he sulked.

I don't have a wide range of techniques for dealing with times when he's grumpy. With Pointy Head, some things are almost impossible to discuss directly. He'll tell you he isn't of the school that says you should love your diagnosis and how he doesn't try to make a career of being a patient. He'll say it's only an illness, not a life-style, and like a compulsory hobby or an unpleasant job, he'll only devote energy to it when he has to. The rest of the time he'll ignore it. It's a philosophy I respect but sometimes, like today, it doesn't work all that well. Unsure of what to try next, I switched into Pollyanna mode.

"We'll go further afield then . . . let's go bush. Up the airy mountains," I enthused. "We'll be like Henry Lawson and John le Gay what's-his-name. We'll go striding through the scrub. We'll take a picnic. We'll drink billy tea and eat damper. We can borrow Diamond Lil's car. She owes me a favour. You're up to driving, aren't you?"

"I guess so."

I should have known better than to expect him to be ready by 8 a.m. He was barely out of bed. Two hours later, I was still descending the stairs with bits and pieces. He was insisting on taking emergency supplies including pillows, blankets, a roll of toilet paper, a beach umbrella, a cocktail shaker and a jerry can of water, all "in case we get lost". My argument that people these days don't get lost going to Katoomba, was ignored. He doesn't trust anywhere west of Ross Street. Like some skinny Toad of Toad Hall, he stood issuing instructions while I carried all his paraphernalia down to the Riley.

I have a proper licence. I bought it about a decade ago for less than double the cost of a legit one. Every year I pay to renew it. I can't drive, there's no need to here, in the inner-city. I have a perfect driving record. Mr Pointy Head, on the other hand, started driving at the age of ten. He doesn't have a licence and says he can't see any point in bothering to get one at this late stage of his life. Whenever we motor, we simply swap identities.

For both of us there was something exciting about getting out of the city. It's such a rarity. We were like a pair of schoolboys, jigging classes for the day. I wanted to make up for lost time but we had to stop to top-up with petrol. We also stopped to purchase some gin. Our next requirement was some tonic water, then a fresh lemon. We had to make two public toilet stops. It was after midday when we finally reached the Blue Mountains National Park.

Pointy Head mixed drinks and we toasted the view of the valley before heading off to walk to the next look-out. We didn't get there. Within a matter of minutes I realized that he wasn't behind me. I turned around and saw that he was way back up the track, just standing, watching. When I returned, he said he'd had enough. He looked worn out and dejected.

"Time to face facts," he said. "Bush-walking is not my forte any more. Come to think of it, I don't believe it ever was. So we'll have to make the best of the situation."

He sat down, lit a cigarette and we watched a pair of sturdy bush-whacking types approach.

"Excuse me," he asked. "We're from Sydney. We've come up here by mistake. Can you help us? My little mate is handicapped. Is there anything around here, other than bush, that's worth seeing and is less than five minutes' walk to get to?"

They suggested the waterfall a little way back down the other path from the car park. We back-tracked, this time more slowly. A waterfall would provide the perfect opportunity to take photos. We've both been amateur photographers for years. Pointy tends to be overly keen on the artistic effects. My speciality has always been portraits. Over the years, I've taken hundreds, with Pointy Head always a willing model for experiments with lighting and angles.

Now it's not so easy. Every day he looks the same to me but, as we've discovered when we tidied up his flat last summer, a decade's worth of pictures, when collected together in a carton, says something else. Photos suddenly ceased being easy souvenirs. He became self-conscious. I began picking reasons, events and locations to try to give the shots an emphasis beyond his declining health. It was too complicated and somehow intrusive. I began leaving the camera at home.

This time, however, he'd insisted I bring it along. He spent ages positioning me right on the edge of the cliff, near the car park. For once I became the uncomfortable-looking still life in front of the scenery.

We made it to the waterfall and photographed each other. An English tourist took a couple of shots of the pair of us. Despite the majestic beauty of our surroundings, I knew they would be very pedestrian pictures. Postcard backdrops and wooden poses. Merely proof we were there.

We sat, depressed, swatting flies, each I suspected waiting for the other to suggest that we begin what would be, for him, a slow trek back up the steep hill to the vehicle. Pointy was the first to move.

"Where there's hair, there's hope," he said and clambered up on to the rock behind me.

I'm not very muscular or fit, facts he enjoyed pointing out as I piggy-backed him to the car park. He also claimed the view was better ascending as opposed to descending. I agreed, to shut him up, that bush-walking was indeed great fun. I grumbled, as expected, and amused us both by complaining about his weight.

Despite our efforts, the picnic was not a success. By the time the camp fire for the billy was set, the ants had discovered the food on the table-cloth. The lid on the jar of beetroot had not lived up to expectations and the assorted cheeses, the salad and bread rolls were stained severely. So was the sponge cake. The billy didn't exactly boil, something to do with altitude I suppose, and the tea tasted terrible. Our total ineptitude, as always, did wonders for Pointy's spirits.

"Some people have an urge to get back to nature," he finally announced. "I have an urge to get back to a pub. There's one up the road. I couldn't help but notice as we drove in that they do a country-style luncheon from 11 to 2.30. If we get a move on, we'll be just in time."

We were.

After several drinks and a decent feed, Mr Pointy Head said he felt much better but needed to rest. We wandered over to the town park and he slept under a tree while I read the paper and contemplated the folly of taking us so far from the security of home.

At sunset he woke and declared himself fit and sober enough to try driving so we set off. It seemed to take much longer to return to the city. He still looked exhausted and I felt guilty. He said it was only the western suburbs of Sydney, they always depressed him.

His mood improved once we began negotiating more congested traffic, a sure sign that we were nearing the grimy back-streets of Glebe and his small flat.

"It's been a perfick day, my dear. Just perfick. But next time you feel like going feral, take me to the Royal Botanical Gardens instead."

KISSING IN THE WHEAT

Richard K. Edwards

NOT LONG BEFORE my eighteenth birthday, I received a letter informing me that I had been accepted at King's College in London. My teachers had told me all year that I stood a good chance of getting in, but the news was all the more rewarding because I would be the first in my family to attend university, and was the only student from Capel Cynon to qualify that year.

It is a small village, resting peacefully in the hills of mid-Wales. Even calling it a village makes it sound bigger than it is – a few rows of houses, some small farms, a post office, and a chapel. I had seen little of life outside the immediate area; a visit to relatives in Cornwall was the farthest I had ever travelled. Although we were not the poorest in the area, my family lived from week to week and relied periodically on the charity of others in the chapel congregation. For the only son of such a family to enter university – with a full scholarship – was an achievement to be celebrated, at least as far as Welsh Methodists celebrated anything.

But I would never see King's College, nor return in triumph with a diploma to be displayed with pride in front of relatives and friends; because that summer I disgraced myself – and my family – in an incident that in my mind marked my coming of age in spectacular fashion, but which caused uproar in the village and destroyed my hopes of studying law in London.

It had been a good year for the local farmers, and record crops were anticipated. Huw Griffiths, whose farm was by far the largest in the area, had offered me work as a farm-hand. At first I was reluctant to accept, thinking that as a scholar I was now above manual labour. But my father spoke up before I had the chance to say anything for myself, and a few days later I was rising at four in the morning, bracing myself for a full day of back-breaking work in the fields.

A widower for several years, Huw had two sons. Dafydd, a short, red-haired boy two years older than me, was soft-spoken and timid, having inherited both his mother's looks and her temperament. Ifan, the younger of the two, was my age, and we had been in school together until our sixteenth birthdays, when he dropped out and I continued to study for the college entrance examinations. Ifan was tall, handsome, and boisterous, with a halo of blond hair and a smile that shone with an air of boyish wickedness. I admired his outgoing personality and his masculinity, and there could scarcely have been a girl within six miles of Capel Cynon who did not share my feelings. But Ifan was also a mysterious figure, known to disappear on his bicycle for two, sometimes three days at a time. Local gossip had it that he had found a girlfriend in one of the neighbouring villages, and although no names were ever mentioned, everyone believed that this was a young man who would break hearts from one end of the street to the other.

On one side of the Griffiths' farm was a field of wheat so large that it would take twenty minutes to walk around it. In the village it was referred to simply as "the big field". Huw, in order to save his neighbours – or the postman – a few minutes' walk, had cut a path through the field, dissecting it into two not quite equal halves, but connecting the farmyard directly to the road. Eventually, the path became known as "yr heol fach", or "the little road". On still, sunny days one could sit on top of the hill overlooking the farm and believe, with a little imagination, that a beach had been lifted off the coastline, coming down in the middle of the valley. Even the gentlest breeze might set the wheat waving, and the beach would be transformed into a silk-like cloth of white and gold. Reverend Walters, the minister at Gorffwysfa, the village chapel, was known to climb to the top of the hill seeking inspiration, and on more than a few Sundays we were subjected to a sermon on "the treasures of Nature".

At the end of one of my last days at the farm, I was riding my bicycle along the heol fach, looking forward to my bed and to my week's pay, when I heard a dog whimpering in the big field. Supposing that it was Cati, the Griffiths' yard dog, I got off the bike and tried to determine where the sound was coming from. I called her name a few times, but heard only some faint panting and whining sounds. Assuming that she must have been hurt, perhaps bitten by a fox, I walked into the wheat, continuing to call and following the feeble responses. When the whimpering stopped, I stood still and tried to get my bearings. I had lost my sense of direction, the wheat being tall enough to obscure all landmarks. I turned around, thinking that it might be best to return to the house and alert Dafydd. In front of me stood Ifan, his white shirt blinding me as it reflected the sunlight. He remained still, smiling at me but saying nothing.

"I heard the dog," I began. "It sounded like she was hurt."

"Wasn't the dog," Ifan replied proudly. "It was me. I've been practising all summer. I must be getting good at it."

I chuckled, adding that he had obviously fooled me, and that perhaps he could learn other animal noises, too. He didn't respond to my comment, but instead told me that he wrote poetry at night, secretly, when his father and brother had gone to bed. "I'm aiming for the National," he said, referring to the eisteddfod held every August. "I'll win one day, make no mistake about it."

I motioned towards where I thought the heol fach was, saying that I had to be on my way or run the risk of being late for supper. Ifan grabbed my arm. "So what?" he said, shrugging. "You'll be leaving for London soon, and I can't let you go without giving you something."

He put his hand on my shoulder and pulled me towards him. With one hand behind my neck he drew closer and kissed me on the mouth. Confused and nervous at first, I began backing away. I wanted to do it again, but I was scared. "I've never done this before," I said.

Waving away my hesitation, Ifan led me to a small clearing, where we passed an hour doing what I knew Reverend Walters would call unnatural and immoral acts. I didn't care; I knew already that it felt very natural to me, and that I wanted to go on making love with Ifan. This was a different Ifan from the one I knew. The brash personality gave way to a tender, subtle character that I found myself unable to resist. I asked him where he had learned such things, but he just winked and smiled at me. When it was over I cycled home at breakneck speed, recalling the thrill of the first kiss and the adrenalin rush that made me light-headed.

Opening the door to my parents' house, I tried to conceal my excitement. I felt so completely changed by what had happened that I thought they would be able to see through me at once. I was surprised, but also relieved, that they saw nothing different in me.

Family meals were usually solemn occasions, but that evening we talked constantly during dinner. With only a few weeks to go before I left for London, my parents argued over who should travel with me to hep me move in. They had just decided that my father would accompany me when someone knocked on the front door. It was the Reverend Walters, asking if he could speak to my father. Almost half an hour later they emerged from the sitting-room, each with an expression suggesting that a matter of the utmost urgency had arisen.

I watched my mother and sister shiver as Mr Walters explained what he had seen from the hilltop that afternoon. An avid bird-watcher, he had been indulging his hobby when he caught sight of my abandoned bicycle, and traced through the big field until he noticed Ifan leading me into the clearing. The wheat, being more than six feet tall, had made us feel safe from the risk of being caught; it had not occurred to us that someone on top of the hill might be looking down at the field, let along through binoculars. With tactful euphemisms Mr Walters described what he had observed, and expressed the hope that I would not be scarred for life. My father joined in, reassuring me that I only had to confirm the Reverend's story and he would see to it that "that evil Griffiths boy" would be punished.

Without stopping to think, I began contradicting the minister's version of events. "It wasn't like that at all," I protested, not thinking of the consequences of what I was saying. "Ifan didn't make me do anything."

I was damned by my own words. My father, almost blue in the face, lashed out with his walking stick, striking me across the forehead and knocking me to the floor. I stayed down, dazed, afraid to risk another one. My sisters were ushered quickly out of the room, while my father and Mr Walters determined that the doctor should be called at once.

Having explained that homosexuality could not be detected by signs of physical abnormality, the doctor suggested that I would just grow out of it, and that a term or two of hard work at college would be the best medicine. But it was not to be: my father, enraged at my complicity with Ifan, had already made up his mind that I would not be going to London. Instead, in the weeks that followed, arrangements were made for me to be sent to Canada, to live with my mother's brother and his wife. My uncle owned a small factory in Sudbury, Ontario, where machine parts were manufactured. I would work in the factory to earn my keep, and was forbidden to return home until given permission to do so.

Life in Canada was difficult; winters were unbearable, and I was homesick constantly. I had been separated from my family and friends, the familiar landscape, and from Ifan. As if that was not enough, my aunt and uncle, who had no children of their own, were strict Calvinists: dour, grey people for whom there was no greater sin than leisure. Though the factory remained in profit, their home life was austere; and money was not spent unless it was essential. My own allowance was pitiful for the first year, but when I turned nineteen they consented to paying part of the cost of my college education, on condition that I should study "something useful". I finally graduated after my twenty-fifth birthday, and against my uncle's wishes moved to Toronto to work for an American company. I had few sexual experiences in Sudbury, and found Toronto an intimidating place. But eventually I developed a small circle of friends, and met Andrew, who became my lover. As time passed, I began to feel more at home in Canada, and came to think of it as my home. Even so, nothing ever hurt as much as when someone would ask, innocently, when I would be going back to Wales for a visit.

My uncle died a few years after I moved to Toronto, and the factory was sold. My aunt decided that she wanted to return to Wales for the summer; after weeks of delicate negotiations my father's resistance finally broke, and he agreed to welcome me back across the threshold after more than nine years, with only one condition – I was not to discuss, or even hint at, my sexuality.

We arrived in Capel Cynon one evening in early August, just as the sun was setting over the hill. At first glance the village had not changed at all, except that the post office now included a small grocery and video store. My father looked much older than I had imagined, an impression made stronger by his slow movements, the slight stoop in his stature, and the crack in his once-imposing bass voice. My mother, though shorter than I remembered, seemed to have aged less. She cried as we walked up the path towards the house, saying over and over how much she had missed me, how tall I was, how handsome. My sisters, both married now, were waiting at the door to welcome us. The table was set for dinner, and we gathered together for the awkward experience of getting to know new relatives, my aunt never having met my sisters, and their husbands having never met either of us. As dinner came to an end, my mother asked what I planned to do the following day.

"I'll probably just go for a walk," I said. "The jet lag will take some getting used to."

My accent was an instant source of amusement to them, leading my older sister Rebecca to proclaim that I sounded "just like a Yank". I pretended to be insulted, and reminded her that I lived in Canada, not America; but the comment had made me feel like a stranger, someone who didn't belong. Except that I had belonged once; I had been a part of the life of this tiny village. I wanted to reclaim that part, to embrace it and protect it; and to renew the old ties: with my family, with the land and the hills, and with Ifan.

Early in the morning I got up and drove, giving up on walking, to the top of the hill. My heart sank when I looked down for the big field and saw only a mass of fir trees, arranged in uniform rows. I closed my eyes and tried to recapture he image of the wheat, as if doing so would bring back the big field. When I opened my eyes, though, the trees were still there. Disappointed, I drove back to the village and towards the farmhouse. It, too, was gone, and standing in its place was a modern red-brick house, in all aspects indistinguishable from thousands of other anywhere in Britain. Where the heol fach once ran was paved road, with a sign stating that the farm was owned by the Forestry Commission. Visitors were directed to the manger, a Mr Tom Stepian.

A beaming, stout man in his late forties, Mr Stepian welcomed me in and explained to me that Huw Griffiths had died, and that his son had sold the farm to the commission.

"Do you mean Dafydd, or Ifan?" I asked.

"Well, I'm not sure of the name exactly. But only one son he had, as far as I can remember. Quiet sort of chap. Red hair."

He had no idea where I could find Dafydd, so I returned at once to my parents' house, where my mother was busy making breakfast.

"What happened to the Griffiths' farm?" I asked her. "You never said anything about it in your letters."

She described how Huw had suffered a heart attack about two years after I left for Canada, how he was found dead in the big field, and that within months Dafydd had sold the farm and moved away.

"And what about Ifan?" I demanded.

"As long as you are under my roof you will remember not to speak that vile name." My father came into the kitchen from the back yard, where he had clearly overhead me.

"But it's been nearly ten years, Dad," I said. "I'm only asking where he is."

"I said no!" He slammed the back door with surprising force. "I want to hear no more about it."

My mother looked at me with pleading eyes; the look meant the subject was still taboo even after all the time that had passed.

But when my father was out of earshot, she whispered that I should ask one of my sisters. She put her hand on my arm.

"Please," she begged. "Don't bring it up again. Your father blames Ifan for everything that happened. He'll never understand. Listen: you've been away too long, and I'm thrilled to have you home again. But your father is a difficult man. Don't let him come between us like he did before."

I agreed to let it go, not to make waves. But I cursed my father for not understanding, and myself for allowing him to get away with it. After all, it was he, not Ifan, who had sent me to Canada. But knowing that my mother was right about him, I promised not to bring up the subject of Ifan again. I decided that I would ask Rebecca for the details, and a few days later went to discuss it with her. We walked along the banks of the river, where Ifan and I would sometimes sit and watch the salmon leaping. The information she could provide was of little help; she knew only that Ifan moved away within a year of my departure, and that he had never returned; neither Huw nor Dafydd ever spoke of him to anyone in the village. Dafydd had married, and was living in Brynfilo, about 30 miles from Capel Cynon. She had no idea what he did for a living; but his wife, she remembered, was a teacher in the village school.

My aunt had arranged to visit an old school friend on Saturday, a woman who lived in a village two-thirds of the way to Brynfilo. I offered to drive her there, but excused myself from visiting the friend and went the extra few miles to look for Dafydd. Just one enquiry at the village shop was sufficient to learn where he lived, and I called him to make sure he was home.

He embraced me on the doorstep, remarking on how well I looked and saying that Canada obviously suited me. I couldn't tell him immediately that I was aching inside, that what I wanted was to find Ifan before returning to Toronto. He seemed surprised that I had driven all the way to Brynfilo, and I explained that I had been just a few miles away anyway. We sat in the living room, which was filled with pictures of his wife and children, and of Huw; but I could see none of Ifan. His wife, he told me, had taken the children to her mother's for the day while she went shopping in Swansea. I wasn't disappointed to have missed them; they would only have been a distraction from the real purpose of the visit. I offered my condolences for Huw's death. It seemed odd to be doing it years after the fact, but in Wales the ritual is what matters. I talked about my career and my life in Canada, and asked him about his own life. When we reached a pause in the conversation, I took advantage of the moment and asked about Ifan. Dafydd's face changed instantly, and I knew from his expression that I should not expect good news.

Slowly, and with a tremble in his voice, Dafydd told me that Ifan had died about two years earlier. He had been living in London, but no one had heard from him since he left Capel Cynon. Then one night someone called to tell them that he was very ill and that they should go to London right away. Upon arriving, Dafydd learned that Ifan had taken a drug overdose, and that he had died after falling into a coma. He left no note, and the inquest returned a verdict of accidental death. Dafydd's eyes were wet now, and I could tell that he was still grieving.

"I wish he could have told us," said Dafydd, weeping. "He was the only family I had left. We could have helped him through it. My father threw him out the year you went to Canada. I don't think Ifan understood that it was your father who made you go. He was so fond of you, you see. And then when Dad disowned him, he must have felt so abandoned."

Sniffling, Dafydd pulled out a handkerchief and dried his eyes.

I was stunned, and thought of the number of times I had tried to write to Ifan. But each attempt had become more difficult than the last, and eventually I stopped trying. Now I felt guilty, as if writing would have changed the course of events. I tried to say that I hadn't gone to Canada of my own volition; but Dafydd already knew that. It was Ifan who deserved the explanation.

"I know I should have written," I said. "But I don't think more than a few days ever went by when I didn't think of him."

It sounded pathetic, an inadequate apology at best; but Dafydd just pushed himself up from the chair and walked to the corner of the room, where he retrieved a large envelope from a drawer in the dresser. "Ifan's friend asked me to send this on to you," he said. "I've been meaning to get your address from Rebecca so that I could send it to you. But perhaps you were meant to collect it in person."

I opened the envelope, and pulled out a manuscript. It was an untitled poem on the subject of young love. I read a few verses, enough to see that the poem was not written specifically for a man or a woman. Finding a reference to ill-fated lovers, I thought my heart would break there and then. I tried to compose myself while Dafydd explained that Ifan had meant to enter the poem in the Lampeter eisteddfod, but he had decided against it. "Not bad for a first try, though," he said, smiling. "And for a nineteen-year-old, too. With a little practice he might have done well."

We talked a while longer, reminisced about the farm, and drank two pots of strong tea, the kind that reminds me of Sunday breakfast at my mother's house, and fortifies the soul for a thundering sermon in chapel. Almost two hours later I announced that I had to go and fetch my aunt, and Dafydd walked me out to the car.

"I miss the farm," he said, looking out at the countryside. "You really do feel closer to the earth. Maybe it's something only a farmer knows."

We embraced again, and Dafydd insisted that I keep in touch. As I opened the car door, he thanked me for coming to visit and then asked me how I would remember Ifan.

"Grinning," I replied, "and full of mischief."

The following morning, I climbed the hill on foot. A soft drizzle was falling, reinforcing my already sombre mood. The news of Ifan's death was beginning to register, and it hurt to think of him, to try to recapture the sound of his voice. Everything seemed different to me; the big field might almost have been an imagined place, my experience with Ifan a boyhood fantasy. I felt foolish for thinking that nothing would have changed after nine years. Perhaps the disappointment was inevitable; having returned to Wales full of anticipation, I was eager to go back to Canada, where at least there would be Andrew, to listen to my stories and hold me while I cried. I knew that I would miss Wales, but the ties that once held me to it seemed less powerful; and it was some time after I returned to Toronto that I realized I had never asked where Ifan was buried. The part of my soul that calls itself Welsh told me that I should go back and pay my respects, that the story demanded closure; but I prefer to picture Ifan as a teenager, untroubled by family squabbles and always looking for adventure.

Occasionally, I fly over the hill in my dreams, looking down on the big field and admiring its smooth fabric rippling in the wind. I swoop down to the field like a bird, gliding along the heol fach and into the wheat, where Ifan is waiting for me, his head framed by soft light, and his smile always beckoning. He tells me he is glad to see me, and as we kiss a surge of electricity buzzes through my body and brings me feelings of intense joy.

I hear someone calling my name faintly at first; but as I open my eyes it grows clear, and I realize that it is a North American voice. Andrew has woken me because our plane is beginning to descend over Toronto. We have been visiting his family in Saskatchewan, where the wheat fields, though larger and more impressive than the big field, could never nurture such powerful dreams in me. He asks how I'm feeling.

"I'm OK," I say. "I was miles away, that's all."

"Oh. And where were you, exactly?"

"In Wales," I reply. "Watching the wheat."

He smiles and shakes his head. He has heard me say it many times before, but I doubt that he will ever really understand.

THE DESTROYER

David Evans

TODAY I MEET the skinhead.

He wears dirty combat-fatigues, once ox-blood bovver-boy boots now much scuffed and split. He wears two T-shirts, the outer one ripped and very torn and held together by a strategic and – happily – artistically placed safety pin. It's coldish and he wears little else. He is, to be fair, far more punk than skinhead. Much, much more so if I'm being precise, although it seems he never abandons either to embrace the other. I have seen the pendulum of his style-loyalty swing radically over the time I have been noticing him. No sooner has he fledged from skin to punk then the direction is reversed. Patently, this is not the first time our paths have crossed in this car park although on previous occasions the guy has been practically non-verbal, stoned entirely one hundred and three per cent out of what remains of his mind and any conversation between us has been limited to the briefest of exchanges.

"Orright then, doll?"

I reply that I'm just fine and thank him.

He would usually be carrying alcohol of some sort. Not usually. Always. Cans of lager sometimes. Today he carries a large plastic lemonade bottle and a green carrier bag.

"Wanna drink? It's vodka, y'know."

I decline. He grins. He upends the bottle and takes a deep swig.

"Y'know what I got in 'ere?" He points to the green carrier.

My mind boggles. I reply that I do not.

"Crickets."

Crickets?

"For me tarantula."

Of course. A tarantula. What else? I wonder if it's on his person, secreted somewhere dark and arachno-friendly or if it's demurely waiting for him to return home with its tea in a green plastic carrier.

"Got 'im for two-seventy-five. Usually they're thirty quid."

I suppose I'm being invited to ask how come the huge reduction. Did, I enquire, tarantula have all its legs?

"Course. 'E's perfect. I did it with the bloke in the pet shop. Out in the back. Massive dick 'e ad."

I think I say, gosh. Or golly.

He grins again. His eyes are suddenly expressive instead of vacantly glazed. However animated his speech, his eyes grab at your eagerness with a zombie's ever-hungry passivity. I feel as though I'm a cosmic explorer cautiously circling a black hole which threatens to draw me in to nothing. To somewhere which doesn't exist.

But, as I fear, his new window of openness is entirely temporary. However, for a moment he could be . . .

He could be any age, any age between twenty and death and I wonder which is closer, his birth or . . . His face is almost skull-like, etched and taut, hollow-cheeked and sallow skinned and yet his mouth is full with generous lips which curtain one of the finest sets of teeth I have ever seen other than on movie stars. He asks and I tell him I am forty-eight; he laughs and says I am as old as his mum. So . . . he could be my son. He's some father's son. That's for sure.

"I jus' come out the 'ospital."

Really, I say with concern. Even alarm. I wonder about pneumonia. As one does. He is inviting me and I ask what is wrong with him.

"Got cut up, di'n' I. Jumped on. On fuckin' Clapham Common. Black bastards did it."

I am shocked. I ask if he was alone and how many of the . . . them there'd been. He shows me his arms.

"Dunno. Forgotten. It was dark, wa'n' it. Look! You count 'em." He thrusts his upturned arms in my face insisting that I examine him. "Used a fuckin' Stanley, din' they. Cut me tendon to me thumb. See!"

I ask him again . . . How many? How many attacked him?

"S'pose arf a dozen maybe. An' two of 'em's fuckin' gay too. One of 'em's called 'inton."

Hinton, I say, including the H.

"Yeah. Tha's right. You know 'im?"

I tell him no. I don't. It was just the way he said . . . Forget it.

I stare at his arms. Nice, good, basic arms. They fit his tall, lean frame. Skin he might be, skinny he isn't. From wrist to elbow and probably beneath the T-shirts too, his body is a canvas worked with livid scars and covered with tattoos. I notice the tattoos are also on his neck. On his head, his scalp. One of the visible neck legends reads: SKINZ. The scalpmotif I see to be – natch – a spider and on the other side of his head there is a bruise-blue device which I can't quite make out. I have a sinking feeling that it might be a swastika. The quarter inch hair crop which provides a fuzz of camouflage for the artwork is one half-bleached blond and the other, so he assures me, his natural colour. Sort of brown.

"I 'ate it. S'nuffin, brown, is it? But I'm not sure at the moment. What I'll do next to it . . ."

The boundary line between the two colours is expertly fine. He is obviously not only a dab hand at dyeing but at all the cosmetic arts, however rough and ready, which come to hand to change, cover or disguise any part of him that he perceives as natural. In another life, he might have made a plastic surgeon. I shrug odd surprise. I know several women who pursue, equally hell-bent, a similar mission but who do it first class in the comfortable and creditable shade of the visa tree.

"I like your 'air, doll," he says, returning to the subject

which made him greet me in the first place. "Wha'cha done to it, then?"

I told him I just put a number two crop on both sides, left long bits on the top and down the back and then bleached the whole lot.

"Ah. Mohican, is it?"

He seems a little confused, anxious to label my ill-thought-out coiffure so that he can understand me. Where I'm coming from. Trust me. See me as the same as him. But I tell him I don't think my hair sticks up naturally that way for me to be able to have a proper Mohican.

"Fuck natural."

His tone is not confrontational but concerned. For me. Rather earnest, as though he were giving last minute good advice to a virgin.

"Use Evo-stick, girl. 'Air spray's fuckin' useless. I 'ad a Mohican 'til last year."

I say I know. I saw.

"Fuckin' eighteen inches it was. Used Evo on it for ages but it all broke in the end. Jus' snapped. The Evo rots it, know what I mean?"

I say I do.

Not.

Of course, I don't. I return to the subject of the mugging.

"Oh, that. Same thing as in Kennington Park. Know about Kennington Park, do ya?"

I say I don't know about Kennington Park. He now sounds rueful. Upset, affronted but also angry. Not in-your-face outraged. More like insulted. I ask where Kennington Park is.

"Where the Pride is. You know!"

I feel ashamed that I've never been to a Pride, but I mumble. I hardly dare confess.

"Well, they all go down there. Once a year. September the sixth or something. Black bastards."

I hear myself asking, Why? Why once a year? Why Kennington? The racism, on the other hand, I cannot face. Yet. Cannot question. Ever? Coward?

No. Pointless.

Pointless.

"Cos they don't believe in gays. They reckon only whites is queer so they go down the park once a year and cut up any ol' dykes or gays they find."

I wonder if there are many. Gays and lesbians that is. I have a picture of a greenfield space seething with blue denim placards and Doc Martens and hair.

"Quite a few. Usually. Yeah," he murmurs.

I say something about such brutal thuggery being so medieval and I'm thinking too about Arabs and then about Indians and a lot of Muslims one hears about these days. And I realize a knot of panic forms in my guts. Fear. I struggle to eschew my own self-protective racism. Banish thoughts.

"I 'ate 'em. I never go wiv blacks, me."

Really, I murmur, thinking I really should just walk away from all this. There is nothing amusing anymore. Nothing I want or need to learn. Is there?

"Used to go with gels, though."

I'm hooked again.

He pauses, his train of thought snagged on a millisecond's reflection.

"Yeah."

He grins again.

"Would'ja believe I gotta kid? She's about nine now. Pretty little thing."

He laughs. I'm intrigued.

"Mind you, she's arf black 'erself."

I'm amazed.

He downs another swallow from the glugging bottle. I wonder how much vodka he's poured into the lemonade. He belches.

"But I've always bin queer, mind. I still got meself married somehow, know what I mean? Used to be BNP too."

He sniffs. He is, at worst, aware of the irony. And at best?

"Crazy, i'n'it?"

He pulls his lower lip down and out, revealing yet another hidden tattoo. An internal one, applied to the soft, fleshy pinkness of the inside of his mouth. The letters are a terrifying trinity. BNP. British National Party.

"See?"

I see. My bum crinkles in a sort of exquisite horror. My mind shuts down as it fast-rewinds through jumbled imagined stills of who, how, when, where . . . How. Needles. Dirty needles, even.

"I jus' bought this. Look."

He is now enthusiastic once again. He obviously cannot focus his butterfly attention-span on any topic for longer than it takes him to forget what he has just said. He rummages in the green plastic carrier bag – presumably the crickets are in a separate bag within – and he pulls out a horrendous double-ended spike, some four inches long, made of shiny stainless steel or chromium which he pulls apart, making two horrendous spikes reattachable, it appears, by a crude male-female push-together joint. I shudder once again to think which part of him this fabulous equipment decorates.

"Cost me ten quid. Look. Goes froo 'ere."

He indicates the cartilage separating his nostrils. My teeth are set immediately and painfully on edge.

"I do all the piercin' meself, y'know. Jus' push it froo. Done everythin'. Tits. Done me tongue."

He sticks out his tongue in the middle of which I see the glint of a metal stud.

"An' me eyebrows."

He fingers some old scar tissue now partly hidden by his eyebrows.

"Some cunt ripped them rings outta me in a fight. I bottled him after, mind. Some cunt in the LA. D'ja go there then?"

Again that grin. That absurdly cheerful, ingenuous grin. Does he know he's being shocking? I am like a rabbit, transfixed in the beam of his smile, trapped by the glint in the serpent's eye. And to think I thought I was daring way-back-when, knowing Adam Ant and buying bondage trousers from SEX. I fancy, briefly, that before punk, the only schism I thought existed between us gay boys was the sort that got spilled on a leather jacket in the dark. Rough trade was never like this. But before that . . . We were queers then. Us and . . . them? Definitely. Oh, definitely. All class and station. And before that, so I'm told, there was merely the love and lust whose

names were spoken on NEITHER side of the station above
or below which NEITHER side was supposed to trespass for
longer than an orgasm.

And now? Us? Just us?

Not.

Ever?

Not.

"Yeah. I got pierced everythin' me. An' I done it all meself
'cept for me cock. Some girl did that but it went infected. 'Ad
to go to 'ospital for that an' all. They 'ad to cut me dick apart
to get the fuckin' ring out."

I wince. Sublimely. I fancy I am now way beyond mere
cringe.

"Gotta go to court next week."

I am confused. I don't know where we are, whether still in
Kennington Park or the unnamed hospital from where I hear
the echo of his bloody cock-ring being thrown with a clank
into a metal bowl.

I ask, anyway, why he is going to court.

"'Bout all this bein' cut up. They charged me, see 'cos I
managed to do one of the bastards meself. Two actually."

I mutter something about self-defence. And who had charged
him. And with what.

"The ol' bill charged me. Shoulda been at Clapham but
'cos I live up Finsbury Park they put me to 'ighbury. Next
week. Tough there, they say. ABH it was."

I ask if ABH stands for aggravated bodily harm. Or actual
bodily harm. I have never heard of ABH.

"Dunno. 'Xactly. But they're tough at 'ighbury, aren't
they."

It is a statement, not a question. But I happen to know
from my own bitter experience that "they", it – "them"
at Highbury – the magistrate's court are tough. I don't
tell him.

I feel myself slipping into the first stages of whatever inured
is called. Listening to my neighbourhood skin-punk is incurring
a certain – admittedly uncharitable – disbelief which I am
beginning to be unable to suspend.

I ask him with what the others involved in the affray had

been charged. I fondly think of affray, in his circumstances, being a complementary offence.

"Nuffin'."

Nothing?

"Nah. I told the ol' bill that I was queer an' all. Look at me, I says, I'm fuckin' queer, me an' y'know what they says to me? They says, 'So fuckin' what!'"

I'm beginning to get a picture here. But it's one which I don't think I can reproduce for him. I'm thinking that the police think he's a National Front, probably part of a gang the rest of whom have skidaddled. They think the black guys were merely defending themselves. And maybe . . . Who knows? Fuck knows and never will. Maybe the police are right?

But the police don't determine what is lawful. Do they? I ask about defence. A court establishes legality. Justice. Doesn't it? Has he contacted a lawyer?

"Naah," he sniffs dismissively. "I got all me fam'ly comin', see. I'll be orright."

I don't see and wonder how much of courtroom drama he's ever watched on TV and how much he's understood. Instead of voicing my thoughts I merely say how good it must be to have that kind of support.

"Oh, yeah. Right. They've always known 'bout me. Always known I bin queer. Since I was seven, I've known. They don't mind."

I hear myself telling myself how lucky he is. Lucky? Shit, yes. In a way. Lucky. He's alive. At least. At best.

"If I get sent down, they'll do 'em. They'll get every one of them black bastards 'cos I know who they are and I can tell 'em where to find 'em."

There is no hatred. It's all quite chilling. He merely states a fact and his matter-of-fact is deadly. I remark that at least he seems to have fully recovered from the physical aspects of the ordeal and I ask how long he was in hospital.

"Coupla days. 'Ad all the tests too. HIV 'an that. I'm negative, of course."

Of course.

What am I saying, "Of course." What would he have felt had he been told otherwise? With his proclivity for self-inflicted mutilation, what would he have thought had they told him he'd tested positive?

"Full of 'oles, I am. I was a smackhead for years, did'ja know that?"

I shake my head.

"Eroin an' all that sorta gear. Don' do it no more 'cos I'm not on the game no more. Used to be a rent boy, see. In the Golden Lion. D'ja know·it? D'j'ever go in there?"

I tell him I don't, didn't and won't but wasn't it in Piccadilly somewhere?

"I was on the streets then. Sleepin' rough, know what I mean?"

I nod. Is there anything that this child-man has not done to his body? Is there no hoop of fire or glass or steel or chrome through which he has not gladly leapt? No dark night through which he has dragged his hopes like an old blanket, drugged and doped and dead to the morning?

I realize too that he is not trying to shock me. He hasn't that facility. This is unadulterated conversation, this series of questions and rhetorical announcements. He merely assumes, as he talks, naturally that I know about Kennington Park and the Golden Lion and bits of metal through tender body parts and heroin an' all that gear because that is life. I, on the other hand, think I should know.

That his isn't my life, he, in turn, isn't to know and he will never feel the lack of that knowledge. He is not even accidentally programmed to think he should know.

"Yeah. I think I'll grow me Mohican back again soon."

I observe that it has been twenty years since punk began. He disagrees.

"Nah. Much longer. Twenty-five."

I know I am arguing with the expert but . . . But fuck it! I had been there, after all. This child had been nothing more than a mewling infant, if that. Suddenly I feel anger. I mention Jordan, one-time punk princess of King's Road, Chelsea.

"Oh, yeah. Went down there the other day. Fuckin' empty now."

He talks as though he has been there, at the beginning. Maybe he's wished so often that he had been, swapped braggadocio with those who had been and with those who, like him, also have wished they had been that he now believes he really was. Maybe the truth is what you make it. Maybe time does concertina. Maybe parallel universes are mutually accessible through black holes. Maybe our truth is someone else's fantasy. His something is my nothing. And vice versa?

He remembers.

"D'you mean 'er with all that blonde 'air? All bleached. All up on 'er head, twisted up? 'Er on the telly the other night?"

I say, perhaps.

"I know 'er!" He speaks with some triumph. Like he's discovered a new element. "She lives in Croydon, don't she?"

Jordan, I ask? Is her name Jordan?

"Yeah. Fink so. Dunno really. Probably, though."

He puts his empty bottle into his green carrier bag. I hope he's not squashing the tarantula's supper.

What am I saying!

"I 'ate litter, don't you? Well, see yer, doll. An' keep that 'air goin'. Suits you."

EPILOGUE

I have just met the skin-punk again.

It is some six months later. He is rather scrappily dressed and the hair is of a uniform shortness and colour. It is recently bleached but below the quarter-inch of blond, his dark-brown roots are growing out and almost disguising the Nazca-like designs of the symbols tattooed onto his skull.

And there is no metallic ornamentation. The holes in his lips, ears and nose are empty. As empty as his eyes in which there is no hint of sadness, self-pity or cynical awareness and not the slightest evidence of a smile. Yet he is not unfriendly. There is, strangely, nothing positive about him at all. There appears to be no lurking aggression whatsoever. Sure, he is hyper, nervous, itchy, jumpy and distracted but underlying this manifest physical energy there is a hint of calmness. Unnatural calm. More drugs, of course. This time legal.

"They put me on Prozac. Twelve tablets a day. It was the wrong prescription. Should'a bin six so I 'ad to come off 'em 'cos it did me 'ead in. Know what I mean. Bouff!"

He made a little gesture, indicating the top of his head exploding.

"So now I'm on . . ." I didn't catch the name of the drug. "Methadone sorta fing," enlarged the man who'd forgotten more pharmacology than most people in Boots will ever be taught.

I nodded.

Like I know from methadone. Please.

For the assault charge against the black boys in the park, he tells me he was sectioned. I have no idea what being sectioned means.

"They fink I'm a danger . . . fret to society, know what I mean. Put me in this little dormitory . . ." – I guess he means cell – " . . .only this big . . ." He uses his arms to show how small his world had been in which his exploding head had to be contained.

"I only come out coupla days ago. Feels like a year."

Being sectioned, I ascertain, is hospitalization in secure confinement. This is no care in the community shit. But, ever resourceful, he found the combination – EF 126 – to his cell door and left twice although on both occasions he assures me he returned of his own free will.

"Course I was able to go out," he adds. "Wiv one o' 'em wiv' me, know what I mean. I'm dangerous, I am." He smiles and for a moment he finds my eyes. I wonder if he's wondering whether . . . If I'm the one. If I could be the one on the other end of his life line.

But then . . . Suddenly he is nothing but positive. Shockingly, unnervingly, only-too-really positive.

"But I don't wan' no more," he tells me flatly. There is no hint of the jocular, egging-me-on tone of our last encounter. "Cut meself up again, din' I. Did me arms in again. S'wunna the reasons they sectioned me." He looks around him. "I don't wan' this no more . . ." He gestures around him. All around him. The sky. He means the world. "I wanna do meself in. End it all. I told me mum, she don' mind. She says if yer wanna do it, do it."

I hear him but I shut my mind. A wriggling memory-worm reminds me of something. It wasn't the black boys who cut his arms. It was him. Realizing that, I know I cannot explode his lie and instead, find myself standing on the edge of an ocean of tears. Beneath a very thin crust on which we are standing, there is a chasm of . . . Not despair. Not hell. Just . . . Nothing. Freefall forever. Eternity. Oblivion. Nothing.

"Wen' over Finsbury Park the other day, y'know. Two black guys were there. D'you think I look nutty? Weird like?"

I reply that he does look different. But weird? By whose standards, I ask?

"They called me a weird cunt. Called me a fuckin' weird cunt. Blew me brain again. Went for 'em and did 'em both. I jus' lost it."

So there is still violence. But there is no anger. No hatred. Merely, still that matter-of-fact violence. What did he do to those boys? Not caring about himself, I fear for what he may have done to them. Would he have stood apart, the other him, watching his brain-dead, conscience-numbed oppo kick the shit out of two boys who wouldn't have known what had hit them?

What other him? The him who told me he has a child? A black child? Maybe that is the answer. He has sown his seed and laid-in his harvest.

I ask if they – the ubiquitous they – helped him at all whilst he was . . . away? Helped him to see if there was anything . . . Anything for him?

"Psychiatrists, y'mean?"

I nod.

"I 'ad six."

All at once, I ask?

He nods.

"One time, yeh. Then the others. Them counsellors. Nineteen. Twenty. Just outta college. Never done a drug in their life. Know what I mean? Couldn' get inside me 'ead, could they?"

He looks me full in the face. There is only one answer. No,

I agree, knowing full well that of course they couldn't. That he was right and they were . . . hopeless.

"Told 'em they should fuck off an' getta life then come back. They might be able to do summink then."

I shudder. I do so because I feel the babyshit smell of the breath of "the system". The smell of something sweet but rotten, so well-meaning and yet so utterly passed. Meaningless.

"I gotta sit down. Sorry. I can' stand no more."

He moves from the thoroughfare and sits on a wall. His hands delve into the front of the track pants he wears and he cups what I can only think is his dick and his cum-less balls. I hazard that so much trank pounding through his exhausted system has long done for any hard-on.

"Just been with some bloke," he says. "Got 'is cock out, din' I? Then I didn't know what to do wiv it. Din' wan' it, know what I mean?"

He is now asexual. I don't anymore even wonder what his oft-boasted ten-inch dick is like because in my mind's fantasy eye it has turned into merely a piece of gristle. A limp once-wonder, like the redundancy of a very, very old man.

I enquire whether he still has his place.

"Oh, yeah. Still got that. 'Ad a burglary while I was away. Smashed a window. Nothing was nicked." He pauses. "Nothing to go really." He sniffs. "Me mum 'ad me video and me system so . . ." He shrugs.

I do not ask who fed his tarantula while he was away in section.

"I reckon it was 'im. Li'l'Ricky, know 'im? Remember 'im?"

I had seen Ricky, the boy he refers to, with an Alsatian the previous week. I say so.

"Yeh. German Shepherd. Not mine. 'S'is. Bastard never come to see me." I ask if anyone did. "Oh, yeh. Me mum an' 'at." He looks slightly up and into the distance. "An' Sue. But she's dead now, too." He sighs. "I wanna be, too. 'Ate all this. Being gay fucked me up, y'know. They asked me that in section. "Ave I bin gay long?'"

I observed that he told me he'd always known he was gay.

"Yeh. Told 'em. Since I was five, I knew. Still fink it fucked me up though."

I asked if he remembered telling me he was once on the game.

"Oh, yeh. Sure. Coupla years."

I ask if that wasn't the problem. I am wondering if he will even allude to love. The most terrible thing to me is that I can feel so much of it inside him. I can't unlock it. The person to release it is not me. I . . . This is terrible. Sadder for me than a hundred deaths. For him? I don't think he even knows. If he does, this is indeed a cruel life.

I ask if it was doing it with people he didn't care about and who didn't care about him that fucked him up.

"Prob'ly. Don' like gays much. Gay people don' really care about'cha, do they?"

I cannot disagree in particular. In general, mind . . . Some do. Some. But do gay people care more or less than green or foreign or Antiguan or rich or poor people?

To disagree with him now would mean that . . . I cared? About him? I know I don't and I am ashamed. But not ashamed enough, it seems to make me care. If I cared, if I asked him to make sure he met me in the same place tomorrow to give him a point to live towards, if I gave him money to enable him to do so . . . If I asked friends to find him work, took over some of the responsibility for him, assumed some of the burden of his life from his shoulders, smoothed the way, became a friend . . .

No. Not. Never.

And this twenty-six year old boy wants to die. He is going to die. I feel it. Economics tells me not to waste effort and money. Psychology tells me that unless he finds god or a faith or a lover to fill the vacuum of meaninglessness at his core, he cannot survive for he is not equipped and has no mind for it and no will. Except, of course, the will to die for that is his one survival, for at least he will save himself.

This is all very hard. Hard for someone who has seen so many NOT want to die. So many with so much to want to live for and who weren't allowed.

Clutching at reasons, straws, I ask him whether he has ever thought of joining up with the travellers. Too late.

"Oh. Yeh. I done that. Yeh. Aw'right that was."

I observe that the travellers are known to look after their own and to not judge. Not wanting to be judged themselves.

"Yeh. Right. Sue was a traveller. We went wiv 'em together. But . . ."

Of course. But. Sue is dead. He's already travelled the traveller's road.

In one way, of course, seeking death is the most constructive achievement any human being can aspire to, given intelligence and free-will. Do we not applaud the old person, crippled with arthritis or cursed with some other wasting disease who simply and in an organized fashion does away with themselves?

In another way . . . But on that other way lies judgement. I have no taste for that.

I murmur that no one can tell him what to do. Whatever it is, he has to want to himself.

"Yeh," he avers. "Yeh. Look. I gotta go. Gettin' dehydrated. Gotta getta bottla coke. I'm always dehydrating these days."

I watch him as he walks away from me. He does not look back. He clutches himself, his arms around his chest, hugging the tattered nylon flying jacket closer to him. Is he cold? I am. He looks neither to right nor left. He walks purposefully to the offie. To a shop. He is someone's child. A father's son . . . A mother's baby.

It is not enough.

And then he is gone.

Of the two of us today, he is not the one with a problem.

I COME WITH HER

James Friel

I AM STANDING at the urinals in a club called *What the Dickens* and this young guy is standing next to me. I pay him no mind but I can tell he isn't ugly and he smells of L'Air du Temps. Although I was there first, he finishes before me and stands back to shake off the drops before zipping up. Then he turns to speak – something I didn't expect, did not invite and do not mind at all.

He wears this grey suit and his red tie is tied tight to his throat. Handsome? Maybe he is. I never know what handsome is. I only appreciate what's pretty. If handsome is prettiness falling into ruin than I am well past handsome and this fresh young man is pretty, I decide, pretty enough for me with his pudgy angel face and a bit of brass in his eyes that catches the light shows me he's no fool.

He smiles. I smile back and he starts to complain about the entrance price as if I owned the place and have done him wrong.

"Six quid fifty to get in here, well, it's a lot, isn't it? I mean, even for a Saturday night and there's other places. And what do you get for it? Two dance floors the size of half-pennies and a bar that doesn't sell Malibu. And these here walls. Not posh, are they? Just brick, creosoted black. This is a dump for six pound fifty."

I shrug my shoulders. What can I do? He's right.

"Still," he says, relenting, "it's cheaper than some other clubs in town."

Yes, I say, but then all the other clubs are straight. He smirks at that and although his manner's easy his eyes tell me a different story. I ask him, if he doesn't like it, why he comes, expecting him to say where else is there to go, but now it's his turn to shrug his shoulders and I go a little weak. They are nice shoulders and he shrugs them rather well.

And maybe I'm leering because then he sort of bridles and says, "Of course, I'm not queer."

At this I am surprised and disappointed. But not very. More amused.

"I come with *her*," he says.

I don't know who this "her" is but, from the heavy way he says it, she must be a girlfriend or even fiancée.

"She's outside, waiting for me," he says, as if it's me who's holding him here, who started all this up. "She likes the music and the men don't bother her."

I nod in understanding, swing my head up and down like it's some big hand-bell I use for tolling yes, yes, yes.

"The men, though, they bother me," he's quick to add, eager even. "All these men looking at me, it's dead weird. It's sick. She's blind to it. She says, so what, take no notice, looking's not touching, but I don't know. Sometimes that's how it feels."

I cluck my sympathy but wonder, if all this is true, why he ever stopped to talk to me. I never would have stopped to talk to him. These days I'm too nervous to go hunting after boys. I've not so much built a wall around me as a ditch.

"Like I said, I come with *her*. She likes the music and it's cheap to get in, she says. Six fifty's not that bad, I suppose. We're saving up. Today we bought a set of dining-room chairs and a linen basket. Habitat, too, not Ikea."

Good, I say and there's nothing left for us to do so we leave together as this guy in leather chaps walks in, his bare buttocks two hairy moons.

"See him," the boy whispers to me, "him with the trousers. I don't know how he has the face to wear them. See how spotty his arse is?"

I say goodbye and so does he – we might almost be friends. he heads off into the dark beyond the dance-floor and I head for the bar where My Old Mate Jason has a drink waiting for me. Jason and I come from way back. We remember this place when it was Dusty Springfield, not Madonna, who got us going. We could have been the original friends of Dorothy and when we met a person we liked we'd shake their hand and, as we did so, scrape his palm with a finger – a signal we were willing to fuck, a secret sign that we'd go all the way.

I look back more and more. It's my disease. I remember people I've known and thought I've loved; from the handful of one-night stands memory always singles out, the two attempts I made at something more permanent, to a guy I used to know at school. We never kissed, never did anything, never held each other in the dark while up above the stars shone bright, just glared at each other during Gym and after Maths. Years melt into one and he passes through my mind most days. He was the template, I suppose.

Not that this boy looks like him. He's not remarkable at all except he stopped and spoke to me, made the first move although he never intended to make the second. He's the type I see on the street, on the tops of buses or behind a shop counter, someone I fancy for as long as they are there. This boy is just something I lack, something I look for and never find. It isn't love, it isn't lust. It something that doesn't have a name because naming it would be to possess it and it's a thing that never can be owned. I wonder sometimes if I did possess it once without my knowing it, something lost to me now like innocence, trust in the future or simply confidence.

This mood of mine won't last. Generally I am happy. This boy is just a cloud passing over the sun, that's all.

Later, I dance with Jason, two old gits creaking and slow, on a dance floor that empties just because we're on it, but we act like we don't care. I see him in a dark corner. He is with *her*. She has one of those drab faces with drooping features, like a reflection on the back of a spoon. She's no more happy than I am but doesn't pretend otherwise. She sucks on a cigarette, exhales and then watches the cloud of smoke as though it's telling her something she doesn't want to know. He sits forwards, elbows on his knees, tie loose now around his neck, top button undone. He's wearing white socks with his grey suit. I hate white socks, common they are, town boy things. If I had him in bed they'd be the first thing I'd take off.

I ask Jason if he knows the boy. Jason knows most people.

"I know *her*," he tells me. "Hairdresser, the back of Boots. Did my hair once. Right mess she made of it. Him? I don't know what he is. Wouldn't want to."

We go on dancing but the boy catches my eye or I catch his. He smiles and turns his back to speak to her. I know he is pointing me out. He is telling her I am the old queen who tried to chat him up in the toilets. She is looking over his shoulder and I can see that she is scowling at me hard.

I dance on but lose my rhythm. I am not angry with him for lying. Not at all. What I most want to do is go over, hold him tight, feel him shiver in my arms, happy and reluctant as I bite into his white neck and suck it like an apple.

But I don't. Kylie Minogue is singing *The Locomotion* and it is Jason's favourite song of all time – at the moment. I stay to dance it with him, recovering my rhythm and my appetite for life. In the strobe light that makes of me a silhouette, I tell myself that I am young and lovely still and that he may have come with *her* but that it's me he wants and will never have. I think of it as my revenge, as if it were a choice I made.

COOKERY

Patrick Gale

A FAVOURITE PIECE of broodily-autumnal Fauré came on the radio. Perry turned it up and sang along under his breath, still unused to the delight of having the house to himself and being able to make as much noise as he liked. He lifted a saucepan lid to check on the leeks which were sweating in a pool of butter. He prodded them with a wooden spoon, turned off the heat, ground in some pepper and grated in some nutmeg. Nutmeg subtly sweetened the taste and blended nicely with the air of slightly-burnt butter. One had to be sparing however; too much, and the spice overcame the taste of the leek rather than enhancing it.

He continued singing to himself as he whisked in eggs, cream and some crumbled Wensleydale cheese. Swathing his hands in a towel, he pulled a baking tray from the oven on which two small tart-cases had been baking blind under a shroud of silicone parchment weighted with earthenware beans. They were done to perfection; dry without being coloured. He allowed the steam to escape from them then, biting his lower lip in fear of them breaking, tipped each of them gently onto the palm of his hand then slid them, naked, back onto the baking tray. He spooned the leek mixture in, sprinkled on a few parmesan shavings then slipped the tray back inside the oven and set the timer.

The cat, Edie, was clawing at the window and, being on the large side due to a diet of culinary leavings and field-mice, threatening to dislodge the herbs that grew on the sill. Perry let her in, kissed her nose in greeting and set her down a saucer of cream. She was the only cat he had known to purr and eat at the same time. The sound was faintly indecent and spoke of appetites beyond the power of man to tame.

"Cookery is power," his mother told him at an early age. She meant it jokingly. Minutes before, she had taught him how to make a simple chocolate toffee sauce to pour over ice-cream (butter, sugar, cocoa, a few grains of instant coffee – he made it occasionally still) and was laughing at how instant a reaction it won with some schoolfriends he brought home to lunch.

He had little sense of humour at that age, even less than he had now, and he asked her, quite solemnly, what she meant.

"I'll tell you when we're alone," she said, and winked.

He asked her again that night, while he sat at the end of her bed and watched her, fascinated, as she teased out her dancing hair in the breeze from the hair dryer. She was taken aback at his earnestness. She had forgotten both sauce and comment. He had thought of little else all day.

"Men have very simple needs," she said. "Sleep, food, warmth and the other thing. But hunger is the most powerful. When your stomach's turning in on itself, you can't concentrate. When you eat something delicious, you're happy, you're grateful. Whoever makes the food, rules the roost." She laughed. "The griddle pan is more potent than the gun, Perry. Why frighten people into doing what you want when you can win their love with a cake? Those women they burned at the stake weren't witches at all, they were powerful cooks who led whole communities by the nose. A witch's cauldron is just an oversized casserole. All that hubble-bubble stuff in *Macbeth* is a parody of a recipe."

With the untutored tastebuds of childhood, he had favoured sweet recipes at first. Happily these tended to be those involving the most magical transformations. Thus his early cookery lessons carried all the attraction of games with a chemistry set. There was that hot chocolate sauce that, once he had learned to let it boil sufficiently, set into filling-tugging caramel on contact with ice-cream. There was the sequence of hot desserts, nicknamed *chemical puddings* by his mother, in which an unpromising sludge would rise through a watery layer during baking, thickening into a rich sauce as it formed a puffily-crusted layer above it. Victoria sponge taught him pride. He learned patience through meringue; those wrist-numbing extra minutes of whisking that divided egg-whites that were merely stiff from those that were said to be *standing in peaks*, and the slow baking in a cool oven which managed mysteriously to produce a confection so crumbly and dry. It was only with chocolate brownies, however, with which a girlfriend's brother was so easily persuaded to drop his jeans for a five minutes *scientific* inspection, that Perry learned the extent of his new-found power.

Adult savoury cookery was taught piecemeal, largely through being asked to help out with occasional tasks. Learning how to brown chicken thighs, roll pieces of steak in seasoned flour, dissect and meticulously de-seed red peppers, he combined his new techniques with what he saw his mother doing and so added *coq au vin*, *boeuf en daube* and *ratatouille* to a still succinct repertoire.

"If you can cook," she told him, "you'll never be hungry, but if you can cook *well*, if you can do more than just feed people, you'll be popular too. You'll be able to choose who likes you."

Thrilled by the potency of such a spell, for he was a scrawny child who had yet to grow into his nose, he hung on her every word. He followed her about the garden absorbing her quirky wisdom.

"Parsley," she pronounced. "Useful but common. The curly one is only really usable in sauce and soup. And never use the flat-leaved one unthinkingly. Often this plant, chervil, will do much better. Taste it. Go on. See? Now try this. Coriander. Superb stuff. You can use it almost like a vegetable, by the hand-ful, but be careful again. Used in the wrong context it tastes like soap and it sticks to the teeth as embarrassingly as spinach."

In season, she led him around the fields and lanes behind the house introducing him to blackberries, sloes, elder bushes, mushrooms, crab apples, sorrel.

When Perry turned ten, shortly after his creation of a puffball and bacon roulade had seduced a new neighbour and demoralized the neighbour's wife, his mother fell ill. For a few weeks, without anyone's appearing to notice, he inherited her apron, and whisked up menu after comforting menu for his father and older brothers, reading cookery books in bed and skiving off afternoon sports sessions at school to race into town on his bicycle before the covered market closed. When she returned, grey and shattered after her operation, she was grateful to have had her wooden spoon usurped, still more to taste his nutritious soups and cunning vegetables after two weeks of hospital pap.

Her gratitude, however, seemed to break the peaceful spell of his father's quiescence. It was as though he were noticing for the first time as Perry stirred his sauces and deftly shredded roots and nuts, swamped in a practical but undeniably floral apron.

"Why don't you play rugger like Geoff?" he asked. "You'd like rugger. Once you got used to it."

"Sport bores me. What do you think of this duck? Was the fennel a mistake? Maybe celeriac would work better, or even parsnip. If I could get it to caramelize properly without the duck's skin burning . . ."

Perry was duly banished to boarding school on the Yorkshire coast, handpicked for its bracingly sporty philosophy and lack of opportunities for any science more domestic than the use of Ralgex and Universal Embrocation. His mother was brought down from her sickbed and set back to work at the kitchen stove. She collapsed there shortly afterwards and died of an internal haemorrhage half-way through assembling a deceptively humble fish pie. Perry cursed his father for his cruelty but laid on a suitable buffet for her funeral and brought his seduction of the neighbour to an electric conclusion with the aid of some witty yet somehow mournful filo parcels of pigeon, leek and sultana.

He hated school and counted off the passing weeks like a prisoner. His impatience to be free had more to do with the liberty to have access to more inspiring ingredients than with any brutalities visited on him. His growing mastery over food continued to protect him like a hero's winged sandals or magic armour. An ability to dress crab and whip up a mayonnaise won him an entrée to the shielding comforts of the prefect's common room in his second week and the older boys soon set him to baking them cakes instead of forcing him out onto icy playing-fields. He even came to look forward to overnight field-trips with the cadet corps, given charge as he was of the campfire kitchen. Since adolescents have always lurched between the kindred demands of belly and groin, cookery also brought him sporadic tastes of rough-handed romance.

His father and brothers had long dismissed him as effetely artistic and were as surprised as he was when he began to specialise in chemistry. Boarding school had given him a taste for independence. Without his mother there, the family home held little appeal for him and while passing through university and qualifying as a forensic scientist, he went there as little as possible. (He made exceptions for his brothers' successive weddings – miserable occasions where the poor quality of the catering made him more than usually grateful that he had kept cookery as a vice and not pursued it as a livelihood.)

He had only the one live-in lover, first encountered in the meat aisle of a local supermarket. Douglas had come out shopping in tennis clothes, fresh, or rather not, from a match. Perry could not help but notice the way the chilled air from the meat cabinets raised goose bumps on his legs and Douglas noticed him notice. After smiling, smirking, and then grinning encounters beside toiletries, Kosher and home baking successively, the evening had ended in Perry cooking Douglas lamb noisettes in a pink peppercorn sauce. Smug and yawning twelve hours later, he made them scrambled eggs and bacon. It took only two more dinners for Douglas to move in.

It was a love expressed as Perry knew best, in generous helpings, judiciously seasoned. Over four years, Douglas added running and secret dieting to tennis as he fought in vain the extra poundage that Perry's devotion was heaping upon him. Then he fell ill and for three years after that, Perry became an expert in nutritional coaxing as he tried in vain to stave off Douglas' inexorable spells of weight loss, vanished appetite or nausea. The most innocent foods – yoghurt, bread, cheese

– would suddenly be branded as enemies. His ingenuity was stretched to the limit. Whenever Douglas was in hospital, Perry would cook enough for them both and make a point of their still sharing an evening meal, even if Douglas could manage no more than a spoonful before sinking back on the pillows in defeat. Never had the preparation of food carried such an emotional charge.

That was the second funeral feast he had cooked, beating tears into cake batter, anger into cream. He intended it to be his last.

After Douglas there had been men, occasionally, but no more lovers. Perry's experience of desire had always been so bound up in the pleasures of the table that he found it hard to surrender for long to any romance that was not essentially domestic. Then the hole in his domestic routine was unexpectedly filled.

A stroke after a hip operation left his father incapacitated. There was a gruesome counsel of war in which the brothers, abetted by their child-worn wives, agreed that residential homes were both soulless and ruinously expensive. Perry had room in his house. Perry had experience of home nursing. They would each pay a nominal monthly sum to their younger brother and he should take their father in. He had never declared his sexuality, assuming it would be taken as read and, as they confronted him with their tidy plan, he sensed it was too late to do so now. He had allowed them to assume he was merely a bachelor, a eunuch with a way with sauces. He had allowed them to assume that, for all their initial doubts, his work for CID meant that he had been vetted as "sound". Playing hard to define, he had played into their hands. He could hardly turn around and complain that visiting a speechless, incontinent, not to say unmusical parent would starve a sex life that was already gaping for sustenance.

At first it seemed like an abominable invasion of his privacy. The old man might have lost control of his tongue and bladder but retained his bullying nature and store of indignation. Gradually, however, Perry saw that there was no cause for fear. He was in charge now. He decided what the old man could and could not eat, when he would bathe, when he would watch television and, indeed, what he would watch. To cover the long hours he spent at work in the police laboratories, he took pleasure in hiring just the sort of camp, Irish nurse his father would loathe. Said treasure wore a uniform he described as Doris Blue. He was delighted when Perry confided that his father had been sleeping with men on the sly all his married life and was a wicked old flirt with wandering hands. Perry often came home to find the two of them watching films in which men loved men or women tap-danced and sang their hearts out. The nurse would be watching, at least, and singing along where appropriate. Perry's father would be merely staring, aghast, in the direction in which he had been so mercilessly wedged with scatter cushions.

Perry opened them an account at a specialist video library. In twelve months his father was exposed to the entire output of Crawford, Davis, Stanwyck, Garland and the Turners Kathleen and Lana. He became a passive expert on the complete weepies of Douglas Sirk – of which the nurse was especially fond – and even the most misbegotten of MGM's musical output. He sat, breathing heavily, through any film that could be remotely described as lesbian or gay, subtitles, Kenneth Anger and all. He watched nothing pornographic, however, at least nothing hard core. Despite Perry's bland assurances, the nurse was sure the excitement would have dire effects on his bladder or even his heart.

It startled Perry to find that he could be so vindictive. Apart from some singularly unhelpful grief counselling after Douglas died, he had never been in therapy and was not given to self-analysis. He had never given voice to the damage his father had done him, so had never given it substance. Even now, he did not immediately seek a retributive justification for what he was doing.

He did not abuse his father physically, although the odd smack might have seemed only the mild repayment of a longstanding debt. He dressed him. He undressed him. He bathed him. He changed his incontinence pads. If he spoon-fed him the kind of food his father had always dismissed as foreign or *nancy*, if he occasionally buttoned him into a violet quilted bedjacket that had been his mother's (telling the nurse to humour a camp old man's little ways) it was done in a spirit of domestic spite not unlike that practised between many cohabiting couples.

As a year went by, then two, during which his father was a powerless, dolled-up guest of honour at several of Perry's more Wildean parties, he came to think of the old man less as a parent than a grouchy partner. As he pecked his father's cheek on leaving for work or retiring at night, as he amused himself by brushing his still thick, silver hair into a variety of fanciful styles, as he meticulously piped a saucily naked cherub onto his heart-shaped birthday cake, Perry would admit that, while still not exactly fond, he had developed a kind of tender dependence on his father's being there. Bereft of any other outlet, his nurturing energies were making do with the only man on the horizon. (The nurse was never an option; Perry had old-fashioned views on the healthy inflexibility of sexual roles and had marked the nurse down as a sister from day one.)

Howard had caught his eye over the contents of a dead woman's intestinal tract. The corpse had been principal stockholder in a toy manufacturing firm due for flotation. She was found face down, fully dressed, in her sunken bath. Her family claimed she had drunk too much, fallen in, passed out and drowned. As detective inspector on the case, Howard mistrusted them and ordered an autopsy. The stomach was duly shown to contain precious little bath water, which indicated that she had died before submersion. There was alcohol in her bloodstream but not enough to knock out, let alone kill, such a hardened drinker. Called in by the coroner to analyse the content of her gut, Perry found beef, onions, red wine, button mushrooms, rice and significant traces of a powerful sedative administered to dogs and horses.

"Her brother's a vet," Howard murmured. Beneath the crumpled, unshaven look of the over-stressed detective, the ghost of a more dynamic person stirred. Leaning against the lab desk, he towered over Perry, who was perched on a stool. "How specific can you be?"

"Very," Perry told him, looking up from flicking through the pharmacology files on his computer screen. "These weren't prescription tranqs. I mean, I can't give you a brand name but

I can narrow it to a choice of six or seven and they're only for veterinary use."

Now Howard smiled, a grin of broad satisfaction that cracked the laughter lines fanning out from his sad, blue eyes. Normally Perry was curt with policemen, judiciously telling them no more than the science they needed. Basking in the big man's approval, however, he would have prattled on for hours if it kept him so close.

"There's something else," he added.

"What?"

"Well, it's much more concentrated in the gut contents samples than in her blood. Maybe it was injected into the meat that she was going to cook? If she ate it rare enough and they stuck enough in, it would still pack a lethal punch. You'll need to check my data with the coroner, but I think he'll bear it out."

"Thanks," Howard said. "Thanks a lot. You've made my week. This could have turned messy." He rubbed a big hand across his tired face and over his stubbled chin. "I owe you a drink."

"You're on." Perry saw the wedding ring as he spoke.

From self-protective instinct he spent the rest of the day curbing his interest. When Howard dropped by late in the afternoon, however, changed, shaven and smelling of cheap cologne, he found it impossible to resist his invitation. Howard was a new transfer and unfamiliar with the area. On the pretext of showing him some countryside but actually to avoid running into any colleagues, Perry had him drive them out to a small country pub which served excellent pork and leek sausages. This proved a wise choice for, mid-way through his second pint, Howard lurched the conversation away from cadavers and poison to his marriage, his teenage daughter and, after much fumbling with a beer-mat, to the reason why his wife had left him. Perry discreetly rang the nurse and persuaded him to tuck his father up in bed and stay late on double time, then they drove up onto the moor and made frantic, bruising and extremely messy love in Howard's car.

Howard cried afterwards, which Perry found utterly bewitching. They continued to meet regularly back in Howard's rented flat. Howard often cried out during sex or would exclaim, "I like this. I *do*. This is what I like."

And he often wept after it for sheer relief. He claimed to find Perry overpowering because he would approach sex with another man so matter-of-factly. He had no idea that the very sight of him shyly unbuttoning his drip-dry shirts made Perry want to tap dance. They always went to Howard's place. Perry found he could not face a meeting between his lover and his father, let alone Howard and the nurse and, when they first discussed their situation, had unthinkingly said that he "lived with someone". Howard's assumption that this was a lover and that Perry was risking a relationship to be with him gave Perry an even fizzier sense of power than Howard's grateful tears.

He said nothing to disabuse him. At first he liked the fact that their meetings were secret, snatched and often in daylight. He liked the anonymity of Howard's drably furnished flat and the sense that it was an area in which nothing was forbidden them. He soon began to grow hungry for more, however. He yearned for evenings together. He wanted to wake up with him. Most compellingly of all, he wanted to cook him a meal, the more so when he realized that Howard was a stranger to cookery and stocked nothing beyond teabags, cornflakes, butter, milk and a bag of sliced white.

Once he had settled upon fungi, of course, he had to wait a maddening four or five weeks until the most fitting ones were in season. He knew precisely the variety he needed to use. Mercifully rare, they happened to be a speciality of the region, favouring the grassy fringes of beechwoods. Remarkably similar, at a glance, to an innocuous variety, the things had often been pointed out to him on walks with his mother. Identifiable only from the way their ghostly flesh bruised blue, they caused paralysis and, in an already weakened victim, heart failure. Taking care to use some kitchen towel to keep the toxic harvest separate from the innocuous field mushrooms he had also picked, Perry made a perfect risotto; arborio rice brewed in chicken stock and mushroom juices – with a dash of cream and three threads of saffron – until sticky without being indigestibly glutinous. He went to some trouble. He lit candles and dressed his father in a jacket and tie.

"It could be our anniversary," he told him as he spooned the fragrant mixture into the old man's eager mouth. "More wine, dear? It's a good one this – nicely nutty without being sharp. There we go. Greedy! You'll have the end of the spoon off . . ."

He was not foolish. He waited, peacefully holding his father's hand as they listened to Mendelssohn, until it was plain that death had joined them at the table, then he went to the telephone and summoned help. When he heard the ambulance approaching, he bravely wolfed down several mouthfuls of the bad risotto on top of the helping he had already eaten of the good. This meant that he was already feeling very cold and barely needed to act when he begged the nice young man in casualty for a stomach pump.

"I don't know how I could have been so stupid," he told his brothers later, his throat still raw. "I've been picking mushrooms since we were children. I've never made a mistake before. I'll never forgive myself. Never."

But he did, naturally. He bade the Irish nurse a tearful farewell, redecorated his father's room, donated two suitcases of old male clothes to Help the Aged and, at last, was in a position to invite Howard to dinner. He made the date for tonight, a Friday, intending for them to spend the weekend together but had kept this last bit a surprise.

Howard brought flowers as well as wine. He dithered, anxiously, in the doorway.

"Is he, erm?"

"He's gone," Perry assured him. "I told him to move out."

"Did you tell him, you know, about us?"

"I just told him I'd met someone else and that there was no room in my life for the two of you. Give me those and get in here. We may be alone but I still have neighbours."

Dinner was delayed because Howard felt a need to impress his mark on what he still perceived as a rival's territory, and he was not a man to be denied. Perry had anticipated this, however, and planned the menu so that nothing would spoil with waiting. He knew from the way Howard sang to himself as he was showering there would be little difficulty in persuading him to move in. It was only when Howard took a mouthful of the chicken parfait on toast that Perry served with their preliminary drinks, however, and Perry asked, "Well?" and Howard's face registered surprise, delight then an unmistakeable greed for more that Perry felt entirely sure.

SHADOWS

Damon Galgut

THE TWO OF us are pedalling down the road. The light of the moon makes shadows under the trees, through which we pass, going fast. Robert is a little ahead of me, standing up in his seat. On either side of his bike the dogs are running, Ben and Sheba, I can never tell the difference between them.

It's lovely to be like this, him and me, with the warm air going over us like hands.

"Oh," I say. "Oh, oh, oh . . ."

He turns, looking at me over his shoulder. "What?" he calls.

I shake my head. He turns away.

As we ride I can see the round shape of the moon as it appears between the trees. With the angle of the road it's off to the right, above the line of the slope The sky around it is pale, as if it's been scrubbed too long. It hurts to look up.

It's that moon we're riding out to see. For two weeks now people have talked about nothing else. "The eclipse," they say. "Are you going to watch the eclipse?" I didn't understand at first, but my father explained it to me. "The shadow of the earth," he says, "thrown across the moon." It's awesome to think of that, of the size of some shadows. When people ask me after this, I tell them, "Yes," I tell them. "I'm going to watch the eclipse."

But this is Robert's idea. A week ago he said to me, "D'you want to go down to the lake on Saturday night? We can watch the eclipse from there."

"Yes," I said. "We can do that."

So we ride towards the lake under the moon. On either side the dogs are running, making no sound in the heavy dust, their tongues trailing wetly from the corners of their mouths.

The road is beginning to slope down as we come near to the lake. The ground on either side becomes higher, so that we're cycling down between two shoulders of land. The forest is on either side, not moving in the quiet air. It gives off a smell: thick and green. I breathe deeply, and my lungs are full of the raw, hairy scent of jungle.

We're moving quite fast on the downhill, so we don't have to pedal anymore. Ahead of me, I see Robert break from the cut in the road and emerge again into the flat path that runs across the floor of the forest. A moment later I do so too, whizzing into the heavy layers of shadows as if they are solid. The momentum is wonderful, full of danger, as if we're close to breaking free of gravity. But it only lasts a moment. Then we're slowing again, dragged back by the even surface of the road and the sand on the wheels.

The turn-off is here. I catch up with Robert and we turn off side by side, pedalling again to keep moving. Ahead of us the surface of the lake is between the trees, stretched out greenly in the dark. The trees thin out, there's a bare strip along the edge of the water.

We stop here. The path we were trying to ride on goes, straight and even, into the water. That's because it used to lead somewhere before they flooded the valley to make the lake. They say that under the water there are houses and gardens standing empty and silent in the currents below. I think of them and shiver. It's always night down there at the bottom of the lake; the moon never shines.

But we've stopped far from where the path disappears. We're still side by side, straddling the bikes, looking out. The dogs have also stopped, stock-still, as if they can smell something in the air. There's a faint wind coming in off the water, more of a breeze really. On the far side of the lake we can see the lights of houses. Far off to the right, at the furthest corner of the water, are the lights of my house. I glance towards them and try to imagine them: my father and mother, sitting out on the front verandah, looking across the water to us. But there are no lights where we are.

"There," says Robert.

He's pointing. I follow his finger and I also see it: the moon, clear of the trees on the other side. It really is huge tonight, as if it's been swollen with water. If you stare at it for long enough you can make out the craters on its surface, faint and blue, like shadows. Its light comes down softly like rain and I see I was wrong – it makes the water silver, not green.

"We've got a view of it," I say.

But Robert is moving away already. "Come," he says. "Let's make a fire."

We leave our bikes leaning together against the trunk of a tree and set out to look for firewood. We separate and walk out by ourselves into the forest. But I can still see Robert a little distance away as he wanders around, bending now and then to pick up bits of wood. The dogs are with him. It isn't dense or overgrown down here. The floor of the forest is smooth. Apart from the sound of our feet and the lapping of the lake, it's quiet here.

There isn't much dead wood around. I pick up a few branches, some chunks of log. I carry them from behind where the bikes are. Robert had already made one trip here, I see from a small pile of twigs. I don't much feel like this hunting in the dark, so I delay a while, wiping my hands on my pants. I look out over the water again. I feel so calm and happy as I stand, as if the rest of my life will be made up of evenings like this. I hear Robert's whistling coming from behind me out of the dark. It's a tune I almost recognize. I start to hum along.

As I do I can see Robert in my mind's eye, the way he must be. When he whistles, small creases appear round his lips. He has a look of severe concentration on his face. The image of him comes often to me in this way, even when I'm alone.

Sometimes late at night as I lie trying to sleep, a shadow cast in from outside will move against the wall and then he breaks through me in a pang, quick and deep. We've been friends for years now, since I started high school, riding past my house in a swirling khaki-pack down to the lake. It hurts me when this happens. I don't know what they speak about, whether they talk of things that I could understand. I wonder sometimes if they mention me. I wonder if they mock me when I'm not there and if Robert laughs at me with the rest of them.

He comes down now, carrying a load of wood in his arms. "Is that all?" he says, looking at what I collected. "What's the matter with you?"

"Nothing," I say and smile.

He drops his wood along with the rest and turns. He's grinning at me: a big skew grin, little bits of bark stuck to his hair and the front of his shirt.

"Do we need any more?"

"No," he says. "That should do fine."

We build a fire. Rather – he builds a fire and I sit against a tree to watch. It always seems to be this way: him doing the work, me watching. But it's a comfortable arrangement, he doesn't mind. I like the way he moves. He's a skinny boy, Robert, his clothes are always slightly loose on him. Now as I watch, my eye is on his hands as they reach for the wood and stack it. His hands are slender and brown. He's brought a wad of newspaper on his bike. He twists rolls of paper into the openings between the logs.

Like me, the dogs are sitting still and watching. They stare at him with quiet attention, obedient and dumb.

He lights the fire. He holds the burning match and I'm looking for a moment at this white-haired boy with flame in his hand. Then he leans and touches it to the paper. Smoke. He shakes out the match.

The fire burns, the flames go up. In a minute or two there's a nice blaze going. We're making our own light to send across the water. I think of my parents on the wooden verandah, looking across to the spark that's started up in the darkness. They point. "There," they say. "That's where they are." I smile. The fire burns. The flames go up. The heat wraps over my face like a second skin. The dogs get up and move away, back into the dark where they shift restlessly, mewing like kittens.

In a little time the fire burns down to a heap of coals. They glow and pulse, sending up tiny spurs of flame. We only have to throw on a stick now and then. Sitting and staring into the ring of heat, it would be easy to be quiet, but we talk, though our voices are soft.

"We should camp out here sometime," he says. "It's so still."

"Yes," I say. "We should do that."

"It's great to be away," he says. "From them."

He's speaking of his family, his home. He often speaks of them this way. I don't know what he means by this: they all seem nice enough. They live in a huge, two-storeyed house made out of wood, about half an hour's ride from us. They're further up the valley, though, out of sight of the lake. There are five of them: Robert, his parents, his two brothers. I'm alone in my home, I have no brothers. Perhaps it's this that makes their house a beautiful place to me. Perhaps there really is something ugly in it that I haven't seen. Either way, we don't spend much time there. It's to my home that Richard likes to come in the afternoon when school is done. He's familiar to us all. He comes straight up to my room, I know the way he knocks on my door. Bang-bang, thud.

My mother has spoken to me about him. At least twice that I can remember she's sat on my bed, smiling at me and playing with her hands.

"But what's wrong with it?" I say. "Everyone has friends."

"But lots," she says. "Lots of friends. You do nothing else, you see no one else . . ."

"There's nothing else to do," I say. "Other people bore me."

"There's sport," she says. "I've seen them at the school, every afternoon. Why don't you play sport like other boys? You're becoming thinner and thinner."

It's true. I am. When I look at myself in the mirror I'm surprised at how thin I am. But I am not unhealthy, my skin is dark, I'm fit. We ride for miles together, Robert and me, along the dust roads that go around the lake.

"It's him," I say. "Isn't it? It's him you don't like."

"No," she says. "It isn't that. I like him well enough. It's you, you that's the matter."

I don't want to upset them, my parents. I want to be a good son to them. But I don't know any way to be fatter than I am, to please them. I do my best.

"I'll try," I say. "I'll try to see less of him."

But it doesn't help. Most afternoons I hear his knock at my door and I'm glad at the sound. We go out on our bikes. This happens at night too, from time to time. As now – when we find ourselves at the edge of the lake, staring at the moon.

"D'you want a smoke?" he says.

I don't answer. But he takes one out of the box anyway, leaning forward to light it in the fire. He puffs. Then he hands it to me. I take a drag, trying to be casual. But I've never felt as easy about it as Robert seems to. The smoke is rough in my throat, it makes my tongue go sour. I don't enjoy it. But for the sake of Robert I allow this exchange to take place, this wordless passing back and forth, this puffing in the dark. I touch his hand as I give it back to him.

"Are you bored?" he asks. "Why're you so quiet?"

"No," I say. "I'm fine." I think for a while, then ask. "Are you?"

"No," he says.

But I wonder if he is. In sudden alarm I think of the places he might rather be, the people he might rather be with. To confirm my fears, he mutters just then:

"Emma Brown—"

"Why are you thinking about Emma Brown?" I say. "What made you think of her now?"

He's looking at me, surprised. He takes the cigarette out of his mouth. "I was just wondering," he says. "I was just wondering where she is."

"Why?" I say.

"I just wondered if she was watching the moon."

"Oh," I say, and smile bitterly into the fire. I don't know what's going through his head, but mine is full of thoughts of her: of silly little Emma Brown, just a bit plump, with her brown hair and short white socks. I remember a few times lately that I've seen her talking to Robert; I remember him smiling at her as she came late to class.

"I was just thinking," he says, and shrugs.

I finish the cigarette. I throw the butt into the fire. We don't talk for a long time after that. I can hear the dogs licking each other, the rasping noise of their tongues. I begin to feel sad. I think of my anger and something in me slides, as if my heart is displaced.

He reaches out a hand and grazes my arm. It's just a brief touch, a tingling of fingers, but it goes into me like a coal. "Hey," he says. "What's the matter?"

"Nothing," I say. "Nothing." I want to say more, but I don't like to lie. Instead I say again, "Nothing." I feel stupid.

The fire burns down to a red smear on the ground. Across the water the lights have started to go out. Only a few are left. I look off to the right: the lights in my house are still on. My parents keep watch.

When I look back, Robert is on his feet. His head is thrown back. I don't stand, but I gaze over his shoulder at what he's watching: the white disc of the moon, from which a piece has been broken. While we were talking, the great shadow of the earth has started to cover the moon. If you look hard enough the dark piece can still be seen, but only in outline, as if it's been sketched with chalk.

We stare for a long time. As we do, the shadow creeps on perceptibly. You can actually see it move.

"Wow," he says.

Sensing something, one of the dogs throws back its head in imitation of us and begins to howl. The noise goes up, wobbling on the air like smoke.

"Sheba," says Robert. "Be quiet."

We watch the moon as it sinks slowly out of sight. It's light is still coming down, but more faintly than before. On the whole valley, lit weirdly in the strange blue glow, a kind of quiet has fallen. There is nothing to say. I lower my eyes and look out over the water. Robert sits down next to me on his heels, hugging his knees. "You know," he says, "there's times when everything feels . . . feels . . ."

He doesn't finish.

"I know," I say.

We sit and watch. Time goes by. The trees are behind us, black and big. I look across to my home again and see that the lights have gone out. All along the far shore there is dark. We are alone.

"It's taking a long time," he says. "Don't you think?"

"Yes," I say. "It is."

It's hot. The dogs are panting like cattle in the gloom. I feel him along my arm. A warmth. I spring up, away. "I'm going to swim," I say, unbuttoning my shirt.

I take off my clothes, and drop them on the sand. The dogs are standing staring at me. Robert also watches, still crouched on his heels, biting his arm. When I am naked I turn my back on him and walk into the lake. I stop when the water reaches my knees and stand, arms folded across my chest, hands clinging to my ribs as if they don't belong to me. It isn't cold, but my skin goes tight as if it is. One of the dogs lets out a bark. I walk on, hands on my sides now, while the water gets higher and higher. When it reaches my hips I dive. It covers my head like a blanket. I come up spluttering. "It's warm," I say, "as blood."

"Hold on," he calls, "I'm—"

As I turn he's already running. I catch a glimpse of his body, long and bright as a blade, before he also dives. When he comes up, next to me, the air is suddenly full of noise: the barking of dogs as they run along the edge of the lake, the splashing of water, the shouts of our voices. It *is* our voices I hear, I'm surprised at the sound. I'm laughing. I'm calling out.

"Don't you," I say, "don't you *try*—"

We're pushing at each other, and pulling. Water flies. The bottom of the lake is slippery to my feet, I feel stones turn. I have hold of Robert's shoulder. I have a hand in his hair. I'm trying to push him under, wrenching at him while he does the same to me. He laughs.

Nothing like this has taken place between us before. I feel his skin against me, I feel the shape of his bones as we wrestle and lunge. We're touching each other. Then I slide, the water hits my face. I go under, pulling him with me, and for a moment we're tangled below the surface, leg to leg, neck to neck, furry with bubbles, as if we'll never pull free.

We come up together into quiet. The laughter has been doused. We still clutch each other, but his fingers are hurting me. We stand, face to face. While we were below, the last sliver of moon has been blotted out. A total dark has fallen on the valley, so that the trees are invisible against the sky. The moon is a faint red outline overhead. I can't see Robert's face, though I can feel his breath against my nose. We gasp for air. The only sound to be heard is the howling of the dogs that drifts in from the shore: an awful noise, bereaved and bestial.

I let go. And he lets go of me. Finger by finger, joint by joint, we release one another till we are standing, separate and safe, apart. I rub my arm where he hurt it.

"Sorry," he mutters.

"'S OK," I say. "It doesn't matter."

After that we make our way to shore. I wade with heavy steps, as if through sand. By the time I reach the edge and am standing, dripping beside my clothes, the moon has begun to emerge from shadow and a little light is falling. The dogs stop howling. I don't look up as I dress. I put my clothes on just so, over my wet body. They stick to me like mud.

I wait for him to finish dressing. As he ties his shoelaces I say, not even looking at him, "What do you think will happen?"

"What d'you mean?" he says.

"To us," I say. "D'you think in ten years from now we're even going to know each other?"

"I don't know what you mean?" he says.

He sounds irritated as he says this, as if I say a lot of things he doesn't understand. Maybe I do. I turn away and start to walk back to the bikes.

"Hey," he calls. "What you . . . don'tcha want another smoke or somethin' before we go?"

"No," I say. "Not me."

I wait for him at the tree where the bikes are leaning. He takes his time. I watch him scoop water over the coals. They make a hissing noise, like an engine beneath the ground. Then he walks up towards me along the bank, hands in his pockets. The sight of him this way, sulking and slow, rings in me long after we've mounted our bikes and started back up the path.

By the time we rejoin the dust road a little way on, the soreness in me is smaller than it was. One of the dogs runs into his way and he swears. At this I even manage to laugh. I look off and up to the left, at the moon, which is becoming rounder by the minute. Its light comes down in soft white flakes, settling on us coldly as we ride.

A TRUE ROMANCE

Stephen Gray

THEY TOOK THE more private back route up in the lift. Other shoppers were ascending and descending the escalators, cool out of the summer. They used the opportunity to peck one another: Johan's lips chapped with the sun, John's smeared with Vaseline Lip-Ice.

"Putting KY on your lips now?" Johan said.

John just clenched his hand around Johan's wrist.

The trouble with Johan was that he liked to exhibit himself; John preferred remaining furtive. The lift-door opened.

John was taking Johan to be tested. Not his blood or his lungs, but his big blue eyes. Johan avoided reading small-print nowadays, probably because he was less and less able. His struggle with map-reading in the car was making this apparent. His chin rested on the device, a beam lighting up his beautiful eye.

"Glaucoma," said the optometrist.

"But he's only twenty-two," said John.

Johan gave a massive blink.

"Just screening – it's mandatory by law."

"Oh," said John.

"Well, I haven't got glau-co-ma either," said Johan.

"That's to be thankful for."

★　　★　　★

At first, with the glasses on, Johan walked as if his legs had shrunk. On the down escalator he gripped the moving rail. Outside in the sunlight the glasses clouded over in a satisfactory manner. Johan took them off to study his double mirror image, stuck them back on cautiously with both hands. A whole new, less active way of life. Now he could read the map, just for pleasure this time . . . and the bright route streaming past. "Check that, just check that!"

At the clothing shop he left the glasses behind in their slipcase on the counter. They had to go back. With the glasses on again, he could examine the weave, the stitching in the seams of his new jeans. He squeezed John's knee as John pressed the buzzer for the automatic gate.

Johan, as it were, tripped up the stairs to John's flat where they had lived together for almost a year. They were still in that preliminary stage of a romance, deeply uncertain of one another. Johan would disappear for days, weeks on end. When he returned, John insisted he be contrite. John had to keep the steady job, mark all those tests, earn to provide – for Johan. In a desultory, undeclared way, they were indeed in love with one another, but the kind of social barriers for which South Africa is famous kept them from settling down as an economic unit too soon.

"*I'll* cook this time," Johan insisted. Which meant scrambled eggs.

He actually peered into the pan. "Crumbs, look how . . . look how it's . . . clotting," he said. "Forming clots."

No instrument could measure the *extent* of their love-relationship, but for both John and Johan it had grown, let us say, in spite of themselves. John had previously been straight and married, so that this was his first gay affair and all that it entailed. Johan had hustled since his teens, lived with a few older men of some status until the thieving departure; mostly one-night stands to keep off the streets. This unlikely liaison with dour John was a big event for him, as well.

In bed they were learning to achieve closeness, sometimes frighteningly so. With less alcohol, and earlier nights, they now could spend hours on each other, at the nooks and crannies of bodies that they had not been really alert to in others before. Occasional ecstasies, but nothing like this engrossment. They were learning to express themselves more through themselves. That is why the stolen buss in that lift was not so much a surprise as a proclamation to themselves that they actually did care for one another.

As they were both in their own ways Puritan (Johan – low class Afrikaans, John – residual Presbyterian stock) and thus not much trained to treat others with delicacy, it had crept up on them: love was now wishing the other greater fortune than one wished for oneself. Clingingly, they had both become so *considerate*.

Given their personal histories, this was all the more remarkable. Johan's was obvious, indeed written on his lissome, creamy body: the chink where his baby head was bashed into a table, leaving a ridge beneath his right eyebrow; the scars which were more than accidents – stripes on his buttocks from reformatory life; also two strokes of the razor-blade at the left inside wrist. Yet he was always undressing as if others could not read the signs, holding his balls, focusing on himself in the mirror. *Needing attention*.

John, twice his age, had every reason to stay covered up. Old freckles lately were turning into eczema. Johan was too tactful to comment on these; all he would say was, "Now I'll really descale – descale your back." John was too light-skinned to tan without burning. In the complex's dazzling pool, Johan would dive in and glide down the tiles. Horseplay was out because, if John got his head wet, he would go deaf for hours.

It was on the tip of John's tongue to say the words – *do you love me?* Just over a salad on the balcony, without a change of register. As if they had no more importance than *are you getting used to your glasses now?* But behind that was a larger question: *what difference does it make?*

And behind that: *is it possible for two men to love one another, anyway?*

They had mothers in common.

Johan was trained to the phone ringing on Sunday morning,

picking it up, passing it over to John without the slightest evidence of his presence if it was John's mother. "Yes, mother . . . yes, mum . . ." John would reach around the table for his glasses. As if he was undressed without them.

Sometimes Johan just dozed on; sometimes to be really objectionable he would take a piece of John's body – a big toe, or the elbow curved upwards – and work on it during an interminable duty-chat.

Occasionally the wife phoned, but at more considerate times: brisk, reasonable. In fact, although she did have her regrets, she thought it quite intriguing that her husband – inevitably she had found out – had undergone what she vaguely thought of as a sex-change. Obviously neither woman had yet met this Johan.

For his part, Johan's mother – to whom he escaped periodically down in Port Elizabeth – had been recruited as a Jehovah's Witness. When she was not ill, she spent her time on the pavements soliciting, as her son had formerly – in her case for Jesus. Jesus was the best bet for anyone connected to a homosexual case, like that of her son.

From time to time she wrote desperate notes to him at the post office box they now shared. John would bundle Johan's kitbag on to the Greyhound Bus and they would squeeze hands – just that – at the last possible moment before departure.

And Johan would call with his phonecard from Colesberg, saying they'd got off for supper, and from the terminus to say he'd arrived, his phonecard running out. He would not call again for a whole week. That was how it went: he needed to revert to that other life to which John would never have access, for a while. Just to help him decide.

Then Johan's mother died, too suddenly for her son to be at her deathbed – Greyhound, phonecard, a staggering sum for the funeral, which John provided. For a month after his return from the peculiar wake, Johan was in an unrecognizable state; true distress, even derangement, over the fact that so little had come of his past. He gave out confused utterances, like "They tell me Jesus doesn't . . . doesn't drink" – whilst falling over the empties in the kitchen.

"Evidently *you* do now," said John, which was vindictive.

Johan had inherited the working class manner of dramatizing his sorrow.

Then he'd kneel on the Tabriz. "I'm gonna ... I'm gonna ..." he'd blink. "Get her a fucking tombstone ..." Which was pointless, since her sour bones had been cremated.

Contrite, Johan passed out, there on the carpet. John had to drag him, undress him, wash him and smuggle his drooping weight undercover for the rest of the night. Protect him against himself.

John had his crisis, too, one night when he had eaten a Knysna oyster that had absorbed some red-tide. Johan, who couldn't yet drive, actually persuaded their general practitioner to make a housecall at 2 a.m., stomach-pump the victim, inject him and generally save him for posterity. The doctor, having separately attended to their venereal problems, and thus knowing more about the involvements of the pair than they did, simply told Johan: *don't leave his side.* He didn't.

That seemed to be the domestic part of loving: nursing the utterly helpless. Being around to relay to the partner what had happened when he was knocked out.

After a long, agonizing commotion John was retrenched from his job. Unexpected new South African factors caused this. Like most of his kind, John had previously lived impervious to anything within touching distance of what may be termed the strictly political. Indeed, the great watershed-crossing of the country from apartheid to democracy had occurred smoothly enough for his taste. In fact, it was the best time to turn out gay: now in South Africa, incredibly enough, he *could not* be discriminated against in the workplace as such.

Nevertheless, he was still a middle-aged white, so that a counter current of affirmative action saw to it that he was replaced by a rather dopy-looking trainee from Giyani, brown as toast and aged all of twenty. Simply put, the new headmaster no longer wanted a stalwart who always got his marksheets in early and commanded such a high salary. John was out, as of the end of the month.

At first all John and Johan could come up with was selling

off John's CD collection. Cutbacks would certainly have to be made. Johan could always go out and get a job – as a welder, the profession he had been taught.

After what in a straight household would be called a bout of marital abuse, triggered by John's despair and resulting in a swollen lip for Johan as if a bee had stung him, the whole debacle blew over. John got a job in the classical section of a CD supermarket run by his distant cousin, nine to five, Monday through Saturday. Johan meanwhile continued to make metal gadgets for the kitchen, which they began to sell together at the local fleamarket on Sundays. Months went by in this way, even years.

John's mother seemed to have rationalized her son's situation. So he had a kind of handyman subletting a room in his flat, paying his way, even taking his shift at the stove as hardened bachelors sometimes do. When her daughter-in-law informed her, no, they were *screwing* one another, she genuinely had no idea what she meant. She thought it had something to do with those ingenious appliances.

John's gawky young boy was the one to normalize the family network. He would charge into the flat on the days they were due to look after him, literally throw himself at Johan: splat! "I do love you, *uncle*!"

Johan was looking his best these days: filled-out but still rangy, blond hair like a handful of pick-up sticks, those devastating eyes behind the clear glasses he had taken to. As a salesman of his work, with his vastly improved English, he had developed an easygoing, appealing manner. From the stall, he could readily pick up younger men. Steering them to the chimney stack on the roof of the parking garage, he initiated them in turn into certain procedures. The difference from the days of his own street-life was that now he was the one doing the blowing.

John of course could tell, by a certain lightness of step on Johan's part, what was up, when, if not exactly with whom, though sometimes he saw the suspects slinking off, the telltale speck on their shorts. To assert his right to revenge, once John took off in the car without explanation, and did not return *until dawn*. Months later, when tricked into it by Johan, he did admit that he had merely stayed in the car, staring at Zoo Lake until the sunrise.

And had tears been running down his cheeks? Yes, buckets full of tears had been coursing down.

It was not yet Johan's turn to cry buckets. That would come after he brought to the flat that degenerate, stoked-up number who, with great dexterity and even violence, insisted on having them both more or less simultaneously. After they paid him off, Johan sank into his armchair and, for no reason whatsoever, simply burst out. They became more faithful to one another thereafter.

When John's three-week annual leave came round, his wife would give them little John for a while, so the three Johns took off on a carefully planned trip. Once this was fishing on the Transkei coast, at some remote spot where they had to camp, living off nature's bounty. In little John's case there was no question that affection was a greater tug than biology. He and Johan were perpetually fastened together, prying off bait, getting a license to harvest their mussels (which John would not eat), building up the driftwood fire. Men at work.

Little John had opted to learn some Xhosa at school, so that when their tent was surrounded by curious herdboys a kind of verbal barter ensued, puffed-up little John taking the lead. Something he came out with had a dozen Transkeians on their backs in the sand with laughter, responding with a chorus of lurid insults. Johan said they were calling one another "stupid fat cow" and other imbecilities. When John saw little John doubled up with mirth, then swaggering into a bout of even worse invective, he felt envious: it would be a happier country, giggling.

On their return the father of staunch little John found himself with the mother. For the first time in over half a decade they were alone together, a circumstance he had avoided; indeed, with Johan as a shield, had prevented.

What made John awkward was her likeableness: she was well-together, so amenable. She now saw her husband (they had not bothered to divorce), if it may be put this way, as at last fully developed. He had quit the CD shop, taking a lesser salary as a music announcer on the new radio station, finding the way to put over exactly the right mix of his knowledge and enthusiasm. She had not thought he had that kind of assurance in him. The greying temples helped. He was not meant to be young any more, and how comfortable he had become in his slack body.

"The programme's going well, isn't it?" she said uncomplicatedly.

"I'm glad you enjoy it," he replied.

Then she said, "John . . ."

That was all. They were back in their old bed again. They forgot about little John and the uniforms Johan was buying with him; they forgot, if that's possible, about the difficult intervening years. For her the experience was shattering, scrambled her poise; for him, although his body recognized the old rhythms and performed well, he was no longer inside it at all, but hovering around rather, wondering why he was thus engaged, down there, beside himself. They were grateful to one another, touched . . . never were going to try it again. In due course they did divorce quite amicably.

Johan benefited. Towards him John displayed a new kind of tenderness, a sort of feminine grace which at last he allowed to emerge. They'd scream like school-girls, letting it all out. Furious bouts of work on "the programme" followed. Johan shifted his shielding activities to the phone: hopeless fans, late at night, wanting the master's voice (all women, much mistaken). He unplugged it when they were in bed together.

Johan was appointed to run a metal sculpture workshop for some foundation past Sandton. This meant driving lesson and a second car. They could have gone on in that style: a cosy twosome, private as all such arrangements are in the bourgeois world, based on a dedication to looking after one another that neither of them had thought possible. Habit certainly cemented them, but more basically each knew the other could still deliver surprises: thus, fascination.

In the outside world they were separately thought of as accomplished. Without any planning that way, they both now performed social functions which may perhaps be considered nation-building: John in education again, Johan out there with the avant-garde. It was part of the fresh climate.

Their true romance would have continued had Johan not been killed in a perfectly ordinary car-crash at the intersection of Corlett Drive and Bompas Road when one afternoon he was a bit late for a session at the workshop. What made it worse was that *he* was in the wrong: he had disregarded the traffic light. Not only was he dead, but due to lack of insurance both wrecks had to be paid for by John. It was all unexpected and unwanted. The man whom Johan hit head-on was unhurt; he could not have been more apologetic. Why hadn't Johan seen him coming?

John went straight from the mortuary to a concert in the City Hall. Every time the light went on beside his mike he spoke unwaveringly, a true professional. Once he'd returned the listeners to studio, his body began to shake. In a sense, it continued to shake uncertainly for ever after. He had had the love of his life; would not have another.

Their experience of this love had been different. For Johan John had been the *whole* of his life; they had met before he had found himself, he had died while they were still in progress. Even little John – and his grief was terrible to watch – was experiencing more nuance to his life: a blank, a Johan period and then after-Johan.

So John had now had two lives. Not being as resilient as his offspring (whom he had wondered about – how was he turning out in terms of sexual orientation, had his passion for Johan contaminated him?), he couldn't forget the ghastly accident that easily. The loss stayed with him and haunted him. Often, in the depths of his being, he felt he wished he had been taken instead. That was the extremity of his love.

They held a memorial service for Johan at the sculpture place, where he was evidently much missed. This was in the courtyard in which a huge work of his, welded together out of industrial scrap, was incomplete. John's ex-wife and son attended, but not his mother (who always knew her son's lodger should never have driven).

Under a jacaranda tree dropping down purple blossoms, the service took its course. They held hands a lot – a very mixed group, some black schoolchildren, housewives, Indians, woodworkers from next door, staff. They sang the first two verses of a heartening hymn.

The clergyman, shaking hands, said he was sorry about John losing his son. "No, there he is," John replied, pointing out the handsome teenager. The clergyman and he had realized what had happened and cringed.

John touched the surface of the statue the late Johan had been building. The spot-welds, sandpapered over, reminded him of the scars on Johan's body. The healing process that left traces of the damage done.

John moved to a smaller flat. All there was left of Johan in the end were a few holiday snaps, framed above the music console.

But one night, in spite of the new location – even the new bed – the ghost of Johan found him out. John had the impression that the door from the bathroom was slightly opened. Presently there was the weight of hands and knees on the counterpane, trying to crawl between the sheets without waking him. Then the cool back edged into position against his chest, ready for his arms to enclose it and the late-night blurt: "Love – love you."

He got up to see if a prowler hadn't broken in. There was no one. But Johan had been there. Of that he was certain.

It was another delayed reaction; his way of saying farewell. That is where their romance as such ended.

DEAR JULIUS

Rufus Gunn

THE DANUBE IN Vienna is a dull river. The city turns its back on the cheerless straight channel that flows through the nondescript eastern suburbs, the price of a flood prevention scheme dating from the last century. And there is only one, scarcely adequate, place to moor small craft. All the more welcome, then, the sudden appearance one afternoon of colourful cohorts of canoes invading the muddied brown waters. One broke away and I reached for my binoculars to observe the powerful strokes that were propelling its occupant in my direction across the strong current.

I am not being completely truthful. The fact the canoeist was male and possessed of blue eyes beneath a shock of auburn hair – magnification is a marvellous thing – also had something to do with it. Surely he couldn't be attracted by the red ensign fluttering over the stern, I remember thinking as he drew closer. But it turned out he was; for no sooner had I hastily replaced the binoculars in the wheelhouse, than he hailed me in English – or to be more specific, English with a Scottish burr. The young man – well not so young actually, more in the prime of life like myself – wanted me to know that he was so very, very relieved to catch sight of a red duster; his German wasn't up to much and he wanted to ask a favour and not risk being

misunderstood. He explained that the others participating in
the international canoe event on the Danube he'd joined these
last three days were bound for Budapest and beyond; but he
had a flight booked back to Edinburgh tomorrow night, and
he wanted to see Vienna first. Would I object to him pitching
a tent on the bank near my boat, and keeping an eye on his
gear while he visited the city?

Half an hour later Alec was all sorted out and I had long
since confirmed his eyes were blue, a hazy cornflower blue.
At the local *heuringer*, not far from the bus-stop for the city
centre, we clicked mugs – mugs is what the young white wine,
grown on the slopes of the Kahlenberg not far away, came in
– and looked down the Danube, and at his tent and canoe
now moored alongside my boat. Alec was telling me about
his trip:

"Well, I had this idea of Austria as being all onion dome
churches and jolly farming folk with time to tend their
flower-laden window-boxes, just the sort of place for a short
break to cheer you up before the winter sets in. But as for the
Danube, I think I chose the wrong stretch. I started off in Linz,
and I'd forgotten if I'd ever known that Hitler went to school
there, and years later rewarded the city for the privilege by
having a jolly good go at creating a new Ruhr immediately
downstream. You wouldn't want to capsize there, I can tell you.
They must have rebuilt all those steel mills and chemical plants
that the allies did them a favour in destroying. And then there
was Melk – *that* I was really looking forward to, the grandest
of the baroque monasteries. By the time I got there I knew
that the cliffs on which it's built are tunnelled with galleries
built by slave labour for a munitions factory. And where did I
learn that? At Mauthasen, the afternoon before. The canoeists
stopped at the pontoon there en masse and I couldn't very well
just carry on. Nor could I not follow everyone up the hill past
the quarry to the camp. I'd never have gone through with it
on my own, though. The worst of it was the clinical efficiency.
That place they brought you across to – for taking details of the
dimensions of your head for that pseudo-science of theirs, as
you thought. Lined you up thinking the dark cavity in the wall
was something to do with the measuring device – and shot you

in the back of the neck. 'Humane killing', they'd call it today. And those so-called showers were the same story. I work in a hospital, and I kept thinking of the machines they showed us in a TV documentary about executions in America: those lethal drips they use. And then there was the Wailing Wall where they manacled you for interrogation, and the memorial plaques now lining it. The sheer scale of the slaughter! Not only of Jews who alas bore the brunt of the horror but of more Spanish Republicans than I ever imagined. And there was one memorial plaque that was very special for me, the most recent addition of all. Only ten years old. From the Austrian Gay Association – to the thousands of gays who died there."

Alec fell silent and turned his back on me to stare at the relentless river swirling sadly by.

"The pink triangle, yes it's good that in the end we are not altogether forgotten," I said slowly, and watched his hunched shoulders gradually relax. "Now you'd better catch that bus or you'll see nothing of Vienna. And Vienna, believe me, can be fun."

I trust I made it clear on the way to the bus-stop that I was not making a play for my blue-eyed boy – we live in difficult times and for me they have been perhaps more difficult than for many others. But let this pass. I hoped that Alec would understand and accept that even innocent flirtation was not currently on my agenda.

"Be good! And don't worry about your canoe and the rest. See you when I see you," I signed off as I left him waiting for the bus, hoping all the same he would not be gone too long.

In the event it was gone midnight when I heard a scuffling on the bank.

"Come aboard!" I shouted and soon after Alec was clambering down the companionway steps.

"How'd you get on?" I asked when he was seated in the saloon and a sailor's nightcap before him.

"I met the most marvellous man," he replied, downing the generous measure of rum straight off, most decidedly a merrier fellow than the one I'd met that morning.

"Well then, what are you doing here?" I felt obliged to say, entering into the spirit of things.

Alec flushed. "No, I don't mean it that way. I met Julius at the bus-stop just after you left. He'd been walking up the Kahlenberg, he called it, and had strolled back beside the river. It was the fact of such an elderly man wearing sneakers that first drew my attention. There was something very puckish about the wee fellow but there was no disguising his years. I asked him if he spoke English and mercifully he did – with a slight American twang acquired, he told me, during the years he'd spent away from Vienna, the war-time years I managed to get out of him by the time we reached the Schwedenplatz."

"Sounds intriguing."

"Even more so than you think. But yes, Julius is Jewish and makes no secret of it with a Star of David on a chain about his neck; and he's very fond of the city which was why in the end he returned. When he heard this was my first visit, he said he'd just time to give me a whistle-stop tour – you could do that here faster he claimed than in any other European capital."

"So you took the number 1 tram from Schwedenplatz, the one that brings you all the way round the Ringstrasse; and you saw Franz-Joseph's tiresome pastiches – the gothic city hall, the classical parliament – on the site of the ramparts he tore down. Ramparts, I've been told, where once the Viennese wined, dined and danced long summer nights away when they were not simply looking out from the congested city onto the romantic wilderness of the Danube's backwaters – a myriad of enchanting channels long since filled in," I interrupted.

"Well, yes, but we could also see right into the old centre – Beethoven's house," Alec protested.

"Ah, of course," I stood corrected.

"And then there was the holocaust monument," he continued. "I didn't know if I was doing the right thing bringing all that up, but it had been so much on my mind; and who better than someone like Julius to put things in context? If it wasn't too painful."

"Rather you than me."

"You haven't met Julius! There's something about him: a lambent integrity in the way he looks out at you from beneath that deep-etched brow, a reassuring familiarity that makes you think you've known him for years.''

"So you went ahead?''

"Yes. And I told him I couldn't understand how the Jews after having come so close to extinction could go on believing in the Messiah.''

"That was in at the deep end!''

"You could put it that way. And Julius replied that there were Jews – and Jews. He amazed me by agreeing completely with me if by 'Messiah' I meant what he thought I meant. He asked me to recall all that business about the Second Coming and the Kingdom of Heaven on Earth that was believed to be so imminent two thousand years ago; and then nothing happened. He told me there were those Jews who came to understand that neither that Messiah nor any other Messiah would come. 'Or rather that the Messiah was man himself. That the revelation and the great winds to come were those of our own history.' Fine words, he said, and added modestly that by the way they were not his.''

"Must be some Talmudic gloss,'' I said wildly, uncertain of my ground.

"Be that as it may,'' Alec continued, "Julius takes it very seriously. He maintains that every one of us has a specific contribution to make to this history. And his is here in Vienna and this is a great responsibility for Vienna is a very special city, not on the periphery of Grossdeutschland as some would have it but at the very centre of Mitteleuropa – from whose pluralist past Julius insisted we had so much still to learn. This was one of the things he discussed with the much younger friends whose company he also enjoyed in the hiking club – the club must also explain his sneakers. Their receptiveness and willingness to face up to a difficult inheritance gave him hope for the future, and Julius believed it was up to him to do what he could to help them. By this stage, I should add, we were well into our second time round the Ringstrasse, and when Julius looked up and saw the Opera House again, it was as if he'd been suddenly stung – he leapt up to strange looks from one of the many matrons surrounding us. The feather antennae of her Tyrolean hat seemed to quiver with disapproval. Had she known that passing the Opera House had reminded Julius he had arranged to be there in an hour's time, she might have been more sympathetic, especially if she were herself becoming more forgetful with the years. Be that as it may, Julius told me he had to get home to change first and then meet up with an old friend from Budapest. They had seats booked up in the gods – his friend was on a much less generous pension than himself. Why didn't I join them, he suggested? Tickets were kept back for sale shortly before the performance and if I queued early enough I'd be sure to get one. How could I be in Vienna and not go to the opera? It was *Lucia di Lammermoor* tonight."

"Well, *The Bride of Lammermoor*! What could be more Hibernian? They must have known you were coming. How could a Scot refuse?"

"Precisely, and a redhead too. Joan Sutherland always did play Lucia in a red wig, didn't she?"

"I suppose so." I wasn't really an opera queen but I knew a few titles and plots. New light on Alec. "And so you met the Hungarian?" I encouraged him to continue.

"Yes, his name was Joel. Now this is what I meant earlier by Julius being more intriguing than you think: he and Joel were old, old friends; they were very sweet together. And in the mad scene where Lucia sings '*a noi sara la vita*'" – Alec did not have a bad voice, even falsetto – "there were tears in their eyes when they heard her pray for the bliss that she and her lover can expect only in heaven. And I was reminded that all this too was my history, and perhaps yours – how an earlier generation of gay men identified so readily with doomed divas. How inevitable it seems when society condemned them to such frustrated lives."

"How right you are. And how I'd like to think things have changed – or are changing," I said.

"Yes, I thought that too. And Julius would be the first to say: thanks to the effort of activists like those responsible for that most recent addition to the memorial plaques at Mauthausen."

"But it's not all a bed of roses," I had to add.

I was altogether unprepared for what then happened. Alec flung his arms about me. He had not had too much to drink, nor was I aware beforehand of anything in his behaviour that might signal sexual interest in me. Perhaps there wasn't any. Not to begin with, that is. For we bunked up together that night, as sailors say; and again as they say, helped each other out. I had the sense that Alec remained distant from me, however intimate I became with the athletic frame I'd first seen straining across the Danube in my direction. Had this impressive torso been the exclusive preserve until recently of someone else's embraces? Certainly, sex could hardly have been safer. Were Alec's few days in Austria a prescription for the end of a love affair? Or for something else? I had no way of knowing.

The following morning Alec was up early and by the time I was fully awake he had his canoe folded up and his tent packed. He'd arranged to meet Julius in the Breughel room at the Kunsthistorischesmuseum around eleven. There'd just be time for a quick look over Austria's equivalent of our National Gallery before getting back to the boat about two, and then carrying straight on out to the airport for the late afternoon flight back home to Edinburgh.

Alec returned despondent. What neither he nor I had known – and Julius had perhaps forgotten – was that today was the annual Austrian national day, the one and only occasion when the state collections could be seen free. The fact was well known in the capital of Slovakia only thirty miles away where the cost of a family visit to a Viennese museum represented a week's wages. In consequence Alec had had the impression that the entire population of Bratislava had converged on the Maria-Theresanplatz. It was something of an achievement to have got into the Kunsthistorischesmuseum at all but as far as a rendez-vous with anyone in front of the popular Breughels went – Alec told me think of Oxford Circus underground station at rush hour and multiply by ten. You were lucky to get away without cracked ribs. Alec had done his best and waited as long as his robust physique could stand but he had had to conclude that if Julius had managed to get into the gallery at all he must have missed him. It had been hopeless. The worst of it was that Alec feared he'd now lost contact with Julius completely for he didn't even know his family name, let alone an address or a telephone number. But Alec had remembered something. It had given him some hope, however little, when he'd finally had to admit defeat; and he'd sat thinking things over with a coffee and a very expensive fudgy cake further up the Ringstrasse. Julius had said he was going to *Norma* in two Thursday's time – he'd be up in the gods again with Joel. And wouldn't I still be in Vienna then, Alec asked me, for I'd told him I had to wait for some engine spares? Would I accept an invitation from him for a ticket to the opera, for *Norma* on Thursday week? Alec thrust what were left of him Austrian schillings into my hands claiming he had the bus fare and no use for what was left. And would I do him one last favour? Go up to the gods and look for someone answering the description of Julius – there'd not be all that many elderly gentlemen sitting in pairs. And give him this.

Alec handed me an envelope addressed to "Julius".

"I wrote the letter inside the café on the Ringstrasse. And I want you to read it before handing it over, which is why it is unsealed. There's lots of time so don't look at it now. But not so much time for me – I must be on my way," Alec said as he glanced at his watch and began to gather up his things.

Alec insisted he cope with everything. But it was running late so he agreed to me helping him up the steep slope to the bus-stop with the folding canoe. And as it was, he nearly missed the bus. There was hardly time to say goodbye. Perhaps it was better that way.

The first thing I did when I got back to the boat was open the envelope. It would have perhaps been better to have waited until Alec was back under Scottish skies but I am not the most patient of men. I smoothed out the single sheet of paper on the chart table. This is what was written below an address in Edinburgh.

Dear Julius,
The Breughels? I didn't even glimpse the Breughels and I only hope you weren't trampled underfoot. But here's hoping you receive this.

How I want to continue our discussions; in particular there was something I very much wanted to ask you. I don't want to pry but by the time you read this I'll be back home where men, gay men, of your generation are coming to be envied – something few of us could imagine given the hell they went through. But there are, so many of them, after all still alive. You see, so many of my friends are dead or dying.

What I wanted to ask you was how to cope with finding myself a survivor. For the time being. Now you know. Today is the first anniversary of the loss of the best friend I'll probably ever have. That's why I came to Austria – for a change of scene. I couldn't have handled waking up in Edinburgh in the bed we used to share on this morning of all mornings.

I didn't tell you either that I'd visited Mauthausen, and when you told me in the tram how much you now enjoyed the company of young people, I couldn't help thinking how few of your Jewish contemporaries have survived. And be happy for you that with Joel at least you can remember old times.

It's getting to the point that so few of my contemporaries are surviving that I'm beginning to question what right I have to remain alive. A scenario all too familiar to your fellow Jews, Julius, and I know full well that some of the most respected among you have taken their own lives. I felt sure as we talked that you had confronted this choice; and that you were for me a messiah, and your wisdom would help me see a way towards a future. And how fitting it would have been on a day such as this.

Well, it was not to be. That too is history, and you would say I must make of it what I can. It does however mean you'll meet the bearer of this letter. I believe he too nurses a secret sorrow. I think you'll like him. But do write to me. *Please.*

Alec

SNOWFALL

Joseph Hansen

ROY CREIGHTON RAKED the yard. All along the street great maples had scattered their red and golden leaves across the dying lawns. At the end of the block the ancient elms of Bryant College had blanketed the campus with brown. The smoke of bonfires was pungent in the evening air.

Creighton paused and leaned on the rake, a little weary, breathing the tang of the burning leaves and smiling to himself. This was the time of year he loved best – summer spent, with its rank greens, its humid heat, its raspy insect hum – the return of crispness to the air, and with it the excitement of a new term's beginning.

But no autumn of his life moved him as did this one. He had so very nearly failed to reach it. Sudden tears blurred his eyes. He brushed at them indignantly with the ragged cotton gloves he wore for gardening. The horror that had overtaken him last June in the dim, hot room of a cheap walkup hotel on a dingy back street of that city where he had gone in search of – what, forgetfulness, love? – an insane search with a nightmare ending – apparently had not only half blinded him and nearly wrecked his health forever, but had turned him sentimental as well.

What a picture he must make for that clutch of students passing now, arguing, laughing, kicking the leaves – Roy

Creighton, Ph.D., clinging wanly to the handle of his rake and weeping in the twilight! With a grimace, he bent, scooped the last heap of leaves into the bushel basket, picked up the basket and carried it to the back yard where a great heap of leaves already smoldered.

He retrieved the rake, poked the bonfire into flame, over-turned onto it the new basketful of leaves, and poked it again. Then he stood for a long time gazing into the flames.

When he slept, his mind was haunted by the hurt that had been done him. Again and again he cowered in the corner of that grubby hotel room, the red neon sign across the street spraying it with spasms of light like blood from an opened artery, and again and again he felt the heavy boots crash against his ribs, again and again woke screaming with the sound of their splintering in his ears.

But his waking mind was haunted by a deeper fear, fear of the insane someone who lived inside him and might at any moment take him in charge once more and drag him to his doom. After all, when the thing had happened he was 47 years old. There had been not one such episode in all his life before – not since he was 18 and had known Bovy Welles, known him to the bare skin, bewildered and afraid but unable to resist going back to Bovy again and again, and luring Bovy again and again to himself, Bovy laughing and embarrassed and unkind except when lust stripped all his fundamentalist conventionality away along with his clothes . . . Bovy who suddenly married and went inaccessible and left Roy Creighton to his own bleak, solitary devices.

In time he smothered his wants in work, in learning, in academic achievement, his loneliness by clinging close to his mother. Mother . . . It had been her death, of course, that had set him off. He'd known it was coming, thought himself prepared for it, and perhaps he was. What he had not been prepared for was himself, how he would feel when she was gone. His tenure had come at the same time as her death. He had been free, really for the first time in his life. And how had he coped with that freedom? In the most bizarre and unexpected way.

Armed with 1100 dollars in cash – the bank had suggested traveler's checks; he had merely smiled and shaken his head –

he had driven to the nearest large city, to that blowsy street, that flyblown hotel, to sleep during the suffocating days, to prowl all night – bar-rooms, neon-crazy, shrieking with steel guitars; public men's rooms reeking of disinfectant and stale urine, with their strange, speechless ceremonials of lust; midnight parks with their furtive, shadowy denizens, young pale faces with the eyes of rabbits, the armed faces of the middle-aged, the wolf faces of the old.

The frail little lad called Chick, in his pitifully spindly dungarees and pointed shoes, blouse like a girl's, plucked eyebrows, paint on his sunken cheeks, always by the fountain rim; the lanky, freckled, easily smiling Oklahoman in cowboy rig; the blond, ruddy-cheeked high-school type with a guitar he never played; the sullen Negro youth with the body of a Watusi prince, slouched lazily against a tree-trunk; and beautiful Covent Blessed, arrogant and aloof, astride his glittering Harley, sometimes with others of his kind, sometimes alone . . .

Creighton had gone among them fascinated, beside himself with lust, not himself at all, in fact, insane, rushing upon his own destruction. One by one he had taken them up to that room and had lived out there, upon that butt-sprung bed, fantasies suppressed so deeply all those years he could not recognize them when they came to life. Night by night, hustler by hustler, stud by stud, trick by trick – adrift in an alien world, he expected an alien tongue – he had them all, until he got to Covent Blessed. Or rather, until Blessed got to him.

"Do you really dig that dirt?" He slid onto the stool next to Creighton's. It was three in the morning. The glaring all-night coffee bar near the park was empty except for the two of them and the pimply boy smelled of leather and of great cleanliness. "You could do better. You're a good-looking John."

"Thank you." Creighton nudged his cigarettes toward Blessed. "Perhaps I could."

"They're none of 'em more than five-buck hustlers." Blessed dumped sugar into the steaming brew the tired boy brought him. He stirred it, sloshed in cream, lit one of Creighton's cigarettes. "Chick don' get that, half the time. So hot for it, he gives it away. Cock's his hangup, like some cats get hooked on junk."

"Yes, and he's half-starved," Creighton said.

"Lunch is all he wants," Blessed grunted. He drank from his cup, little finger extended. A tough lady. "He told me you gave him twenty bucks."

Creighton made a noncommittal noise. He had – and to all the others too, and each time with mumbled apologies that it wasn't more.

"You want to make it with me?"

Startled, Creighton looked at Blessed and saw that the color of his eyes was almost violet. It was, of course, precisely what he wanted. Night after night he had studied this Bellerophon straddling his motorized Pegasus – hair a tumble of basalt curls, face of Zeus, skin white – no riding in the burning wind for Covent Blessed. Did he ever ride, or merely sit? The body, inside the tight pants and immaculate T-shirt, was that of a late, slightly gynandromorphic Apollo – marble.

"Yes, I want to – very much." Creighton's heart gave great laboring thuds and his hand shook so that his cup rattled like an alarm bell in the saucer and the counter boy came like Lazarus with the coffee urn.

"OK, only I'm expensive."

"How expensive?" Creighton waved the counter boy away.

"If they're worth twenty . . ." Blessed rose, boots creaking. "I'm worth ten times that. Right?"

"Doubtless, but I haven't that kind of money." With a twinge of guilt – remembering this was his mother's life insurance he was squandering – but only a twinge, and only for a moment, he offered, "Say twice twenty?"

"Make it fifty and you're on," Blessed said.

"No, forty, but—" And here he made his mistake. "Again tomorrow, same price."

Blessed stood very still. "And the night after?"

"Yes, yes," blurted reckless Roy. "However many more nights you wish."

"Cash? You got it on you?"

Creighton smiled wryly. "Did you expect me to offer you my personal check? I have cash in my room."

Blessed turned toward the door. "Let's go . . ."

It was the corner of the dresser drawer that had cost him his right eye, the drawer he had opened to take from his hoard two twenty-dollar bills for Blessed, who sat in the dim red dark on the edge of the broken bed, tight Levis on again, thrusting his feet into his boots. Creighton had no time to shut the drawer. He was flung aside, flung hard against the bed's iron foot, and Blessed was clawing out the money, all that remained – what, 600, 700 dollars?

"No, now wait, be fair," Creighton cried, and stepped toward him.

It was then, with a grunt, that Blessed yanked the drawer free and swung it, slashing, into Creighton's face, the cheekbone crumpling, the eye springing from what remained – what, 600, 700 dollars?

"Professor?" Mary Lou Bendo came toward him now across the dark yard, a mousy girl of 15 with taffy-colored hair, the housekeeper's daughter. "There's a Dr Hubbard on the phone. Wants to talk to you. Brr!" She hugged her frail self. "Aren't you freezing out here?"

"No, the fire—" he began, then saw that the fire had died and that all around him was darkness. He shivered in his old cardigan, and followed the girl back toward the house, the kitchen window bright where Mrs Bendo washed the supper dishes.

"Hubbard here, Dr Creighton. Remember me? We met last spring at Dean Brubaker's, but I haven't seen you so far this term."

"I'm on a light schedule," Creighton said. "I haven't been well. But of course I remember you, Hubbard. How are you?" Receiver in hand, Creighton sat down at his desk in the book-lined study. The furnace had been cleaned during the summer. Its smell was metallic with this, its first use since. But he was grateful for the warmth, the lamplight, the fine old sameness of the place. All it lacked was his mother to look in now and then and enquire if there was anything he needed. He asked Hubbard, "How's that book of yours coming?"

"That's why I'm calling," Hubbard said. "I've finished the

chapter on the Northwest novelists and I'd like you to look it over. That's your corner of the country."

"I like to think so," Creighton smiled. "I'll be delighted. Why not bring it by right now? I'm free."

"Thanks. That's generous. I'll be right there."

Creighton remembered Hubbard as small, dark, vital, perhaps thirty-five. The man for whom he opened the door ten minutes later had changed. His boyish shock of black hair was streaked with gray. Was it pain or grief that dulled the dark eyes, once alive with laughter? Creighton remembered the compact muscularity of Hubbard's body in its thin white shirt when he'd removed his jacket in the heat of the afternoon at the Dean's garden party. The suit now hung on him loosely. He was thin. He'd had a fine, brown, gypsy color last spring. Now he was sallow. The hand that accepted the whiskey and soda Creighton served, trembled.

"I was sorry to hear about your . . . accident," Hubbard said.

Creighton sat down and smiled ruefully. "It's all over now, but I spent my summer in the hospital."

"Mugging, robbery, that sort of thing, was it?"

"The wicked city is no place for a provincial pedagogue." Creighton reached out for the manuscript that lay on Hubbard's knees. When the younger man handed it to him. Creighton was unable to resist a personal observation of his own.

"You don't look at all well, yourself."

"I've been working pretty hard," Hubbard said. "Book's damn near done."

"Don't let them pressure you too much on the publication thing," Creighton advised. "It's been attacked too often in the press lately. The accent will be on classroom performance in future, I expect."

Hubbard lit a cigarette. "It's my own pressure, not Bryant College." He suddenly looked straight at Creighton, and his voice was harsh. "It's been a rotten summer for me. Work was the only way I knew to shake what happened."

"It's a good way," Creighton with a wry smile glanced aside at the shelf of his own books, a dozen of them, that represented his own flight from disappointment and frustration. "What happened – or would you rather I didn't ask?"

"No, I wouldn't rather you didn't ask." Hubbard's wide mouth broke into a harsh grin that showed strong, straight teeth. "I'd rather you did, doctor. In fact . . ." He rose abruptly and picked up the sheaf of papers he'd brought. He held them by the corner and shook them. "I'll be honest with you. This thing was completed weeks ago. I didn't come to talk about it. I came because—" He broke off, sat down again, drank deeply from his glass. The look he gave Creighton was that of a begging dog.

Creighton was oddly moved and disturbed. He blinked in the lamplight. "Because?"

"No . . . the paper does need your reading," Hubbard said lamely. He tossed it onto the desk again. "That's . . . that's all. Don't pay too much attention to me. I'm upset, as I said. It's been a mean summer." He ground out his cigarette, tipped up the glass and drained it. Setting it down, he rose once more. "I'd better clear out and let you read."

"Let me understand," Creighton said. "You want someone to talk to. That's really why you came?"

"Yes . . . but I feel cheap. You see, I'd never have come, only today I ran into Apperson – you know, Germanic languages."

"Yes, I know Apperson." Creighton experienced an inward chill. Apperson had come to the hospital to visit him this summer, all the way to the city simply to gloat. A notorious homosexual, he had been in trouble with the college several times during his twenty-eight years on the faculty. His victims, students, a basketball coach, had been dismissed. Somehow he had survived, fat, disgusting, but always companioned. Creighton avoided him. But this summer he had come mincing, smirking, into that white hospital room, to sit beside Creighton's bed, ostensibly as comforter but really as tormentor, reconstructing with lip-licking avidity and astonishing accuracy the circumstances that had brought his ailing colleague to disaster. "Apperson has a very loose mouth."

"That's why I feel cheap," Hubbard said. "I agree with you – he's loathsome. but he told me—"

"I can imagine what he told you,' Creighton interrupted. "Did you believe him?"

"I . . ." Hubbard shifted uneasily. "Would it make sense if I said I . . . wanted to believe him?"'

"Why?" Creighton squinted baffled. "Why should you? And why should you then come here? No." He stiffened and his voice went cold. "I'm afraid I don't understand."

"Oh, Lord." Hubbard got up and picked up his manuscript from the desk. "I'm sorry. There's no excuse. Ah, the hell with it!" He turned away. But with his hand on the doorknob he swung back, agony in his eyes. "Look, please let me explain. It'll only take a few minute. I've got to. If I can't tell you, I'm washed up. You're my only hope. Melodrama, huh?" He tried for a smile and missed.

Creighton watched him, mystified. "If you want to tell me something, Hubbard, of course do so. I simply cannot understand what Apperson and his vile imaginings have to do—"

"Look, Dr Creighton – I'm gay." Hubbard came back to the desk and leaned over it. "Do you know what that expression means?"

Creighton stared into the tormented face, unable to trust himself to answer, shocked beyond measure, yet with a strange feeling of joy leaping in him. It made him laugh. Hubbard winced. "No, no – excuse me." Creighton reached out to him. "I'm laughing at myself, not you. Yes, yes, I know the meaning of the word gay. And now I see what you meant, why you're here. When Apperson told you about my misadventures in the city—"

"I jumped at the idea there was somebody at Bryant I could talk to," Hubbard finished. "Of course I knew Apperson's gossip couldn't be trusted. I came intending to feel you out on the subject somehow. Instead I got clumsy and wrecked everything. I'm sorry . . ."

"No." Creighton stood. "There's nothing to be sorry for. While Apperson's tale is fictional in its particulars, it has its element of truth. He's perceptive."

Hubbard sighed relief. "That's what made me believe him to the extent I did. He knew about me. First day I walked on campus. He knew, and he knew I knew he knew. He's uncanny."

"Yes," Creighton smiled. "I'm afraid the fact of your very pretty wife easily deceived me." He saw pain flicker in Hubbard's eyes again, and picked up the empty glass from the desk corner. "Sit down," he nodded. "I'll just fix us another drink and we can talk."

2

Frank Hubbard told his story.

At the Wisconsin college where he taught before transferring to Bryant, he had met an exceptional student named David Warsaw. The boy was intent upon writing, absorbed and talented. With surprising suddenness one evening he had turned to Frank Hubbard for love, physical love. It was to Hubbard a fulfillment beyond his powers to have imagined. He was married, but the marriage was conventional and the girl herself extremely so. A nice girl, happy with him. But David Warsaw was like some other kind of being. Special. Set apart. And he and Frank Hubbard were very happy.

"Then this chance came, right after my doctorate – my book. David would have transferred too, wanted to. But there was this chance for him to work with two important poets there this summer. He'd been talking of nothing else. I made him stay . . . You should see him. No beauty. Wait."

Hubbard dug into his wallet, took out a dog-eared photograph, and flipped it across the desk to Creighton. It pictured a tall, gangly lad standing to his ankles in snow, hands thrust into the pockets of a mackinaw. He was squinting against the white daylight, but even in the small photograph Creighton saw, or thought he saw, extraordinary sensitivity in the boy's face. He gently handed back the snapshot. "I see . . . And?"

"Like a colt, highstrung, all taut wires, all nerves." Hubbard bent his head and busied his hands pushing the picture back into the wallet. His voice was muffled. "This summer all the wires broke." He looked up, eyes swimming in tears. "They were very thin wires, and when the slightest thing . . . the slightest wind passed, they hummed. You had to be gentle with him. Very gentle." Hubbard rose quickly and stepped into the shadows, stood staring at the nearly invisible backs of books along the shelves. "I don't know what somebody said or did . . . or maybe he read a great stupidity in a newspaper . . . or maybe he saw some great horror (God knows the world is full of them) . . . I don't know what happened. But all the wires broke."

"He's . . . in an institution?" Creighton asked softly.

"Raving," Hubbard said. "Completely gone. Utterly disoriented – that's the word, isn't it? Disoriented. Out of it, as the kids say."

"There are remarkable new drugs."

Hubbard grimaced, dropping again into the leather armchair. "There are, but the doctors aren't hopeful." He felt for another cigarette, then pulled the pack from his shirt pocket and crumpled it. Empty.

"Do they really understand enough about these things to write the boy off?" Creighton opened a desk drawer and found a dusty package of cigarettes. "They've been here a while," he apologized, "but perhaps the cellophane has kept them fresh. They haven't been opened."

"Thanks," Hubbard said. "No, maybe they don't. But it's too remarkable a brain to cut into or shock. His people won't allow it. So the best prognosis they'll offer is that little by little his lucid periods may lengthen. Maybe. After a while." He tore off the celophane, opened the package top, talking. "It hit me hard. Twenty-sixth of July. A bright Monday, 8.30 in the morning. His mother wrote. Good woman. It hit me too hard to hide it. Betty wanted to know what was wrong. Hell, when the man you're married to sits down and cries, you want to know. And I told her. I had to tell somebody."

"And . . . that was that?"

"She left. Went back to Wisconsin." He lit a cigarette. "Divorce is under way. I keep getting papers from lawyers."

"I'm sorry," Creighton said.

"So," Hubbard smiled warmly, "it was a lousy summer."

"It was, indeed," Roy Creighton said. "But, perhaps, now, the worst of it is over."

"Yes, you lost your mother in June, and then there was this other thing."

"Mother had been failing. It wasn't a shock. As to 'this other thing,' I had an artfully rebuilt right cheekbone and an artfully matched glass eye. My ribs once more work as required. But I brought it all on myself out of sheer folly, I alone am responsible."

"How responsible is anybody when, as the storybooks say, flesh calls to flesh?"

"You don't blame yourself for this boy's condition?"

"Not in *my* lucid periods," Hubbard said grimly. "But things get to you at night, alone, in the dark."

"I know," Roy Creighton said.

Virgil Apperson, balancing his weight like a hippo on a tightwire, crossed the faculty dining room. With hands jeweled as a late Roman emperor's, he set down his tray of luncheon, drew out a chair, and seated himself opposite Roy Creighton. Creighton cursed inwardly. He ought to have gone home for lunch but, mentally involved with a student's question after his morning lecture on poetic method, he had forgotten that Frank Hubbard had gone up to the city to see his lawyer today.

"You're all alone," Apperson smirked. Like a priest performing a rite, he lifted one dish after another from his tray and arranged them in an occult pattern on the table before him. "That's seldom the case these days."

"I guess it is," Creighton said.

"You and young Hubbard seem to have struck up quite a friendship."

Creighton took a mouthful of food and grunted.

Apperson studied him ironically, a dainty wedge of chicken croquette balanced on his fork. "Hubbard must have a gift. You've always been a solitary, *n'est-ce pas?*" He popped the bite into his rosebud mouth. "Certainly you and I have never been able to get close – for all we have in common."

"Hubbard's writing a book on the decline of regionalism in the American novel," Creighton said stiffly. "I've done some work on the Northwest men, H. L. Davis, Ernest Haycox. Hubbard asked for my help."

"All work," Apperson twinkled, fat face rosy, "and no play?" His eyebrows made the query arch. "It seems to me I saw you together last Saturday evening at the Budapest Quartette recital, didn't I? And Evalina Finch tells me you were at the opening of the new exhibit at the municipal art gallery in the city the weekend before – together. I know you two never miss a football game."

"I'm sure *you* don't," Creighton said caustically. Apperson's young man this year was the Bryant team's left tackle, a gigantic, square, blond youth named Halverson. "How did Halverson like the Budapest?"

"He finds Beethoven conducive to sleep," Apperson sighed. "Mercifully, he doesn't snore." Apperson blinked his eyes rapidly. "Does Hubbard snore?"

"Tell me . . ." Creighton glanced around the big, drab dining room. "I see a lot of vacant tables. Wouldn't one of those have suited you as well as mine?"

Apperson's rosiness faded. "Well," he said, "really! Your air of moral superiority would be laughable if it weren't so rude. What right do you suppose you have to sneer at me? After what you did this summer? You'd better come off it. We're not as unlike as you think. If I were you, I'd cherish the friendship of a man in my profession, on my own campus, who shared my predilection, who understood." Then the anger subsided, replaced by taunting wit again. "Besides, I was Dan Cupid for you and Hubbard – somewhat oversized for Cupid, but none the less, my arrow went straight. *Nicht Wahr?*"

"I apologize," Creighton said softly, hopelessly.

"I'm florid," Apperson admitted, actually reaching out and squeezing Creighton's hand – who looked around, the blood rushing to his face, afraid somebody might be watching: no one was. "I'm florid, but I do have a good heart."

Creighton made an effort to smile. "Sorry," he said. He nodded at his plate. "I'm afraid I've finished. Some work to do in the library. Will you excuse me?"

Apperson made a move. "Of course. Who am I to keep you sitting idle?"

Crossing the campus in the dismal rain, Creighton's mouth twitched. *Does Hubbard snore?* Apperson's impudence rankled, but not so deeply as his own unspoken answer: *I don't know.* Apperson was mistaken – he and Roy Creighton were very different. Apperson was not afraid. The campus, the whole academic works, the world of books and critics too, knew he was homosexual. And he didn't care – or made a good show of not caring. But Roy Creighton cared. Apperson was happy, or at least fulfilled. How, with that gross, quivering body of his, he managed to lure into his bed the strong and stupid youths he favored, Creighton couldn't imagine – nor what they did once there. His own body was spare, largely unchanged from his teen years. Naked he wouldn't strike the absurd figure that Apperson would, or most men crowding fifty. Yet he was afraid.

He came under the shelter of the library portico. The drizzle was a cold one, and he shivered in his mackintosh, but he had no wish to go inside. He stood watching the slow drip from the blackened tree branches onto the brown, soggy lawns and leaf-clotted paths. Small birds, unseen, rustled in the dry shrubs at his feet, sheltering. Friday afternoon. The campus was nearly empty, students almost all on their way to Pierce College in the next state, for tomorrow's football game. Only an occasional gray figure moved along the paths, shoulders hunched, mournful.

But his fear was a habit, thirty years ingrained. There had been excuses for it, justifications – one justification paramount: he had not wanted to hurt his mother. Mother. With what sharpness, suspiciousness, she had questioned his occasional very tentative associations with certain students in whose faces, voices, manner he read unmistakably a likeness to himself at their age, a likeness of emotional need. With these he had reasoned there could be no force to the scruple about "corrupting youth."

Yet in the end he had lacked the courage to make sexual overtures. Why? Complications. Endless. Where, for example, could such episodes take place, where that would be safe? He grimaced at himself now, gazing sightless across the campus veiled in gray rain. Even if the way had been smooth and simple, he wouldn't have dared. Too much at stake. Young people were unstable. A careless word to the wrong auditor and Roy Creighton's world would have crumbled around him in ruin and disgrace.

But Mother was gone now. He had tenure plus a reputation

in the wider world that made his presence an asset to Bryant they would not relinquish if there were any way around it. And Frank Hubbard was no nervous child. And . . . he loved Frank Hubbard. The word came reluctantly to his mind and made him shift his feet uncomfortably, shrug, become aware again of the cold, and shiver. He found it romantic and absurd, that word. He a man of 47, Frank a man of 35 – two grown men. Neither young, neither in any way beautiful – ah, except that Frank was beautiful, wasn't he? His glowing eyes, his dark skin, his taut, small compact body, his quickness, keenness, laughter . . . Whatever anyone else might think, to Roy Creighton he was beautiful. Chemistry. Somehow – and he had bleakly feared himself no longer capable of such an emotion – somehow, he was in love with Frank Hubbard. And how did Frank feel?

Well, Frank had sought him out in the first place. And the fact was that Frank had arranged all their subsequent meetings and excursions. There was every reason to take courage from this. Yet could he find it? Wasn't his cowardice a habit too entrenched to overcome? No. He must try. Being with Frank – oh, for example, in the warm car with the music on the radio, driving to the art exhibit, and in that pleasantly paneled restaurant by, of all romantic things, candlelight, he sometimes wanted so desperately, it brought tears to his eyes, to reach out, to touch the younger man, to kiss his mouth. . . .

Roy Creighton's face burned in self-derision. But that was wrong. This was an honest emotion, a fine thing. he must not smother it with sophistication, must not, as the young people said, play it cool. This might be the last possibility for happiness his life would offer.

He would never forgive himself if he did not try. There was the risk of being turned away: it had been, after all, a boy Frank had lately loved, no gray-haired man. Yet he must try. He would try. Tonight.

Mrs Bendo, square and ruddy, hair dyed flaming in vain mockery of its vanished girlhood glow, opened her honest blue eyes at him. "Why, Professor, what's wrong? You've hardly eaten a bite. Mary Lou? Anything wrong with the fritters?"

Roy Creighton laughed apologetically. "They're wonderful.

I'm sorry to be dilatory." He forced himself to act hungry. He was not. He was absurdly nervous. His stomach was full of butterflies. He could think only of Frank Hubbard and how he must, tonight, tonight, speak to him, make his bid. Under Mrs Bendo's doubting stare, he repeated, "They're delicious," and crammed his mouth.

"You act like you're having trouble swallowing. Face painful again? You should have given yourself time for another highball before dinner."

"My face is fine," he said.

"Well, I know the rain'll play hob with an old wound. Mr Bendo's bad knee always—"

"Oh, Mother," Mary Lou said, "the Professor doesn't want to hear about Daddy's knee again." Then she turned her head. "What in the world is that?"

Thunder, Roy Creighton thought. But no. Rain – a sudden downpour? Not that, either. This mutter was mechanical, a low, steady, deep-throated thrum. Engines. Aircraft? Mary Lou pushed back her chair from the table and went to the dining room window, pushed aside the curtains, cupped her hands around her face against the glass. The noise grew, beating the hushed evening air in pulses like a great, angry heart.

The girl said, "I can't see . . . Oh, look!"

Roy Creighton rose to stand beside her. He saw nothing but his own reflection and Mary Lou's in the dark glass. he went to the light switch on the wall beside the kitchen door and pushed it, darkening the room. Mrs Bendo made a sound and stood up too and joined them. Outside night had not quite closed in. It was still possible to see darkly what passed along the street with its ominous rumble. Motorcycles. Heavy, brutish, a crawling double file. How many? Ten? Twenty? No headlights. Only the great throbbing sound.

Roy Creighton felt as if something had struck him a terrible blow in the chest. Dimly he was conscious of Mrs Bendo's voice:

"What are they – policemen?"

And Mary Lou's: "No, it's one of those awful clubs."

"You mean like they wrote up in the paper? Them that wrecked that little town up in Connecticut or wherever it was?

Why, Professor, what's wrong? You *are* sick." Her strong hand gripped his arm as he started to sway. "Here, Mary Lou, take hold!"

But he caught and steadied himself, though his voice wobbled. "I'm all right. Thank you. Just giddy for a moment, there." They were going away – on up the block, on through the campus, following the curving drive, on out through the sparsely settled town fringes with their chicken farms and dairies, on across the red steel bridge spanning the river, on to some other place. They were going away. He gave a laugh and stepped again to the light switch.

But they came back.

It was nearing eight. Frank Hubbard should arrive shortly. He bent to the cabinet where he kept the whiskey, opened the door, lifted out the bottle. Nearly empty. He peered at the seltzer siphon. Adequate. Straightening, he started for the door to the hall to summon Mary Lou – and he heard the rumble again. Ah, but they'd simply be going past once more. Wouldn't they?

"Mary Lou? Another bottle of White Horse, please?"

Her voice from the back of the house. "Coming."

They would go past. Surely he was mistaken. He was indulging fantasies. His experience had made him too associatively vulnerable. Motorcycles. Why, there were hundreds of thousands of motorcycles in this country. Mary Lou came running lightly, smiling, with the bottle. He took it with thanks and turned back into the study, aware of Mary Lou going on along the hall to the oval of glass in the front door, and peering out.

"Why, professor," her voice came, muffled, "they've stopped, some of them. And the rest are going around and around in the middle of the street."

He stood arrested in the act of setting the bottle down on the desk. Cold sweat trickled down his ribs. Like a panicked child, his mind shrieked, *No! No no, no no!* But there came the clump of boots on the porch. There was the doorbell.

"No!" he heard himself shout aloud.

But the door was already open.

Doomed, he walked into the hall.

Covent Blessed stood there, grinning.

3

"Hello, Dr Creighton," Blessed said. He turned and shouted out into the dark, "Yeah, this is the place. Come on in." Others, dressed like him, peaked caps, black leather jackets glittering with zippered intricacies, steel-buckled boots, began to file into the hall. Mary Lou stared at them, wide-eyed. At the other end of the hall and the kitchen door twanged and Mrs Bendo appeared, dishtowel in hand. Her mouth dropped open. Outside on the porch someone echoed Blessed's words: "This is the place. Come on in." The house was surrounded by the thunder of engines, roaring up, then spluttering into silence.

Creighton said, "Now, just one moment. What's the meaning of this? If you suppose that I'm going to permit—"

"Permit?" Blessed, still grinning, came toward him and Creighton had to brace himself, clutch the doorframe at his back, to keep from – what? – running, falling? "Why, hell, doctor, you invited me, man. How could you forget? Make yourselves at home, friends." He jerked his thumb toward the dark living room. They shuffled in, turned on lights, gaping, grunting. One of them held a case of beer. He carried it past Blessed and Creighton and confronted Mrs Bendo.

"Where's the cold box, lady?"

"Professor?" she said.

Creighton turned decisively toward the study. "I'm calling the sheriff."

Blessed gripped his arm. "You have to be kidding. Have you forgotten what I can tell the sheriff of this town about your summer, doctor?"

"You can't – t-tell him . . ." Creighton's teeth chattered. He clenched his jaws. Even then his voice shook. "You can't tell him your part in it. Assault with intent to kill is a crime punishable by long imprisonment." Blessed moved past him into the study. "What are you doing?"

Blessed yanked the telephone wire from the wall. "You're

not talking to anybody you wouldn't, because you don't want to lose your job, wreck your reputation. That's why you never spilled your guts after what happened. But, just in case you get any silly ideas –'' He dropped the phone into the waste basket. "Sit down." He jerked his head at the desk chair. "What's this?" He picked up the Scotch bottle. "White Horse, huh? Unopened too. They don't let 'em get this dusty in the store. You must keep a case around, huh?"

Roy Creighton said, "It's too good for you."

Blessed eyed him up and down. Then, without warning, his hand shot out and lashed across Creighton's face. His voice was softly reproachful. "There was a time this summer, doctor, when you didn't think anything was too good for me."

It was true. In that cheap hotel room, lighted by the soiled scarlet pulse of the neon across the street, he had worshipped the naked body of this scum. Bleakly now he wished that had been the full extent of his folly. To talk there, lying naked in the darkness, talk and talk and talk – of this place, oh, down to the veriest particular – that had been insane, truly insane.

Two more cyclists clumped down the hall bearing cartons of canned beer. Blessed walked to the door. "Get the old bitch to put some chow on," he told them.

"And look around for booze. Like this." He held up the bottle. One of them whistled, the other chuckled. Red hair. A smear of black grease across a forehead. In the living room somebody howled laughter. The television set blared. Boots thundered on the stairs.

"Lady, we're hungry. We been ridin' all day. Start cookin', lady."

"You know," Roy Creighton said as Blessed turned back into the study, "I really don't have to call for help. You've surely attracted notice. Next door is a fraternity house. There's another across the street. Several. Don't you suppose those boys will be coming over to see what's going on?"

"Not many," Blessed said. "Bryant's playing football tomorrow with Pierce. Your little boy friends are all on their way up there. What's left can come look if they want to." From his pocket he drew a knife. His thumb pressed a button. The blade sprang out, glittering. "They want a fight, we'll fight."

Creighton shut his eyes an instant and hoped the boys were all gone. All.

Blessed pushed the bottle toward him. "Open it. Let's have a drink. To old times." He glanced around the book-lined room. "Yeah, this is cool. Boss. Like a movie set. You read all these books?"

Really not knowing what else to do, Roy Creighton numbly opened the bottle, poured whisky into glasses, splashed in soda. He handed one to Blessed, who dropped into the chair where, these last weeks, Frank Hubbard had so often, and so warmly welcome, sat. Frank. Lord, what would he think, walking into this? The true sordidness of Creighton's summer "accident", its lack of a single mitigating quality, would be apparent to him at once. Roy hadn't told him.

"Yes," Creighton sighed. "I've read them all. But they haven't made me wise."

Blessed laughed, swallowed some of his drink, asked, "Where do you think you're going?"

"I'd better reassure Mrs Bendo. She—"

"My boys'll manage her," Blessed said. "Sit down." He lay back in the chair, stretched out his legs and gave a smug grin. "Yeah, when you told me about this place, I figured it sounded about right for us. You don't want too big a town, too many fat-bellied constables. Nice, quiet little place. And, with the college kids, maybe a little action. And when you said you got a big house, you wasn't putting me on. We can fit in here fine. Great weekend." He jumped to his feet, went to the door again, yelled down the hall, "Hey, Krebs, she cooking or what? Christ, I'm starving man?"

"She's cooking. We found the Scotch. Six bottles."

The knife lay on the desk forgotten. The initials C. B. were burned into the bone handle. With sweaty fingers Roy Creighton picked it up. He knew he lacked the courage to use it. Yet he got up from his chair and rounded the desk. His knees were wobbly. His heart gave great laboring thuds in his chest. He clutched the knife at waist level, the evil blade pointed at the center of Blessed's back. He moved like a sleepwalker.

Down the hall came a querulous female voice: "Professor Creighton? What's going on here?"

Blessed turned, saw the knife and with a sharp, chopping
motion struck Creighton's wrist before the older man could
make a move. The knife fell with a clatter. Twisting the same
wrist, he brought Creighton's arm up painfully behind his back
and pivoted him into the doorway. "Tell her it's OK," he
growled. "Get rid of her."

"It won't seem natural if I don't go to the door."

"All right, we'll both go to the door."

The woman was Angela White, house mother for the Pi
Rho boys next door, a sharp-faced woman, but not clever.
Why couldn't it have been Mrs Hobbs from Theta across
the street? She wouldn't have been easy to fool.

"What's going on here, Dr C.? Are you all right?"

Dared he blurt: *Call the sheriff?* No. That would only endanger
her along with him and Mrs Bendo and Mary Lou. Dear God,
in the midst of all this, where was that child? He forced
a smile.

"This is my nephew, Covent Blessed, Mrs White. Some
time ago I told my sister that if ever Covent rode up this way,
he must consider my big, empty place his home. Perhaps he's
rather overdone the guest list this time."

"Well, Harry and I are on our way to Pierce. Wouldn't want
to have to try to sleep through this racket."

"Have a nice trip, ma'am," Blessed said.

Mrs White regarded him skeptically, and looked again at
Roy Creighton. She started to ask a question, then decided
against it, and turned away. As she went down the porch steps
into the darkness, he heard her say, "It's OK, I guess, Harry.
Professor Creighton says it's his nephew."

Blessed shut the door and turned hard eyes on Creighton.
"OK," he said, "back to the study. I came up here to relax.
I can't enjoy myself if my lousy host keeps coming up behind
me trying to run my own shiv in my back." He jerked his head.
"Move, professor." At the study door he shouted down the hall
again. "Krebs!"

"Yeah?" The redhead appeared in the kitchen door, pushing
food into his mouth.

"Get some clothesline from the old dame. On the double."

"What the hell for? You gonna wash something?"

"I said, 'on the double', Krebs!"

"Yeah." He turned back into the kitchen. "Hey, lady . . ."

The house roared with sound. Creighton made out the persistent television underlying the shouts, the laughter, the curses. Someone had a guitar. Songs were bellowed and bawled. Later the tiny speaker of a portable radio strained is throat with the snarl and shriek of electric guitars. Feet stamped. Dancing? There was the race of heavy boots along the hall past the shut door of the study where he sat lashed to his own chair behind his desk. Panting. Some kind of struggle. Low laugher. Someone's weight falling against the wall. Half giggle, half whine: *Naw, lay off, you son of a bitch*. A sudden deafening clatter – the crash of empty tin cans. Beer cans. Had they dumped them down the stairs?

He fought with his bonds. The triple length of clothesline that bound him across the chest – that was the loosest, mercifully. For if he could squirm so that it gradually slipped down to his waist, then he could bend forward and work with his teeth on the ropes binding his wrists to the chair arms, the hands after an hour of cut-off circulation swollen, purple, nerveless. He expanded his chest and wriggled his shoulders against the ropes . . .

9.30. It was hopeless. The rope at his wrists was new and tied too tightly. He had only succeeded in making his mouth bleed. He sat back, panting, great pain in his back from the twisted position that chewing the ropes had demanded. His face streamed with sweat. Tears of frustration and chagrin blinded him.

But did not deafen him. What was that? Outside, coming down the hall, a struggle of kicking feet and – his heart contracted – a girl's voice. "No, let me alone, let me alone! Mother! Professor!" Mary Lou. In a fury of despair, he shouted out:

"Leave that girl alone! Do you hear me?"

The door burst open. Covent, with Krebs and the hulking boy with grease smeared across his forehead, stood there with the struggling, weeping girl between them.

"Professor, help!"

"Shut up!" Covent slapped her. He was very drunk. They were all drunk. Great waves of beer stench blew into the room

"If you do this thing—" Roy Creighton shouted.

"If? What can you do about it?" Blessed sneered. He swung away, jerking the girl after him. "Come on, baby, upstairs. What we want is a big, fat bed."

The door slammed.

Roy Creighton gave a furious heave to his body and, chair on his back, lurched to his feet. They too were bound so tightly at the ankles that they lacked any feeling now. It was an absurd thing to try. He could go nowhere, couldn't even really stand. The great weight of the chair – oak, padded leather – dragged at him, he tottered, helpless to reach out, then fell with a crash to his side on the floor. He heard Covent's boots, the boots of his friends, the ineffectually kicking feet of Mary Lou, pass up the staircase.

No, this must not happen, his mind cried. *It's all my doing, my responsibility. And it must not be allowed to happen. Oh, God, somebody help me! Mother . . .*

"Roy! Where are you?"

His heart leaped. That was Frank Hubbard's voice.

"In the study!" he shouted. "Hurry, Frank." And when the younger man was bending over him: "Thank God you got here at last. Cut me loose. Scissors in the desk drawer. Hurry. They've taken the little girl upstairs – Mary Lou. They're drunk. If they're not stopped—"

Hubbard said, "Better do that first," dropped the scissors on the desk top, ran for the hall.

"Not alone!" Roy Creighton cried. "They'll kill you."

But he was gone

Virgil Apperson, in a vast tweed overcoat, hat, gloves, galoshes, came toiling through the snow that lay new and white – the first snow of the winter – across the cemetery. Roy Creighton watched him come without resentment. He was drained, it seemed, forever now, of the capacity to feel any emotion.

Frank Hubbard was dead. He had clung to life for ten days in Bryant infirmary without regaining consciousness. Covent

Blessed, Krebs, or the big, grease-stained boy, or perhaps all three, had stabbed him brutally, a dozen times. They were in custody. Covent had told every detail again and again. The papers had printed every detail.

Now Roy Creighton stood beside the ugly, raw mound of winter earth that was Frank Hubbard's grave. At his feet were two suitcases. In fifteen minutes he would be catching a train out of Bryant, never to return. None of it would be hard to leave except this grave.

Apperson stopped beside him, his breath frosty. "You must reconsider," he said. "It will all be forgotten soon. Anyway, you're mistaken to think anyone blames you. What could you have done? You were helpless. The girl testified that. What could you have done?"

"I could never have met Covent Blessed," Creighton said. "Or, at least, I could have avoided telling him who I was and where to find me."

"Ah, you're too harsh with yourself. Who hasn't been a fool now and then? Which of us? The dean doesn't—"

"I know. The dean wants me to stay. Did he send you?"

"I came because I'm your friend and I understand," Virgil Apperson said, "whether you think so or not. You're upset and depressed now. That's to be expected. But why not wait? In time – it will be forgotten."

"By whom?"

"By everyone."

"Everyone but me," Creighton said. "Every place I turn – in my house, on the campus – will remind me forever. No, I've got to clear out."

Apperson studied him a moment, then turned to stare mournfully at the grave. He sighed and his voice was a breathy wheeze. "I see. I see . . . Ah, it *is* sad. And who can understand it? Certainly not I. So unjust. Those animals . . ." He looked earnestly into Creighton's face, doing his clumsy best. "But you did have him for a time. I expect he was – I'm sorry to be impertinent, but I've some experience in these matters, some intuition – your first lover. Am I correct?"

"Forty-seven," Roy Creighton said, "is too late for a first anything, Virgil."

Apperson looked upward. "Snow again?" He held out his gloved hand. One by one, fat flakes settled upon it. He lowered the hand and turned again to Creighton. "How gently it covers everything. How beautiful it makes all that it touches, even the ugliest things."

Grimly, Roy Creighton wished that it did.

"I mustn't miss my train." He shook Apperson's hand, picked up the suitcase, and walked down the hill toward the station, through the falling snow.

CHINESE CAMP AND REBUFFS AT THE D'JOCKEY PUB, PENANG

John Haylock

PRETTY, SLIGHT-LIMBED Roger, who is Chinese, has been smiling and flicking his dark eyes at me while leaning against the wall, smiling, glancing, and at the same time chatting to his friends, all Chinese, habitués of the place, who are sitting at the bar. I know his name is Roger as soon after I had gained a bar stool he came over to check me out. He is wearing tight white pants that end just below the knee and a dark-blue silk blouse open in front; a coral necklace adorns his slim neck and round his head is a red bandeau, one end of which dangles over an ear. The bar snakes across the room, and at the far end of a curl sits, among others, mostly Chinese, a Tamil, who stares.

Suddenly, Roger skips over to the Tamil, exchanges a few nods and then comes up to me and whispers, "You like him? He like you."

"The Indian?"

"Yes."

"I prefer you."

Roger goes back to smiling, leaning against the wall, and

chatting to his friends. One of these is matronly. "She" is heavily farded, has an Eton crop, gold earrings, a white blouse, red trousers, wrists loaded with bangles and the look of a youngish mother amused by her outrageous son to whom she is anxious not to appear her age. "She" sports a long cigarette holder in one hand and a crème de menthe in the other. Roger and his companions are drinking beer. I go on looking at Roger.

He skips across the room again, talks to the Indian, who rises and approaches. He is very dark and has fine delicate features; his hair recedes a bit and I notice when he occupies the empty bar-stool on my left that he has a slight paunch, but it is slighter than mine. I guess he is about thirty-five.

"Do you like me?" he asks.

"Well, er . . ."

"You don't like Indians?"

I hesitate. His English accent is almost perfect. If it weren't for his face I might be talking to a compatriot. "You're wrong," I say. "I think Indians are often attractive."

"You like me then?"

"Yes, but not tonight."

" 'Not tonight' means you don't like me."

Trying hard not to offend, I say, "No, it doesn't. I'm tired."

" 'Tired' means you don't like me."

"Perhaps tomorrow."

" 'Perhaps tomorrow' means no."

"Oh dear!" I exclaim more or less to myself.

"I understand."

I sigh and after a silence he says looking at Roger, who now and then sneaks a regard at us, "You like the Chinese?"

"Yes."

"His name is Roger Foo. He works in a tailor's shop."

"He told me he was Roger but he didn't mention the Foo." I gave a feeble laugh.

"You don't like Indians," the Tamil repeats accusingly.

"Oh yes, I do. I told you I often found them attractive."

" 'Often' means never."

"Oh dear!" I exclaim again.

"I understand," he says, glowering. He returns to his place

on the other side of the room, but he continues to stare at me. I look at Roger, who is still leaning against the wall, smiling and listening to his friends, but no longer do his darting eyes take me in. "What did you say to the Indian?" I ask him.

"I say noth-*ing*," Roger replies. "He say he like you."

"I'm afraid I made him angry."

"Never mind. Who care?"

All at once Roger begins to do a *pas seul* to a spirited American pop number the blind guitarist is loudly singing. On my way back from the lavatory into which I was not followed either by Roger or the Indian, I bump into Roger in the middle of a pirouette. "Sorry," I say.

Eyes open as wide as possible, he throws back, "I am Alice in Wonderland."

"I'm the looking-glass. Come through!"

"Tonight is tomorrow," he says and dances away.

An oblique refusal?

When I rejoin my bar-stool I notice that the Indian has gone. I am sorry he has. One likes to be admired. I rise to go. I want to ask Roger if he'd like a lift into Georgetown. My hired car is parked up the lane just past the garden of this converted suburban villa. But annoyingly, he is away through his looking-glass of dance and incommunicado. *En route* to the door I pass a witch-like "dame" in black tights, black blouse and a black wig. "She" is perched on a stool and casts disdainful glances at the general scene. Roger has told me that "she" is a Filipino, runs a flower shop and is very rich. I wonder whether if I lift the wig a bald head would be revealed. I do not, of course, but I enquire, "Are you in mourning?"

Indignant, "she" straightens "her" back, pushes "her" chin in the air and replies with hauteur as if addressing an ignoramus, "*This* is late church bazaar."

I leave, hoping to find the Tamil in the garden waiting for me. How vain one is! I drive back to the E and O Hotel on the outskirts of Georgetown alone.

DIRTY STORIES

Tim Herbert

Surf side sex

HARTLEY WAS COMING down. At level 24, in came the man in the black tuxedo, catching the mirror reflection of Hartley before turning his eyes to the front panel. Both men were heading for street level.

There wasn't much time to get an overview. Comparisons in a lift are always subject to the fleeting glance, but a man in a black tuxedo invited longer stares, or so Hartley figured. It was just after midday and a Sunday too. Hartley was dressed in beach gear with Greek sandals and a leather knapsack. Not quite right for September in Sydney, and it had the other man thinking, forgetting how the rain had eased out overnight and the forecast of a balmy spring. Hartley knew the days of lust were coming.

It was one minute past when the lights went out. A hard jolt into silence, and without a rasp or buckling of steel, Hartley was surprised. Not like the days on the wheat farm when the grain elevator went bung. City life was always unpredictable.

Hanging out somewhere between levels four and five with a stranger in the black.

"Oh no," whispered the man, with a tone of displeasure. Hartley picked it up and the fact that the fellow was a claustrophobe – or maybe something worse. He had better salve him over. Mention the woman who fell through the Empire State in the Thirties. All floors to the buffer zone and not a scratch. But instead he reached for the red button, now a dusty grey and with the words 'Emergency Stop' just visible in silhouette.

"What are you doing?"

Hartley had brushed the man's trousers as he reached across for the button.

"If you're stuck this can often get things going again." Hartley was glad that his big grin was shadowed. Innuendo matched the smug swelling around his crotch.

"First comes the alarm," said the other man, who then complained about the lack of an intercom and that he'd be late for his sister's wedding.

Hartley mentioned the two-metre swell at Curl Curl, which had the man in the black tuxedo opening up a little, telling Hartley that his name was Michael and that he swam laps on summer mornings at Boy Charlton.

"Surfing strengthens your gluteus maximus," insisted Hartley.

Michael shrugged and Hartley sensed his response.

"Your muscles in your butt," he explained.

The silence was becoming an obstacle. Keeping them isolated in a kind of antiseptic void. For Hartley, passion was brimming like a backroom encounter, but he needed the carnal moans and weavings of other men, or even just the bubbling of a cistern in some goluptious beat.

He wondered about the other man's fantasies and whether it was a wise move to advertise. Expressing the surfie mode, Hartley could show off his glorious calves, or at least talk about mastering that tricky goofy-foot technique. But Michael might just cast it off. Too much craft spoils the appetite when the issue was something as simple as sand or a speedo tan, with a dab of fluoro zinc for living colour. Hartley refused to be disappointed and thought once again about the Boy Charlton reference. Yes, there was no doubt. That was a solid kind of come-on.

His fingers toyed inside his board shorts, while Michael pressed the alarm another time.

"Getting stuffy ain't it," said Hartley, and Michael sighed, unfastened his bow tie and took in some deeper breaths.

"This is Security. We've got the message. Don't keep pressing the button please."

The voice was middle-aged, semi-boozed and angry, Hartley decided.

"How long is this going to take?" Michael's voice sounded less agitated now.

"Forty minutes. The technician's gotta come from Alexandria."

The security guard had shone a torch across the split between the lift doors and a transitory beam of light drew out the bulge in Michael's trousers.

"How many are you?"

"Just the two of us," replied Hartley.

"Keep cosy then. Won't be long boys."

The words became a spur for Michael and Hartley was astounded. At the same time he was annoyed that Michael needed approval from outside, as if some prison warden had cocooned them in with lights out for the night. Time now defined the limits on what might have been a pure and spontaneous display. No, buck up and get on with it, he said to himself. This was still a radical act.

Michael's penis was small and uncut, with his pouch shaved smooth and heavy. Hartley felt the taut folds of his stomach leading up to a smattering of chest hair. The waft of "Fahrenheit" cologne reminded Hartley of insect spray, though it fitted in well when sand-fly bites from sex at Wanda had become a regular thing.

Michael was a merchant banker, or a broker. The dealer's fingers were unmistakable. But no questions were posed. Tongues were preoccupied in flecking the crude sweat from each other's unladen bodies.

A prod in the cranny and Michael rubbed up the surfer's torso. He couldn't recall if Hartley was blond or dark, as their tongues grappled before the silent mirrors.

Hartley had a few salty dog stories to relay and then thought about moving doggy style on the acrylic mat floor. He almost wished that Michael had kept his tuxedo on and that there had been another speck of light to catch the image of a ribald out-of-work surfer fucking a stockbroking wedding-guest trapped in the folds of his glossy tuxedo. Subversion. Power re-encoded in a truly dramatic setting. But thinking this way had him losing his erection. Intellection throws a spanner in the sex.

"So what's your fantasy, Michael?"

The question stopped him. His lips running around words instead of Hartley's shaft at half mast.

"Why this comes pretty close."

"Being stuck in a lift without any light," and Hartley laughed, "you always do it in the dark and lock the door right?"

Michael bellowed and gathered the other man's swelled nipples with two sets of fingers. The pinch was a little vicious and when he moved his thumb behind and jammed it hard up Hartley's arse, Hartley broke back and left the elevator swinging.

"Take it easy will you."

That was Michael's voice, though Hartley could have followed up with the same, as Michael retreated to the opposite wall.

"Best sex for me was the orgy room, the one at 'The Steam Palace'. Mirrors everywhere and we forced the door so hard, we locked ourselves in."

Michael's voice carried a nervous slant once again: "It was great for two hours, but we had to call for help."

"Sounds embarrassing," said Hartley.

"Especially for this conductor from Paris with a concert on that evening. A whopping great dick like a loaf of French bread and we really got carried away. Ended up keeping his orchestra waiting too, and they mentioned it in *The Age*."

"And it might happen to you too eh?" said Hartley.

"The wedding you mean? No, I gave myself plenty of time. There's always diversions in this town you know."

"Gotta be prepared," said Hartley. Very matter of fact.

"You bet. I've got condoms and lube up my inner sleeve."

"Hey presto, let's do it."

Hartley took the signal with a hoarse grunt and then opted for riding high, Michael's thighs straddling his belly. Michael bucked while Hartley mouthed the script from some vintage Stryker porn.

"Yeah! Take that cock all the way."

Back home on the lounge such words would be enough to empty the mood. One hollow yawn of regularity. Here it was different. Desire and danger lifting up the mundane.

Hartley slapped the other man's balls and turned sensual fingers about his ears and nostrils to the erogenous strip along the back of the neck.

"I love that," and Michael was crying out as a rush of semen peppered Hartley's chest.

Coming down and their groans altered key. A major panic as they broke apart and began lashing the darkness to recover their clothes.

"Quickly!" yelled Michael.

They banged heads, ripped a shirt and lost a button or two. It was ten minutes before time but the elevator was moving again.

"Where's my fucking sandals," pleaded Hartley, tossing a bow-tie at the human shadow and tripping through a pair of trousers.

"What a disaster," he added, though he had to laugh when the lights came on, just as the lift reached street level.

There was the technician and the security guard. Side by side and waiting. The technician wore blue overalls and make-up. She smiled at the man decked out in half a tuxedo, with a pair of lurid board shorts holding him close underneath.

"That's a nice tight fit," she said and winked at Hartley.

The security guard shuffled his feet. Very straight and innocent.

"It's a great day for the beach," he said.

Libertine

Hartley was coming down. At level 24, in came the man in black leather, catching the mirror reflection of Hartley before turning his eyes to the front panel. Both men were heading for street level.

There wasn't much of an overview. Comparisons in a lift are always subject to the fleeting glance, but a man in black leather invited longer stares, or so Hartley figured. It was just after midday and a Sunday too. Hartley was dressed in slave gear with bound feet and cufflinks. Not quite right for September in Sydney, and it had the other man thinking, forgetting how the look in rubber had eased out overnight and the forecast for a sluttish spring. Hartley knew the days of cruelty were coming.

It was one minute past when the lights went out.

Contracts of power never form in the darkness.

When the lights came on again, the issues were bright and clear.

   i. Innocence of youth (Days on the wheat farm)
   ii. Urban alienation (City life was always unpredictable)
   iii. The neurotic waves authority (He loved a man in a uniform)

Hartley sought an alliance with the stranger in the black. He reached across for the button.

"If you're stuck this can often get things going again." Hartley was glad that his contract was almost drafted. Innuendo matched the smug swelling around his crotch.

"Pornographer," said the other man, stifling a yawn as he then proceeded to destroy Hartley's contract.

Another cock and balls story.

SOMEONE IS CRYING IN THE CHATEAU DE BERNE

Andrew Holleran

HADLEY VAN NESS had the most beautiful hair – he went to a barber on Astor Place who charged only two dollars (Hadley loved a bargain, and could afford little more), but his hair was so thick and luxuriant that he always looked better than the people who paid fifteen dollars at Sebu. There were those who, out of envy or cynicism or both, claimed he was the only person they knew who once stayed in bed for three days with a bad haircut. It is hard to imagine this being true, but what they meant by this tale, of course, is that Hadley was shallow, too sensitive about his appearance. But who among us has not, on some days, considered his barber as only a shade less important than, say, his doctor? Hadley was always a pleasure to look at, and when I caught sight of him at Grand Central Station one morning last March (we were going up the Hudson to visit friends of his), I noticed as I approached that the color of his sweater – a cinnamon crew neck with touches of gray – matched the color of his hair. The effect, as he looked up from his newspaper with a warm and reassuring smile, was stunning.

"*Darling!*" he said to me and held out his arms.

"No longer late for trains," I murmured as we embraced.

"No longer late for trains," he said with that dazzling grin, "and smart enough to travel with very few things." He hoisted his canvas overnight bag. "And considerate enough to bring gourmet cheese and appropriate books for our hosts. God!" he said, holding up an illustrated survey, *The English Garden*, "in the old days I was awfully rude, but now I'm so thoughtful I could puke!"

He took my arm and fed me toward the gate to our train to Brewster. Only Hadley van Ness could have produced me on the spot with only twenty-four hours' notice; only Hadley, despite my deep affection for the country, could have persuaded me to visit a house of people I did not even know; for whenever Hadley van Ness pulled up on his motorbike, or telephoned, out of the blue, to ask for a loan, or a coat, or my company at a party, I always said yes. There was something about him I could not resist.

"Now I must explain," he said, as we sat down in our seats and he took my hand and patted it, and looked straight at me, smiling, "I must give you a little history. I don't want you to be alarmed, but these are *not* my favorite people we are going to see. They're perfectly nice, and ten years ago I wanted to belong to their little group more than anything on earth. In the last decade, however, I've grown up – we've all grown up – and they strike me as just a teensy bit dull. This used to be their summer house, but now they live there permanently and they're even duller. They've always thought *me* mad, anyhow. Wilcox is fun, and Roger I *adore*, but the rest are beasts. However," he said, "once a year – the way other people go to San Francisco, or Provincetown, or wherever – I go up to see Roger's new lover. He always has one, and he's always worth the trip. We'll just stay one night, play charades or something, and leave, and anyway, you *do* adore the country, don't you?"

I assured him that I did. He patted my hand again and said, "Well, it's all right then, Brewster is *aw*fully pretty," and with that he settled back to read a back issue of *L'Uomo*, and the train lurched forward and began to slide out of the station.

The journey we commenced was up the Hudson into the countryside north of those crumbling, mellow towns along the river whose mansions are now open to tourists on Sunday, up into that peaceful farmland dotted with reservoirs (lakes on which no sailboats sail, no swimmers intrude, since they contain Manhattan's water) like the covers of packages of butter: the sombre forests of Brewster, where horses, farmers and homosexuals retire when they have been too long in the city pent.

The journey takes an hour, and we read the entire trip, exchanging magazines, newspapers and letters from mutual friends, with the comfortable silence that is one of the legacies of a long friendship. So pointless did talk seem that Hadley merely handed me his calendar for the month, and I read the news that way. Not only was each event – dinner, opera, cocktail party, tryst – noted, but each was rated in the corner with an "Ugh!" or "Golden!" I asked why he even did things that were an "Ugh!" He said: "Well, one doesn't know in advance, darling. If one did, one wouldn't. But sometimes you find yourself in a loft in SoHo with two video artists waiting for a hustler with a ten inch dick to show up. You know."

I handed him the calendar and said: "Of all my friends, Hadley, you're the only one who hasn't changed. You still go out to all these parties, you still go to SoHo and wait for hustlers with ten inch dicks."

"*And* he had a pimple. Here," he said, and with that the train came to a stop in Brewster. It was lightly snowing and there was no one to meet us. We called a taxi company and sat down on a bench.

"How like them to meet us at the station!" he said. "How courteous, how chic!' He sighed, and said in a quiet voice: "You know, in all my years in New York, I've never fitted in to any group. I never felt I belonged."

At that instant the taxi appeared.

We were silent as we drove through forests of fir, over hills which gave us views of little lakes, and finally to a white clapboard house which sat at the end of a long driveway.

"Hello, Hadley," said a man with reading glasses and a magazine in one hand when the door opened. "Welcome to *la casa de las Reinas Muertas* – a name too silly to translate.

There's just two of us here now. Roger and Nick are out, and Wilcox is sleeping. Let me show you your rooms."

After introducing me, we went upstairs to a room whose two windows looked out on an enormous oak.

"Oh darling!" said Hadley dramatically. "It's too divine! It's so pretty I could die!"

When the door had closed behind our host he said in a low and serious tone: "I won't get a minute's sleep. I have to have a *very* firm mattress for my back. *I'm* sleeping on the floor," he said grimly.

"The floor?"

"Absolutely," said Hadley. "Otherwise I'll have lower back pain for days."

It was not my first contact with Hadley's whims, but it brought to mind a remark made by a man who did not even know him, but who said, on learning I planned to attend Hadley's birthday party: "You mean you still know Geminis? I got rid of my Geminis years ago!"

I asked why.

He said: "They're all very charming, but so inconsiderate!"

To concisely describe life in the house its occupants had christened *Casa de las Reinas Muertas* (a name I won't translate either), let me simply say that that afternoon, after introductions and gossip had dwindled to silence and we all sat reading in the living room, I looked up to see Harry sitting in an old red armchair as he stared into the fire with an index finger to his lips.

"What are you thinking about?" I smiled.

"I was trying to remember if I've masturbated today," he said. He looked up at me. "I don't *think* so – but perhaps I did. Oh well," he said, and went back to his book.

Hadley looked up from the scrapbook on his lap – he loved scrapbooks more intensely than anyone else I knew – and said, "Here's Joe Clark! I haven't seen him in years! I wonder how he's aged."

"He's dead," said Clayton.

"I see!" said Hadley briskly. Then after a moment: "Who got his apartment?"

Clayton looked at him.

"That divine apartment on Twelfth Street," said Hadley. "Who got it?"

"I haven't a clue," said Clayton.

"What a steal that place was," said Hadley. "Five rooms for eighty-seven dollars, and trees on both sides of the block."

"Why, at the age of thirty-seven," said Clayton in his foghorn of a voice, a voice from the tomb, hoarse from cigarettes, slowed by life in the country, "is one suddenly a horse that has run free till that moment, but which is now saddled, bridled with guilt, discontent, self-reproach, and the nervous awareness that one's time is limited? Why does that become evident at once?" he said with his head back as he addressed the grandfather clock against the opposite wall. "Why isn't it gradual? Why is it overnight? To suddenly realize one's time is up, that one is about to be whisked offstage by one of those hooks they used for bad vaudeville acts?"

Hadley put down the scrapbook. "I've always said there are two things one should never talk about – hemorrhoids and age. Both may be troubling you, but do not mention the fact to others."

"I'm sorry," said Clayton, "but sometimes I get frightened."

"So do we all," said Hadley. "But calling attention to the dreary fact only makes it worse. So let's remember, these *are* our golden years."

"Hadley," said Clayton, "you said our twenties were our golden years."

"Darling," said Hadley, "they are *all* golden. Life just gets better and better."

"Hadley," Clayton said as he removed the cigarette from his lips with the slow, measured dignity of a man who deplores haste, "is it true you collected money for a Christmas tree from all the people in your building and then gave a dinner party with it?"

"Well," said Hadley, "it doesn't take news long to travel from city to farm, does it! It *is* true, darling," he said as he looked up from the scrapbook, "I'm a van Ness – I *must* entertain! Besides, I *got* them a tree. I took it from the lobby of the Emigrant Savings Bank on Fourteenth Street."

"Was it a pretty tree?" said Harry.

"Very," said Hadley. He put down the scrapbook. "A girl's got to live, don't you see! I was destitute and it was Christmas and the apartment was *so* pretty! I used white poinsettias. Simple. Classic. I had twelve for sit-down, twenty-four for charades, and got nothing but raves. I've saved *all* the thank-you notes! I've put them in my scrapbook. Wish I could remember the cutest," he said as he stared off into space. "But I have no memory. That's why I left the theater. I couldn't remember my lines."

"You have no memory?" said Harry.

"For most things," said Hadley. "I can remember the veins on the wrist of the boy I spent last evening with – every one! To recall the veins of the wrist of Pablo Marcovici, the neurons rush to collide with one another. Not for *Hamlet*." Hadley stood up and ruffled the back of his thick, beautiful hair with the fingers of one hand. "Mmm," he said, "it's three o'clock."

This fact elicited no response.

"Would you like to take a walk?" I asked.

"Adore to," said Hadley and started up the stairs. "Let me just get my shoes."

Hadley disappeared upstairs. Clayton sighed and said, putting down his copy of Mary Renault: "Where would Hadley be without his hair?"

"I beg pardon?" I said.

"Where would Hadley be without his hair? That magnificent head of hair."

I had never thought about it, but when Hadley descended the stairs I could not *stop* thinking about it: indeed, as we went out into the snow I stared at his magnificent head of hair and wondered if it did *not* explain his life. It was impossible to imagine Hadley bald, and it was evident he never would be. As we walked down the snowy road, the wind parted his hair briefly like the fur of an animal blown into tufts by a breeze, and then it fell back into place.

"To think," said Hadley, "I once wept that I was not included in that group! I used to see them in their blazers walking down

Ninth Street on spring evenings with daffodils and champagne in hand, on their way to dinner! *I* was on my way to the Upper West Side to give some old man a massage! Well, weep no more! Just so boring. Don't get me wrong," he said, turning to me, "I know there are far worse things to be, they are not mean, or selfish, or thoughtless, but darling, they are *dull*. Do you know they watch a soap opera?" he said.

"Clayton told me," I said.

"I asked them what they did during the day," said Hadley, "and Clayton said 'Well we all watch *Another World* from two-thirty to four.' Can you imagine? That's why I live in New York. In New York one doesn't watch soap opera. One sleeps with the actors!"

He threw out his arms to embrace life. I took a tree branch in hand, shook it, and watched the snow shower to earth. A sparrow flew up from an evergreen and perched on an oak limb to watch our progress. The air was sharp and clean. Hadley pulled a train schedule out of his pocket and read it.

"I don't know about you, dear," he said, "but I'm going to take the one o'clock tomorrow."

"Oh, Hadley, no!" I said. "You have to relax, they're all very nice, you have to undergo a sea change and give the place a chance."

"A sea change?" he said.

"Yes," I said. "New York is so fast that it takes a while for you to slow down, to get into this other rhythm. You see we're – or at least, you're – still going sixty miles an hour, and they're all going ten. But it's so beautiful here," I said. "Look at those distant hills! Just breathe the air! How clean it is! Feel the cold on your face, look at the pheasants grazing there!"

"*Aren't* you good," said Hadley in a flat voice. "Aren't you the perfect house guest! I suppose I will give it another go," he sighed.

But when we returned to the house after our invigorating walk, filled with energy and good spirits, our hosts were in the same chairs and seemed hardly to have changed position, nor did they look up from their reading at our entrance, nor at the appearance of Wilcox Trent at the top of the stairs as we stood unwrapping the scarves from our necks.

Wilcox stopped on the stairs held out his arms, and said: "Darling."

"Sleeping beauty," said Hadley, holding out his arms. "Were you wakened by a kiss?"

"Gas," said Wilcox as he descended the stairs. "We eat nothing but bean sprouts and I fart day and night. When did you get here? What time is it? What day is it? What is my name? And where are we?"

"We're in Sleepy Hollow," said Hadley.

Harry looked up from his volume of Plato's *Dialogues* and asked "Do you think happiness is a virtue or a sensation?"

Wilcox and Hadley looked at each other – years of madness between them – and then Wilcox said: "*I* think happiness is a pair of silken balls, resting on my chin. If you want *my* opinion."

"Well," said Hadley, with a smile, "I wouldn't go that far. I would say it's the right sweater on my way to a Tea Dance."

And the two of them sailed off to the kitchen to gossip about people Wilcox had not seen in months. Silence descended over the house. Hadley came back to the living room to retrieve his cigarettes, and, after lighting one, sighed and said, "Will we ever get to Moscow?" He rolled his eyes and went back to the kitchen. A deep log shattered in the fire. The domestic peace deepened. Around the window seats stood pots of flowering azaleas, bright pink against the snowy panes, and African Violets. A white cat dozed in the corner. Completing the decor were a birdcage containing a stuffed parakeet, two walls of books, and little alcoves in which a comfortable old chair and a floor lamp promised hours of happy reading. It was an old farmhouse, and even the fact that the floors slanted was charming – like an imperfection in hand-made lace. Wilcox went up to bathe, and Hadley fell in with the regimen by leafing through old copies of *L'Uomo*.

"Hadley, can you cook yet?" asked Clayton.

"No, I've never really got beyond jello," he said.

"Who's cooking tonight?" asked Harry.

"Roger," said Clayton. "He and his boyfriend should be back soon. He's doing an Argentinean pancake called *pantouche*. They are just delicious. And some fowl. He hunts, you know."

"I'll say," said Hadley. He put down his magazine. "Tell me. What is the new lover like?"

"Like all the others," said Clayton.

He elucidated this remark no further, but Hadley made a face at me behind the newspaper he held. We both knew that – at least in his opinion – all the others had been glorious.

"He knows a lot about plants," said Clayton. "He knows, for example, that a waxy begonia requires partial shade. I just learned that today."

But this was all he offered, and as silence resumed, Hadley picked up the newspaper and read parts of it he never glanced at in town – the business section, for instance, sports, science, obituaries – and the log in the fireplace hissed and popped. The white cat rose, arched her back, and, receiving no inspiration from the humans around her, lay down again in the exact spot, as if, having completed her exercises, she could now go to sleep. The light grew dim in the room, and when I looked outside the sunlight lay in long, low, slanted bars across the snow. The trunks of two oaks glowed a ruddy brown in its light and then they faded to pale gray and the early winter darkness arrived.

Just then there was a piercing shriek, and we ran upstairs to the room from which it came. Wilcox stood in the center of his bedroom, arms outstretched to a Delft vase of flowers on the mantelpiece.

"These azaleas," he said, putting a hand to his head, "drive me *mad*! Did nature have to go *quite* this far to attract a bee?" He swept out of the room and left us standing there.

"Aren't these people mad?" said Hadley. "I feel like an appraiser for Sotheby's," he said in a whisper as we went into our bedroom to nap. "In the mansion of a mad old woman whose silver we want to auction. I've only come to see the pieces, and then I've got to leave. Where *is* Roger? And his new beau? What is taking them so long?"

We lay down on the comforter and he began to recall Roger's past lovers he had admired: the Japanese swimmer on a scholarship to Columbia, the Argentinean cab driver who had left the seminary in Buenos Aires, the carpenter from Colorado, the naturalist from Oregon, those creatures so rare in eastern shores, those silent blonds with whom he had always fallen in love.

"They were so special, you see, because they had a quality, a quiet masculinity, a lack of pretence," said Hadley. "They were not always *brilliant*. I remember the boy in Montauk in . . . 1966." He sighed. "The last time I was in Montauk was fifteen years ago. I find it most upsetting that fifteen years separate me from *any* event other than my birth." He drew the comforter to his chin. "Well, he had absolutely nothing to say. I once had to spend the day with him, and I found it a chore. But the others were all, let's face it, mere gods."

There was a noise downstairs and we raised our heads: voices in the kitchen, stamping of boots. We sat up and listened.

"It's Roger!" Hadley said as I heard a hearty voice asking if we'd come. We got off the bed and bounded down the stairs like children about to meet their father.

"Hello!" said Roger.

"Hello, Roger, hello!" we warbled.

A young man with curly blond hair on which snow was still dusted came through the door and stopped. A single drop of water zig-zagged down his temple, golden in the firelight.

"Nick this is my old friend Hadley, and Steve," said Roger, and in the silence that occurred after we shook hands, and after Nick said "Hi, Hadley," and "Hi, Steve," in the great breathless silence that sometimes follows the apprehension of beauty, or the peculiar knowledge, like the moment you know you have caught the flu again, that you have fallen in love, one heard with utmost clarity the single pop of a log in the fireplace. We turned to Roger and went on with life, as one must, as if the earth had not opened and swallowed us up.

Hadley behaved as if Nick were not there; he interviewed Roger about his teaching post, his car, his plans for the summer, and mutual friends now living in Carmel, Key West, London. It was not until Hadley and I were setting the table, and we were alone, that he put a knife between his teeth and bit it. "Darling, he's *direct* from heaven," he whispered to me as he passed on his way to get more plates. Hadley began to pale, and I sensed this was more that the usual delight in a comely young man; in fact, a few moments later he held his temple and said, "I've got a splitting headache." Half an hour later he grinned and touched his spine. "My lower back," he said.

"Next you'll have fever blisters," I murmured, familiar with this succession of symptoms.

By dinnertime Hadley had retired upstairs and told everyone not to worry. Nick went up with a tray. Downstairs we talked about New York until Clayton, coming in with a tray of hot biscuits said, "Who wants to take these to our sick friend?" and I volunteered.

The dialogue within the bedroom stopped me just outside the door: "You *must* go to Flamingo once," Hadley said, "if only once. I hardly go more that twice a year myself, I used to go every week, but now there's Studio too. And the White Party next week, and the Sleaze Ball after that, and the opening of Pravda. These are things someone of your age *must* see, just as you must see Paris, Rio, the Sistine Chapel. You understand. They are wonders of the world! Imagine a gigantic space filled with perfect men at six in the morning; at nine they are still dancing, glistening with sweat! Everyone should experience it once, and who knows how long it will last?"

"I would like to go to the city," said Nick in a quiet voice. One could hear his smile. One could feel the joy flooding Hadley van Ness (the wrong van Nesses, a cousin from Cincinnati once said coldly) at that moment.

"You know, you're quite welcome to stay at my flat," said Hadley. "I've almost always a houseguest from somewhere but it's no problem to find room for another. We'll have *such* fun! But you mustn't delay! In two months it will all be over, and they move to Fire Island, which is a spectacle of a different sort. Have you thought of living in the city?" he said.

"Well, Roger— "

But this was too much: I entered just at that moment and yelled, "Look at these biscuits!"

Hadley shot me a look.

"My food must be cold," said Nick, getting to his feet.

"Has Hadley been enchanting you with fairy tales?" I asked.

Nick smiled. Hadley narrowed his eyes.

"I hope you feel better," said Nick. He then excused himself and went downstairs.

"You *couldn't* have entered at a worse moment," said Hadley in a gloomy tone, putting his hands to his temples.

"Hadley," I said, "there are ethics. Roger is your dear friend, and— "

"I *merely* invited him for the weekend," said Hadley in that same dead serious tone. "I think he should be seen. One rarely finds things like this in the provinces. That boy is magic."

"Earlier this evening, Hadley, you spoke of *The Three Sisters*. May I remind you of another play by Chekhov? *The Seagull*?"

"Is that the one," Hadley mumbled through bites of his chicken Marengo, "where the boy commits suicide—"

"And the girl falls in love with the sophisticated writer from the city, follows him to Moscow, and then returns, a broken bird, when he has tired of her."

"Darling, *I'm* not going to do that! *I'm* not sophisticated! I'd just love to have him for three days, and put his thank-you note – next to a photograph, of course – in my scrapbook. Some people collect butterflies."

"Some people *are* butterflies," I interrupted.

"I collect thank-you notes," he went on. "You know very well I'm not interested in the kind of long, deep relationship which is Roger's forte. I live for my scrapbooks! And I always will! The reason why Roger has all these exceptional lovers, these gods, these angels – you must have wondered how he does it," he said, dropping his breast of chicken and picking up a buttered biscuit.

"I have," I said.

"Is simply that *he* is as single-purposed about having an intimate relationship with a serious young blond as *I* am about having twenty-four for charades and twelve for sit-down. Now you must realize that because Roger *has* this genius – for that is what it amounts to – because Roger *can* give himself to these fellows, he is never without one! Simple as that! What most of us fail to realize is that each and every one of us has a talent— "

"Which is death to hide," I said.

"Death to hide," he mumbled through his second biscuit, "and that we aren't competing with each other! And remember dear, a young man *wants* to be attached to an older guy: he feels secure, he learns, he meets people he never would otherwise – people like us! Remember how attractive *we* found older men when we were two-and-twenty? Thirty-five was the *acme* of attractive, in our eyes. A graying temple, a slight puffiness beneath the eyes, was *heaven*. Now we have the graying temple, the bags under the eyes, and we're looking for a recent graduate of Long Island University! Altar boys! No matter! *I* can't give Nick what Roger can. *I* haven't the time! A weekend with me in the city is *hardly* the plot of *The Seagull*, dear. Try again." He finished his biscuit, licked his fingers and sighed. "That was absolute heaven," he said, looking as happy as a child. "I feel quite restored. Do you think if I went downstairs after coffee, we could persuade these girls to play a few charades?"

But this remained only a thought – even he decided they were too heavy a mass to raise to the heights Hadley demanded on charades – and he was still beside me leafing through an issue of *L'Uomo* when I dozed off. I was awakened by his hand on my arm.

"Shhh!" he said.

"What is it?"

"Someone is crying," said Hadley.

I listened harder and discerned the sound; it grew louder, then subsided.

"Someone is crying in the Château de Berne," said Hadley.

"What?" I said.

"Someone is crying in the Château de Berne. That was the name of our house at the beach, summer of seventy-one," he said. "I remember lying in bed one night after a marvellous party, in this house filled with young, stylish, drugged beauties – and hearing that sound. Someone had just broken up with his lover. He wept. Who could it be now?" He turned to me with a frown. "Do you think Wilcox is weeping over the crow's foot he found this afternoon?"

"Of course not," I said.

"Then who? These people are full of gloom to begin with. They've retired to this house in complete despair, having concluded that they are no longer young – as if a messenger from the gods knocked on your door one day with a telegram to that effect – retire from the scene. *Tant pis! Quelle domage!* They're so loaded with regret, nostalgia, and remorse over their wasted youths, I suppose weeping in bed in not uncommon around here!"

"It *is* sad," I said.

"What?"

"That even among friends, even among families, there is often a secret sadness, a grief we can share with no one."

"But one does not *sob* over a receding hairline," he said.

"Over what then?" I said. "It *is* sad that so many of the men we considered wonderful, handsome, are now recluses. Replaced by eight-hundred boys with black moustaches, who are all twenty-two and named Luis."

"How thrilling," said Hadley, returning to *L'Uomo*.

The house was still but for the tapping of an oak branch against our window. Hadley, untouched and unperturbed by the passing of the years, sat upright, ears alert, like a detective in an English murder mystery; only it was not murder he wished to detect, it was grief. There was a knock on the door.

"Come in!" said Hadley.

Roger entered. His face was calm. He said, "Hadley, I have a favor to ask. Can Nick go into the city with you tomorrow, and stay a few days? He's been wanting to for a while now, and I think the two of us should have some time apart."

"But darling, of course!" said Hadley. "I'll show him all the sights, we'll have a marvellous time!" Hadley put down his magazine, and went pale. "Roger, I must be quite candid. May I be perfectly frank?" He took Roger's hand and laid his over it.

"Of course," said Roger.

"I invited Nick to stay with me, and urged him to come to the city, and told him he'd have a wonderful time."

"I know," said Roger.

"You do?" said Hadley.

"Yes, he just told me."

"Oh. Well, let me just say I in no way wanted to cause a rift between you two, dear. I would never forgive myself. I do find him dead attractive, as who does not – the angels weep – but relationships, rare as they are, are sacred to me, and— "

"Our relationship is over," said Roger calmly.

We gaped.

"No!" said Hadley.

"Yes," said Roger. "You'll be doing me a favor to take him to the city. We've simply been alone out here so many months, we've devoured each other. I'm grateful to you for your invitation." Roger squeezed his hand. "Thanks for your concern."

Hadley sat forward and embraced Roger and said, "*What's* a friend for?"

Roger said good night and closed the door.

Hadley turned and said, "Now I know why I was asked this weekend. Roger knew this would happen."

"What?" I said.

"This! I wonder what's wrong with him."

"With whom?"

"Nick! I wonder why Roger has finished with him. Kind of like buying a house, don't you see? You always want to know *why* the owner is selling."

"Roger isn't *selling* Nick to you," I said.

"Of course he isn't, dear," said Hadley, as he put a finger to his lips and frowned.

"Hadley," I frowned.

"Yes?"

"You shouldn't think of Nick as a used car."

"Well, one *does*, don't you see?" said Hadley, with a frown and a sigh.

"What exactly *are* your plans for the boy?" I said.

"Nothing unusual," he said. "Just take him around. The weekend was all I had in mind, although it would be so easy to fall in love with that one. His eyes - I simply swam in them. Did everything but wear flippers and a face mask."

I broached the wisdom of painting the city such bright colors, in describing positively a life whose limitations we all saw very well by now, in leading him to believe that there was happiness to be found in such places as Flamingo, or the White Party, or the Sleaze Ball.

"Oh," said Hadley, "I won't send *him* to the Sleaze Ball. These things must be done in stages. I'm not sure he even shaves every day. He'll go to the White Party. And anyway, you all say these things are empty and meaningless and emotionally void, but dear, you didn't think so when *you* were twenty-three! They were fabulous! They were ecstasy! You had a ball! I find it very amusing that all you boys suddenly decide in your middle and late thirties that the life you lately led was silly, sordid, and a waste. Easy to dish the host, dear, after you've left the party! Anyway, that's your opinion of it all, not mine! I want to die on my knees in a back room with dead babies oozing from my lips!"

There was a crash in the corridor – I leapt up, opened the door, and found Clayton kneeling among the tea things, which lay around him and an overturned tray on the carpet. "I . . . was just . . . putting these away," he mumbled, and, after helping him put everything back on the tray, I returned to bed.

"Well," I said to Hadley, "what do you think happened to all of Roger's previous lovers?"

"They're probably buried in the basement," said Hadley with a wave of his hand. He turned out the light. "At any rate, it's clear to me who was crying."

"Roger?" I said.

"Nick," he said. "He's scared, probably of leaving what is, no matter what else it may be, a very stable home. But the break-up was not our doing. It never is. My conscience is clear, my calendar for next week *black* with entries. I shall take Nick everywhere!" And with that he sighed and – as only he could – fell asleep at once. Hadley could fall asleep in discotheques. He snored beside me in noisy slumber oblivious to melancholy, regret, nostalgia, or concern over the price of veal.

In the morning we ate blueberry pancakes and shortly afterwards caught our train back to the city. Nick told Hadley the story of his life. Hadley composed drafts of his thank-you notes as he listened.

"I was *born* to write thank-you notes," Hadley explained to me.

I did not see Hadley for several months after our return. He owed me over two hundred dollars, but I could not find the words to tell him so. That summer I saw Hadley in Central Park.

"What happened to Nick?" I inquired.

"Nick?" said Hadley.

"Roger's boyfriend. From Brewster! The weekend in January!"

"Oh, Nick!" he said. "He's living with a man and his mother in Brooklyn," he said.

"He was so handsome!" I exclaimed.

"But very dull," said Hadley. "The magic wore off pretty quickly, dear, and thank God I placed him with someone who loves him."

"Hadley, you're not talking about a pet."

"I know, dear," he said. "But the man is very rich, and has already bought Nick ten thousand dollars' worth of stereo equipment. And a BMW. Nick stays at home with the mother. They're all Greek, and she's a great cook and Nick is as big as a house. But he wrote the most charming thank-you note after he left! I have it in my scrapbook next to a nude photograph of him – when he was skinny!"

And with that we parted, and went our separate ways; eventually I came to see very little of Hadley, except from a distance, on the street, and on those occasions I did not stop him to ask for my money, my lamp, or my parka. Of Hadley a friend once said: "He tries so hard to be superficial that he has *depth*." But the friend who said this has long since disappeared up the Hudson, to one of those sleepy little towns with an abandoned factory beside the train station, on which the late afternoon light becomes ruddy gold on those quiet autumn afternoons when you step down off the train and stand astonished by the silence and the beauty. He lives now in one of those little towns that recall the stories of Washington Irving, where the bricks of the buildings are faded and the aqueduct that runs down to Manhattan forms a bridle path between slender sycamores shedding their leaves on a warm October day, and where the river is flat and blue and somnolent. He lives there now – as do I – and only Hadley remains in the city, and Nick who has also been swallowed up by it, sequestered in Brooklyn, fat and no longer beautiful.

THE STEAM PARLOUR

Witi Ihimaera

NIGHT AND RAIN. The street is busy with buses and traffic streaming up from Queen Street. I pull the car out of the flow and across the intersection. Headlights dazzle like golden showers. Ten minutes later, I park the car down a side-alley. Get out and lock. Quick steps take me away from the rain and along the pavement, following the curved wall of glass frontages. Each window is a mirror of desire. The headlights pinion me, popping flashbulbs like a photographer leaping out of the darkness, Gotcha.

The anonymous black door to The Steam Parlour is a street-level entrance set back from the glass wall. On one side, appropriately, a pharmacy sells late-night supplies. On the other side is a menswear shop. Opposite, a twenty-four hour video rental joint. Car doors slam as young guys, whistling nonchalantly, hands in pockets, saunter to the latest X-rated epic.

There is no sign on the door. Only logos which indicate that Bankcard or American Express are accepted. You have to know the door is there. Nobody goes there by accident. You go in because you want what's inside.

I push open the door. Get away from the searchlights of the traffic. Leave the other world behind.

The warmth envelops like an old friend. A brightly lit stairway leads up to a closed window hatch. There is a sign above it:

LET US STEAM CLEAN YOR BODY

The words are large black ejaculate, and the "u" in the "your" is missing.

The hatch slides open. The Spaniard's face appears. He watches as I ascend. Grinning. Gold tooth flashing. Earring glittering in dyed black hair.

Waiting.

None of us who are regulars has yet worked out how The Spaniard knows when clients are coming up the stairs.

"There must be a beam when you come through the door," The Bald One offers. The steam turbans his head. He always avoids the single red bulb in the steam room. If he sits beneath the light his pate will glow like a red beacon and put off the young hunks. First impressions are everything and baldness is not attractive currency in this world of hair, curls, moustache, chest, armpit and pubic thatch.

"Nah," Wet Dream Walking disagrees. "I reckon he has a sensor on the stairs." He hunches forward, the red light limning his chest and washboard stomach. His pectorals pop like mountains in the steam. He needs no darkness to obscure any physical deficiencies, for he has none. He is an athlete of smouldering proportions, the stuff of adolescent desires, and wherever he goes both men and women follow.

Then Hope Springs Eternal says, "Oh, chaps, we all know he does it with mirrors."

That cracks us up. Not just because of Hope Springs Eternal's upper-class delivery but also because it could well be true. The Spaniard is suspected to be a voyeur, but aren't we all? We are fairly sure he has two-way mirrors in the cubicles, where one-on-one action takes place, and in the bunk room at the back. At least, that's what we think or like to think. In this place imagination is as potent an aphrodisiac as the reality. Imagining someone looking turns us all into performers. Turns us on. Cranks up the exhibitionist nature. Makes us strut and spout.

Poor Hope Springs Eternal starts to remonstrate against our laughter. Then, good-naturedly, he flaps his hands.

"OK, OK, you fellows know better."

Although Hope Springs Eternal is around my age, thirty-one, he somehow seems at least ten years older. Jester to our court, he is a blind albino bat peering out from the darkest corner. Never approached for sex, he has accepted a role as onlooker. But if he takes his glasses off he won't see anything and if he leaves them on they steam up. Windscreen wipers are no solution. The onlooker who needs glasses in the steam room must be the most frustrated man in the world.

We are still laughing when, outside the door, there are sounds of footfall. Then the muted spraying of sound of someone in the shower.

Of all the times at The Steam Parlour, this is the one filled with expectancy.

Who knows who will come through the door? Someone youthful, bringing hope. Someone strong, bringing power and domination. Someone handsome, someone to worship. Someone pliant, bringing succulence. Someone smiling, bringing love. Someone shining, bringing destiny.

Someone.

Anyone.

A hiss. An eddy of steam.

The door opens.

The Spaniard may grin but he never smiles. Although he knows who I am, he still checks my membership card. It is as if he has never really looked at me, looked at us. He grunts and hands me a key to a locker.

I am puzzled at the spelling error in YOR. It is totally out of character for The Spaniard. When I telephoned him, five years ago, to ask if the establishment was exclusively a steam parlour or steam parlour combined with a sauna, he had replied, "The former."

I had almost gone somewhere else. One never expects such formality in places like this, where machismo reigns.

"I know what you're thinking," The Spaniard says as he hands me a towel. "Schools teach kids nothing these days."

He jerks his head and, behind him, I see a new Young Thing. Who knows how The Spaniard finds them, these young men to hand out towels, keep the place clean and, by being decorous, titillate and titivate.

The Young Thing pretends indifference. He is wearing a cap back to front and a T-shirt which has been carefully ripped. His jeans look as if they've been bashed to death to get the right torn and weathered look. His body language is defensive and he refuses to look me in the eye. His petulant silence says more potently than words that he is above all this. He is only doing it because he wants a job. Fuck, do you think he really wants to be here? He only came because the advertisement promised good money.

His look of innocence is refreshing. Even so, there is a sensuality that marks him as being one of us.

I try to put him at ease.

"Hi," I call.

But he ignores me. Frozen, my greeting snaps in mid-air.

"So," I ask The Spaniard, "what's his name?"

The Spaniard looks to heaven.

"Three guesses."

Another Mark. Jesus.

The Spaniard presses a button. There is a buzz, the door to the right of the hatch opens and I am in.

Journeys into places like The Steam Parlour are always accompanied by diminishing lighting. Nothing blazes, nothing glares or explodes. Light dies here, becomes ambient. The discreet darkness hides who we are. Hides what we do. Gives us anonymity and glosses us with glamour. In the netherworlds the wattage is always way down low.

Not even the low lighting, however, could ever transform the vestibule of The Steam Parlour. Like others of its kind, it exhibits wall-to-wall tackiness. On the left is a mural, presumably of a Spanish hacienda, complete with lurid red flowers suggestive of sex. On the right, a giant plastic cactus. In the middle is a bar selling watered-down beer, Coca Cola and stale potato chips. Four stools next to it are where you can catch your breath or use the telephone, and on the bar are bowls of plastic-wrapped condoms. Be careful you don't eat them with your chips.

But the vestibule at least serves its purpose. It provides a moment to get ready, to check out the scene, to pose and breathe in the heady sweet-sour smell that only places like this have. To acclimatize before moving on to the locker room. Extend your tongue and you can lick the warm sweat off the air.

Through the door to the locker room.

"Hey, man," a voice greets me. Snake Charmer is climbing into his sweat pants. "How ya doing?"

"Pretty good," I answer. I look around. There are just the two of us.

"Things are slow," Snake Charmer says.

Some nights are like this. But you can never tell. The potency of The Steam Parlour lies in its promise, the infinite possibilities. I shrug my shoulders. Begin taking off my clothes. We got it on together once, Snake Charmer and I. Now we no longer interest each other. With some men once is enough to tell you all you need to know. There's nothing to boost you beyond the climax, as stunning as that might be, to wanting to know more − where they live, what they do, what animates them − all those curiosities which hook us into each other, which take us from anonymity to having names. After it's done, may as well shake hands.

That's not Snake Charmer's fault, nor mine. The chemistry just isn't there. Despite the intrigue and glamour of his Indian ancestry and the aromatic scent of curry in his sweat, nothing. Just skin, bone, being given sex and giving sex, and five minutes of his life and mine. That's all.

"Well," Snake Charmer says, slamming the locker. "See you around."

And is gone.

Snake Charmer is right. Exit the locker room and there is hardly anyone around in the space euphemistically known as the lounge, which connects to the showers and the steam room itself.

Hardly anyone except, of course, for Always A Bridesmaid and Fat Forty And A Fairy. There they languish, carefully draped in towels, staring at a dead television screen. Obviously, The Spaniard hasn't hooked the latest Cadinot sexpic into the video yet. Do they ever go home? Do they ever move from this place of flickering magic?

I wave to them. We have only exchanged a few words, ever, but I know their wit to be devastating. Once, Fat Forty And A Fairy, after a playful bout with a partner, called out, "Thank you very much. Have a nice day. Next please." His voice cut through the entire establishment and filled it with mirth.

I am ashamed of my attitude to them but add another prayer to my list: Thank you, Lord, for the equipment I have, but when I reach forty cut it off so it doesn't control my life.

Always A Bridesmaid smiles across the room. Like two boatmen at the River Styx, he and Fat Forty And A Fairy wave me through into the passage leading to the shower room.

There but for the grace of God go I.

The shower room is small and octagonal. In total contrast to the preceding dimness, the light is bright here, razor-like, flashing off the eight enclosing steel walls and white ceramic floor. The showers are silver stalks attached to a central pillar in the middle of the room. Each stalk is topped with a shower nozzle. A bouquet of metallic roses. Beyond is the closed wooden door unnecessarily labelled "Steam Room". To the left is the corridor leading to the cubicles and bunk room beyond.

Nobody is showering. I take off my towel and put it on the hanger. There are two other towels. The Spaniard hasn't done his round yet.

When I first came here and was exiting the showers, I saw that my towel was gone. I thought someone had taken it until, on subsequent visits, I caught The Spaniard removing all of them.

"The house custom," he winked.

There is no room for coyness or embarrassment here. Seeing guys either striding or sidling back to the front desk, either swinging it left and right or cupping it in protective hands, adds to the titillation.

"Uh, you got another towel?"

You learn a lot about a guy that way. How easy he is, how comfortable or uncomfortable he is with his nudity. It's all part of the fun. And The Spaniard makes a buck fifty on every fresh towel.

Once you're in the know, however, and if you're still coy, you stash your towel in the empty rack just outside the shower room.

Move over, guys.

I step up to the shower and my reflection flashes around the entire room. Suddenly I feel alone and yearn to fill the room with other men. I try to will them to appear, all those wonderful men, laughing and shining in the glory of their years.

Most are dead now. Or dying.

Quickly, I turn on the shower, close my eyes and try to forget. Reach for the soap. There is always just the one bar of soap in the shower room. It is meant to be shared, passed from one man to another, to help start up conversations between strangers.

"Hey, have you got the soap? Great! Do you come here often?"

In all my times here I have never found the soap missing. It belongs here. To take it would be an act of selfishness. Of unsharing.

The Spaniard shows impeccable taste. The soap is fragrant, blossoming into rich lather. It is talismanic. Its magic is collected from all the bodies that have slipped it around the curve of buttocks, beneath and around and along the sweetmeats of our thighs. Sharing this intimacy makes the soap sacramental. So slide it everywhere, spread the potency and add to it.

The water streams in rivulets down my face, rushing over the planes of my chest, down through the matt of pubic hair, around the tube of my cock to the testicles beneath, pouring between my thighs.

When I open my eyes again the light dazzles. And suddenly I see my naked reflection shooting off the glistening octagonal wall like a steel honeycomb. The uneven planes make my face sphinx-like, shimmering, remote. On each face is the question: What is it that walks on four legs in the morning, two legs in the heat of the noonday sun and three legs in the evening?

The shower room is the place to respond to the sphinx's age-old riddle. To say either "Yea" or "Nay" to desire. The creature who crawls, then strides on two legs and then on three is not only a man in infancy, maturity and old age with a walking stick. He is also man driven by sex from crawl to walk to full erection.

But one might not need to respond to desire tonight. Don't predict the auguries. They will, after all, depend on who comes bearing them.

And it is already too late to say "No." Muted laughter comes from behind the door of the steam room and, somewhere else, the sounds of soft sighs in the humid night. They quicken my desire to be part of the action.

So. Quickly. Five in the steam room, huh?

Turn the shower off. Nostrils flaring.

Two strides. Already, tumescence.

Into the steam room.

After midnight, and I am driving back to my flat from The Steam Parlour. But first, turn off at the motorway and travel the rain-slicked streets through Parnell to the two-storeyed house at the top of the rise. Around the corner, the wheels slipping on the steep incline, and there it is.

Silhouetted against the sky, the house is a Ship of Dreams, a galleon set full sail toward the shining star second from the right. The forward sails are luminous with the moon. The mainsails are unfurling, sprinkling stardust as they billow and swirl.

I turn off the engine and freewheel into the accustomed watching place, beneath the trees on the other side of the street.

All the lights are out.

My two princesses are sleeping.

Suddenly there is a menacing movement. Adrenalin pumps my body with alarm and I am ready to leap out of the car and—

But the movement is only the wind gusting against the shutters.

Has Annabelle remembered to check the doors and windows? Has she put the safety locks on? For something wicked may come this way. Something with slavering jaws to huff and puff and blow the house in. Or something bearing a red apple poisoned to send my princesses to eternal sleep. Or something with a needle to prick their fingers. Something.

The wind comes up, swirling the midnight tides of the night universe. The sails snap and bell into fullness. The house is like a shining fairy galleon, spun of dreams and laughter, tugging at the moorings and ready to weigh anchor.

Turn the key. Start the motor.

Dear Lord protect my little ones. Always.

I close my ears to the filigree of silver laughter. As I leave, the sound of tiny bells tinkles in the wind.

Away from that Ship of Dreams.

A VISIT TO THE GENERAL

Francis King

THE SUN-BURNED hand with the freckles and the clean, closely-cut nails moved across the chess-board. "Check," the general murmured. He was sitting bolt upright in a plain wooden chair.

The boy opposite to him stirred lazily in the recesses of the sofa, pushed the hair away from his eyes, and glanced at the game. "Oh, but you've exposed your king," he exclaimed, massaging one thin blue-veined wrist against the fingers of his other hand. He was slight, with a stoop, and when he gave his faintly malicious smile, as he did now, one corner of his mouth twitched oddly upwards, almost in the snarl of a cornered animal. "Don't you see?" he asked. "You can't do that."

The general scraped his chair backward and rose to his feet, his face moving out of the shadows in which they had been playing and striking a transverse beam of sunshine from the open window. It was a fine but rather terrible face, one cheek covered with scars, and the whole divided by a few resolute lines. "I give you the game," he said. "You're too good for me. I'm becoming rusty."

At the words the boy again gave his curious smile, more to himself than to his opponent. His eyes, surrounded by dark rings, glittered. He yawned.

The general, who had gone to the window to see if it had stopped raining, stood there for many minutes looking out to the garden, now steaming in the late evening sunshine. The syringas were dripping water onto the narrow paths. The eaves of the dark Victorian house were dripping also; there was a sound like invisible kissing whenever the water plopped into the butt. The general turned: "Shall we go out now? It's rather pleasant in the summer-house."

The boy nodded, but there was an unwillingness in all his movements as he made for the door. He was twenty but looked sixteen, with his smooth chin, oddly immature voice, and almost girlish features. When he walked, he balanced on his toes: but the impression this gave was not one of sprightliness, but rather of an excessive, almost elderly caution. The general found himself far ahead of the boy, and had purposely to adapt his strides to that bird-like stepping. There was something ludicrous in this. He was a man whom one could not imagine acting lethargically, for whatever he did was done quickly, almost brusquely, as though that sinewy, much-tried body was incapable of indecision.

The boy looked about him, at the rose-beds, where each bush had been pruned to only a foot or so from the ground, then to the distant pond where ducks waddled and quacked, and finally to the grey and ivy-covered façade of the house, with many of its windows boarded up and one lace curtain billowing outwards from an upstairs room. As he made this scrutiny, he had a sensation of decay and scrupulous order, the two oddly compounded in the dilapidated house and its tidy garden. It was a paradox which teased and puzzled him.

On reaching the summer-house, with its trellis of tea-roses and creaking weather-vane, the general began to put up a deck-chair and then motioned the boy into it. "Sit down," he said, as though he were giving a command. This was a habit of his. The boy sank into the place offered to him so peremptorily, again with that privately malicious smile on his face. The general took a cane chair.

At that moment an aeroplane tipped dangerously over the house and roared upwards. The boy shaded his forehead with both his hands and looked disapprovingly at it, his eye-lids flickering incessantly at the white dazzle: but the general stared fiercely without screwing his eyes together, until it had passed far into the distance. Then he turned away with a shrug of his broad shoulders: "Things are different," he murmured. "Ever since my day." Although he was only sixty-six, he always talked as though he were a relic of a far-distant age.

The boy made some remark, in an effort to conceal his boredom, and the general, imagining that he was interested, began to talk of all the changes that had taken place in warfare. He spoke shyly at first, but later found the words that he was looking for. All the time he sat erect, his face turned from the boy, his eyes still fixed on the gap of blue between their chairs and the house. The trees spattered the summer-house at sudden intervals; the afternoon sun caught the study windows and made them flash angrily; birds moved precisely across the lawn or tapped snails on the floor of the terrace to break their shells. The boy made sympathetic noises.

Flushing a little under his tan, sweating even, but never moving or changing his position, the general became eloquent. The ravaged face glowed as though there were a flame beneath it. The voice ceased to be brusque. Slowly, by degrees, he passed from the general topics of warfare to talk of his own part in the Great War, the terrible but undeserved disgrace, and compulsory retirement. This was the first time that he had spoken of the matter for several years, but his voice was steady, almost conversational. He was not a man to show his feelings. All that puzzled him was that he should be making this confession to the boy: this he could not understand.

At last it was over; the fierce eyes fell to the ground. He felt ashamed, said nothing, did not look at the boy. He waited for some question or remark, the inevitable sympathy. But when the silence stretched out between them and grew big, and still nothing came, when the patter from the trees had begun to oppress him, and he could feel the perspiration breaking again on his forehead, as though he were suffering from one of his old attacks of malaria, he turned his head slowly.

The boy was asleep.

The general watched him for many minutes: still maintaining that rigid pose in the cane chair while his dark face continued to trickle with sweat. The boy lay with his head turned sideways, the fingers of one hand lightly touching his cheek, and his collar creased. He was still smiling to himself.

Then he awoke, gradually, gracefully, without confusion, opening his eyes on the mass of tea-roses and the frothing syringas as though he had just been called, in bed. "Oh dear, I am sorry, sir. You must forgive me. The truth is I've been sleeping badly – and my exams . . ." He massaged his leg and then stamped; he had pins-and-needles. "I don't think I've slept as well as that for ages. But it was very rude of me. You were just going to tell me about the differences – between now and then . . ."

The general nodded. Then he helped the boy to his feet and took him in to dinner, propelling him by the elbow as though he were an invalid.

After dinner, when the only servant had said goodnight and left for her cottage in the village, the general and the boy sat uneasily together in the dining-room, the boy sipping a vintage port. The general did not drink. They talked in fits and starts of the only topic they had in common – the boy's dead father, the general's friend. The general would ask abrupt questions which the boy would answer a little tremulously, almost impertinently, turning his glass in his hands or looking up from under veiled lashes. They had both eaten sparingly, the general because he was naturally ascetic, the boy because he was tired.

Eventually the general rose to his feet: "Shall we go into the study? I have some maps that might interest a scholar like you."

The boy put a hand to his forehead in a gesture of fatigue. "If you don't mind - I really think I should go to bed. I feel so desperately tired. I might go to sleep again in your study. And if I have to be off again tomorrow . . ."

"Yes, yes, of course." The general turned on the hall-light for him and watched him mount the stairs, one hand trailing lightly along the bannisters, the other in his pocket. Disappointed, angry even, he went into the study and sat down at the desk, covered with the articles which he now wrote for the papers – "If Kitchener had Lived", "The Twelve Decisive Battles of the World", "The Six Greatest Generals", "If Marlborough had Lost Malplaquet". They were never published. But tonight he could not concentrate on the hypotheses which usually filled his solitude. He fidgeted round the study, lit a cigarette, though he never smoked, puffed at it, and then put it out. He crackled *The Times* and filled in a corner of the crossword.

Then he walked hurriedly into the hall and went upstairs.

"Come in!" His sharp knock was followed by a preoccupied murmur, as though the boy were doing something else and did not wish to be bothered: and when the general opened the door, it was to discover him before the window, in his pyjamas, a hypodermic syringe in his hand.

"I – I'm sorry," the general stammered. "I came up to see if you had everything that you wanted."

"Yes, thank you." The boy still did not look up. "I've got to give myself one of these wretched injections."

"Diabetic?"

"Yes. My mother usually does them."

"Shall I do it for you?"

"If you like." The boy was off-hand. The general took the syringe, and drew back the boy's pyjamas sleeve, revealing a thin yellow arm, whose skin was oddly soft. His firm, competent fingers felt the brittle bone. "About here?' he asked. The boy nodded and turned away.

As the needle plunged into the tender flesh, there was a sharp "Oh!"

"Sorry. Did that hurt?" The general put down the syringe, and patted the boy's shoulder. He still spoke abruptly.

"When you offered to do it, I thought you knew how. It's a matter of finding the right spot." The boy was sulky with the pain.

"Perhaps I should have let you do it yourself."

"I don't *like* doing it. But I know the place." The boy climbed into bed, still rubbing his arm, curled up, and turned to the wall.

"Good night," the general muttered. "Sleep as late as you like."

"Good night."

Meditatively, the general walked to his own room, the attic in which of all the rooms in the house he chose to sleep. In one

corner there was a plain deal chest of drawers, and in another
a hard bed with one blanket. There were no ornaments, no
pictures but for the photograph of a young woman, dressed in
the fashions of the Edwardian era, with oblique, rather stupid
eyes and pouting lips. She was his wife who had died childless
after they had been married for two years – after his disgrace.
He looked at her face for a long time, almost in perplexity, as
though he were expecting those lips to cease pouting and tell
him something. Then he crossed to the chest of drawers and
opened it. Slowly, caressively, he fingered a faded snapshot
with one end torn from it and the surface gone blotchy. It was
a young man in a subaltern's uniform, his weak face divided
horizontally by a moustache.

He, too, was dead.

The general was up at six o'clock, his usual hour, the
following morning. First, he did exercises for fifteen minutes
before his open window, taking an oddly sensual delight in the
co-ordination of a still athletic body. Then he had his cold bath:
and again it pleased him that he should not yet have become
flabby. He ran a hand down his side, staring at his body with
its many wounds as though it were not his own.

Then he dressed and tip-toed downstairs to get the breakfast.
He began by laying the table for them both, but later changed
his mind and put the boy's things on to a tray. He was
extraordinarily meticulous, taking out a clean tray-cloth and
putting the marmalade and sugar into special little pots.
Then he fried an egg and bacon, and made the toast. He
moved swiftly, competently, with obvious experience of all
these things.

At last the tray was ready and he began to carry it upstairs.
But then an after-thought came to him. Flushing a little with
that same glow under his tanned skin, he went into the garden
and cut some white roses. These he arranged in a vase and put
on the tray. He tip-toed upstairs.

But the boy met him on the landing, fully dressed. He must
have been watching him as he climbed the stairs, so careful not
to make the slightest noise. "Oh, goodness!" he exclaimed.
"You really shouldn't have done this, sir. I've been up for
ages, packing."

"I thought you'd like your breakfast in bed," the general said rather foolishly. He walked into the boy's room, the boy following. "I'd hoped you'd sleep on. You seemed so tired . . ."

"As a matter of fact there's nothing I loathe quite so much. I can never balance a tray on my knees and crumbs always get into my pyjamas. But as you have brought it up, I might as well eat it here. Have you had yours?"

The general nodded. He never had more than a cup of tea and a biscuit. "I'll leave you then." As he closed the door, the scars on his cheek gleamed oddly as though dragged downward by the two sagging lines of the mouth.

The general walked down the corridor to his attic room. Slowly he stretched out on the hard bed and buried his face in the pillow. One hand twisted the blanket in a soundless anguish.

BILLY & BUD

Michael Leech

IT WAS VERY curious how he suddenly recalled things long
past . . .

Billy stood staring at the foot of the stairs as he entered the
house, remembering an event of twenty years before.

He had come home, on a warm spring evening with the
chestnuts in bursting bud in the park, with a man – not an
uncommon experience at twenty-five, when the blood ran hot
and a pickup wasn't hard to find – and as they had entered his
hallway, this hallway, the new friend had commented on the
curiously carved finial of the staircase. He had explained later
that he was a maker of furniture, working in an East London
factory, and he was interested in woods.

His name was Bud, he was twenty-two, and he was, Billy
recalled with a tug at his heart, very beautiful. Lean and
well-made, with a mane of long blond hair. They had made
love in romantic, exciting ways, rolling about on the worn
carpet before the gas fire, knocking over a vase of flowers,
eventually falling into bed breathless with anticipation to get
down to a bout of passionate love that had lasted for *hours*.

Oh, thought Billy with a gasp, those times when you could
do it all night! How strange that he should suddenly recall and
so vividly, Bud – the beautiful carpenter, with the funny accent,

the finely-made lips, the lean body like a young lion . . . and all, until this very moment, practically forgotten.

Oh well, a couple of decades before there had been many visitors to the narrow house on Bramwell Road. Now there were no footsteps on the stairs, no letting out of exhausted, satisfied men at six in the morning, to tom-cat back to work while he, smiling Billy, went back upstairs to repair the ravaged room. He didn't regret one of those episodes – well, maybe one, but who was to know which of your lovers would turn out to be a dark card in the pack? Billy was a fatalist, calm even in the face of catastrophe – and there had been one or two of those in his life. Even the events of the past month, traumatic though they had been, had not thrown him into despair.

Yet how strange it was that he should forget so completely such an incident, only to be reminded of it by the carving on a staircase. It was not as if Bud had been a one-night stand. They had met again, and again, and over several weeks it had developed into what Chicky, Billy's bosom friend and a marvellous chatterbox and observer of life from his corner bar-stool, had even started to call an affairette.

No. It hadn't been that. It had, potentially, been much more dangerous. So much so that Billy had become afraid – an old problem, and the fresh eagerness of Bud, looking at life from the starting viewpoint of a new arrival, had made him feel he was being backed into a corner. There was not much difference in age, but Billy had far more experience.

He moved away and the look of hurt puzzlement in Bud's beautiful grey eyes had not helped. It lingered. It made Billy feel guilty. Guilt made him back right off: he had dropped Bud with his naive ideas of love – well, they had seemed naive at the time – and not seen him again.

Chicky had made him feel better – "He's young, darling, he'll get over it" – during one of their nightly bar chats. It was just another episode and Billy had reassured himself by saying that they weren't really suited. His search for "the right one" would go on – and then he and Chicky had turned to a favourite occupation, dishing friends. Chicky had a wide acquaintanceship and his lines of communication stretched everywhere. Billy had often said he really ought to be called Spider, sitting at the middle of a web, but Chicky felt that having a hairy body and eight legs ("Eight darling – imagine *them* all waving in the air at the same time!") wasn't really his style . . .

Bud, the flame of such a short time, was forgotten. Well, not quite. Almost a year later Chicky had had a piece of news, quite a shocking piece of news, but by that time Billy had put not a few men between him and the leonine young carpenter with the golden skin and the magic lips . . . even another affairette as Chicky again deemed it, with a South American flight attendant, and his memories had become glazed and faded. Funny how memories came back. "Proust's madeleine" Chicky would have said – he read voraciously, claiming he had nothing else to do in bed – if Chicky was still around. Maybe he was. Billy had lost touch with him long ago. Poor old Chicky, always gossiping and gazing, always expected to be the clown – yet no one ever wondered if Chicky had had any love life. Boy, thought Billy, I really seem to have lost touch with so many people. I wonder why. Chicky was a sweet fellow, even if he had been, in his own words "Camp as a cockroach's arsehole dear" and no I have no idea where he is. And we were such close chums all those years ago.

He looked again at the wooden finial and then mounted the stair, slowly, a little uncertainly. It was a shock recalling that crazy time, it seemed to have made him a little short of breath. In his flat he made some tea, looked out over the darkening garden as he drank it, and suddenly felt a need for some air. He'd take a walk in the park. Early spring, the air would be good, and even though he no longer considered the possibility of cruising, he might meet someone to have a chat with. He had felt increasingly lonely of late, and even with his strong character he couldn't always rely on his own company. Some friends might retire into bouts of television and video watching, others to self-imposed projects, still others to exercise and health foods, or bizarre religions, but these were not his ways. As he grew older he had indeed become more self-reliant, and it was only now after the recent discoveries that he had felt a need to re-establish friendships. Fatalistic Billy may have been, but he didn't believe in giving up. Even if he ws nudging forty-seven he liked to keep up. Perhaps he'd pop into the pub later.

It was something he hardly ever did now; with no one like Chicky to chat to he felt odd and out-of-place. He was still good-looking in a severe, masculine way, but he knew well that to the mainly trendy young men who crowded the Princess of Wales' bars he was just an old fart, someone to be looked through. Billy had few vanities. He had had a yard-full of fun when he was young, now it was really quite nice just to look and watch others enjoying themselves. Besides there was no possibility now anyway, he had started the slide into middle age, and with the new discoveries about himself virtue was a necessity. "Just because you've had a positive test," the medic had said, "doesn't mean that anything will develop." It might all go away, he might well live for ages. One had to be strong and sensible. There was no point in letting things get you down. He had a lot to live for, even on his own, he would not give up. No, he would not.

It was very peaceful in the park. Great trees were beginning to push out tender leaves, the soil was damp underfoot and here and there flowers glimmered against the dark clumps of bushes. Billy recalled with a grin the impromptu meetings he had had over the years in those shrubberies. They had been fun, all of them, he had nothing but pleasure out of his sexual adventures, good healthy pleasure, celebrations of sex for some mysterious deity of the old ages. There was no one here tonight, and under the yellow light of the lamps no shadows appeared. Then, as he turned a corner beside a lilac bush, he saw a figure on a bench. It was odd, for he knew this particular path went nowhere, and he had seen no one walk by, and certainly the bench had been vacant when he had glimpsed it through a gap in the undergrowth a moment before. He walked on and approached the figure, its face towards the ornamental lake from which a few ducks still quacked now and again. As he did so the figure turned and the light of a street lamp struck full down on a face, thin and handsome, maned with golden hair, a face so suddenly and shockingly familiar that Billy stopped dead. A face that looked at him from his past, with eyes of softest grey, Bud's face undoubtedly Bud's face, but one that had been arrested at about twenty-three or so, just as young as Billy recalled it. Suddenly Billy found strength in his limbs, and without a second look he turned and bolted along the path, across the wet lawns and over a low fence, not stopping until he came to the relative safety of a pavement. He was gasping and perspiring, his breath seemed shorter than ever, and he had to lean up against a tree for long moments before he could trust himself, still trembling, to cross the road and return home.

When he got home he cursed himself. How stupid and silly he had been – ghosts, who could believe in them? A gay ghost at that, a shadow from his past. It was obviously a mistake, he had canned himself into imagining that the almost-forgotten Bud had reappeared in the dim setting beside the lake. It was a look-alike, obviously, someone who, somehow, uncannily resembled the long-dead Bud.

For Bud *was* dead. Chicky had clipped the newspaper and brought it into the pub to show him. One of those screaming Sunday papers – he could see the headline now. *Lovesick Chippie Sawn to Death* and the ensuing couple of paragraphs. He had had a nasty accident with machinery, cut himself up, bled to death when working late at the furniture factory. As he remembered another sentence danced before his eyes, quite forgotten, like Bud, until now. "His employers said that Bud Evans had been morose and involved over the past months, and seemed to be having emotional problems. He tried to overcome these unknown problems, some broken love affair they thought, by working long hours and never going out."

Poor Bud, surely he hadn't met his death because of being in love with him, Billy? It was all so long ago, and Bud had never said anything, nothing at all, just looked reproachfully at him with those large, clear grey eyes that cried for love . . . No, thought Billy, I can't believe he died because he was in love with me. And if he died how could he come back? Nevertheless, it was several weeks before Billy attempted another stroll in the woods, and this time he borrowed a neighbour's dog, ostensibly as a kindness, to take for a walk. It was again evening, the weather warmer, the ducks more vociferous, and while the dog did behave a little oddly as they passed the bench by the lake there was no sign of a figure, ghostly *or* real.

The incident faded in Billy's mind, and suddenly there were other things to think about. He had been feeling a little tired, a little weary, but that could be work which had become dull and routine-like. He was looking after himself well, he did not smoke or drink, he had never, apart from a brief fling when he was a teenager, taken drugs, and now he was following a healthy diet and getting lots of rest. He looked well, he didn't feel out of sorts.

He was in his bath one morning, luxuriating in the warmth while rain beat on the skylight and promised a rather dull, wet day – Flaming June! thought Billy with a laugh as he lazed in the water surveying his body. He had learned to think well of himself too, in a series of classroom meetings with other positively-tested men. Now he looked down at his well-formed chest, his flattish stomach and muscular legs, and gently stroked his flaccid cock recalling for a moment all the pleasure it had given him, and pleased that it still reacted well to fantasy, for his now solo sexual bouts. Pleasure was mounting, as we gently soaped and played with himself, when he became aware that there were two or three purplish blotches on his feet. In sudden shock he pulled one foot towards him and stared. He could perhaps, fool himself that it wasn't what he thought it was, he could pretend it was a chafing shoe, a minor infection. In his heart he knew better. Slowly he dried himself, dressed, and called the office to tell them he would be late since he had a medical visit to make. The hospital would confirm all too quickly what his painfully thumping heart already feared.

It could of course be slow, it could be fast, he told himself over and over again. He informed a couple of friends, and they were duly shocked and promised to help, but he did not want assistance. He'd lived a lone life too long. He had his own ways of facing up to this tragedy, and he would not be too sentimental or silly about it. He tidied up his life, he organized things – there was time for that. Oddly enough he was not regretful, or angry, not even depressed, except at certain quiet midnight times. One of these bouts attacked him as he was slowly preparing for bed one late September evening. He suddenly hated the confines of the house and wanted to get out. Pulling on jeans and boots and a leather jacket he went down stairs, let himself out, and walked.

He did not know how he came to take the way to the park, but before long he was there, under the trees he knew well, still thick leaved, yet dripping damply. A mist cloaked the bushes and hung over the pale street lights, making their illumination soft and diffuse. He passed two men sitting on a bench, holding hands, although they attempted to slide away from each other as he walked by. He grinned at that, the first time he had smiled for some time. "Don't worry," he said aloud to the surprised pair. "Just have a good time!"

He chuckled as he walked and before long his feet took him by the lake, and along the path for the bench. It was odd, he felt as if all this was predestined – somewhere among the clustering trees the ancient arbored spirit was guiding his steps. When he saw, quite suddenly at a turn in the path, the figure seated on the bench, he knew that this was not a foolish notion. Now it was turned towards him and the remembered face was illumined with a smile of welcome. He came nearer, yet slowly for suddenly he was tired and his feet felt unbearably heavy. This time he was not at all afraid. It was as though it had had to happen. He could see that the figure was clothed in some sort of coat, pulled over his shoulders, and as, painfully and fearfully, he drew closer, the coat fell away. Two arms were lifted, and stretched out towards him. In the silence of the quiet path Billy felt sure his sharp intake of breath must be heard. It *was* Bud, indeed it was Bud, and under the loose coat as glowingly beautiful as he had been more than a score of years before, in that park, that very same park . . .

Billy stopped, breathless, and gazed at the young man, marvelling at the blond hair, the skin sweet with youth. Could it be true? Was it really happening? Here was Bud, just as he remembered him, body unmarred with time or accident, and when he very slowly stood up he was really as perfect as Billy so blindingly remembered. For a moment he felt as if he would faint. he stumbled and fell to his knees, he had trouble getting his breath, he could not for a full minute it seemed, lift his head. He just could not believe this was happening – yet, what did it matter, for surely this showed that past mistakes can be rectified, that life still has more secrets than man can fathom? He gazed at the figure above him, wide-armed and welcoming, and felt his eyes filling with warm tears. It was unbelievable, but it was happening. Two gentle grey eyes stared into his, and then the real world dissolved beneath the pressure of an urgent mouth as young and eager as his own once had been.

The two men described how they had found Billy to the attentive yet not very interested policemen. "He was just lying there beside the bench," said one. "No sign of a struggle, no, he just looked very peaceful, very happy." He paused. The other man, still shaken and upset at this encounter with death, broke in. "He was smiling, really smiling. You know I don't think I've ever seen a smile as happy as that . . ."

GINGER ROGERS'S PRIVATE COLLECTION

Robert Leek

For Tim

ONE NIGHT A few weeks ago I was in the middle of explaining about Niord's feet to some friends in The Bar when Ginger came rushing in. His real name is Reginald Rogers, but since he's a redhead and proved to be something of a twinkletoes in drag on the occasion of one of our fancy-dress rages, "Ginger" has clung.

Ginger appeared to be hyperventilating. He calmed down a little over a tall L&P with something strong in it, while I continued my tale. It was about a Nordic giantess – I'd forgotten her name, but it was something like Skating – being given the chance to choose a divine husband by his feet, which was all she could go by, for the rest of him and of the other contenders was hidden. So she chose Niord, the God of the Sea, mistaking him for Baldur, the God of the Sun. Because presumably his were the fairest and cleanest. They did get married, but in the end split up, like the Waleses, because they couldn't sleep in each other's company, and she went into the mountains and became a ski-goddess. End of story.

It went down like a cup of cold sick, I'm afraid. Shamus just said "awesome', giggled, had a coughing fit and rushed to the loo; only old Warren thoughtfully confessed to having been something of a foot-fetishist himself, in his day. After which they toddled off in search of more entertaining company and I was left with Ginger, who was nervously sipping his drink.

"What's eating you?" I asked, hoping at least he would stay.

"I wonder . . . if you could help me, Michael." (He always uses my full name, just like my sexy social science teacher at college used to do – he was a redhead too.) "I'm in a bit of a fix.

"Pleased to oblige, Ginger – though I must confess to being a bit hard up for cash just now . . . I know that even millionaires have occasional liquidity problems, but . . ."

"Oh dear, oh dear, no, no, nothing as . . . sordid as that. Don't you run a print gallery?"

"I do. The best assortment in town. Ask Shamus – he's an expert. Shamus!" (My pixie'd emerged from the toilet, but seemed disinclined to rejoin me; perhaps he thought my ski-goddess story reflected unfavourably on the usual state of his feet.) "The trouble is, no one these days seems to be much into buying prints."

"I'm sorry to hear that. So I take it you have a fair collection in stock?"

"Far too many, I'm afraid. Framed and all."

"Oh – excellent." Upon which, apparently much cheered, he told me something about his urgent problem. Earlier that evening he'd received a phone call from his mother in Tauranga, to tell him that his favourite cousin was about to fly in from Uganda the next night. Cousin Aidan, coming home for the first time in seven years.

"A diplomat?" I asked.

No – that would have been all right. Aidan was, of all things, a missionary – a very ardent and successful one. Besides, they had been really close when they were striplings. And since the flight came in so late – in the middle of the night in fact – Aidan could hardly be expected to travel straight on to Tauranga. So Mum and Aunt and Uncle had assured him that dear Reggie

(Ginger, that is) would be only too pleased to collect him and put him up for the night. Ginger was indeed more than happy to do so; but it presented him with the problem of extensive and urgent redecorating.

"Why? I've never seen your apartment, but I gather it's quite choice."

"So it is." He sighed and drained his fortified L&P. "There's no point in talking about it: you've got to see it for yourself. Mind coming along for a quick perusal?"

It sounded temptingly like being invited to inspect Ginger's etchings, something I'd long since been dying to do; but I was mordantly aware that there was nothing like the usual *double entendre* to be inferred. It so happened that etchings were my special domain, and that Ginger's pressing problems really had something to do with something like etchings. So I sloshed down the last of my pink gin, and called out to Shamus, who was chatting up someone at the other end of the bar. My part-timer, I explained to Ginger.

"Work or play?"

"Both. He also is a part-time student, majoring in art history."

"Nice." There was a speculative glint in Ginger's eyes as he said that. Just as well I'm not the jealous type.

"Not bad. He looks as if he's set up for the night. Good for him. Let's go." I followed Ginger down the stairs and to his car – and felt heartened by hearing him muttering: "Oh Michael, oh Michael, you're a godsend."

It was a short ride to Herne Bay; the apartment, with a panoramic view of the bridge and the upper harbour, proved indeed quite choice: wall-to-wall dove-grey shagpile as lush as a Waikato paddock in spring, custom-made Swedish-style furniture, and so on. But Ginger's problem was immediately apparent. His beautifully stark walls, and there seemed to be many square metres of them, were covered with images – mostly photographs, both black-and-white and colour, but also oils, gouaches, charcoal sketches and lithographs – of penises. Dozens, scores of penises, of every conceivable shape, size and colour. Flanked and backed, of course, by an eye-scorching array of balls.

He stood there in the middle of his living room looking quite crestfallen, while I gazed at this extraordinary display of male pride with bated breath.

"My portrait gallery," he said at last. "My hall of fame, if you like. A true representation of every lay in my life."

"Good God," I said.

"Yes," he said. "Hardly the thing for a missionary, don't you think? Let me pour you something. What was it again? Pink gin?"

"Yes, thanks, Ginger. Make it a stiff one," I said, at which both of us broke out in hysterics.

Ginger busied himself behind his well-stocked liquor cabinet, while I examined his collection of wall decorations. They were superbly hung – oh sorry! – and lit by expertly placed individual ceiling spots. One would expect a certain monotony from such a singular subject, but there was a surprising degree of variety: jaunty, sullen, gross and delicate dicks; hooded and unhooded dicks; gnarled, coarse-skinned and wrinkled dicks alongside ones sleek, silky and juicy like French asparagus spears; dicks boldly swinging from their bushes between parted thighs. Dicks barely glimpsed amid Rembrandt-esque glooms, and others gleaming like polished trophies in a blaze of light.

"How did you get them all?" I asked. "They're quite splendid."

"Aren't they?" Ginger said smugly, handing me my drink and placing a bowl of Japanese rice nibbles on his glass-topped mahogany coffee table. "I'm proud to say: but for a few, I took them all myself. I've got a wonderful camera, and though I have no pretensions to being a second Robert Mapplethorpe, I'm a pretty deft hand with the shutter. Besides, even as an amateur one can perform minor miracles in the dark room with the enlarger. And these days, with photocopiers. In a few instances, when I felt I, or my camera, hadn't done the subjects justice, I commissioned artist friends to enhance the best of the shots – pictorially or graphically, as you can see. There were just one or two who preferred to take . . . self-portraits. And one who presented me with an entire portfolio of magazine pics for which he'd modelled. One of the self-portraitists is a commercial photographer, but I'm none too pleased with his product. The image is grossly flattering; I suspect he used a trick lens."

"And . . . can you really put faces to them all?"

"Pretty well. Though I must confess, some of the faces were decidedly less memorable than the private assets."

"That full-colour one looks familiar . . ."

"The one with the gold ring through the prepuce? Yes he makes the rounds, I believe. Frankly, that adornment did nothing for me; it proved to be a decided nuisance. I suppose it depends on what you're into. But I'm pleased with the shot, and the print; it's almost surreal."

"Not as surreal as this one here. Does he really have tattoos all over it?"

"Oh yes. A miniature tiki on the glans, a manaia crawling up the shaft, and intricate spirals on the scrotum. God knows how it was done, on all that mobile skin. It must have been sheer agony, too. And those spirals were hardly worth the bother, they're all but hidden behind the hair. He's got splendid matching designs on his buttocks, and around his tits. Delicious. A walking work of art. Dear, silly Timoti! Lovely hunk, though."

"Hmm. They're all wonderful, wonderful. That black one with those highlights on the skin and that intriguing little wart to the left . . . well! Interesting, though, there are no . . . uhm . . ."

"Erections?"

"Yes. Don't you . . . ?"

"Of course I do, Michael. Nothing like a good one. But – no. Not on the wall. A little quirk of mine, I admit. I can't fully account for it. Except, perhaps, by wanting something left to the imagination. And memory."

Carrying our clinking drinks we toured the rest of the apartment. The kitchen, where wall space was limited to some narrow panels between the cupboards and the dresser. The master bedroom, for which Ginger had reserved some of his most spectacular pieces that, I reflected, might well have an inhibiting effect on the space's less generously endowed overnighters. There was even one in his walk-in wardrobe. Black and white dominated in the coolly functional en suite bathroom, in a series of finely executed lithographs from the hand of a well-known artist; whereas Ginger had dedicated his study to sumptuously erotic colour, mostly in oils, pastels and gouaches. One pseudo-Caravaggio number, all pale umbers, deep velvety browns and purples, in a heavily embossed burnished-bronze frame, stationed between Ginger's leather-bound first editions of Dickens, Thackeray, Trollope and Eliot, really took my eye. It all but dripped off the canvas.

"Holy Mother," I muttered.

"Hush, Michael," Ginger said sternly. "No profanities, now; I know you're of respectable and devout Irish stock. Yes, I must say, he was quite a find. Not much of a stimulating intellect or conversationalist, I'm afraid . . . but one can't have everything, can one? And, well: this speaks for itself."

"In lieu of conversation." We had another fit of hysterics, and Ginger tinkled off with my glass to top it up, leaving me to drink my fill of this particular, almost three-dimensional pictorial dork. I was sure it would have sent Shamus – an idolater of Italian mannerists and large dicks – into ecstasy, and almost wished he were there. Its brushwork was nothing short of masterly. Every pubic hair had its own distinctive highlight, and one could almost feel the weight of that boyish scrotum in one's palm. There was a slight reddish discolouration on the foreskin, to the right, as if someone had over-eagerly, accidentally bitten it. The delicate blue marbling of the veins along the shaft had been caught to perfection. Magic realism. My lifelong allegiance to abstract expressionism went soundlessly down the gurgler.

"I wonder," I said, when Ginger came back with both our glasses refilled to the brim, "how on earth you can . . . concentrate on your work. With this to look at. It must be very distracting."

"Not at all. Consider the relationship between my desk chair, my desk and word-processor, and this picture. In order to see one, I resolutely have to turn away from the other. They function like perfect antidotes in my thinking space. Very salutary, I can assure you."

"So – do you select your partners simply on the basis of this? Their potential?"

"Good Lord, no – of course not, Michael. One never knows.

No more than that giantess of yours, when she picked Niord, because he had beautiful and well-washed feet. My collection is strictly retrospective. The live joy is always in the surprise if the full revelation. So may be the disappointment, of course. But neither of them, in my book, have much to do with shapes and sizes. I've been bored to sleep by foot-sized monsters, and experienced delight upon delight with dainty little dicks that lasted the distance. Ultimately personality is all that counts.''

"I'm with you there," I sighed, thought of Shamus and felt relieved when Ginger took me back to his living room, and the airy view of the Waitemata and the bridge.

"I take it you can see my problem," he said, after we'd settled down in piles of silken cushions, and nibbled some of the nibbles from the bowl on the glass-topped mahogany coffee table. "Even without those pictures he'll find my lifestyle obscene enough, used as he is to squatting in mud huts and sharing bowls of rice and porridge with Aids-ridden natives. Dear Aidan – he really is a treasure, you know. I wouldn't offend him for the world. But it's not my fault I made a few handy millions on the stock market before the crash, and now earn heaps with my silly TV soap scripts. I *have* taken on half a dozen Tear Fund children, mostly in his part of the world. I've got the most adorable photographs of those boys . . .''

"?"

"Oh, shut your wicked mind, Michael! Of their angelic wide-eyed innocent faces, of course. I don't subscribe to AMBLA. Now: can you help me? I assure you, I'll pay you generously for your services. A couple of days' work at top consultancy rates, plus a premium hire for all your framed prints. I'll even throw in a reception of sorts, after Aidan's left for Tauranga, if you like. Admittedly, time is short, but I'll do a quick ringaround of all my capitalist art-collecting friends, and if you come up with the goods, you may just sell your entire surplus stock.''

I gave that some shrewd thought. We both sipped our drinks over some quietly tuneful Mozart from Ginger's remote-control CD sound system. The lights of the Waitemata twinkled in my eyes, and my two-or-three-too-many pink gins pinkled in my brains.

"I'll make you a counter offer," I said. "I'll charge nothing for my two days' work, nor for the hire of the prints, provided you give me a free hand, and throw that party you mentioned. In exchange for your permission to exhibit an anthology from your collection – if you like, anonymously – in my gallery. Just for a couple of weeks. The next couple of weeks."

"It's a deal," he said. And ordered a stretched limousine to take me home. "Seventy-eight prints I need. I'll expect you at ten-thirty tomorrow morning. I'll have strong, black coffee ready. And give my regards to Shamus."

Needless to say, I didn't go home to sleep that night. I even phoned Shamus out of bed, much to his chagrin (and that of whoever was snoring alongside him), to help me deframe and reframe appropriate items from my stock. I rang through an ad to the *Herald*, and a message to the arts page editor. I designed a stark yet effective black-and-white poster. DICKS – A PRIVATE COLLECTION I called my forthcoming exhibition, and my mind was filled with them.

Shamus, still thick-eyed for lack of sleep, was off seeing to the printing and distribution of the posters by the time I got to Ginger's Herne Bay apartment. It was redolent with strong coffee, but Ginger wasn't there. He'd been called out early for a TV script revision session, the housekeeper told me; the meeting might take all day. The housekeeper, by the way, was not your usual prim middle-aged motherly type, but a spunky young Rarotongan, with the most wonderful conspiratorial grin on his face. He introduced himself as Douglas and was helpful and obliging in a most charming way. I tried to match him up with one of the unmistakably Polynesian privates in Ginger's collection, but he never gave himself away.

Although it was a mammoth job, I managed it with a great deal of satisfaction and pride. By mid-afternoon Shamus – fully recovered by then – came to collect Ginger's pictures and, eagerly assisted by young Douglas, carried them off in a discreet little rental van. When Ginger finally came home, at five-thirty, all his dicks had been replaced by land, sea and cityscapes, still-lifes, flower arrangements, genre pieces, a fair sprinkling of abstracts and – I confess, tongue-in-cheek selected – devotional prints. To fill the space of that provocative oil-painting in the study, I'd found a modern expressionist crucifixion featuring the two thieves on either side, with copiously filled loin-cloths. And I'd managed to match the number with the gold ring through the foreskin in the living room with a crude woodcut of a horn-clad and arrow-pierced Papuan highlander, representing that most ambiguous of all holy men, St Sebastian. Ginger was elated and took me out for dinner at the Regent. Meanwhile, Shamus and Douglas had set about hanging the rest of Ginger's prize collections of dicks around the exhibition space of my gallery.

I can only relate half the sequel at first hand. Ginger presumably drove out to Mangere Park to pick up his cousin late that night, after our sumptuous Regent dinner; meanwhile Shamus had had to prevent a small community standards posse from ransacking my Parnell gallery. I'd never in my life enjoyed such publicity; by the time I got there, about ten the following morning, I found the footpath thronged with Remuera ladies furiously objecting to the deliberate destruction of our moral standards, and my usually quiet gallery aswarm with people scrutinising Ginger's marvellous dicks. Shamus had shown the good sense to stick red dots alongside all the works we'd put on display, but I hate to think of the fortunes we could have made if any of them had been for sale. The centrepiece was the one from the study; Shamus and I took turns standing guard over it, that first day, and explaining its artistic qualities to the gawping multitudes. The brilliant play of light and shadow, the sophisticated composition, the delicate sensuousness of the colours used, the wonderful brushwork. It was a treat to watch some of my less inhibited patrons - and matrons – thoughtfully lick their parted lips and succumb to an erotic trance, in the course of listening to our recitals. This was, indeed, the Mona Lisa of dicks. I must confess that, in the course of all this, I became quite obsessed with a desire to know who its live model had been. So, I suspect, did Shamus.

Meanwhile, the missionary from Uganda had come and gone. Not long before closing time – the gallery was still buzzing with visitors – Ginger strolled in, hiding behind a pair of large shades. He gave me the thumbs-up sign and waved in the direction of the café across the road. I pointed at my wristwatch and signalled the number of minutes it would take me to join him.

It took longer than I'd expected. My staunch supporters Myra Scofield and Jean Littlejohn, who never give their extensive circle of friends and relations anything other than prints bought from my gallery for birthdays and weddings, had jointly homed in on the Kodachrome tattoo job, the one with the tiki on the glans and the spiral designs – only just glimpsable through the pubic thicket – on the balls, and insisted on postcard-sized reproductions, to mail overseas to all their friends for Christmas. Something earthy and truly indigenous, they both felt, ever so much more interesting than pohutukawa blossoms and views of Mount Egmont ("Taranaki!" Jean corrected Myra vociferously, "Who was Egmont anyway?"), so all I could do was tell them that I'd have a chat with the collection's anonymous owner and let them know.

I finally managed to clear the gallery by a quarter-to-seven, having sent Shamus home with a bonus, a bottle of Dom Perignon and the suggestion of a good night's sleep, and joined Ginger in the café. I was worried that he might have grown impatient, but after installing himself comfortably under one of the red-and-white umbrellas on the tiny outdoor terrace, he'd had a perfect view of the goings-on in the gallery and thoroughly enjoyed himself.

Dizzy with fatigue, I was grateful for the stimulation of a kingsize *caffe latte*, and got him to tell me about the visit of his missionary cousin. Yes, Aidan had arrived last night at 0.40 a.m., had been delayed for a couple of hours, and it had been well after 3.00 a.m. before they got to Herne Bay. There, the carnal and spiritual cousins had caught up on one another's lives – or as much of those lives as each was prepared to give away – until dawn had announced itself behind the imposing silhouette of Rangitoto. Ginger had not found himself nearly as discomfited as he'd expected to be: Aidan clearly revelled in his return to comfort and civilization, and had not even blenched at the popping of a bottle or two of champagne in his

honour. They had retired, pretty sozzled, about five – Ginger
to his chastened master bedroom. Aidan to the spare one.

"Oh my God," I said at that point in Ginger's account.

"Precisely. The one room overlooked. I never even gave it
a thought. I got up at eleven – I'd given Douglas the day
off – and set about preparing brunch. Aidan emerged soon
after, a little jetlagged of course but suffering from nothing
some healthy exercises on my sundeck and a bracing shower
wouldn't fix. He was in great spirits when he joined me in the
dinette for fresh croissants, juice and coffee. He made a point of
commenting on my – your – wonderful collection of prints and
then suddenly came out with it: still wide awake, at five, he'd
spent half an hour studying the array of dicks on the walls of
his bedroom. He'd been bewildered, astonished . . . delighted.
"What a wonderful celebration of life, Reggie," he said. "What
variety, what splendour. So . . . uplifting, after those rather
sterile abstractions in your lounge, and those floral pieces
and old-hat landscapes. The Lord gave us cocks! Aren't they
marvellous? The one true sign of His yielding the ongoing work
of creation to humankind. You shouldn't hide those enthralling
pictures in your guest room – they should be displayed boldly, all
over your lovely apartment! I was particularly taken by the long
arching one, evidently uncircumcised, with that prominent vein
meandering all the way from the blond jungle-down – the very
river of life!'"

And so on. Aidan turned out to have a passion for penises.
He gave Ginger graphic accounts of spectacular specimens he'd
come across in Africa. Monumental black cocks decorated
with garish colours for tribal dance rituals and initiation
ceremonies. Runes inscribed on the butts of chieftains, and
their significance. The pride young men took in the size and
shape of their balls. The idols they carved to celebrate their
masculine endowments. To conclude, he undertook to send
Ginger some of the prize pieces from his own collection of
African genitalia. He had offered them to his mission for a
fund-raising exercise, but the response had been negative.
"You've no idea how stick-in-the-mud some of those people
are," he'd said. "They seem to be unaware of things going
on right under their very noses. Oh Reggie, these croissants

are scrumptious. And those wonderful Ferndale cheeses, and Kerikeri honeys! How shall I ever again be content with a subsistence diet of rice, soya beans and milk powder?"

Ginger had only just managed to get Aidan back to Mangere in time for his domestic flight to Tauranga, but he'd wrenched from him a commitment to stop over for a night before returning to the dark continent, ten days hence. It provided the perfect sanction for my fortnight's exhibition – or did it? In retrospect, Ginger wouldn't have minded having his private collection back where it belonged, but on the other hand he felt inspired by Aidan's missionary zeal. He should not deprive the art-loving public of Auckland of its opportunity to share his delight in this most potent emblem of creative power. Also, he thought Myra's and Jean's desire to broadcast the cultural essence of our country in their Christmas cards was worthy of consideration. Our vibrations, it seemed, were beginning to harmonise. Once again we dined expensively and elaborately up the road, and once again a stretched limousine saw us home in the early hours of the morning; for both of us are principled opponents of driving whilst under the influence.

The next morning Ginger and I (or rather, Shamus, Ginger and I: Ginger confirming my hunch in The Bar, took rather a shine to Shamus, so I expect there will be a new item in his collection) conferred at length about the postcard issue, under the watchful eye of charming young Douglas, who'd come along to the gallery to look after our creature-comforts in the form of fresh coffee and delicious Danish pastries. We settled on a dozen of Ginger's most spectacular dicks – including, of course, the pseudo-Caravaggio; my obsessive question was burning on my lips, but I realised that this was not the proper occasion to have it answered. For most of our selections Ginger merely needed to supply the negatives; he himself took excellent photographs of the remaining items. My backstreet printers, who'd taken care of the exhibition posters at such short notice, fast-tracked our designer Christmas cards too, and we could offer the results to our clients before the week was out. Myra and Jean were most gratified, and so were many of their fellow customers: the reproductions were selling like hot cakes. What's more, the news appears to have spread like wildfire. Orders are coming in from

dealer galleries and card shops in all the main centres. It looks
as if after eighteen dire months of penury I can finally phone
my bank manager to black out my overdraft. So although I'm
far from sure about that of my country, my personal economy
is decidedly looking up.

But I'm running ahead of myself. There was still Ginger's
cocktail party, the following weekend. It turned into quite a
grand occasion. The kerb outside his apartment was lined with
late-model continental, British and American cars (none of your
Japanese trash; I shamefacedly hid my twelve-year-old little
Datsun rustbucket up a side-street), and the apartment itself
was bristling with money. Douglas and Shamus joined forces to
serve the delectable goodies and the manhattans, white ladies,
daiquiris, margaritas and blue angels, while Ginger himself saw
to my and my print collection's public relations. And he did a
sterling job: little red dots were appearing everywhere, inspiring
me to the impromptu announcement that I'd donate ten percent
of the gross takings to Aidan's mission in Uganda. After which
the takings got even grosser: my Papuan St Sebastian fetched
twice the price I'd dared ask for it in my gallery.

I hadn't been in such high spirits for months – years. Who
wouldn't be, doing as well as I was by doing good? Besides, I
must say, the ambience had an exhilarating effect. In one fell
swoop, I'd acquired a class of clients I'd courted in vain for years.
In order to keep my wits about me, I'd let all those dangerously
fancy cocktails pass by and confined myself to Ginger's ample
supply of unadulterated chilled Veuve Cliquot, the sparkle of
which perfectly matched that of the Waitemata at our feet on
this fine early-summer afternoon. I was surrounded by financial
wizards, corporate lions and TV celebrities; some even stopped
for casual chats. One of the electronic media's grand dames,
who had invested in one of my finest abstracts, introduced
herself as Catherine ("just call me Cath") and confessed that she
had visited my exhibition in Parnell earlier that week, and had
been most vexed that all the items on display had already been
sold. "Any time you get a fresh supply of that . . . genre," she
said, thoughtfully wiping a smear of lipstick from her cocktail
glass, "will you promise, Michael, to let me know?" And she
wrote her address and unlisted phone number on her lace

handkerchief, and tucked it in my breast pocket. After which we discussed, at length, the various merits of small and large, plain, ringed and tattooed, light and dark dicks. I could not escape the distinct impression that she was almost as much of an expert on the subject as Ginger was. But then, after downing her last daiquiri she was, to my surprise, helped down the steps to a waiting cab by her very butch-looking ladyfriend.

The excitement of two weeks that had begun in The Bar, with the story of the Giantess and Niord's sexy feet, suitably culminated in Aidan's visit to the gallery on the eve of his return to Uganda, to take receipt of the generous cheque for his mission. The two cousins walked in together, and there was no mistaking the family connection. Aidan was red-haired and brown-eyed, too, and I'd never realised how spectacular the combination of a permanent African tan and a copper-coloured mop can be, particularly when offset by the stern, spotless white linen of a missionary's outfit. I'd fancied Ginger in frustrated silence for years, but I went positively weak-kneed at the sight of Aidan. Yet – dare I confess it? – the enthusiasm he inspired in me was of an aesthetic and spiritual rather than a sensual nature. Only fleetingly an image of something luscious curled about by copper-coloured pubic hair crossed my mind, but I sternly dismissed it with a stinging slap on my own wrist. When he gave me a startled brown-eyed look at this, I told him that at this time of year and time of day, we were occasionally plagued by mosquitos.

I took him on a guided tour of the exhibition – which he loved, without knowing where the collection came from. On this occasion I found myself not much interested in the display; most of the dicks had lost their charm. I had eyes only for the beholder: the strong, slim, graceful figure in white, his expressive hands, mouth, the tilt of his flame-coloured head. Every trim hair on it had its own distinctive highlight. He had wonderfully spiritual things to say about all those anonymous genitals – mostly quotes, I believe, from the Song of Songs – but they have slipped my mind. All I remember is that sonorous, humorous voice, that beautiful face, its radiance, its ineffable innocence. I realized why Ginger, who truly loved his cousin, had wished to chasten the walls for him; I also, finally, understood the meaning of all those dicks for Ginger: they had constituted a wry memorial, never a prospectus. Aidan himself brought me back to earth when, near the end of our perambulation, he halted in front of our riveting centrepiece and became quite absorbed.

"The Mona Lisa of . . . don't you think?" I offered meekly.

"Quite. A perfect realization of the . . . Platonic ideal," he agreed. "It verily radiates generative power. Wonderful, wonderful. A great work of art. Oh, uhm, alas . . . it looks like the time has come for my return to duty and sordid reality in Africa. Thank you, Michael, for this truly delightful and inspiring exhibition. And once more, of course, for your generous donation."

"My pleasure, I assure you." We solemnly shook hands and Ginger took off with Aidan for a quick meal on their way to the airport. I was left alone – well, not quite, Shamus was still there – to gaze upon my favourite dick. When was I going to find out whose it was?

"Isn't it awesome?" Shamus whispered, behind my shoulder. I turned and looked at him. His freckled pixie face bore an expression of something close to reverence, and he licked his lips as if he imagined tasting it. Then he caught my eyes and blushed. "Sorry, Mike," he said.

The next day Ginger phoned to tell me that he'd agonized all night after Aidan had left, but finally had decided to sell the entire collection. I exulted: it would make him a fortune. It would make both of us a fortune. I remembered the lace handkerchief tucked in my breast pocket at the cocktail party. Still, I was mystified.

"But why?" I asked him. "Aidan loved them. He told you to plaster them boldly all over your walls. As you used to."

"Isn't he a darling? I know. That's exactly why, though. He's made me realize I don't need them. Besides, I've become attached to your prints. I realize most of them were sold, at the party, but they deserved to be. You *have* got the best assortment in town. I'll spend a day, next week, selecting some new items from your remaining stock. I'll happily commission some more. So: for the time being, keep my privates on display, and remove the "sold" stickers. I'll tell you something, Michael: we could turn this into an annual event. I'll continue to photograph the dicks of my lays. It's become a ritual of sorts. But you can have them, in future. The prints, that is."

"I'm confident, Ginger, that there's a market for them."

"I know. Wonderful, isn't it? Just think of the funds we can send to Aidan for his mission."

"My sentiment exactly. I'm going to call some prospective buyers straight away. But before I do that, I *must* ask you . . ."

Unfortunately, he'd already hung up.

The media-woman of the handkerchief was the first one I phoned; I also got in touch with Jean and Myra. I went through my regular client mailing list and spent the whole evening on the blower. The one person I failed to get hold of was Shamus, whom I meant to ask to come in early, to help me remove the red dots. It occurred to me that I'd seen little of Shamus after five o'clock of late. I felt a little peeved, for it obliged me to drive in, close on eleven, to remove those stickers myself. My grumpiness was relieved by this unlooked-for late-night chance to have another look at the matchless pseudo-Caravaggio. I'd already determined an exorbitant price for it, but reflected that I might forego the profit and keep the masterpiece myself. I left a message to that effect on Shamus's answerphone.

When I arrived at the gallery at ten in the morning, a number of my prospective buyers were already queuing up – including the eager television producer. I returned the lace handkerchief to her, with thanks, and let her and the others in. They dispersed around the gallery like hounds after their respective hares. Ginger's collection of dicks gleamed in the early-morning sunlight, and I felt on top of the world. I enjoyed hearing Jean and Myra squabbling over the modestly-priced original of the Kodachrome tattoo job. However, Catherine, the handkerchief diva, descended on me like an unforseen thundercloud.

"Michael! How come *my* priceless picture's already been sold?"

"Sorry, Cath . . . which one?"

She imperiously seized my hand and led me to her – our, my – favourite painting. I distinctly remembered removing the "sold" sticker the night before, with some misgivings. Now, not just one but three red dots blazed from the virginal white wall alongside it. I was dumbfounded.

"It looks like someone has beaten you to it, dear lady. Though I must confess, I haven't the faintest idea who! – How about the one with the little gold ring?"

"I don't care for ringed cocks, I like them unadorned, *au naturel*," she muttered crossly, and left me in a huff. I felt mortified; but fortunately Jean and Myra had meanwhile resolved their differences. Jean had yielded the tattoo job to Myra, and consoled herself with the large black prick with the intriguing wart alongside it. It would look just splendid in her hallway, she felt, between the mirror and the umbrella stand.

Still mystified, I phoned Ginger and told him the story about our Mona Lisa. There was a moment of uneasy silence on the other end of the line.

"Ginger . . .?"

"Yes, Michael. Yes: I'm afraid it's sold."

"You mean . . . you're keeping it yourself?"

"No. How much were you going to ask for it?"

I named the exorbitant price I'd had in mind – and, I was sure, it would have fetched.

"Goodness me . . . well, I'll see to it that you get your commission on that. Someone put a deposit on it, last night."

A bright light started flashing in my mind.

"The . . . model? Please, do tell me, Ginger. I've just got to know who . . ."

"No . . . Michael. No, he didn't. Anyway, don't be silly. I told you that he has his . . . limitations. No: his new partner bought it. I'll send you a cheque. Why don't you come for a drink at The Bar tonight?"

"All right, I will . . . thanks, Ginger."

* * *

Within three days, the entire collection was sold. The formidable Catherine, to my relief, did come back and buy the bathroom series of lithographs. I was preparing my Christmas exhibition, and advised my clients they could come and collect their purchases. Ginger's dicks were making place for post-modern representations of the sacred-season's icons, such as Madonna-and-Child in a supermarket and another one in a women's refuge, shepherds herding their flocks to the abattoir, and the three Magi riding tanks through the desert under a sky full of scud missiles. My thoughts often, devoutly, went out to Aidan, eating porridge and lentils in Uganda, but in more profane moments I still was often drawn to the contemplation of my Mona Lisa of dicks – the last one to linger in the stock room. I wondered when the new owner would turn up to claim it.

Shamus continued to be helpful around the gallery. In fact, he was as diligent as I'd ever known him to be, but he invariably left early, and he'd become secretive about his private life. What on earth was the matter with him? Nothing untoward, I could tell, because he was as bright as a button. I was beginning to feel extremely frustrated, but I kept my cool. And since he fully deserved it, I decided to present him with a generous gift for Christmas. He was in all day, on the 24th of December, and as closing time loomed after ten hours of record sales, I asked him what he would like to take home from our collection. His freckled pixie face beamed at me with delight.

"You're a darling, Mike," he said, kissing me on both cheeks. "But a bottle of after-shave will do, honest. I'm just going to wrap up my prize."

Upon which he went into the stock room and came out, a moment later, with the Mona Lisa. He carried it to the counter, solemnly, as if it were the Holy Grail. I must have looked the epitome of bafflement.

"Isn't it just awesome?"

"You . . .?"

He nodded and began to pack it expertly, meticulously in brown paper. "Mustn't damage that beautiful frame, must I now . . .? I paid off another instalment last night. Here's the receipt. Ginger told me I could forget about the rest. *His*

Christmas present for us. Ginger's gone all religious, you know, just like you."

"But who do you know, then, who . . ."

"Of course. A perfect likeness, I can assure you. There he is now."

I turned round. In the open doorway, radiant, stood Ginger's Rarotongan housekeeper, Douglas. He looked absolutely adorable and was festively dressed, all in cream, with a tinsel wreath around his black frizz, and he too treated me to a chaste kiss on both cheeks.

"We'll take this home, Shamus and I, and then we're off raving," he said. "You're only young once, they say, don't they? Ginger asked me to ask you if you felt like joining him for the midnight carol service at St Matthew's and a glass of champagne at The Bar, to follow."

"Oh . . . yes . . . of course I do. What an excellent thought . . ."

"Merry Christmas, Mike," Shamus said.

"Merry Christmas, Michael," said Douglas. Their two faces were wreathed in seraphic smiles.

"Merry Christmas . . . boys."

And off they went, carrying the precious parcel between them.

BUTCHER

Simon Lovat

. . . So I WAS in Waitrose, doing my weekly shopping, as you do. Well, not exactly shopping *as such,* I have to admit. More sort of window shopping. I had dropped a single lemon into my wire basket, to avoid suspicion, and was having a marvellous time trawling the aisles for special-offers. Come six-thirty on a Friday evening, it's amazing how many "single gentlemen" are choosing their meat for the weekend at my branch. Naturally, I was dressed in the manner appropriate to my purpose – a pair of black Levi's, a white vest, DMs, a leather jacket, and stubble. I'd omitted the Muir cap, dismissing it as outré.

I patrolled the smooth, calming aisles for some time, trying to establish the butchest way of holding a wire basket containing a single citrus fruit, and at the same time looking out for new friends. I engineered intimate exchanges over the sweet potatoes, and meaningful looks over the mixed herbs, but to no avail. All my targets seemed impervious to my charms. Worse, I squandered an opportunity to strike up a conversation with a cute shop assistant because I couldn't think of anything witty to say on the subject of cat litter. It was going to be one of those days. Sighing, but undeterred, I embarked on yet another circuit of the hushed, sepulchral arena, avoiding eye contact with the dogs.

Ten minutes later I was passing the vegetarian cheeses – for what must have been the fourth time – when I saw this handsome guy at the green counter, where you find all the environmentally friendly products. So I went over to where he was standing, and noticed that he seemed undecided about which colour of recycled toilet paper to purchase. Now if you ask me, I think it's fabulous, all this recycling business. But recycled toilet paper? I just hope it wasn't toilet paper last time. Anyway, the man didn't seem to notice me and moved off, but by this time I was transfixed and trailed off after him, at a discreet distance, feigning interest in whatever I found in front of me every time he stopped to look in my direction. It's what I call the paradox of cruising. You look, but you have to pretend *not* to look. It's an art, and I don't have it. I'm usually caught gawping straight at the object of my affections, and believe me, that's a no-no. In a desperate attempt to make it seem as if I was not, in fact, following this man around the shop, I found myself loading into my basket whatever I happened to be faced with on each occasion that we stopped, like some reverse game of pass the parcel.

This cat and mouse routine continued for some time. By now, I'd acquired a more or less random collection of toiletries, pastas, condiments and so forth, none of which I'd usually buy, and loverboy hadn't so much as smiled my way. Typical. So I gave up and consoled myself with a family pack of M&Ms, which I shoved into my basket on the way to the check out.

As my somewhat eclectic shopping was hurled through the laser by a surly, gum-chewing adolescent wearing too much make-up, who looked as though she hailed from Beckenham, I considered my singleness with a sigh. Perhaps I'd lost the knack? Perhaps I'd lost my looks? Heaven forbid that I had lost both! I resolved to practise my smouldering stare in the mirror as soon as I got home, and promised myself that I'd renew my gym membership. These were my preoccupations as I paid for my goods and loaded them into the brown paper bag provided at the check-out – the kind that rip as soon as you pick them up. Needless to say, I had given up all hope of dinner for two.

Just as I was placing my lemon atop a four-pack of bath

cleaner, I felt a warm presence at my shoulder, surrounded by an aura of Farenheit. Ever the optimist, I turned round with my best "fuck-me" smile plastered across my face, and was confronted not by loverboy, but by a gorgeous Dirk Bogarde lookalike whom I had failed to spot in the course of my wandering. He was looking at me with an intense expression that I recognized at once.

Well, I thought, *it's been a long time coming, but my ship has finally come in.*

Dirk followed me to the lift, and I brushed myself against him as the doors parted for us, and I smiled winningly, in a butch kind of way, over the top of my shopping, which I was clutching to my chest like a hard-won prize. But he wasn't responsive. As the lift ascended to the level of the car park, he didn't say a word and pretended not to look at me, which had me hyper-ventilating into my economy sized yoghurts. I love it when they're silent.

As I was going through the automatic doors to the car park, which sighed open before me like depressed flunkies, he laid a firm, hairy hand on my shoulder.

"Excuse me, sir," he said. "I believe you've been shopping in this store?" His voice was toneless, flat as a sea oppressed by rain.

"Yes," I said, thinking: *ten out of ten for observation.*

I immediately replotted the evening. Discussion of Wittgenstein, over pasta carbonara, was unlikely. A witty conversation built around old Bette Davis movies was probably a more realistic goal . . .

"Would you mind coming with me for a moment?" Dirk asked, cocking his head in the direction of the building from which we'd just emerged. He raised his eyebrows and made off towards the electronic doors, guiding me forward with that gorgeous hand.

"Where are we going?" I said, breathless, my heart banging against my sternum.

"Upstairs to my office," he said.

Of course, he worked there! Smiling to myself, I had visions of having him over a cardboard box in the store-room, but true to his word he led me to a genuine office, whereupon I decided that a desk would provide an acceptable alternative. Once we were in the office he shut the door, and I looked at him for a moment, wondering whether or not to make the first move. I tried another of my butch, stubbly smiles.

"It's no smiling matter, sir," he said in his toneless voice.

"What?"

"I'm afraid I must ask you to show me the contents of your shopping bag."

I stared at him, dumbfounded.

"Why?"

"I have reason to believe that you've been shoplifting, sir."

It was then that I realized I'd made a dreadful mistake. My libido ebbed away. Dinner for one again.

"What nonsense!" I cried.

I pulled out the pasta, recycled toilet paper, yoghurt, bath cleaner, lemon, M&Ms, and the My Little Pony video that I'd bought and laid it all out on the desk in front of him.

"Is that all?" he said, eyeing me with suspicion.

"Yes, of course it is. See for yourself," I said, proffering the patently empty bag for his inspection.

"May I look in your other bag, please?" he said.

I'd bought a few little bits and bobs in Woolworths, immediately before coming to Waitrose. The latest Kitty In My Pocket – that sort of thing. "Be my guest," I said.

He ferreted about in the Woolworths bag for a moment, then pulled out, from god knows where, a bottle of mascara.

"Have you got a receipt for this?" he crowed, his eyes aglitter.

"Well, no," I said, "I've never seen it before."

"You shoplifted it from this store," he said. "I was following you."

"Don't be ridiculous, I'm not a shoplifter," I said.

"You put it into your basket, then let it fall through the wire mesh into your Woolworths bag," he replied. "It's a well known technique."

I was speechless, and hugely affronted. I drew myself up to my full five feet six inches, and looked him straight in the eye. "Do I look like a person who uses mascara?" I said.

Sometimes I say absolutely the wrong thing. It's a shame, really, because I liked Waitrose, and shopping at Kwik-Save just isn't the same . . .

IMPROPERLY DRESSED

Joseph Mills

I KNOW IT'S been absolutely ages but I've been trying hard to find out how best to explain what's happened. In fact I've written dozens of letters to you and torn every one up when something changed (it's all been happening so quickly) or when a better theory came to mind. Those letters were actually very helpful in my decision to let things go on. I could/can pretend I'm merely observing a strange phenomenon for your entertainment.

As you well know, I have always believed that obsessive romantic love is like measles – once you've caught it and got over it/didn't die from it, you're immune forever. I remember telling you and all those other friends, poor weak fools, I thought, who succumbed a second, third or even fourth time, "Once is allowable: you didn't know what was going to happen. You had to see it through to the bitter end. But more than once and you're addicted."

Then I met David. Father David to be precise.

(A nice irony, that "Father", since the Catholic Church is into unfettered rampant reproduction for everybody *but* their Fathers. And yes, I promise I won't go on about Catholicism.) I should explain how we met. It happened outside his church. I'd been having what the Church (sorry) calls impure thoughts. I don't know if you ever noticed (joke!) but every summer I turn into a mental rapist. I don't just fantasize vaguely about being with the amber-gold, half-naked bodies I see in the street. I fantasize about raping them. I feel like a fake – a clean-cut, angelic-looking young man like me, politely giving the barman with the Gillette-ad looks the time when I'm dreaming about muddying his pristine designer shirt and tie, marking his face with warrior streaks as we thrash about on the ground.

I could never figure this out and never asked you but I am now. What does this mean?

In my defence I should say that I don't wonder where I would take victims if I could overpower them, don't really plan for a second a real attack. It's always mutually consenting "rape" – a game we're both playing.

I'm really dreaming we're lovers.

So trusting of each other we could do all that. And rape, by definition is not that. By definition it's mutually exclusive with consent. Nevertheless, why don't I fantasize we're holding hands or having nice quiet safe sex. Why is it always quick and rough and violent and painful – for both.

What does this mean? (I wish you were here.)

Then I hear other people's stories (nobody you know – in just two years all our mutual friends have drifted off the face of the Earth, or at least – same thing – stopped going to the same pubs as me). My straight male friend (yes I have one at last: very plain) says he likes women on top so he can fantasize he's volcanoing spunk out of her head and I think it's a male thing, we're bastards. Then a straight girlfriend says she imagines cutting off her lover's nob with her cunt once she's satisfied and then ramming it down his throat. So I think lesbians are the only pure-sex type left in the world and my lesbian friend shows me her Damaging Dykes S&M video.

As I say, impure thoughts.

Ten minutes before I met Father David I was in Safeway. It was ninety-degrees outside. Ninety-nine in my head. I was following a guy in scarlet shorts. And nothing else. No shirt, trousers, socks.

Or underpants.

You could tell. Believe me. Angle of the bulge: down the leg rather than across the crotch.

He was buying ice-cream. The incongruity of the near-nakedness and the setting was so sexy. I was so close to him in the busy queue that I could feel the heat of his body at the checkout, jostle sweat from his shoulders onto my cheek, smell the gel on his hair (Brute), and on his neck the aftershave moisturizer (Obsession by Calvin Klein – a name the sound of whose cool phonetics and the sight of which on a page can give me an erection, conjuring up those beautiful black-and-white Weber advert models).

If I or some strong randy female raped this guy would we have our sentences diminished due to his contributory negligence in dressing so arousingly? Just a thought.

Sexual beauty: a strange, maddening old thing. (I don't understand how you could just take it or leave it.) I can pass endless uglies on the street, offended at the ill-attention to clothes and body – especially if the body and face has potential: a perfect face destroyed by long hippy hair (male baldness there is no cure for. But there is *No Excuse* for long hair); the obviously taut, lithe Indiana Jones body obscured by grungy jumpers. And yet, when I chance upon the undiluted perfect face, the flawless body, there is always that fathomless sadness, and the knowledge that not even a shared orgasm would make it go away: you'll just have to come again hours later, he'll still exist, there's plenty more of his kind in stock and more being produced every second. And that's by no means the worst of it. Jealousy and competition certainly has much to do with this sadness – which is why so many gays (no names . . .) spend so much time in the gym, on their appearance: but it's also a documented fact that heterosexuals feel it too, this ache (see ninety percent of Art). And it's not only the envy of the plain for the attributes of the beautiful. Perfect dark-haired gay male feels it for perfect blond. I suppose it's why the human race evolves.

And age is in there somewhere too; desire for youth/maturity/immortality. David looked like the sort of young teacher I'd have had a crush on at school (remember Mr Anderson?) – a great part of that desire being the power and masculinity his ten years over me gave him. From the other direction my late twenties approach to dread three zero, embryonic laughter lines and grey hairs would now make his early-twenties' smoothness as desirable and unattainable as the secret of life.

Sex and death. Love and hate. Sex and hate. Love and death. You can't will away or satisfy the wonderment: it's like when me and you used to lie in bed and think – *really think* – about there being nothing in the universe than there being all this. I mean absolutely nothing. And then a beginning. Or no beginning and no end. It's not a thing a human can conceive of or deal with. Like absolute beauty. You just have to stop thinking about it eventually and accept that there are some things you will never be able to deal with to complete satisfaction. Your brain tilts. Better settle for God (God can understand eternity so we don't even have to try to: phew!)/ promiscuity or prostitution/ facelift and the gym: do your best to improve what you can, forget what you can't. And if you can't forget: look and look until you drain enough beauty with boredom to escape.

I followed the supermarket guy outside until we came into the street of the church. The priest saw me watching the guy and something instantly told me that he knew. And knew I now knew about him. I had caught him looking at the guy before he looked at me. He was staring at the nape of that thick shaven neck, a part of a man that no other het male ever stares at, unless there's some football tattoo on it they can get het up about (forgive the pun). The stare lasted only a second, the time it took for Thomas to doubt Christ, Eve to tempt Adam, me to realize finally that you really were leaving. I only saw it after I saw the guy glance back at me – he'd been following the priest's eyes.

"Oh Christ he's seen me," I thought. One of those. So embarrassing, that I-know-you-need-me-but-I'll-never-need-you look. As you know, I'm usually so discreet. But he would have recognized me from the supermarket and perhaps he glimpsed me getting on his bus. Now he knew all – even the look in the priest's eyes – in an instant. Straight guys are so knowing these days.

Well I did my indignant you're-very-mistaken-pal butch offended look (based on the many examples I'd experienced to model it on), didn't bother to check if it had worked, and just went up as brazen as hell to the priest, the nervousness giving me strange false confidence.

I was also annoyed with myself, with the ridiculousness of it all – following the guy who, now that I had time to study, I saw was no better-looking than half the bodies we passed, whose main attraction had been his incongruous nakedness, a nakedness that was now, in the oven-baked streets, as common as a lamppost. There is some great metaphor for sexual desire in that, but damned if I can think of it. Maybe it's more a metaphor for love-fever – the way you chase the original obsession that refuses to succumb, long after it's lost it's initial attraction, not noticing that you're chasing just for the sake of the chase. The cancer gets cured but the pneumonia it left kills you instead.

I asked the priest about the jumble-sale there was a notice outside the church for, if he needed any workers. My mother had told me there was a nice new young priest. Up close he looked like a baby, by priest standards, who you always think of as older than you, like policemen. His looks and station in life were as incongruous as a fifty-year-old and a sailor suit. He told me he was just out of the priest school. Which, presumably, was why he was trim-muscled, crew-cut, and as fit and healthy looking as a teenager doing National Service. His handsomeness seemed such a tease. So unfair. (Even worse in a way than a handsome het.) He wasn't wearing his priest garb (the gold chain with the crucifix, and the prayer book was all that had given him away) but a tight black T-shirt and tighter silky-blue training-trousers. He had sepia-coloured hair, as groomed as a model's, shaven ever so precisely over the ears; and the face of a devil. A handsome devil.

I followed him about the church helping him stack things.

The building had too many rooms for an entire family, a big Catholic family even, let alone a couple of priests and a housekeeper.

"This all seems rather obscene," I said. The Church was in the poor South. It would have housed dozens more of the destitute and homeless than the paltry profits of the jumble-sale would pay for. "And you've the expense account car out front too haven't you . . .?"

He just smiled, didn't say anything until I kept on picking at all the fancy antiques and saying how much they'd fetch. "Look I can give you the complete lecture on my beliefs or none of it. What do you want?"

"The complete lecture."

"Fine. But not now."

"When?"

"Tonight. I go for a walk every night in Queen's Park."

"That's more like it. The boring life I expected."

"I can't win, can I?"

"You sound like Derek Hatton."

"Well he's not exactly my role-model but he has a point. If everybody had to be perfect before they espoused morality or equality we'd be living in the jungle."

And that was basically his line that night, said over and over and over and in different colours; thankfully there were no tired religious metaphors. No Evening Call Crap. It was nice. We walked and walked. There was a great late sunset. Purple rain liqueured the streets and later I learned pubs weren't off-limits and, well, I fell in love. Ridiculous. No excuses. The next night he arrived dressed in a big black jumper and leather jacket – you'll love this - on a motorbike. ("Paid for by me.")

Then I did my number on him. Immediately criticized/tried to change the thing that had interested me about him in the first place. "So did you become a priest to kill off your homo desires?"

"Not at all. It wasn't an issue – for me. I'm just not very sexual. I like the life style, the job, the chance to pontificate, to give my version of the message."

"So you would do it then?"

"No. I'm a religious Stephen Fry." He said this sentence as though it had been perfected with argument. With whom? Wasn't I the first?

The egotism of love.

David would annoy my friends by getting drunk and not being a boring priest, coming out with as much drunken nonsense as the rest of us – "I am not a number! I am a letter of the alphabet!"

"What letter?" I would always play along.

"'A' of course, the Scarlet Letter of the Sinner."

It annoyed me that his mind never strayed too far from God, even when he was at his most heathen. "I don't want to sound like Bridey Brideshead," he laughed when I told him that. "But you have no idea how ironic that is."

Maybe I was just annoyed because he was better-read. Devastating looks and brilliant intelligence had been the irresistible attraction the last time too. Ha, ha. (And yes, you are still The Last Time.)

He could also be as philistine as the rest of us, though, loving *Neighbours* and all the films and books we did and even contributing to our erotic gossip. "David this is the sort of thing that ends up in the *News of the World*," I would warn him. "There's probably someone in here with a tape up his backside."

"Good. It will bring it all to a good head."

"Do you want to be un-priested! Is that it?" I suspected then his vocation must be a parents thing – but then, of course, I suspected all middle-class parents forced their children into doing things they didn't want to do. He told me no, they were lapsed, had wanted him to be an accountant or a TV star.

That was it!

"You want to be an ex-priest. On TV. You want a scandal for publicity. This is all some brilliant long-range media career plan."

"Nope. It's as simple as what I've told you. I like the job."

"Bring what to a head then?"

"I don't really know. I think I want to see what you can get away with saying, criticizing."

"But not doing?"

"Of course not. That would make it all too simple for them."

We were on a bus the next day (I was scared of the bike – claustrophobic with the helmet – and David never let me in the expense account car – "Don't want to bring your morals down to my level." This thrilled me: I could hurt him.) The

conductor was going to put three bare-chested boy-teens off
for being "improperly dressed". It was one of those really sad
dramas you wished you'd never seen. Why did the conductor
do it? Was it a mad impulsive memory of some silly bus law
he'd learned? Some latent scary paedo feelings? I felt sorry for
the boys and, eventually, the conductor.

"They're putting their T-shirts on now," a woman said
as the bus drove off and the conductor was lambasted, even
though he eventually let them on after David, the Leader Of
The Gang, stopped the bus and argued that all they had to do
was put on their T-shirts and it would be OK. Amazing what
a priest can do in his uniform – which I hated him wearing –
so unerotic.

That night in bed he was too sexy, in faded denim lying
next to me, to ignore. He had an erection. I rubbed it. He
stopped me.

(Sorry, but this isn't going to be one of those letters: I'm
sticking completely to the facts – which, come to think of it,
are more arousing than the fantasies in the other letters.)

"What if I look at you and masturbate."

"OK."

"And you masturbate."

"OK."

"What's the difference if we touch?"

"I prefer masturbating myself."

"It's not a religious thing?"

"Nope."

"You know, it's just as much a sin if you masturbate
alone."

"Maybe."

"I could tell on you."

"I know. I live my life as though The Church is watching
over me every second."

"Which of course God is."

He started rubbing at the denim bulge.

Another night David had said he would hate just to be a priest
and hate just not to be. The thrill was the in-between, the

disguises. And it occurs to me now (*i.e.* now that I write it down) that that is my problem too, not wanting the full story: the romantic addiction to Mystery. And it will go on – ecstatically – until they find the cure. Which I'm not sure I want. Why? Because of what you told me and I refused to believe. I thrive on contradictions. Questions.
Such as.

1 The way he only ever drinks Diet Coke through a straw because he heard it was terrible on the teeth, yet he drinks alcohol every day.
2 The seemingly incidental unthought-out beauty and yet obsession with age and decay – "When you're young," he said sadly one day, looking at an established author's long credit list (your copy of *Live from Golgotha*), "all you want is all that behind you. When you're old you'd give anything to be that wanting, that young."
  "But you're perfect."
  "I found my first grey hair today."
3 Why is he really a priest? It is maddeningly mysterious. All I can say is, he's not acting when he accepts all my criticism. He agreed that being a homo/adulterer/alky was almost a prerequisite for the priesthood, laughed at that and all my other jokes – those trillions of unused sperms priests were supposed to keep, frustrated and unfulfilled in their balls for a lifetime. The unnaturalness of stopping post-pubes from having sex (why give them genitals at fourteen if they're not to use them); the sick illogical joke that the rhythm method is not contraception; the nightmare of an uncontracepted world.

I've been holding off writing until The End. But which end? And how do we ever recognize that? And do I want *this* one to end? First time since you I've wondered that. Will you ever come back? I think I've made it clear that all the ingredients are in place for an ending. And a beginning to move on. If you let it. No bluff.

The latest so far: the cute thing he did before he went to sleep tonight. Perhaps it's as much of an explanation as I'll get. Or there is. I said, "When you look like a priest you're not a real one, when you look sexy you're untouchable."

"Improperly dressed," he mumbled sleepily, then turned over and scratched that beautiful right bicep, the one with the tattoo on it, which said "Father".

THE LAST PIECE OF TRADE IN AMERICA

John Mitzel

BY THAT TIME, all America had gone fluffy.

More than just a passing fad or fancy, effeminacy of the most outrageous sort had arrived, spread and stayed. Rooted in a successful political and ideological foundation, the merchandizers had made their logical move and completely transformed a once virile nation of taciturn, self-sacrificing pioneers and steel-tough workers into a giggling mass of disposable, squeezable and *cuddly* citizens.

To be elected "First Lady" was now regarded as the highest honor in the land. Accommodations for the new life style were everywhere apparent: football players of both sexes wore larger helmets to hold their *coiffures* in place while on the gridiron – The Saturday Night Date was more important now than the game itself. The most disturbing industrial injuries were Broken Fingernails and Dry, Scaly Skin. The most serious public offense was Unwanted Body Hair. Police officers, army recruits and all other uniformed personnel were required to watch their diets and keep their torso measurements within a strict proportion. This they eagerly did with Smart Lunches of dressy lettuce, spam, cottage cheese and jello. The only major crimes the constabulary had to deal with were wig-shop heists and people being ugly in public. It was felonious Not To Try To Be Beautiful.

Material success alone was no longer the Big Dream of the populace. This was the age when Elegance and Good Taste were the capstones of The Great American Experience. Even tough contract bargaining between union leaders and management in the major tertiary industries – catering, swimming pool repair, interior decorating – were thoroughly polite and strictly followed the established rules of etiquette. Not only *could* everybody become a Society Lady, *everybody had*! The last pair of baggy white men's drawers had long since been hung in the Smithsonian's new Antique Couture Wing (aka a "Campy Clothes Collection").

And yet somewhere in the hinterlands of this frilly, fluffy culture, hidden away in some bleak mid-western state, Stanley "Butch" Markman was just about to quit his rural cabin where he'd many years before been left as a foundling and where he was raised by a craggy hermit straight out of an early misanthropic strain of American Literature. After the old man died (Stanley had wrapped him in a sheet and buried him aside the Old Oak Tree), Butch decided the big city was the place for his future, the place where a man could make a fair and honest wage with hard labor. His hair combed back and matted down with bacon fat, three days worth of face stubble, a dirty T-shirt, grubby coveralls and mudcaked boots, he put his thumb out as he paced the country road, watching the spiffy cars spin toward the metropolis.

It wasn't long before a creampuff, the driver that is, pulled over his lavish, highly-personalized sedan, filled with a fashionable fragrance.

He leaned over to speak out the passenger's window:

"Going my way, baby?" asked the teased head. "Hop in! What's your name, cutie?"

"Butch."

Heaven!" shrilled the silly billy. He swelled his eyes. "I can *certainly* see *why*. Have a cigarette and relax, toots."

The car raced down the highway, a metal and glass bubble filled with loud music and the strains of the familiar seduction

of The Last Innocent to the ways at the end of Big City
Living.

In town, Butch walked the streets for awhile. An idle and
curious crowd, many with painted faces and hard voices,
slowly grew in his wake and followed him. Brash, vulgar,
short-lived, these harlequins of the streetcorners, even after
they had had what they wanted from him, were probably the
least calculating of the bunch Butch was to meet, ultimately
too stupid to be deeply malevolent. And, after the first nights
of revelry, drinking, doping, hanging-out and petty theft, the
police vans descended – the vans had been painted by America's
leading cop-art designers, each pattern coordinated with its
district's distinctive characteristic (theatres, antiques, leather
goods, hi-tone dining, secure investments, etc.). All were
pinched in the bust except Butch; he was left alone out of
admiration for the novelty of his manliness.

This same manliness was to get him into the chic apartment
of the last gentlemanly Metropolis bachelor – thirties "sophistication" being his hold-out against the new decadence of Fluff
and Elegance. He took Butch in and, though Butch had not
yet learned it, kept him separate enough, even if as caricature,
to give him an Identity that could bolster fantasies. For this,
others would be grateful.

"It's kind of you, sir, to do all this for me, but I want
you to understand that I'm just happy when I can hang
out in a bar and listen to the juke and strike up talk with
the other guys."

"To begin with: there are no 'other guys' and haven't been
for ten years. Trust me, and keep to your own number and
you'll do all right."

"Huh?"

Through this connection, Butch would walk into dance
bars and cause a riot of desire; stud service fees reached
unprecedented levels (or so it was said; no one had any
memory of anything that had happened before yesterday).

One night, Butch came home in a svelte, open-necked, red
nylon jumpsuit and a shell necklace. His keeper thwacked him
good with a riding crop. "You are never to allow anyone to
buy you or give you anything, do you understand? Once you

get sucked into *that*, you'll turn out just like the rest of them, vile creatures."

"Aw, hell, I thought he was just trying to be nice to me."

"Kind, yes. Kind of subversive. What your pea-brain can't grasp is that they actually *hate* you deep down. That's why it'd satisfy them to make you a replica of *them* in a flash if they could. As good citizens, they must possess and destroy you. Why do you think they all became 'fluff' to begin with? They're like you, *dumb*, and they got caught up in a game the end of which they could not foresee. The results of which *you* see. So, ride 'em good, hillbilly. Don't listen to a word they say. There's nothing inside their bubbleheads but that incessant chatter of everything that is unimportant in life. Tomorrow, I want you to get your hair cut in the old-fashioned military style."

The jumpsuit – as well as the soft sweaters, scarves, floppy hats and tiny jewels – that Butch had received went into the rubbish, and for one week he was obliged to keep to an itinerary which comprised only bus stations, greasy spoons, gin dives and pool halls. This was done to maintain his contact with his roots, such as they were, to make sure he stayed *plain* white trash and didn't catch the contagion of *haute elegance* of the uppitty trash. It was hoped that this punishment would become his pleasure.

Yet, even in the these sleazy emporia he wasn't safe from the contagion. Small, *cute* conspiracies had formed to trick him into getting his nails trimmed and lacquered, his pants custom-made, his hair tinted and styled. These were great temptations to one as easily conned as was Butch; in fact *he* thought many of his temptresses quite nice folks.

The time came, alas, when Butch had serviced every orifice in town which had sought the attention. Butch soon became somewhat *passé* for the trendy, garnering only the flattery of those few not indelibly fashion-conscious. Others would wait years for him to return again as a "new" item. In the most chi-chi circles, his making messes, passing out drunk, cutting up expensive fabrics with beer can lids was not only *not* funny or amusing anymore, it was not tolerated. Much fluff, of all sexes, simply barred him and treated him as though he didn't or even *shouldn't* exist.

Having been consumed, transformed from The Latest Thing

to mere litter junking up the city. Butch became subject to harrassment from the very same fluffy fuzz who had earlier thought him The Most. A few times he was arrested for no reason and held overnight, during which he was introduced to the vicious side of fluff constabulary – *the humiliating things he was made to do*! Fluff decadence need not be as flabby as it appeared.

His use to his master diminished, and, with a gift of cash, Butch was sent packing. It was suggested he return when he could cut his own way.

Butch fell back onto working the streets, going with strange creatures who were visiting from all parts of the world, gabbing with sorry faces, living in the manner of an unconscious exile, the wretched fate of a discarded bauble in Fat City. Even after months of exposure to their culture, he was still amazed how much everybody looked alike. What people thought were other people *he* knew were grotesques: talking heads with powdered faces in sleek and unnaturally taut bodies (wrinkled by booze even so), clad in couturier-copies and having a fabulous time.

He turned more aggressive and met with indifference. He tried starting fist-fights in public places and found absolutely no social support. After a particularly destructive brawl, Butch was hauled into a tastefully done-up courtroom, found guilty of being A Big Nuisance, and was literally *slapped* on the wrist by the presiding judge and told to stop it. In its way, it was a devastating sentence.

Alone in his room one night he fell apart. He cried, snivelled, moaned. He tossed and turned. He heard accusing voices. By daybreak, a new resolution steeled him. He studied his face in the mirror, shaved more closely than usual, trimmed his sideburn. He ran his comb through his hair and dropped it into bangs on his forehead. Instead of tucking in his shirttails, he knotted them at his navel. Trouser legs rolled, loud striped socks, no shorts, Butch went out dancing. It was a straight line from that step into being just another shrill voice, once yokel, now elegant, matching itself with the masses in all but the most minute matters, having fully learned fast what is actually written in small type at the base of the Lady in the harbor: If You Can't Be An Event, Play Safe.

TAKE IT LIKE A MAN

John Patrick

STEVE SHOWED UP on my last trip to New Orleans in November. He looked so young; I guessed not even of legal age, and green as far as river-barges went, but at least he knew port from starboard. He claimed to have spent two years in the Navy, but I doubted it. There was something not quite real about him that I could never put my finger on. He made me think of a handsome actor from one of those TV comedies, playing the part of a barge-worker.

That month we were shipping taconite ore from the mines up north, to be loaded on some Japanese freighter and then hauled back to Louisiana in a year as a boatload of Toyotas. The *Daisy May* was not the largest barge I'd ever worked, but I knew her skipper, Earl, and had actually saved his life. Well, maybe not saved his life, but pretty close. I'd walked out of the Torchlight Bar in Memphis one night and seen Earl passed out beside a dumpster and a couple of really young guys rolling him. The kids ran off as soon as they saw me coming, and I'd heaved Earl over my shoulder and carried him to his hotel room to let him sleep it off. I hadn't known who Earl was then, but since everyone who went to the Torchlight worked the barges I knew he had to be a riverman. The next morning Earl hired me on.

I had kept pretty much to myself until Steve arrived on the scene. Why he became so chummy with me I could never figure. Why with twenty-six men on the *Daisy May*, had Steve chosen me? I asked him that once, after we'd spent a night drinking and we were walking back to the barge at 5.00 a.m., guided by the rank, flat smell of the river. Steve just laughed and threw a couple of phantom punches to my ribs. He said it must have been the twinkle in my baby-blue eyes.

Bullshit, I thought. It was more than that. I began watching him more closely. When the other guys went to town, he'd split and say he had something he had to take care of. By the time we were in the next port, I discovered what he was taking care of was his cock – and not in the way most rivermen do either.

I'd always wondered about gay guys, but that was about it. I was never highly sexed, I just did what was expected of me. When I was very young, my shipmates would invite me along and I'd watch them fuck their whores and then turn 'em over to me. When they saw the size of my cock when it was hard, they always wanted me to go last. "After you've been in there, they'd be stretched for days," one of them kidded me. Some whores didn't even want me to do it. "You ain't sticking that in me, honey," they'd say. In a few towns, guys had regular girlfriends who would put them up for as long as they were on leave, but I met few girls that weren't whores and when I did most of 'em didn't want anything to do with me after they saw my dick.

I began to develop a complex about my horse dick. I began to think of myself as a freak, that my prick was downright ugly. But Steve was the one who set me straight. It began by his talking about my hands. We were a couple of days out of Rock Island. My shift was over, and I was sitting in the aft lounge, the "ass lounge" the crew called it, watching some porno-flick on the VCR and smoking Camels with the chief cook and a couple of older bargemen. Steve walked in, sprawled over the chair beside me. There was something almost too perfect in his features, his jeans were too perfectly worn and faded, his T-shirt dirty in just the right places, and I found myself attracted to him.

Much to my surprise, he asked for advice. Steve always wore gloves topside, but he said he'd heard your hands would toughen quicker, and so be less likely to get injured, if you went barehanded. "You've got the biggest, toughest damn hands I've ever seen," he said with a quick grin. "So what d'ya think?"

I shrugged, embarrassed, and glanced over at the other guys, but they were engrossed in the movie. I looked at my hands. I hardly thought of them as part of my body. They were huge and the palms were covered in thick yellow ridges of callous from years of fighting ropes the size of a man's wrist. All my fingers had been broken at least once and jutted out at strange angles. Even my fingernails were deeply creased and hard as horn. Between the callouses and the fractured bones, I had little feeling left in my hands. Now I felt like I was in high school and one of the popular kids had just said something nice to me. I wasn't sure whether this was a compliment or perhaps he was setting me up for a joke.

"Oh, I dunno," I said. "I had gloves when I first started on the barges, but I left 'em on deck one day when I went down for lunch, and they were gone when I came back. Didn't have money for a new pair." I held my hands up and laughed. "Yeah, they're pretty fucked up."

Steve took one of my hands in his and squeezed it. "But they sure are meaty." Then he laughed, "I bet you're meaty everywhere."

I pulled my hand away and stood up. "That's what the whores all tell me – too damn meaty!"

The next night, a thunderstorm had blown down from the Dakotas and the river was running high, rocking the *Daisy May* and sending deep clangs and hollow booms through the length of her. We were heading into Des Moines and had a game of five-card-stud going in the ass lounge. I was playing more recklessly than usual. Steve just sat with his chair tipped back against the wall, but I could feel his eyes on me all night. In the end, I had lost nearly my entire paycheck. Steve told me not to worry: "Your luck will improve." It was such a stupid comment I ignored it.

The next evening, as we were heading down to mess, Steve stopped me in the stairwell. "Hey, Meaty, let's do the pizza thing tonight, my treat."

I shook my head. "Nah, I hate bummin' off people."

Something about Steve made me jumpy, reminded me of the sensation I got driving over really high bridges, when guard rails pulled at me so hard I sometimes felt I had to fight the steering wheel to keep the car between the lines.

"Come on," Steve urged. "You can owe me. Besides, I got somethin' I want to show you."

In the end, Steve convinced me, and we shared a couple of thin, greasy pizzas and two pitchers of draft beer at a windowless Italian place on the pier. As we left, Steve whispered, "Check this out," and beckoned me around the back. We stood near a loading dock, next to a dumpster overflowing with crushed pizza boxes and empty beer bottles. A half-dead florescent lamp shot a cold blue light over everything, and I had to force myself not to blink in time with its flickering. Steve opened his coat and flashed a dog-eared phone book.

"What?" I said blankly. "This is what you wanted to show me? That you could rip off a phone book from a pizza joint?"

Steve chuckled. His eyes framed by long girlish lashes, looked flat and wet in the jittery light. "I have a plan, my man, if you're up to it. It's something that'll take care of your financial problems."

Shit, I thought, I could see where this was headed. Over the years I had collected half-a-dozen misdemeanour counts for public drunkenness and disturbing the peace. The last thing I needed was serious trouble from the cops. The smell of rotting pizza and sour beer floated up from a pile of garbage at my feet. Steve watched me and grinned, his sleek black hair looking blue in the weird light. I knew what he was thinking; *I dare ya old man . . .*

"What the fuck," I said. "Let's do it."

"Yeah, all right."

Steve ripped the blue government section and the city map from the front of the book and threw the rest behind the dumpster. He studied the pages for a moment, then took off down the alley.

We walked for half an hour through a quiet residential area of square white houses with bicycles in the front yards. From somewhere to the south, I could hear the clanking of boxcars being unloaded. The sound was faint but incredibly clear in the crisp air. I even thought I could hear voices sometimes. In truth, I hated trains. That was why I'd ended up on the river instead of the freightyards like my old man.

We had to move a lot when I was a kid because my old man was always getting fired. The winter I turned thirteen, we moved to Rockwall, Texas. Like always, I pumped myself up to go out and face whichever gang of boys ruled that neighbourhood. After three or four fistfights in a vacant lot, they decided to accept me. I'd been initiated along with another new kid, from Austin, at midnight along the train-tracks. I had no trouble slipping away; Dad didn't care and Mom was passed out by 6.00 p.m. every night. Our initiation was to stand on the tracks with a freight coming at us until Chuck, the leader, said jump. If we moved a muscle before then, we'd be out of the gang and probably get the shit beat out of us on top of it.

A train was due at 12.20 p.m., and the kid from Austin went first. He stood on the tracks, arms stiff at his sides and stared straight ahead. His breath came out in cottony puffs. Me and six other guys stood with our fists stuck in our pockets, shuffling our feet in the frost-blackened weeds lining the tracks. The gang passed around a pack of Luckys, but deliberately skipped me.

When we heard the train, everyone stopped moving and peered intently down the tracks. Soon I could see the big headlight barrelling towards us. It was an express, moving fast, making no stops in Rockwall. I glanced at Chuck then back at the kid from Austin, who was breathing faster. He had carroty hair and a pinched freckled face. His bottom lip was swollen from a recent battle in the empty lot.

When the train was still a couple of hundred yards away, I could feel the rumbling through the soles of my shoes. The other kid hadn't twitched. His eyes glittered but he didn't blink. I knew somehow that he wouldn't move, no matter what. Panic rolled through my guts. I glared at Chuck, planning to yell at him, "Say jump!', or even shout it myself. Chuck's face stopped me, though. Chuck also knew the kid wouldn't move. The look on his face was hungry, ravenous, the expression of a starving man about to get a feast. The boy's curly orange hair was blowing wildly as the freight bore down. I thought I saw the same look on the kid's face, the same determination, the same hypnotic hunger, just before the train hit.

At the last instant, the engineer saw him and slammed on his brakes. The steel wheels threw a high-pitched shriek into the air along with arcing lines of blue sparks. I felt the sound like an ache in my groin, like finally pissing after holding it in for hours. The kid exploded into a cloud of red mist.

We all stood transfixed, until the last car had blown by. I kept thinking, "I'm next! I'm next!', and I felt a weird sensation, half dread and half anticipation surging through my body. I realized dimly I had an erection. One of the gang was puking in the weeds and we went into the woods nearby. Chuck made me take my cock out. He held it in his hand, stroked it. "God, that's the biggest one I've ever seen," he said. "You could kill a girl with that."

"Nah," I said, so embarrassed I couldn't look at him.

"Yeah," he said, continuing to stroke it. I came almost instantly.

Walking back to join the others, he swore me to secrecy.

"Damn right," I said.

I was in the gang after that, but I found myself avoiding them, especially Chuck, as much as possible. Then my old man got fired again and we moved to Waco. Two years later, I left home for good.

Me and Steve entered the school through an unlocked classroom window. Schools were perfect, Steve said. No alarms, no safes, and all that lunch money, a couple of bucks per kid, six maybe seven-hundred kids, all of it just waiting in the principal's office.

"Betcha ten bucks," Steve said, "it's in the top right-hand drawer."

But he hadn't counted on a security guard. The guy must have been about seventy, thank god. No gun. Steve acted on instinct when the old man turned a corner, cold-cocking him, then slamming his head against a locker. I stood for a moment, stunned and breathing hard, more from shock and excitement than effort, and glanced at Steve, who winked and said, "Hurry up, Meaty."

We counted the money in an alley near the river. I leaned against the cold bricks, ruffling the bills, wondering if the old watchman was OK. I felt super-charged with energy, then realized I had an erection. Steve noticed it too. Just like Chuck, he just put his hand over the bulge and squeezed it.

"God, *meaty* is right." Unlike Chuck, Steve couldn't wait for me; he unzipped my jeans and took my cock out. Like Chuck, he'd never seen anything like it either. Stroking it, he said, "I'd love to see this goin' into one of them whores."

"Most of 'em say it's too big."

"I know some that'd love it. Sure enough do." He continued massaging it, stopping every once in awhile to admire it. He fondled my balls as he jerked it until I came. As the cum slid down his fingers he laughed. "Big load, too. Yeah, I know some whores that'd *really* love this. C'mon."

We walked a few blocks and stopped in front of a club that Steve said was "not for the faint of heart". The bar was off the main strip of the downtown red-light district, set between an abandoned warehouse and an old flour mill, at least three miles from the docks. It was hardly a riverman's hangout. I paused at the door, my hand going to my back pocket where I always kept a knife and a set of brass knuckles, but Steve grabbed my arm and pulled me inside.

We ended up at a pay-by-the-hour motel with a slim boy in a red satin dress named Kitty Kane. If not for his too large Adam's apple and the fact that the bar was full of drag queens, I would never have guessed that he was a man. In the room, I slumped against the wall, holding a bottle of tequila, and watched Steve fuck the guy's ass on the creaking little bed. "I'll warm her up for you," he said, going at it energetically.

"I'm used to that. Go ahead. Fuck your little heart out." I felt light-headed and a little sick at the sight, like the first time I saw a bull mount a cow, or spied my parents through a crack in their bedroom wall. But just like those times, I was mesmerized. I could already feel a hard-on fighting the effects of the booze. The sound of their breathing and the squeaking of the bed springs seemed too faint for the cramped space.

I knew I shouldn't have taken the second bottle of tequila. Steve, I recalled fuzzily, hardly had anything to drink the whole night.

Suddenly, Steve's face was in front of mine. "Come on," he said, taking the bottle from my hand and grinning, "it's your turn now."

I moved a little unsteadily towards the bed and looked down at the damp, wrinkled red dress and a hard angular hip. Steve came up behind me and unzipped my jeans. Slowly, he drew my cock out and told Kitty to roll over. Kitty grinned when he saw my pecker, now stiff and coated with pre-cum.

"Didn't I say this was somethin'?" Steve said.

Kitty nodded but didn't say a word, just took the whole thing in his mouth, all the way down to the pubic hairs. Nobody'd ever done that before; most of the time, whores just licked and sucked a little on the head. I held his head while he continued. Then I realized Steve had gotten on the bed next to Kitty and the two of them were taking turns. I could scarcely believe my eyes: the kid who'd been working alongside me for weeks had jacked me off and now was giving my cock a bath. I ran my fingers through his hair and groaned as he began nibbling on my balls while Kitty deep-throated my cock once again. Kitty could hardly wait to get my cock up his ass. Even though Steve had been in there, it was still tight, tighter than any whore I'd had. While I fucked him, Steve jacked off beside the bed, but tight as Kitty was, I just couldn't come. I'd had too much tequila. Steve finished inside Kitty, but it was to me Kitty gave his card. "You're welcome any time, honey," he said, patting my crotch as we left the room.

When we got off the *Daisy May* in St Paul, Steve said he wanted to go to Minneapolis, across the river. Winking at me, he said he knew a place I'd like. The Pussykat Lounge had black cinder-block walls painted with naked pink bodies. Cheap vodka, straight-up. Steve didn't find anybody to his liking, but as we were leaving around two, he found a guy passed out beside a dumpster near the bar.

"Come on," Steve whispered. "Let's have some fun." Steve kicked the man in the stomach and he rolled over, groaning. I realized he looked a lot like Earl laying there by the dumpster; same beer belly, same thinning brown hair. Steve kicked the guy again and he staggered to his feet, clutching his stomach. "Don't kill me," he begged.

I began gulping air like water. I felt I was going to faint, but I could tell I was getting the biggest hard-on I'd had for weeks. Steve waved me over. "He doesn't want us to kill him. What should we do with him?" he panted.

Steve forced the guy to his hands and knees beside the dumpster. "My buddy's not going to kill you, but it'll seem like it at first." Steve came up behind me and undid my pants. The man's eyes bulged and he began begging, "No, no, not that!"

"You'll love it, shithead," Steve snarled and he guided my cock into the guy's ass, then stood over us, jacking off. By the time I got my cock deep in him, I went crazy with it, fucking the hell out of him, but only for a couple of minutes. The guy in the red dress was one thing, but this fat old man was something else. I stood up, swaying a little. The vodka burned in my stomach. I felt like I was going to puke. "Are you done?" Steve demanded, his voice tight. "Is that all?"

"Yeah. I feel sick. Why don't you fuck 'im?"

"Okay, I will." Steve grabbed the guy by the hair and shoved his cock in him. The man was now hysterical.

I went behind the dumpster and heaved.

I woke the next day to find Steve and a short Mexican-looking guy standing in our hotel room staring down at me. Only a dim, grayish light came through the curtained window, but my eyes ached and I was momentarily blinded.

"This is my friend, Lupé," Steve told me. "Lupé, meet Jake."

Lupé snorted and said, "Yeah, right. *Big* Jake."

I swung my feet, still in my work boots, to the floor and sat up groaning, trying to get my mind into gear.

"Got a surprise for you," Steve said. "Lupé drives limos. He's got one outside right now. Thought you'd like to take a little ride."

About half an hour later, I was pulling my forehead back

from the window and looking at the faint smear of grease left on the glass. Then I stared at my hands laying motionless on the creamy leather seat of the limo. Rubbing the back of my hand across my eyes, I realized my hand was covered with dried, flaking vomit. I wondered briefly if it was mine, then the memory of the previous night hit me and I thought it might be from the guy in the alley. He had really looked a lot like Earl. I stared down at my blood-stained jeans and the rips in my work shirt. Hell, it could just as easily have been *me* passed out next to that dumpster. The thought sent a ripple of nausea through my stomach.

I glanced over at Steve, and was suddenly sick of the sight of him, ready to tell him to fuck off, when he buried his head between my legs.

Soon the limo rolled smoothly through a tight right-hand turn and my body followed it, pressing against the armrest. We were leaving the suburbs now and heading into the countryside. It was a bright, very warm day for May and our Mexican driver switched on the air conditioning.

I looked down at Steve's head, now bobbing up and down, my cock between his lips. I leaned back and closed my eyes. God, I thought, the guy sure loves to suck dick.

Before long, Lupé had parked the car in what looked like a forest. In all the years I'd shipped out of St Paul on the river barges, I'd never seen the countryside. In fact, I'd never seen the countryside anywhere. Somehow, no matter where I lived, I always ended up on some dusty street that reminded me of towns I'd known as a kid in west Texas. In town, my hotel on Payne Avenue was flanked by bars, strip-joints, gas stations and beauty parlors. Their windows were filmy with dust, the signs cracked and faded as though they'd been exposed to the blazing sun of the desert instead of the mild pale light of the north. I always half-expected to see a tumbleweed skittering along the crooked sidewalks.

But here we were awash in lush, cool green. "Let's have a picnic," Steve said, letting my cock plop from his mouth and thud against my belly.

Lupé lead the way, carrying a basket, a blanket, and some towels. "But first we go swimming," Steve said. It didn't take much encouragement. The pristine pond shimmered in the bright sun, reminding me of a picture I'd seen in a book once. Besides, I thought a swim in the chilly water might cure my hangover.

While Steve and I undressed, Lupé began laying out a banquet on the blanket.

I dove into the pond and Steve was right behind me. We played in the water for awhile and my head was beginning to clear. Steve reached down and stroked my cock occasionally. "Lupé loves to get fucked," he said, giving me that lewd wink of his. "I told him all about you, so I hope you can stay on him for more than a couple of minutes." The memory of the man next to the dumpster came back to me. And the boy in the red dress. I dove under the water and swam away from Steve.

After a few minutes, I came up for air and looked back toward the shoreline. Lupé was getting undressed. I saw the poor man on his knees. "It coulda been me," I said under my breath. I watched Steve emerge from the water, really noticing his tight little ass for the first time. "How'd he like it?" I wondered, and my cock stirred to nearly full attention.

As I walked toward the two of them, Lupé was now naked, reclining on the blanket, sipping some wine from one of the plastic cups he'd had in his basket. He looked up at my erection and blinked. Steve, wrapped in a towel, grinned and began pouring me a cup of wine, then one for himself. Lupé took a few preliminary licks on my cock and then we sat there quietly eating the fried chicken, French bread and drinking the wine. When we finished eating, Lupé returned his mouth to my cock, sucking hard, showing almost as much talent for it as Steve. Satisfied that he had me as hard as I could get, he rolled over. Steve ran a hand up and down the back of the young Mexican's hairless thighs. "I'll warm him up," Steve said, stroking his hard-on with his other hand.

"Go ahead," I said. "Enjoy yourself."

While he was fucking Lupé, I stood over them, jerking my dick, dropping spit on it, getting it ready. Steve was close, his body trembling, I got behind him and took his asscheeks in my hand.

"Hey!" he shouted. Spreading him, I shoved the head of

my cock into the incredibly tight hole. He screamed, "What the fuck— ?!" But it was too late; he was having his orgasm.

I showed no mercy. I was in him in a flash. He was hanging on to Lupé, coming down from his high, crying hysterically.

I laid across him and brought my hands to his neck. "Quiet asshole. Take it like a man."

"No, no," he cried, fighting me. "You bastard! You fuckin' bastard!"

He wouldn't stop shouting, calling me every bad name he could think of.

I couldn't stop fucking his tight ass. And squeezing his neck. I just kept squeezing, choking him. "It coulda been me," I kept saying, unable to let go.

When I came, I realized his screams had stopped.

With thanks to SLS, whose real-life encounter inspired this story.

THE WAR OVER JANE FONDA

Robert Patrick

WHEN MY LEASE on Wax Wit' Wix expired, my rent tripled. I flung all my candles out onto Christopher Street and phoned my sister out West. "You've been begging me to visit since Aids was still a diet candy," I said. "Does it still hold?"

"Why we'd love to have you," she shouted (because it was long-distance), "that is if you can stand us."

Homeless crack-addicts with running sores were performing New Age rituals curb-side with my candles. "I can stand you," I said, and headed for the bus depot.

Breakdowns, a strike, flats, and a collision stretched my three-day bus-trip to five. My grinning brother-in-law collected me from the Greyhound depot in the big town (pop. ten thousand) near Backwater (pop. four-thousand retired Air Force officers like him), and said, "Welcome home. I hope you're comin' for a nice long stay. Your sister is so happy she cried." He let me sleep until the blank freeway delivered us into Backwater. I could trust him to drive; he'd survived being a navigator in Korea and Vietnam. He woke me to point out the great globe of the water-tower, the one two-storey structure in town. The Class of '90 had just painted it with a world map in pink, blue and yellow, "for educational purposes," he said. "Beats defacin' it, huh? Ain't that artistic?" It revolved until we pulled up in the moonlight before my new low-slung suburban home.

In a pink patchwork housecoat, my pretty sister stood on the green lawn, waving. Behind her on a slender staff waved an American flag. I hadn't seen one since the one they left on the moon. I thought she was listening to a Walkman, but as she tiptoed to kiss me, I saw it was a shrimp-like hearing aid. She touched my face with one hand. The other marked her place in a volume of condensed true-crime books. She thanked me for a box of fancy candles. "I'll give them for birthdays," she said as the garage door opened before, closed behind us. "You'll tell me if I forget and give you one."

She guided me to my spacious bed and bath, indicated the ice-box, then sat down at the kitchen table to smoke Parliaments, munch M&Ms, and read her brief books. After a while she looked up. She called me by the name of one of her long-grown, long-gone children, laughed, corrected herself, pointed across a low room-divider at the family room, and said, "Go turn on the TV if you want to. You won't bother me." She pointed at her hearing aid and twiddled the dial to show that it was off.

"I'd rather talk," I said directly into her face.

She turned her ears on and flipped her reading glasses up onto her hair. "Well, all right," she said, "what would you like to talk about?"

We hadn't seen each other for twenty years. I'd been all over the world fighting for peace. She'd retired from a cosmetics-dealer franchise with a bigger pension than her husband got from the Air Force. Our lives, I would have said. Then I remembered our last, ancient exchange of letters. I had told her I was quitting my political work because Nixon wasn't impeached. She had replied that she had realized I must be gay, but no Christian could cast the first stone if they'd done the things she did with her husband before they were even married.

So I said, "Oh, television. I haven't been near a set in a decade."

"He watches," she said. "I can't stand the ads. TV is just trying to sell you stuff.

"No," I said, "it's you they sell. The broadcasters sell you to the advertisers. You are the product. They should pay you to keep a set in your house."

"Well," she said, "we subscribe to the cable . . ."

She had one hand on her volume control, one holding up her reading-glasses, and an elbow holding open her bloody book. She had nothing free with which to smoke or munch.

My brother-in-law came striding into the family room, sat in his chair, started sorting his newspaper. "What was that I heard on?" he asked, referring to my Sis's loud conversation. "Two of them experts tryin' to prove they was each one smarter than the other?" He waved a little black box at the TV and a sit-com blared and glared. Sis lowered her glasses like a visor, raised her book like a shield.

"This here little tough kid on this one," he said. "I just love him. He's a little wise-ass. Don't nobody never put nothin' over on him." The kid in question insulted someone. My brother-in-law roared along with the laughter track. For a half-hour, interrupted by commercials for cars and weight-watchers, didn't nobody put nothin' over on him.

Sis looked up only for a brief announcement that there would be live reports of a local murder at ten. By then my brother-in-law was asleep under the carefully sorted sections of his news.

A schedule emerged. I sat in the family-room while my brother-in-law shuffled and chortled. I read a few of my sister's books. All her true-crimes were family murders, white suburban stuff. Each day my brother-in-law added another newspaper to the recycling pile in the garage. Each month a new true gore book was lined up on sister's shelf.

But things in the family room livened up whenever President Bush decided to throw an expensive war to compensate the arms industry for the income they'd lost since Russia's bankruptcy slowed down nuclear stockpiling.

Well, heterosexuals are people to watch a war with. "Man's stuff," my sister shrugged. "I guess they know what they're doin'," and returned to her condensed carnage.

Whenever my brother-in-law was not lawn-mowing or counting cholesterol, he was slouched before CNN, knees covered in newspaper, watching the blood on the sand and huffing, "Haw! They got 'em!" or, at announcements of treaty negotiations, "See! Them Reds is tryin' to put it over Bush, but he ain't fallin' for it! He got round the UN and he got round the Democrats in Congress and he'll get round the Russkies! Haw!"

In the early days of this tired re-run of late Roman history, I mentioned that Bush seemed to be systematically taking out the leaders he helped install while in the CIA: first poor Noriega on the pretence of doing something about the then-much-publicized drug-lords, and now Saddam Hussein.

This casual observation was greeted by Sis and BIL with puzzled faces. They didn't know Bush had been in the CIA and could not conceive that the US had puppet rulers anywhere. Further chat revealed that they didn't know Bush was oil-rich or from Yale. Yet they voted for him. Or perhaps they just voted against Dukakis (whose name was always followed in Backwater by "that was goin' to let all the murderers loose on us on furlough!"). Well, that is, after all, what Dukakis was set up for, the rich having tired of pretending there are two parties.

I asked which of Bush's platform planks had swayed them. They didn't recall. Understandable; he never said anything definite enough to register, except that he was personally against abortion. The rest of his time was spent slinging mud against poor patsy Dukakis. They had watched the debates, but didn't remember details. They don't exactly listen to the TV; or rather, they do, but some mechanism installed while I was out in the streets filters out anything that might trouble them.

When one pointed out that Bush's envoy (named April, could you die?) was sent to tell Hussein that if he attacked Kuwait we wouldn't interfere, they frowned, briefly troubled, then brightened and said, "But we're there to help Saudi Arabia."

"That's not what the UN License to Kill says," I countered.

"Well, I suppose the United Nations knows what they're doing," Sis said, and turned a sticky page.

If tens-of-thousands were shown protesting the war, BIL said,

"Shit, them's the same people protest ever'thing American."
He now wore a big Walkman radio like Mouseketeer ears.
Pointing at it to indicate that this news came from his favourite
talk-show host, he went on, "They's just a few of 'em, you
know, an' they go from city to city, with their transport
supplied by Russian agencies. They don't work. They're paid
to protest."

When I commented that his pro-War host also gets paid,
and very well, for putting down all protest and dissension,
he replied, "You bet he gets paid! He started out local here
and now went national. He's got millions of listeners. Them
marchers, hell, they're just after publicity!" BIL fulfils F Scott
Fitzgerald's definition of a first-class mind, by being able to
hold contradictory ideas and still function.

They trust the media to make things bearable for them, and
they can. According to polls, the public was about evenly
pro- and anti- this Arab roast, so then the media began to
equate "being against the war" with "not supporting the
troops." Instantly the polls began to tilt toward the killing,
even as the respondents insisted they were not for the war, but
for the troops. Yellow ribbons, a popular symbol of "support"
derived from some popular song about a returning convict
(go figure straight people) began to proliferate on every
perpendicular object.

Our handsome paperboy wore a yellow ribbon T-shirt. Once
when BIL was unwrapping his paper and hooting in glee at a
front-page statement that peace demonstrations were no longer
increasing in size, the paperboy recited, "Well, I and my friends
are all against the war, but we won't protest because we support
our troops." He smiled, thrust his charming chest out, and
looked back and forth at us adults, expecting smiles, a pat on
the head, probably not a good clutch at his buns, most probably
a tip. I said one of the great media-manipulations in all history
was this administration's use of the ambiguities surrounding the
term "support". The paperboy and BIL stared at me blankly.
They did not seem to have heard me. It was more as if they
had heard silence when they were expecting a certain answer
to a cue. I suppose I was supposed to say, "Well, of course, we
ALL support the troops." How terrifyingly uncertain they must

be of what they think, to be so afraid of even the existence of another opinion.

Once we were sitting sipping diet root-beer (for they have diet root-beer; they also have a fisher's magazine called *Bassmaster*), and some token intellectual on CNN (for whom my heart ached) said, "We must look for the origins of this war in the psychological needs of George Bush." BIL spewed foam across the family room, shouting, "What does she mean, the reasons for this war are the psychological needs of George Bush?"

I went for paper towels and responded, "Well, one has to look somewhere, because there certainly is no rational need for us to be over there."

He clutched his foaming news-sections. "No reason?" he replied. "No reason? But Saddam Hussein is just like Hitler!" That's something else Bush put on TV when the polls still showed resistance to his war. The suggestion seems to be that we can atone in retrospect for not having nipped Hitler in the Bund (ha-ha) by tearing up Hussein, as if this was an early stage in his allegedly proposed world-conquest. Of course, at the same time, to whip up ire, we're told that he's been the Beast of the Apocalypse for years and years and years (funny how we were never told until now). Babble babble babble.

I tried to get the conversation on a light and sound basis by pointing out to BIL that if anyone is like Hitler in his early years, it's his talk show host, because he, like early Adolf, is starting out as a glib unprincipled fascist idiot articulating the rage of a lot of dupes in a depression.

Well, it was like telling someone who's mortgaged his condo to buy Pop Art that Andy Warhol is a fraud. My BIL just gaped, then gasped, then smiled pityingly and said, "Well, he tells the truth; that's why don't nobody like him."

I pointed out that since his ratings are getting right up there with *Wheel of Fortune*, somebody must like him. (I had no idea what we were talking about; that's the usual effect of any prolonged conversation between me and BIL.) "You damned right they like him," BIL gloated, and left me to mow his lone and level lawn. It's a technique he uses by instinct; to act as if he has won a point makes him feel he has. It's called "sympathetic magic," I think. It's part of the Protestant need to pretend to be perfect, coupled with the standard Machismoist heresy that all relationships are conflicts necessitating a winner and a loser. It's a combination which could make it impossible for one to think at all. No wonder they invented the computer. And the CIA. Shudder.

Another time, a soldier came on TV to announce that she wanted to be listed as a conscientious objector. She was willing to fight for her country and for democratic principles, she said, but it was against her conscience to fight for racist, sexist, sectist Muslims (remember, our invasion of Iraq was justified as being to protect Saudi Arabia). BIL scoffed, "Yeah. You notice she was willin' to take the money 'til the war started, huh?"

I laid down my fork and stupidly said, "But that question, whether we should defend a theocracy whose daily practices offend the UN's Human Rights Resolution, is the most important moral question of this war." He stared at me over a suspended forkful of spinach.

My sister, who had not gotten all of this, said, "Well, I think women can be just as good soldiers as men."

Then an ACLU lawyer came on to claim that there were actually thousands of US troops applying for conscientious objector status, but that the government was sitting on the applications to avoid demoralizing the troops. "Yeah," said my distracted BIL, "Why don't he produce the applications, then?"

I started to point out to him that the lawyer had just said, in words of comparatively few syllables, that they were being withheld, but my sister sighed, turned off her ear and opened a book, and I shut up. Minutes later, mention was made of the hardships of families of bread-winning service-persons who'd been snatched away to play with missiles and whistles. Feeling sure BIL would certainly support service families, I ventured, "The least the munitions makers, oilmen, and bankers could do would be to pay a soldier's rent while he killed gets for their shareholders."

"Yeah," BIL said, "but when they find out the government'll pay for it, they'll all move to expensive apartments."

"BIL," I cried, "if you believe all the Americans are corrupt, why did you fight for them?"

He turned scarlet and leaned toward me over the steaming casserole. He screeched, "Yes, yes, yes," trembling as he screeched, "they are that corrupt! And I don't know why I fought two wars for them! It wasn't for them! I fought for this house! I fought for my family!" He shoved his face into mine and huffed and puffed like a horse. I heard the dishes on the table rattle. He reared back and stalked out through the garage to work on the lawn. It was 8 p.m. in February and pitch-black out.

My sister sighed and said, "Don't worry, we can all watch *Jeopardy* together on the other channel later after he cools off," and began clearing the table.

The next day he was especially nice, asking if I wanted a ride to the nearby big town while he got his lawn-mower fixed, told me interesting stories about how to deceive radar during low-level bombing runs, named the fixed stars he navigated by and the unchanging constellations they appeared in, and did not discuss the conflict. Neither ours nor the one in Iraq. Clearly a point of no return, or no deposit, or whatever the nautical metaphor is, had been reached. He could not kill me. He could not even consider it. I am family.

That night I even made him laugh at dinner when I suggested that George Bush had started the war because his son's crooked Savings and Loan company had acquired a yellow-ribbon factory. BIL likes anything that confirms that everyone is stupid or dishonest. He repeated the joke several times to himself and suggested I call it in to the talk show. Given time, I could learn to entertain him.

If it had not been for Jane Fonda.

When CNN started showing (over and over like a hit music video) those nightmare shots of civilian corpses being dragged from a bombed bunker looking like the pasta special, my BIL assured us it had really been a military bunker and that Hussein had stuffed it with corpses of political enemies he'd killed himself. I swear he said it before the TV did. I said nothing. Corpses are corpses to me. I just wanted it to stop.

However, on the talk-show that evening, responses were wild. BIL turned the sound off on the constantly-bloody TV and tuned in a small portable so we could all hear. Most callers echoed avant-garde BIL, but there was one who actually made him and me smile together. An old, angry woman said, "I don't think they should show us corpses; there's too much violence on TV already."

BIL and I were just enjoying the sort of shared peace that can only come to two enemies who realize that there is a third party stupider than either of them, when the next caller, a lady older and crazier than the last, said, "No wonder Ted Turner on CNN is showing all of Saddam Hussein's propaganda; Turner is going out with Jane Fonda, and she's poisoned his mind against America!"

BIL and I looked at each other and our smiles exploded into laughter. It was a wonderful moment. I looked at Sis to see if she saw us getting along. She was quietly reading.

The talk-show host was still laughing at the lady. I wanted to prolong our shared moment. I had to say, "Jesus, what an idiot!"

BIL said, "Yeah, she probably slept with Saddam Hussein." It was extraordinary for him to use sexual terms, "shit" and "son-of-a-bitch" being more his style. I actually looked over to see if he had embarrassed my sister, but she seemed tuned out, lighting one Parliament from another.

"That old lady caller?" I cackled.

"No," he said, "Hannoi Hannah."

"BIL," I said. "You can't be referring to Jane Fonda. The woman is adamantly against tyranny everywhere."

"Don't talk to me about that whore," he growled, "she betrayed her country."

"Good God," I said. "How?"

"She sided with the enemy," he said.

I was stunned. "Do you mean when she risked her life going behind enemy lines to publicize the possibility of peace?"

"She's a traitor," he affirmed.

"BIL," I protested, "she was trying to end the war as fast as possible."

"Yeah, she swallowed them lies that we was bombing civilian targets."

"Lies? My God, the stories are still coming out."

He turned off the radio as if to keep the host from hearing.

"I never bombed no civilian targets," he roared, "and if I had, all them so-called 'civilians' was hidin' grenades in their shirts and comin' walkin' into GI bars."

"BIL," I said. "Not all of them. And in their hysteria over such sabotage incidents, American soldiers, among a swarming populace they couldn't classify as friend or enemy, went paranoid and massacred who knows how many innocent— "

"They was none of them innocent!" he screamed. "They didn't want us there and they killed as many of us as they could!"

"But, BIL, we shouldn't ever have been there at all!"

"Damned right we shouldn't have!" he said. "We never had no business there!"

"BIL," I cried. "That's wonderful! That's exactly what Jane Fonda believed. You see, you agree with her!"

"Don't talk to me about her, I told you. She's a traitor!"

"But she thinks like you! She hated the war!"

"So all our soldiers was treated like shit when they come back because she turned the people against them!"

"BIL! Long before she entered the peace movement, hundreds of thousands of us had marched against the war for years. I myself marched hundreds of times."

"But them marchers called our soldiers pigs."

"BIL, not all of us. Most of those kids were very young. When they learned we were carrying on an unjust war they marched against it. And they were beaten and gassed and jailed for it. They were baffled, hurt, confused. If some few of them took it out on soldiers— "

"Against our will! Without our consent! And we were fighting for freedom, too, for freedom, for your life! And we were unarmed!"

I hated quarrelling with him. I looked to Sis for help, futilely. Some exec. must have been gutting his whole family, because she had her eyes glued to the page while patting the table looking for her M&Ms. Sometimes holding the book flat with one hand and holding an M&M suspended over it during a suspenseful moment, she looks like she's playing Bingo.

BIL persisted. "Armed? What did you need to be armed for? Where was the violence against you?"

"BIL! Everywhere! Three Green Berets threw paving stones at me in Greenwich Village. I was carrying a giant picture of soldiers in Vietnam with the slogan, 'End the War! Bring them back alive!'" There was a long pause. He stared at me. He had newspapers in both hands. "Here," I said. "I had to have stitches." I pulled back my hair to show him my scars.

He was very quiet. An airborne elite navigator, he had never taken a wound. "So you can see," I said, pressing my presumed moral advantage, "although I was too sensible to hate all soldiers for what only a few did, some frightened young kids might well have, just as frightened young soldiers over there might have come to hate all Vietnamese. But you shouldn't in turn hate all protestors just because some of them turned ugly."

"How do you know," he asked, "that some of them was Green Berets?"

"They were in uniform," I said.

"Shit, that don't mean nothin'. Anyone could of bought a uniform. Them could have been commie agents. Or anyone."

"Well, yes, and those might have been card-carrying Republicans dressed as hippies ridiculing returning soldiers! But we can't assume everyone is – " I was going to say "corrupt", but thought better of it. "Anyway, you see, there's no reason for you to hate Jane Fonda. She was a latecomer to the movement. She was one of millions." We stared at each other, limp and hot. I said, "You might as well hate me."

"You're family," he said. He turned away, sat down, rearranged newspapers on his lap. "But that woman is a traitor." He picked up the control box. "Let's watch the war," he said. He put on his Mouseketeer Walkman. "It's a just war," he said, turning up both the TV sound and his earphones. "That man is just like Hitler. And we can win it. By bombing. Civilian targets. And we will. This war ain't like Jane Fonda. Like Vietnam." He pointed at his earphones. "Everyone's behind it. And we can win."

Rejections of peace proposals rattled out of the big box. Refusals to participate in cease-fires buzzed out of the earphones. "Analysts predict all offers will be rejected," BIL intoned, simultaneously translating for me. "A ground

war will commence." In his own voice, he added, with a big
smile as if talking to his friendly talk-show host, "Shit! I guess
Bush has showed them people that predicted he was a wimp.
He's got 'em all hornswoggled. Don't nobody put nothin'
over on him."

I looked around. My sister was munching, smoking, reading,
flipping. "I think I'm going out for a walk," I said. She
looked up, with us after all. "Wear something," she said.
"It's cold."

It is cold. The flag is still. The earth hangs in the starry sky.
I feel like I'm on the moon.

A SON'S STORY

Tony Peake

IT WAS THE gardener who first caused Jake to talk to his neighbour. He'd brought home a box of bibles from the church – bibles which he intended handing out on his next round of visits in the area – and as he struggled to extricate the box from the car, which he'd foolishly parked where there wasn't sufficient room for this manoeuvre, on the narrow strip of sun-baked concrete that separated the two houses, he became aware that his difficulties were being observed through the hedge by a pair of very large, very dark eyes.

"Memphis!"

The eyes flicked instantly away, and as Jake straightened up, the box of bibles angled awkwardly under his arm, he saw the tall, thin figure of his neighbour cross the lawn to where the shorter, squatter gardener hovered behind his camouflage of hedge.

"You look like you need a hand."

At first Jake thought it was the gardener the neighbour was addressing, but immediately the voice continued: "Shall I come round?"

Hoisting the box onto the roof of the car, Jake turned to face the unexpected Samaritan. "No, really. I can manage now. Thanks all the same."

Closer up, the neighbour's disbelieving face – unusually pallid for Johannesburg and tending, at a distance, to insubstantiality – revealed itself to be as finely hewn as a piece of statuary. "Well, if you're sure."

At the neighbour's side, his flatter, less expressive features still largely obscured by the foliage, the gardener continued to regard Jake unblinkingly.

"The name's Paul." The neighbour made to extend a hand over the hedge, only to find that its height prevented him. Withdrawing his hand with a chuckle, he used it instead to encompass the gardener. "And this is Memphis. I feel very bad I haven't been round to introduce myself. Welcome you to the neighbourhood. You know."

"Please!" As always happened when people approached him too directly, Jake felt a hateful blush burn across his cheeks. "No need to apologize." And then, so the introduction would be complete and he could escape to the safety of his house: "I'm Jake."

Paul took this as an invitation to pursue the conversation.

"From England, yes?" he enquired; and when Jake nodded, continued blithely: "What part?"

"London."

"Ah!" Paul ran a languorous hand through his long blond hair. "Now that's a city for you. The city to end all cities! No?"

"Well," said Jake uncertainly. "It's big, certainly, and I suppose . . ." The truth was he'd never much cared for London, found it far *too* big, too big and too anonymous, was even – though he'd never articulated this – obscurely frightened by it. But Paul didn't let him finish.

"I spent a month there last year. Staying with friends in New Cross. Now New Cross I could have done without, but the rest . . ." Words obviously failed him, and for a minute he was silent, paying his respects to the remembered wonders of London. Then, shaking his head sadly, he added: "Too expensive, though, for us South Africans. Five rand to the pound. Well, almost. It'll be years before I can afford to go again. Especially now I've got you to support – hey, Memphis?"

"Yes, Paul." The gardener nodded solemnly, apparently oblivious to the joshing tone of this last remark.

"Anyway," said Jake, reaching for his box. "I'd better let you get on." Standing in the blazing sun under Paul's equally direct gaze was causing his head to ache. He longed for the cool interior of his house. "Nice to have met you at last."

"No but listen!" Paul patted the top of the hedge. "I've got some cold Castles in the fridge. Come over for a drink."

"Well, I . . ." Jake was undecided whether to make his excuse the fact that he wanted to unpack and inscribe the bibles, or that he didn't touch alcohol.

But Paul was adamant. "I insist. When the Malherbes left, they made me promise to be neighbourly. Ten minutes, all right?"

Out-manoeuvred by this mention of the Malherbes, Jake was obliged to dip his head in half-hearted acquiescence. "Ten minutes. Right." He heaved his box off the roof of the car.

"Don't bother to knock," Paul shouted after him. "I'll be in the kitchen."

Jake turned to indicate he'd heard this last instruction, and was just in time to catch Paul's gaze complete its blatant inspection of his body.

"Ten minutes," repeated Paul, and then – apparently unfazed by Jake's interception of his scrutiny – turned and began issuing instructions to the silent Memphis.

Inside the house, Jake dropped the box onto the kitchen table, and leaning against it for support, closed his eyes and waited patiently until his breathing had returned to normal. Then, pulling out a chair, he sat down and – eyes still closed – let his throbbing forehead fall against his palms.

He was remembering the last time he'd seen that look, on the face of his father as together they'd walked to the pub where Jake was planning to break the news of his South African trip. As they'd approached the pub, a young man in ripped jeans, the hair on his legs clearly visible through the tattered denim, had come spinning out of the public bar and his father, on the pretext of holding the door open for Jake had stood back to follow the young man's jaunty progress down the street.

Jake got up and went to the tap, where he poured himself

a glass of water. At least, he thought grimly, the obviousness of his father's action had made telling him about the trip to Johannesburg that much easier. Fuelled by what his father liked to joke of as his "unbiblical" anger, Jake had come straight out with it over his father's first pint: that a certain Danie Malherbe, a leader of his church in Johannesburg, was coming with his wife to London on sabbatical, and that he, Jake, had volunteered to look after their house.

"Goodness!" His father's eyes had teased Jake over the rim of his pint. "Am I to take it you've become political?"

"What's politics got to do with it?"

"In South Africa?" Placing his glass carefully on its mat, his father had patted his pockets for his cigarettes. "Quite a lot, one way or the other. Or are you so busy reading your bible that you don't have time for the papers?"

"I'm going," Jake had said slowly, trying to contain his anger, "because our church has links with the church in Johannesburg, and because according to Mr Malherbe, who came to talk to us last year, there's a lot of work to be done out there, particularly amongst the blacks."

"Such as?"

"Bringing them news of Jesus."

"I see." His father's lips had twitched with the most momentary of smiles. "Just the sort of news they need, especially now."

"It's the sort of news," Jake had said stiffly, "that everyone needs, no matter who they are, or where. The time and place are immaterial."

He couldn't remember what his father had replied to that, or even whether they'd continued to discuss the subject – he rather thought he'd said what he so often had to say at a certain point in their discussions, that he hadn't come to argue, and that his father had given his customary reply: "Certainty without argument. How convenient."

Still, he thought, rinsing the glass and placing it upside down on the draining board, it was a blessing really that his memory was so selective where his father was concerned. What, after all, was the point of remembering all that pain? Indeed, he sometimes wished that the other, earlier memories,

which came unbidden and when he least expected them, were
likewise incomplete. Not that he allowed them to trouble him
unduly, but all the same, their vividness could be unsettling:
the smell and texture of his father's jacket as he nuzzled his five-
year-old head into the crook of his father's arm, the sea-like
rise and fall of his father's voice as he read to him at night, the
entirely uncomplicated smile in his father's eyes when he, Jake,
had walked into the living room on his eleventh Christmas to
see the train-set laid out on the carpet. Not knowing, then,
who's idea the train-set had actually been; not knowing who
had helped his father lay it out with such painstaking care.

He looked at his watch. Twelve-thirty. His ten minutes were
up. Time to be neighbourly. He went into the hallway to check
out his hair in the mirror.

Indifferent as a cat, the bungalow lay cool and silent about
him, waiting patiently on the return of its rightful owners. It
allowed but didn't accept his presence; the precise arrangement
of ornaments on the many surfaces, the cupboards in every
room that had been left locked, the list of instructions (one
to twenty) that Mrs Malherbe had pinned to the notice-board
in the kitchen, all conspired to remind him, lest he forget the
fact, that the house was merely on loan.

He stared at the image he presented in the glass: the
severity of his haircut, the old-fashioned spectacles which,
or so his father had said, did nothing for the fineness of his
features, the button-down shirt, the grey flannel slacks. On
impulse, he twisted round to verify what it was that Paul had
thought to admire. Then, satisfied that his slacks, unlike ripped
jeans, clothed rather than unclothed his twenty-three-year old
frame, he gave a quick pat to his hair and let himself out of
the house.

The midday sun was as vituperative as ever, and he had
to shield his eyes against its glare. In the garden of the
house opposite a middle-aged man, T-shirted gut spilling
over a pair of khaki shorts, stood watering his dispirited
lawn, a beer can on the wall at his side. Further up the
street another man, younger by the look of him, but in the
same, almost regulation suburban shorts, was leaning into the
open bonnet of his car, whilst the street itself, a shimmering

mirage in the heat, ran like a silent river between the squat, square bungalows.

Memphis was standing on the verge outside Paul's gate, chatting to a maid in a starched green uniform who made a little bob at Jake's approach.

"Molo, baas."

Jake returned the maid's greeting, taking care to include Memphis in the greeting. The gardener, however, his youthful face no easier to read in the open, merely regarded him with those same watchful eyes.

True to his word, Paul was in the kitchen, mashing an avocado into a bowl.

"I thought you might like some dip with your beer. My guacamole is much admired."

Paul's kitchen, as indeed was the case with what little Jake had seen of the rest of the house on his way through, was a carbon-copy of the Malherbes', except that where in the Malherbes's bungalow everything was clinically ship-shape, in Paul's version haphazardness reigned. The Malherbes' kitchen furniture was stark and tubular; Paul's an admixture of country pine, Victorian oddments and down-right junk.

"Now!" Paul forsook the avocado and skipped to the fridge. "One cold Castle coming up!"

Jake cleared his throat. "I'm sorry," he said. "I don't drink alcohol. Do you have something soft?"

Was it his imagination, or did Paul, ever so slightly, flinch?

"Especially at midday," he continued quickly. "It would put me to sleep."

"And we don't want that," said Paul, "do we?" He opened the fridge and made a pantomime of inspecting its contents. "Well, we have ginger beer, coke, apple juice."

"Apple juice," said Jake. "That would do nicely. Thanks."

Moments later, having supplied Jake with his juice and thrusting a bowl of crisps into his other hand, Paul took up his beer and the guacamole and led the way into the living room.

"Excuse the mess," he said airily, pushing aside a pile of books on the coffee table to make room for the dip. "I'm not much good at house-keeping and neither, I'm afraid, is Memphis."

Jake set the bowl of crisps alongside the dip, then headed for an old armchair draped with an Indian shawl.

"Sit on the sofa, rather," instructed Paul. "The springs in the armchair are shot to hell."

"Right!" Jake perched himself as instructed on the edge of the sofa whilst Paul threw himself on the offending armchair, which sagged under his weight, almost swallowing him whole.

"So!" Paul raised his glass. "Welcome to Bez Valley!"

A silence followed this toast, during which the two men gave more than necessary attention to their respective drinks.

"Memphis," said Jake eventually. "It's an unusual name."

Paul laughed. "His parents are mad about the King. He has a brother called Elvis, one called Presley, and a sister called Grace. At least they had the sense to drop the land."

Jake didn't understand this last reference. "He seems very young to be working. Shouldn't he be at school?"

"He is. In fact I'm tutoring him. Paul gestured towards the books on the coffee table. "He just does the gardening at weekends. As a way of saying thank you."

Another silence ensued, broken this time by Paul, who struggled out of the armchair and offered Jake the dip and the crisps.

"I don't believe in servants," he said. "I know it makes work for people, and God knows they need it, but I wouldn't feel comfortable." He shrugged. "Liberal guilt. Scourge of my generation. But I'm sure the Malherbes, responsible citizens that they are, have left you well provided. Servant-wise, I mean."

Not sure how to take this, Jake popped a guacamole-laden crisp into his mouth. "There's a maid who comes three times a week, if that's what you mean."

Paul returned to his armchair. "You haven't told me," he said, "what brings you to our fair and glorious country? How do you know the Malherbes?"

In view of the way in which Paul had just spoken of them, Jake wasn't sure how to reply. In fact, so uncomfortable was he beginning to feel in the other man's presence, he wasn't sure it was a good idea to be having any kind of conversation with him at all. Still, he thought, the quickest way to get this over

is to give the fullest account of myself. That way there can be
no misunderstanding about who I am, or what I stand for.
So, fortifying himself with a sip of his apple juice, he plunged
right in.

He didn't, of course, give an absolutely full account – that
would have been foolhardy – but he told his host in reasonable
detail how he came from London, how his mother had died
when he was two, how his father had brought him up, how
they were estranged because, at the age of twelve, he had
joined the church, which was how, in time, he had come to
know the Malherbes.

"I see," said Paul when he had finished. "Another born-
again."

"If by that you mean I have been born again in Christ's
love," said Jake sharply, "then yes. Though it's not a term
I'd use myself."

"And is this because the first time wasn't to your liking?"

But Jake had decided he wasn't going to be put out by his
host's hostility. He had, after all, encountered such hostility
before. It was his job to cope with it.

"Only through Christ the Son," he said, "and through a
personal, living relationship with Him, can we hope to come
to the Kingdom of God."

"And fuck the Father?"

So startled was Jake by this riposte that for a moment he
fell silent, and it was his host who picked up the thread of the
conversation.

"That box you were carrying," said Paul. "Let me guess
what it contained."

"No secret," countered Jake. "I'm here to spread the word.
They were bibles."

Paul grinned into his beer. "Your spiritual calling card."

Jake put down his juice. "If, as you say," he began,
"you're a liberal, if you care about what happens to the
people of this country, then how can you not want their
salvation?"

"Oh," said Paul quickly, "I believe in salvation too. Make
no mistake. In liberation, even. Which is perhaps what makes
me wary of any form of servitude."

"The love of Christ," said Jake, "is the greatest liberation there is."

"I'd sleep happier," said Paul, "if man could first learn to love his fellow man." He finished the last of his beer and got to his feet, the perfect host again. "But how about a top-up?"

Jake looked at his empty glass. "I think," he said careful, "it would be better if I went home."

"Oh please!" Paul was suddenly contrite. "You mustn't mind me. It's perfectly true I don't have a lot of time for the Malherbes. I could swallow their guff about God if I saw them behaving in a more Christian fashion themselves. Particularly to their maid, whom they pay less than anyone in the street. But that's no reason for us to argue."

Jake had made up his mind, though. "No, really!" He got to his feet. "I've things to do."

Paul followed him to the door, where he extended his hand.

"We South Africans," he said, "we get too defensive sometimes. A heritage of the damage we've done to our country. I didn't mean to upset you."

"That's quite all right." Jake took Paul's hand and shook it firmly. "Thanks for the juice."

He didn't see Paul again for a month. Not that he made a conscious effort to avoid him, it was more that their hours didn't seem to coincide. When Jake went jogging in the early morning, Paul's curtains were always drawn, and even when he set out on his rounds an hour or so later, the chances were that his neighbour was still not up. And in the evenings, when there was a likelihood they might meet, well then yes, perhaps he was avoiding him: he'd taken to parking the car in the street so he didn't have to use the strip of concrete that separated the two houses.

It was greatly to his surprise, then, returning late one night from a youth group, that he found Paul sitting on his doorstep.

"Goodness!" he said. "You startled me! Is anything wrong?"

"I'm sorry to do this," began Paul, the words tumbling over themselves. "You're probably all done in after all that bible bashing. But I need to talk to someone. I won't keep you long."

He had risen to his feet at Jake's cautious approach, his thin figure made startlingly gaunt by the light of the naked bulb above the door.

"You'd better come in," said Jake. "I'll make some tea."

In the sterile kitchen, Paul flopped onto a chair and took out a cigarette. "Is there such a thing as an ashtray in this hymn to cleanliness?"

Jake handed him a saucer, then plugged in the kettle. "So?"

Paul drew deeply on his cigarette. "What I didn't tell you about Memphis," he began slowly, "is that his family are Zulus. His older brothers are Inkatha members. You know about Inkatha, of course?"

Jake didn't, as it happened, or not in detail anyway, but he'd heard the word and knew that Inkatha and the ANC were politically opposed. He contented himself, therefore, with a nod.

"In fact Memphis' political sympathies, if they lie anywhere, are with the ANC, though the truth of the matter is that our Memphis isn't a particularly political animal. More interested in literature. But he can't say anything to his brothers, naturally, and what he tends to do is keep his head down. His brothers, however, are firebrands, and I don't know if you've heard the news, but in Soweto this afternoon there was an attack on an ANC hostel. By Inkatha members. Prominent among them, Elvis and Presley."

"So how does this affect Memphis?"

Paul flicked his ash into the saucer. "A group of ANC supporters came to his parents' house and set fire to it. Luckily it was Memphis' afternoon for Eliot. He was with me. But when he went home, he found the house in ashes. His mother and father and sister . . ." Suddenly the tale became too much for him, and grinding his cigarette into the saucer, Paul put his head in his hands and began to cry. "Memphis didn't dare show himself, of course, so he couldn't ask the immediate neighbours, but someone further down the street thought they'd all been in the house at the time. All three of them. His sister was only nine."

Jake abandoned the kettle and pulled out a chair next to

Paul's. Reaching tentatively for his neighbour's hands, he squeezed them in his and said gently: "And where is he now? Memphis, I mean?"

It took Paul a moment to recover himself. "At home with me."

"And what is it you want me to do?"

Paul wiped clumsily at his face with his sleeve. "There's a good chance they'll come looking for him. The Inkatha people. They'll ask the servants in the street, and people are so scared of what will happen to them if they don't do what's asked of them, they'll say anything, give anyone away."

"You want me to talk to the maid?"

"No!" The word exploded from Paul's mouth. "That's exactly what I don't want. Say nothing, and if she asks you, which she might, say you haven't seen Memphis for ages. Or even" – a sudden light came into Paul's eye – "yes, say I told you he's gone to Zululand to see his grandparents."

"And meanwhile?"

"Meanwhile," said Paul grimly, reaching for another cigarette, "I'll keep him hidden. Until it's all blown over. Whenever that might be."

Jake stood up and went to the counter, where he began to fill the tea pot.

"Well," he said. "Memphis is certainly lucky to have you. Not everyone . . ."

But he wasn't able to finish the sentence.

"Lucky?" Paul sounded amazed. "I'm the one who's lucky."

And in that instant, Jake knew, knew everything there was to know about Paul and his relationship with Memphis; knew that Paul's last remark, properly completed, should have been: "I'm the one who's lucky to have him."

It was only by a supreme effort that he managed to reach for the cups, slop them full of tea, and hand Paul his.

"I'm sorry," he said, his voice seeming to come from a million miles away, "I've spilt some." And when Paul didn't reply: "Don't worry. Your secret is safe with me."

Paul, however, appeared not to have heard him. "When I think of what that boy has been through. When I think of what his life has been like." Then he started to cry again.

"I think," said Jake slowly, "you should go to bed. Try to get some sleep. Things will look better in the morning."

Paul smiled crookedly through his tears. "You have a comforting quote for me? From the good book?"

Jake allowed himself the faintest of answering smiles. "A great many. Though I'm not sure you'd welcome them. I'll come by in the morning, though, I promise." And taking Paul by the elbow, he steered him to the front door and waited on the doorstep until his neighbour had been swallowed up by his house. Then, turning slowly into his own, he bolted the door behind him, and unable suddenly to take another step, fell to his knees on the cold parquet.

"Dearly beloved Jesus," he prayed, "sweet, loving Jesus, son of your Father, help all poor sinners in their time of crisis, show them the way of your truth and righteousness, guide them to your ever-lasting love and to eternal life."

The familiar words, honed to incantory perfection by repeated use, failed, however, to obliterate the memories that were crowding in on him: how, on that fateful Christmas, the very day of Christ's birth, the day of the train-set, an unexpected guest had come to lunch – the man whose idea, it transpired, it had been to buy him the train, the man who, when he'd been asleep the night before, had helped his father set it up, the man who had come to take his father away from him.

Not that it had happened that quickly, of course. On that Christmas all he'd been aware of was a slightly unsettled feeling in the pit of his stomach as he watched his father and his father's new friend; something, he knew not what, unusual, inexplicable, about the way in which his father, normally so quiet and reticent, had bustled about the flat while Gareth had shown Jake how to change the points and link the carriages.

No, the full horror had only come later, on the evening of his twelfth birthday, when – as a special treat – his father had taken him to a grown-up restaurant, and over a glut of profiteroles, had said: "You know I loved your mother very much, and that I hold her memory enormously dear, but I think you're old enough to know something else about me. Gareth and I are in love."

Kneeling now in the Malherbes' hallway, his knees beginning to ache from the hardness of the floor, he wondered what had given him the strength not to run crying from the restaurant – and what, in the months that followed, as Gareth slowly but inexorably moved in, had allowed him to carry on at school as if nothing untoward had happened, to make the lightest of excuses as to why he couldn't take his friends back to play with his train, and to tell his form mistress, when she kept him back from school one day to ask him if everything was all right at home, that he supposed he was simply embarking on a difficult adolescence?

This uncharacteristic joke at his own expense made him smile as bitterly now as it had then, and reminded him of course where he *had* taken strength: from that self-same form mistress and his introduction at her hands to the church, from Jesus Christ, the only begotten son of God, who loved the world so much that He gave His life to save all sinners.

Lowering his head, and ignoring the ache in his knees, he thanked his saviour for sending Miss Ash to rescue him, for opening that door on Jesus' love – even, in time, for arranging with Jake's father that he should live with her. And when he'd finished offering thanks, he prayed with an added fervour that this self-same Jesus, who'd never failed him yet, should now show Paul the correct way forward, should release him from sin into righteousness. Then, getting stiffly to his feet, he went into the kitchen, cleared away the cups, checked the back door, switched off the light, and made his way down the darkened corridor to his bed.

He woke the next morning feeling as if he hadn't slept at all. Although he couldn't recall any of their images, he knew that his dreams had been vivid and troubled, and his body, when he swung it out of the bed, felt heavy and torpid; unpleasantly, hopelessly mortal. He'd rather hoped, after his prayers of the night before, that he would have woken knowing how to help Paul, how Paul could help himself – but it seemed that Jesus had not been among the figures who'd haunted his dreams. He took a cold shower, and getting into his running gear, let himself out of the house.

It was only a quarter to seven, and the air was pleasantly cool still, and crisp – no hint in it yet of the heat to come. He set off in the direction of the shopping centre, barely registering the clusters of servants chatting idly on every street corner prior to entering the houses where they worked. His mind had returned to the events of last night, was restlessly seeking guidance of the son.

He reached the shopping centre and was about to cross the road when, in concert with a car hooting noisily at him to step back on the verge, the answer suddenly came to him, in exactly the flash that he'd hoped it would, as it always did, when he put his trust in Jesus – and without breaking stride, with only a quickening of his step to indicate his mounting excitement, he made a sharp about turn and headed for home.

He was completely out of breath when he reached Paul's front door, and he had to pause a moment, leaning with his head against the wall, before he was ready to press the bell. He heard it chime deep within the house, followed immediately by the sound of Paul's footsteps.

"Who is it?"

Paul's voice sounded as cautious as it was weary, and if he hadn't come with a message from Jesus, Jake might have been compromised by pity. As it was, though, with salvation at hand, he was able to say brightly: "Only me."

The key sounded in the lock, and Paul opened the door.

"Come in," he said dully, "and shut the door after you." And without waiting for Jake, he vanished into the living room.

Jake paused a moment on the threshold before following his neighbour. Not so easy, now that he was inside the house, to explain to Paul that what had happened was God's will, that painful though it seemed at times, God truly did move in mysterious ways to bring His children unto Him. That what God clearly intended, in what he had caused to befall Memphis' parents, was that Memphis be reminded of where he came from, and where his loyalties lay: in Soweto with his people, not here in Bez Valley with Paul. And that what Paul had to do, if he cared for his gardener, was release him from the bondage in which they languished into a state more nearly approaching grace. To renounce the body, to let go of lust – that was all Paul had to do. Something so easy, now that God had helped stage-manage it, as to be almost miraculous.

"I've come here this morning," he began, still in the passage, but raising his voice so that Paul could hear him, "because I know what Jesus would have you do. In answer to my prayers, and in his infinite love . . ."

By this time he had reached the living room, where the sight that met his eyes caused him to stop in mid-sentence. In a huge, untidy pile in the middle of the carpet, and strewn too, about the room, on the sofa and the armchair, were torn remains of what looked like an entire library-full of books. Some had been ripped into tiny shreds, in others the pages just hung drunkenly from their spines, but there wasn't one that had not been viciously attacked.

Paul was standing woodenly by the window, his back to Jake.

"He won't be needing them anymore," he said quietly. "No more books for Memphis. When I got back from your place last night, he wasn't here. Just a note on the kitchen table, telling me he had to go and find his parents and his sister and give them a decent burial. Though of course, when he shows his face in the township, it won't be to bury his family – it'll be to get buried with them."

For a moment, Jake didn't utter a word. He was still acclimatizing himself to the scene in front of him. Then, as the full extent of what had happened began to sink in – and with it the realization that not only had Jesus come to Jake on his run, but that He'd visited Memphis also, had shown Memphis the way to turn from Paul – he took a tentative, half-joyful step forwards. All that was needed to complete the miracle was for Paul to understand that what had happened was for the best; that Jesus was beckoning.

"Paul . . ." he began.

He didn't have to say another word. At the sound of his name, Paul slumped to his knees at the window – and though, at first, Jake hardly dared believe the evidence of his eyes, when Paul remained on his knees, rocking metronomically to and fro, then, ever so gradually, Jake allowed himself to say it: that Jesus had indeed completed the miracle; and pushing impatiently through the violated books at his feet, he ran to lay his hands on the head of his praying neighbour.

HUNTER

Felice Picano

IT WAS SUNSET when Ben Apres drove up to the hanging shingle that read "Sagoponauk Rock Writers Colony", and, on a smaller, added-on shingle, "Visitors see Dr Ormond". An oddly autumnal sunset, despite the early summer date and no hint of dropping temperature, as Ben stepped out of the ten-year-old Volvo that hadn't given him a bit of its usual temperament on the long trip. He urinated on a clump of poison ivy until it was shiny wet, surveying what appeared to be yet another rolling succession of green-humped New England hills.

The muted colors of the sunset fitted Ben's own fatigued calm following weeks of torment, his final uncertain decision to come, and his more recent anxieties since the turn off the main road that he'd never find the place, that he'd driven past it several times already, the directions had seemed so sketchy.

He found himself gaping at the sky as though it would tell him something essential, or as though he'd never see one like it again. Then he made out some houses nestled in a ravine. The colony. He'd made it!

Dr Ormond was easy to find. The paved road that dipped down into the colony ended at his front door in a shallow oval parking lot, radiating dirt roads in several directions. The lot contained two cars with out-of-state-plates and a locally licensed beat-up Baby-blue pickup.

The active, middle-aged man who stepped out of the house chomping an apple introduced himself, then looked vaguely upset when Ben asked where he would be staying.

There appeared to be a mix-up, Dr Ormond said. Another guest – and here Ormond threw the apple down – and went on to mention a woman writer of some repute – had unexpectedly accepted the colony's earlier invitations, thought by them to have been forgotten. She had taken the last available studio. They hadn't been certain Ben was coming this season either. Victor Giove hadn't heard from Ben in weeks. Of course, Victor hadn't heard from Joan Sampson either, and she'd come too, though naturally they were all delighted she was here.

Ormond motioned behind him vaguely. Ben saw a white clapboard, pitched-roof house standing alone on a patch of grassy land. He supposed that was her studio, the one he was to have lived in.

Before he could ask, a plump middle-aged woman, her apron fluttering, her hair in disarray, was waving to them from the doorway. She'd already telephoned Victor, she called out. He was on his way. Mrs Ormond, Ben guessed.

He leaned against the Volvo. Darkness was quietly dropping into the ravine. One or two lights were turned on in the Ormonds' house, other lights appeared suddenly in more distant studios. Ben wanted to wake up tomorrow morning in this enchanted glade, to spend sunny and rainy days here, long afternoons, crisp mornings, steamy nights. He would not allow the mix-up to affect his decision. After all the inner turmoil, he was glad he'd come. He wasn't leaving.

Above all, he was grateful to Victor Giove, who was jogging toward them now, accompanied by a large, taffy-colored Irish hound, the two racing, skirting the big oak, circling Ben and Dr Ormond, the dog barking then nuzzling Ben's hand for a caress, Giove hardly out of breath, glad to see Ben. He took Ben's hand, clasped his shoulder, smiled, was as openly welcoming as Ormond hadn't been.

Victor was tan already; his curly dark head already sparkled with sun-reddened hair; he looked healthier and more virile than he'd ever looked in the city, an advertisement for country living with his handsome, open-featured face, his generous, beautifully muscled body that loose clothing like the old T-shirt and corduroys he was wearing couldn't disguise. Ben felt Victor's warmth charge into his own body as they touched, and he knew that all things were possible this summer, even the impossible, even Victor.

"There's no place for Ben to stay here," Dr Ormond protested once they'd gotten inside the Ormonds' living room.

"What about the little cottage," Victor said. "That's empty."

"What little cottage?"

"By the pond. I passed it today. It's all closed up. You don't need a full studio, do you Ben? Of course, he doesn't. He'd love the little cottage."

"It's a fifteen minute walk from here," Ormond said, unpersuaded.

Ben suspected he'd be crazy about the little cottage.

"He's young," Victor said. "it's not far for him."

"But it isn't ready for him."

"Sure it is. You helped clean it up yourself. Remember? It can't have gotten more than a little musty in the meanwhile. Besides, he can't go all the way back now, can he?"

Ben told them he'd already sublet his apartment in the city. He had nowhere else to go.

"You see!" Victor said. "Come on, Ben, dinner's ready. I'll take you to the little cottage after."

"Victor!" Ormond said, in a strange tone of voice. "That cottage was Hunter's."

"It belongs to the colony."

"You know what I mean."

"Ben's here," Giove said firmly. "Hunter isn't."

"No. I guess you're right."

"Then it's settled."

Four of them ate dinner. Joan Sampson was to have joined them but she called to cancel, saying she had work to do.

Ben did know they had no such thing as community dining

at the colony, didn't he, Frances Ormond asked. Everyone took care of themselves. Except of course, everyone dined with whoever they wanted to. She hoped that Ben would feel as welcome at her table as Dr Giove was. It was impossible for Ben to not like the transplanted urban woman who'd evidently found peace at Sagoponauk Rock. Like Victor, she radiated health and happiness. Ben would later discover that was a rare quality at the colony. Others had brought their sufferings and neuroses, unable or unwilling to let them go. They argued around kitchen tables just as badly as they had in Manhattan bars. They outraged and scadalized each other in country bedrooms with infidelities and treacheries as though they still lived in West Side apartment complexes. Over the following week, Ben sized up the colony members quickly. Only Mrs Ormond was judged to be sound.

And Victor, of course. Victor, who was the reason Ben had come to Sagoponauk Rock, and the reason he had almost not come. Even after Ben had sublet his apartment. Even after Ben had turned off the exit from the New England Thruway and had driven north for what seemed hours.

After dinner, Victor got into the Volvo's driver's seat and drove through the dark, rutted road to the little cottage. Ben held an extra kerosene can Frances Ormond had given him, unsure whether the electricity was turned on.

It was, they discovered, after a long, silent ride through the deep darkness of the country, passing what would later become landmarks to Ben on his night walks and night drives: the community house, the first two studios, then Victors, the apple orchard, then the fork past the pond.

The cottage was L-shaped: a large, bare bedroom separated by a small bathroom and cavernous storage closet from a good-sized study area opening onto a small one-wall kitchen with a long dining counter.

Victor built a fire to help clear out the unseasonable chill. Ben went through the kitchen cabinets and found a bottle half full of Fundador. They sipped the brandy, talking about the program they'd tentatively set up the past April at school, which Ben as an apprentice writer would follow at the colony. He was only to show Victor a piece of writing when he was satisfied with it, or unable to find satisfaction in it. Some of the others at the colony never shared their work with each other. Victor and Joan had agreed to meet regularly to read to each other. Ben could join them.

Although it was only a three and a half month stay, Ben had decided he would write day and night. Not only the few short stories Victor asked for, but a novel too, *the* novel, the one he'd planned, the one he believed he'd been born to write. Free here of most distractions, he felt certain he'd get much of it done before the last school year rolled around again. He already loved the cottage.

Only the bedroom, after a second look, didn't seem as cozy as the rest of the house. Ben thought the bedroom's coldness was due to its appearance: low ceilings, uncarpeted dull wood floor, only a few pieces of furniture: hardly inviting. Perhaps a single night's sleep would warm it up. The double bed – higher and wider than the one he was used to – was firm yet comfortable when he tried it out.

Victor had gone into the bathroom. He found Ben stretched out on the big high bed and stopped, lingering on the threshold.

For a long minute they looked at each other. Ben, his hands under his head for a pillow, felt suddenly exposed, then seductively positioned, inviting. Giove seemed suddenly bereft of his usual composure, uncertain, fragile, even frightened. Neither of them moved. Ben could feel the tension of the possible and the impossible filling the room like mist.

"It's getting late," Victor said, his voice subdued, his hands suddenly gesturing as though controlled by someone else. "I'll come by in the morning to show you around the colony."

Embarrassed himself now, Ben quickly sat up and got off the bed to see the older man out. In an attempt to cover over the shame he felt he asked, "Who had this cottage before me?"

"Stephen Hunter, the poet," Giove said, looking out into darkness.

"You're kidding. I didn't know he stayed here at the colony."

"Oh, everyone important comes to Sagoponauk sooner or later."

Ben was about to say something about how happy he was that the cottage had a literary past, but Giove said goodbye and was gone.

Ben settled into the dank chill of the sheets they'd found in the big closet and thought of that moment in the bedroom, of Victor's suddenly coming upon him, his hesitation, his distracted gestures, the quiet tone of his voice and his sudden decision to leave. If he had remained another minute, come into the bedroom, come closer to Ben, the impossible would have been possible, in this very room.

Ben climaxed with a sharpness he hadn't experienced masturbating in years, not since he was an adolescent. Wiping his abdomen with a hand towel, he wondered whether it was the fresh country air or seeing Victor Giove again after so long.

Victor didn't come by in the morning to show Ben around. Ben didn't see him until dinner time. But that was only the beginning: Victor's fluctuations of intense consideration and total aloofness eventually formed themselves into an inescapable pattern.

That first morning, Ben didn't care. The bedroom faced east and he awoke to a sunny spendor of nearby trees and bright clear sunlight flooding every inch of what seemed to be a really handsome though sparsely furnished room.

After a breakfast of bread and honey provided by Mrs Ormond the night before, Ben wandered around the colony. He was still too awed to approach any studios closely, believing the other colony members would be intensely concentrating on their writing, and thus not to be disturbed. But he had enough to look at: the pond, surprisingly large, still and lovely, quite close to his cottage; the apple orchard stretching far into the distance; the lively stream that formed a tiny marsh at the pond; the large old trees, many he'd never seen before; the young saplings everywhere; the fruit and berry bushes in demure blossom; the wild flowers surrounding the house; the cottage itself, beautifully crafted of fine wood, so that built-in tables, drawers, and cabinetry were integrated perfectly by color and grain, all of a piece.

He skirted the colony later on, driving up to and along the

two–laned highway, following Frances Ormond's instructions, locating in one direction a truckstop all-night diner, a gas station and after another five or six miles the tiny hamlet of Sagoponauk – where he purchased a backseat full of groceries and supplies. Driving in the other direction, past the colony, Ben found another gas station and an old clapboard roadhouse, containing a saloon and an Italian restaurant.

The peace that had settled on him momentarily the dusk before, returned when he drove back to the colony, and arrived to see the little cottage – highest of the houses on the property – aglow with fuschias and oranges, its western windows reflecting a brilliant summer sunset.

Victor apologized when he saw Ben. Besides doing some writing that day, he said he'd fixed a propane gas line to Joan Sampson's oven and hot water heater, and had helped Mrs Ormond pick early apples for saucing.

Ben was embarrassed by the apology. He could spend all day with Victor. That was why he had come to the colony. But now that he was here, he could not justify deserving Giove's attention. Victor wasn't merely gorgeously unself-conscious – he was altruistic, giving his time and energy to anyone who needed it. Obviously there were others in the colony who needed it as much as Ben.

So Ben contented himself. Especially after the first few weeks, when he began to realize that the impossible love between them could only occur suddenly, impulsively, unforgettably, like any other miracle.

Victor's comings and goings appeared to fit some obscure plan. Ben wouldn't see him for days, only to come upon him mowing a shaggy patch of lawn, or wrapping heavy black tape around a split waterpipe of one of the studios. Then Victor would come by the little cottage early one afternoon, spend all day, remain for a hastily concocted dinner, talk about people and writing and books until midnight. Only to disappear for days. Only to reappear again as suddenly, stretched out on the yellow plastic lawnchair at midday as Ben returned home from a walk, or suddenly diving past Ben's surprised face into the clear water of the pond and swimming to the other shore. His appearances were unpredictable. The hours he spent with Ben

so full of talk, of intense attention that Ben would be charmed
into persuading himself that Giove was merely being careful,
getting to know Ben better, making sure of him before he would
suddenly turn to Ben, put his arms around him, and . . .

That was when Ben would feel frustrated all over again, full
of lust, and he would have to go into the bedroom, to lie down,
to picture how it would be, sometimes masturbating two or
three times after Victor had been with him, feeling his fantasies
becoming so real that the impossible *had* to happen.

Once, Victor came by after dinner when Ben was writing.
Giove lay down quietly on the sofa, began to read a magazine,
and fell asleep. When Ben realized that, he couldn't concentrate. Even sleeping, Victor was too disturbing. Ben wandered
around the cottage, trying to wake the older man by the noise
be made. He even tried to fall asleep himself, but it was an
absurd attempt – the bedroom felt as cold, as uninviting as
the first night he'd spent there.

He finally decided to wake Victor: he was so tall, he had to
sleep bent up; he awoke with cramps and pains. Ben didn't
say it to himself, but he suspected that once they were in bed
together, Giove would relent.

Victor stretched, got up, looked once at the bedroom hallway
as though trying to make up his mind whether to stay, then said
he wouldn't hear of it.

It was hours before Ben could fall asleep, even after he'd
taken a mild sedative.

He had purposely not touched himself during those
tormenting hours of unrest. During the night, however,
half-awakened, he felt heat emanating from his genitals,
couldn't fight it away, and worked groggily but efficiently
to bring himself to orgasm. Dazed, exhausted, he sank back
into slumber.

The following afternoon, Victor was at the pond again when
Ben arrived for his daily swim. With him, sitting on the tiny
dark sand beach, wearing a huge sunhat, was a chaperone,
Joan Sampson. Ben remained with them only long enough to
be polite.

After that day, Victor and Joan were always together, Victor
seldom alone.

Even without her interference, Ben thought she was the least sympathetic person he'd met in the colony. She epitomized all he disliked in the others, their utter sophistication and real provinciality, their brusqueness, their bad manners, their absorption with themselves and lack of interest in anyone else except as reflections of themselves. Her frail child's underdeveloped body and the expensively casual clothing she wore, her bird-like unpretty face and unfocussed blue eyes that seemed to look only with disdain, her arrogance, her instant judgments and devastating condemnations of matters she couldn't possibly know about, her artificial laugh, her arch gestures and awkward mannerisms – she might have been a wind-up toy. Next to her, large, naturally graceful, athletically handsome Victor, his Victor, looked bumbling. Together, they were grotesque.

Ben made certain he wouldn't see them together. He pleaded work when they asked him to join them for dinner, didn't show up for readings of their work, never went where they were likely to be.

The impossible, he began to see, was impossible. He had to forget Victor, to forget him, and above all to stop fantasizing about him.

When the cold showers and extra work he made for himself around the cottage no longer served to keep his mind off Victor Giove, Ben began to run miles every day along the two-lane road, to swim hours at a time in another, larger pond he'd discovered a short drive away. When he realized these methods were no longer working Ben got into the Volvo late one night and drove to the all-night truckstore diner.

Two cars – one he recognized as belonging to the owner – and a large red Semi, were parked in the gravel lot. Ben pulled up close to the truck, hidden from both the diner and the road and waited. When the truck driver finally came out of the diner, Ben rolled down his car window and asked for a light for his cigarette.

The trucker was close to middle-aged and heavyset, but he had kind brown eyes and an engaging grin. He lighted Ben's cigarette. When he asked if Ben weren't a little young to be doing this sort of thing, Ben shrugged, then leaned back in the car seat with a loud sigh. A second later, the trucker's lower torso filled the car's window frame, the worn denims were unzipped, not another word said. Ben sucked him off and came without touching himself.

The following night, Ben stopped at the roadhouse and struck up a conversation with a travelling salesman who had a suitcase full fo encyclopedias. After a few drinks, Ben was able to convince the man he wanted something other than books. The salesman was younger than the trucker, thinner, better looking, just as obliging. They drove separately away from the roadhouse, met a mile further at a turn off, and made love in the backseat of the salesman's car for over an hour.

Ben drove out late every night. One time he picked up a long-haired hitch-hiker who offered him grass. They smoked and Ben drove twenty-five miles before he got the courage to ask if he could blow the kid. Sure, the hitch-hiker said, unzipping, I was wondering when you were going to ask.

Several times he repeated his first night's success at the diner. He also discovered that the Esso station outside of Sagoponauk had a removable plank at exactly the right height between the two booths in the men's room. High school boys who came there after unsuccessful weekend-night petting sessions with their girls and local older men furtively used his services at various odd hours. Ben became bolder, picking up strangers leaving the roadhouse. He was often misunderstood, sometimes threatened. The bartender, a married partner in the place, offered to guide likely men Ben's way in return for occasional favors. A week later he took his first payment sodomizing Ben on a shiny leather sofa in an office after the roadhouse had closed.

During all of these experiences, Ben never felt less frustrated, less craving of sex, or less in love with Victor Giove. But he told himself that whatever else he was doing, at least it was better than fantasizing about Victor and masturbating. That seemed to help.

Although he had gone to sleep very late, and was even a little drunk when he'd finally gotten back to the cottage, Ben awakened instantly, fully, as soon as he thought he heard the footpads in the darkened room. Fully alert, tensed, he kept his eyes closed, pretending to be asleep. Whoever had stopped at the foot of the bed was looking down at Ben.

Despite his terror, Ben didn't panic. Then, oddly, he felt a wave of intense lust passing through his body. Odd, since the young man he'd spent two hours with on a blanket inside a clearing they'd driven to had been both passionate and solicitous of Ben's pleasure: so that Ben had felt both mollified and physically exhausted when they'd parted with a long, lingering kiss at their cars again. Despite that, Ben now felt a biting, itching erection, a pressing need to masturbate as though he hadn't had sex in a month.

The fear returned. Ben almost shivered. He pretended to be disturbed in his sleep, mumbling loudly, rolling onto one side before waking up.

During his exertions, whoever had been at the foot of hs bed left the room. Ben felt alone again. He listened for noises in the other rooms, waited a long time hearing nothing, then got out of bed, and crept first into the corridor, then into the rest of the cottage. The doors were all locked, the rooms empty. Puzzled, wondering if it were a dream, Ben went back to sleep.

Several nights later, he again awakened sensing someone at the foot of his bed. Once more he felt a scalding, sweeping lust over his lower limbs, the need to touch himself. Then fear reasserted itself, and he was cold again. While he was sleepily trying to get out of bed, whoever it was got away. He was certain it wasn't a dream this time.

Ben thought about the matter for the next two days and determined to ask Frances Ormond who else had a set of keys to the little cottage. Walking to the Ormonds' house, he came upon Victor Giove, surprisingly alone, sunning on a blanket spread over the grass behind his A-frame studio. Victor was clad only in a pair of red, worn swim trunks.

Ben moved on with a wave, but Giove hailed him over so insistently that Ben reluctantly joined him, and even took off his shirt to get some sun.

He was "pale as February", Victor told him, and would burn

unless he put on some suntan oil. When Ben began to splash it on, the older man said he was doing it all wrong: he would show him how. As Ben lay on his stomach, he expected to feel the large, strong applicating hands transformed into messengers of caresses. They weren't. They were brisk, efficient. They spread the lotion evenly: nothing more.

Giove didn't seem to have noticed that Ben had been avoiding him. Their conversation was the usual: what Victor was writing, what Ben was doing, what was happening among the others at the colony.

Ben stayed for almost an hour – his disturbance at their near-nude closeness had vanished. When he got up and put on his shirt Victor said: "You ought to get more sun. And rest more. How are you sleeping? You look sort of done in to me."

Ben was so stunned he couldn't answer. Why would Victor say that to him – unless it was Victor himself who was visiting him every night?

When Ben finally did say he was sleeping well, Giove seemed skeptical, then added, "Well, you know best." When he rolled on his stomach, his wide shoulders, his long, muscled back, two solid buttocks stretching the bright red nylon of his swim trunks, his thighs and legs – honeybrown and flecked with sun-bleached hairs – all jumped out at Ben. He wanted to fall down there and kiss and lick every inch of that body for hours on end. The black curly ringlets of Giove's hairs shone like white gold in the sun. Shoving his itching hands into his trouser pockets, Ben managed to mumble goodbye before tearing himself away from the spot.

He was imagining things, Ben told himself, walking away. Victor had only asked how Ben was sleeping because he'd probably heard Ben driving past his studio late every night for the past three weeks and was concerned.

Frances Ormond confirmed that she had heard Ben's Volvo at two and three in the morning at least a dozen times. She was far less subtle about it.

"That's the way Stephen Hunter began his terrible descent," she said, "staying out late, getting drunk in roadhouses, coming home late. Summer after summer. Night after night toward the end."

Ben thought it was none of her business, but defended himself by pointing out that he had written the two required stories and had already begun his novel. Late hours helped him work, he said.

She pursed her lips as though to counterattack, but changed the subject, feeding him coffee and freshly baked berry pie instead.

She told Ben no one else had keys to the little cottage. None were needed; the locks didn't work; anyone could get in if they wanted. Stephen Hunter had once told her he'd had enough of locks in the city. He wouldn't have functioning ones out here. It was his undoing, she added, because it enabled his murderer to get at him so easily.

Without much prodding, she narrated the grisly tale of three summers' past. The young vagabond had been captured in a saloon a few towns away. He'd confessed and was imprisoned. At first he made some foolish claim about Stephen owing him money and refusing to pay, about them being friends for years. Under pressure, his story changed into one of revenge. Stephen had molested him, he said. It wasn't convincing, even to the unsophisticated local sheriff.

Back at the little cottage, Ben discovered she was right – all the doors could be opened, the locks just flapped on their hinges. Ought he have them repaired? Yes. But whoever was visiting him at night did nothing but look at him. Was that reason enough to change something Stephen Hunter had done? Ben would never bring anyone back to the colony. He congratulated himself he never had. And he still couldn't get Victor Giove's words earlier that day out of his mind. He was almost certain it was Victor.

So he didn't repair the locks. And the next time he was awakened in the middle of the night and sensed the figure at the foot of the bed, Ben felt only a few seconds of the usual fear. The figure remained motionless. It seemed to be the right size for Giove. Then Ben began to feel the intense warm itch sweeping from the tips of his hair to the soles of his feet.

Slowly pushing down the light blanket, Ben let the dark figure warm him with its gaze, then began touching himself on his legs and groin. He though he heard a sharpened intake of breath from his visitor, and Ben let go, slowly, luxuriously caressing and stroking himself, thinking of Victor at the foot of the bed watching him, wanting him, not daring to touch him. His climax that night was shared: he was certain of it.

When he opened his eyes, the room was empty.

He was visited every night for several weeks. Every night Ben awakened, sought out the outline of the figure against the lighter darkness of the room and succumbed to fantasies and sex.

During the day he often told himself he ought to be sure it was Victor and not someone else. But who else could it be? He searched the eyes of the other colony members he saw, looking for any signs of guilty, secretive interest. He found none. Then he would come upon Victor, racing around the lawns with the big Irish hound, or sitting reading in a hammock strung outside of Joan's studio, and, though they seldom exchanged more than a few words, every word, every phrase seemed so couched with meanings relevant to their shared nights, Ben was convinced that it was Giove.

Didn't everything point to it? Victor's insistence that Ben remain at the colony that first night? His friendliness? His increased reticence with Ben since the night visits had begun? He seldom spoke to Ben of Joan, or of their work – as though it had only been an excuse. Ben came to believe that their new silence – when they met at the local grocery store, or out on walks – was more eloquent than words. It spelled content.

Ben would be a fool to spoil it. The impossible had become the possible. Not in the open way he'd at first naively imagined, but tacit, secretive, and for that reason somehow more passionate than he'd ever fantasized. Victor must still have hurdles of attitudes, ingrained prejudices to jump before he could admit what he was wanting, feeling. Ben would give him time. Who knew what the next step would be in their growing closeness – so long as Ben didn't force it.

Ben had been visited that night as usual, all his lust and wakefulness drawn from him, as it always was, replaced by deep, calm, dreamy sleep.

People were marching down a small town street. Batons

twirled, trumpets blared, signs and crêpe-covered floats sailed past. Children bounced eagerly behind. The drum passed by very close, going bam bam BAM! bam bam BAM! again and again, sounding lovely and rich and mellow at first, then ominous, then emergent.

Ben awakened to someone hammering on his front door. He thrust open the bedroom window to the cool mountain summer morning. It wasn't quite dawn.

"Ben! What do you know about drugs?" It was Eugene Ormond, evidently recently awakend. If he hadn't looked so panic-stricken, Ben would have laughed.

"Joan Sampson's taken a pile of them. We're sure they're some kind of sleeping pills."

"What did they look like?" Ben asked.

"We found one that fell on the floor." Dr Ormond showed Ben the red and blue shiny capsule – Tuinals.

Ben dressed and ran out to Ormond's pickup idling in front of the cottage.

"She's got to vomit them up, I suppose," Ben said as they drove toward her studio. "Then black coffee, to keep her stimulated."

"Frances thought the same. I hope she's all right."

"Where's Victor?" Ben asked. "He would have known."

They pulled alongside the studio. Ormond looked at Ben oddly, then said, "Didn't you know? He's back in New York. Has been for three days. That's what all this is about."

Before Ben could register the news, Dr Ormond had stopped the truck and was urging him to come inside.

Joan was audibly vomiting. Frances, as audibly, was cursing about the stupidity of trying to kill yourself over a man, for Chrissakes, even one like Victor. There was a final spasm of vomiting, quiet, then Frances Ormond half dragged the small woman out of the bathroom and, spotting Ben, asked him to help her walk Miss Sampson around a bit while Eugene made coffee, doubly strong coffee.

Their charge was light, but weak, her arms were useless, her head kept lolling against Ben's shoulder, words and saliva dribbled out of her mouth.

They wheeled her around for another five minutes. Another

fifteen minutes were spent feeding her the coffee and ensuring she didn't vomit that up too. Then more walking around.

Joan was visibly recovered by the time the phone rang. She still looked awful and had allowed Ben to bring her into the bedroom where she was noisily sobbing, but at least she was safe.

"Get that, will you Ben?" Mrs Ormond asked, looking up from where she was cleaning the bathroom's tiled floor.

Ben lifted the receiver and said hello. There was a confused mumbling from the other side. Then: "Joan. Is that you?" Victor Giove, perplexed.

Ben looked away from the phone, unable to say anything for a minute. Holding his hand over the phone, he barely murmured, "It's Victor." Saying the name was more difficult than almost anything he could remember in his life.

"Of course it's Victor!" Frances Ormond said, and came to take the call.

"You see!" Joan sobbed, standing at the threshold of the room. "He's seeing her again. He was with her all last night. He couldn't stay away from her. That's why he went back."

Frances Ormond hushed her. Ben moved away from them, feeling as though he were on the set of a movie where everyone was playing a role and only he didn't know the scenario. He couldn't believe that Victor was in New York; yet there he was calling long distance in response to a call Mrs Ormond had put through.

Ben walked slowly back to the little cottage. He felt dazed by the morning's events, but not so distracted that he didn't notice it had rained the night before: the dirt around the cottage was still damp, though drying fast. Two sets of footprints led to the tire tracks of the pickup. No other marks of someone walking around were visible.

That night he drank some brandy which kept him awake longer and made his sleep lighter than usual. When he was awakened during the night by the urgent panting breath at the foot of his bed, he immediately turned to the bed table and turned on the lamp. The room was empty.

Energized by a need to know, Ben leapt out of bed and ran out into the other rooms. He even looked outside. When he returned to the bedroom a few minutes later, he thought he saw a wisp of smoke curling into the lower edges of the large storage closet. The closet was empty, but the morning chill caught up with him there, and he began to shiver so badly that he had to get back into bed and pull up the covers, waiting for sunlight.

"Stephen Hunter was homosexual, wasn't he?"

Frances Ormond looked across the distressed oak parquet of the old table at Ben.

"I guess they still don't talk much about those matters in college do they?" she asked, instead of answering him.

"The vagabond who murdered him was a hustler, wasn't he?"

"You seem to know all the answers. Why ask?"

"In the bedroom?"

"Stephen tried to get away," she said. "In the closet."

Ben wasn't surprised to hear it, only vaguely chilled to know his line of reasoning had been so on target.

"And Victor and Stephen were friends, weren't they?"

"Not by then, they weren't. They had been close friends. That summer they had a falling out."

"Because Victor wouldn't sleep with him?"

"You do have all the answers, don't you? Yes, Victor looked up to Stephen as though he were a god, but he couldn't bring himself to love him that way. Generous as Victor is with himself – I sometimes think he's too generous – people want more than he can give."

"And that's when Stephen began picking up hustlers?"

"No he'd done that long before he met Victor. You've read the sequence called "Broken Bones", haven't you?"

"Years ago," Ben admitted. He'd never thought it was about hustlers.

Frances got up from the table and went to another room. She returned with a copy of Hunter's *Collected Poems*. Ben found the page and reread the first few poems in the sequence. He was shaken by the harsh, beautiful images of lust and fear.

"And this is why you said you thought I was heading in the same direction?" Ben asked her.

"I don't care what you do. Just be careful."

"I've never brought anyone back to the cottage."

"Borrow the book," she pleaded. "Read him again, Ben. He has a great deal to tell you. All great poets do. But I think he has a special message for you."

Like every literature student of his generation. Ben had read several of Stephen Hunter's poems in class, and had even memorized one – a sonnett: "August, and the scent of tragic leafburn". Aside from that one, however, Ben had always thought Hunter overrated. He had preferred the more formal poets, Stevens and Auden and Aiken, to what he termed the wild men. Dylan Thomas, Lowell, and especially Stephen Hunter. Not that his opinion made any difference. Hunter was in every anthology, his work written about, eulogized, discussed, reinterpreted.

Ben rediscovered him, reading through the poems in two days, rereading them, then selecting out single poems and analyzing them.

Hunter's famous *Odes to an Unruined Statue* were suddenly opened to Ben as though they had been written in a language he could never understand until now. Victor was the beautiful man/object, the unattainable; Hunter, the critical observor and adoring fantasist. The *Window Elegies*, that dozen intensely wrought series of dense metaphors and precise, yet oddly angled images were illuminated as though a light had been switched on in a basement room. Their visionary style and metaphysical message were all held together by carefully delineated details of different windows through which the poet had seen a loved one. The description in the second elegy was clearly that of Victor's A-frame studio here at the colony, the window Hunter had looked through night after night, spying on Victor.

Ben didn't go near the large closet, which he never used anyway. Nor did he sleep in the bedroom.

He felt safe on the living room sofa, even though it was cramped. And, whether it was because of his intense new fear, or whether there was a natural boundary to the presence, Ben was not awakened once by his nocturnal visitor while he slept there.

The locks were repaired, of course, just as a precaution. And he began to haunt his previous places of fast, usually anonymous sex, returning home late at night and sleeping deeply. When he didn't go out, he would stay awake at night, working, and sleep during the day. Everything he did seemed tinged by an undercurrent of excitement, as though anticipation were slowly building, but toward what end he couldn't even begin to say.

Giove returned to the colony. Ben sometimes came upon him swimming at the pond. Although Joan was no longer with him, and the older man waved Ben over to join him, Ben would plead an excuse and quickly leave. The one time Ben and he were thrown together, for dinner at the Ormonds', they found they had nothing to say to each other.

What Ben had thought to be a mutual secret content, he now saw otherwise. Victor was perceptive enough to understand what Ben wanted from him; he was trying to avoid having the same kind of problem he'd had with Stephen Hunter.

Ben knew that evening he'd fallen out of love with Victor. The golden aura that used to light the other man's steps through the tall grass, the sparkle that used to dapple his dark curls as he lay in the sun were gone. His eyes seemed tired, his face lined, his laughter constrained.

Ben knew why too. No man he could ever deem desirable would have been fool enough not to give so simple a matter as his body to a once-in-a-lifetime genius like Stephen Hunter.

It was August when Ben moved back into the bedroom. "August, and the scent of tragic leafburn," he reminded himself, when he awakened once more out of a deep sleep. He knew instantly that the presence at the foot of his bed was Stephen Hunter.

His body was beginning to tingle warm under the blanket cover he had protectively pulled up in that instant of realization. But Ben still shivered. The air about him stirred in cool eddies unlike any air he'd ever known. He heard what seemed to be fragments of whispered lines from poems, pleas, demands, obscenities. Stephen knew Ben, knew who he was, what he wanted, what he'd given up. Ben's teeth began to chatter. All he had to do was to reach over to the lamp table and put on the light, and he'd be alone, well, out of harm's reach. But if he did that, Stephen might never come back to him. Ben wasn't sure he wanted that either.

He suddenly thought of Victor Giove. Large, muscled, beautiful generous Victor. He thought of Victor's smile, the bulge of his crotch in those tan worn corduroys, the roundness of his buttocks in those scarlet swimtrunks, his rippling chest, his furrowed back, those ringlets of black curls, his Florentine profile.

The room became warm and still. So warm. Ben had to push the blanket away from him, letting the heat seethe around his body.

Keeping his eyes closed, Ben thought of Victor walking, running, swimming. Then someone else pushed Victor out of the picture and came into focus: a broad-shouldered, tall, thick-bodied man with intelligent deep-set eyes of indeterminate color, a craggy face, long, straight, honey-colored hair, straggly moustache and beard, the face, the body, the very photograph from the frontispiece of the *Collected Poems*.

Stephen Hunter was a great poet. A genius. He'd filled himself with wisdom and suffering equal to any philosopher, any monarch. Compared to him, Victor was an oversized primate

Ben relaxed, seeing without sight, the figure moving in front of him, as though undressing, feeling the figure reach out and slowly caress Ben, the multicolored eyes gleaming softly, the mouth working to form wonderfully original words of manlove lewdness. The raking gaze swept over Ben's body like electric fire. Only such a genius could provoke, could produce such utter pleasure, Ben thought, as he gave in.

He was only slightly jolted when Stephen Hunter accepted. The sudden touch of large warm hands pressing upon his spread thighs, the brush of warm skin on either side of his loins, like a soft large cat. But the tongue that invisibly licked before engulfing him was that of a man, the long bony nose and unkempt facial hair, when Ben reached down to gingerly touch them, those of Hunter's photo images; and Ben knew he had finally found what he'd come to Sagoponauk Rock Colony for, and why that first sunset had been filled with implications he could not at first decipher.

By the end of the summer Ben was a complete recluse. He had not been seen by anyone on the colony in weeks when most of the members went back to their teaching posts around the country. Joan Sampson and the Ormonds – the last to leave, in mid-September – tried to find him, but gave up after a series of attempts.

Both the Ormonds and Victor Giove used the house on a long, late October weekend. The little cottage was empty, lived-in, although increasingly messy, dusty, ill-cared for. Victor felt guilty about the boy, and waited for hours one afternoon, then searched the area until sunset made it impossible. He left notes that were never answered and were never found on subsequent visits.

On his Thanksgiving break, Victor again drove up to the colony, this time to close off the water pipes against the winter and to make certain that all of the houses were locked. He once more drove to the little cottage, hoping to find Ben and to talk him out of his foolish decision to remain isolated. He didn't find the boy; but walking away from the little cottage, he gasped when he noticed the roof of Ben's Volvo sticking up out of one edge of the pond.

Although the pond was dragged by State and local police for two days no body was every found.

Victor relayed the sad, ambiguous news to Frances Ormond, who contacted Ben's family in Eastern Long Island. Neither of them heard from his relatives again.

The last two days of the Christmas holidays, Frances Ormond drove up to the colony by herself. She found several studios broken into: cans of tinned food opened, eaten, discarded. She cleaned up, repaired the windows and doors with local help, gathered all the remaining canned foods in the studios, bought more at the grocery store and dropped them off in a large cardboard box near the little cottage. She never told anyone she did this. Secretly, she was proud and envious that Ben had gone and done what she'd always wanted to do – live here all year.

It turned out to be an extremely fierce New England winter.

Storms raged weeks at a time. All but main highways were blocked by high snow drifts and after by ice layers most of which lasted until late March. Livestock froze in heated barns. Old people were stranded and died. Children and stragglers from stalled cars were lost in blizzards. Many local farmers closed up their houses and went south. Others remained indoors, barely surviving.

Even though they managed to get into the colony by early March, the snow plows couldn't get anywhere near the little cottage.

Easter brought on the first thaw. Victor drove up to the colony, bitterly hoping he would find the boy, and that he would finally listen to reason.

The door to the little cottage was still iced over and had to be kicked hard to open.

Inside, the main rooms were icily cold. Fires had been built, tin cans charred over the fire. Kerosene litters and sterno cans littered the living room floor. But Victor couldn't tell how long they'd lain there, a day or a month. It did seem as though the boy had gotten through the winter. That was a relief. He'd probably suffered so much he'd return with Victor to the city without much urging. Victor sat down to wait.

Although it was still cold, something else seemed to be missing from the cottage that Victor couldn't at first define; a disturbance he'd almost subconsciously felt every time he'd been here since they'd discovered Stephen Hunter's corpse in the storage closet.

When it finally was too cold to stay seated, Victor got up to leave the cottage. He wrote a note to Ben saying he would be at his studio; Ben could find him there. He was about to walk outside when he realized the bedroom door was closed.

Could the boy be hiding there?

Victor opened the bedroom door and remained quite still for a long time.

The nude emaciated body of Ben Apres was stretched out as though in utter ecstasy on the bed. His skin was ashen, pale blue with frost, perfectly preserved down to the few frozen drops of semen that had splattered his gaunt abdomen and hung off the tip of his penis.

Victor understood why he no longer sensed the supercharged presence. The insatiable Stephen Hunter had finally found someone worthy of his love.

LUV, G

Neil Powell

LUV, G

Neil Powell

THE FIRST THING he sees, as a gust of onshore breeze flusters the curtains and tickles him awake, is that George has typically turned away from him in the night and is now engrossed in intermittently snoring communion with the pillow. The second is a vivid salmon-pink brilliance, glimpsed just beyond the open window when the curtains dance apart. Matthew eases himself out of bed, pads almost surreptitiously across the room, and peers between the curtains. He had forgotten the window-box, or rather scarcely noticed it in yesterday's dusk, and discovers that it is packed with ivy-leaved geraniums in flagrant, outrageous bloom.

George will sleep for an hour or two yet, so Matthew slips into the bathroom to wash and dress as quietly as possible, although there is little danger, or even chance, of mere noise waking his friend. Their daily cycles seem hopelessly incompatible, but this curiously strengthens their relationship, providing for each periods of respite and freedom whilst the other is sleeping. Thus Matthew doesn't know what George got up to after he left him at about ten yesterday evening in a thoroughly doubtful establishment called Benjamin's Bar; and, since neither of them plays dangerous games, he is disinclined to worry about it. He merely reflects ruefully that George has reached that difficult

age at which he can no longer resist even the ironic attention
of the young. As he silently closes the bedroom door behind
him and sets off, cheerful and clear-headed, on an exploratory
walk, he feels almost virtuous.

He has time. He is reading at one of the festival's morning
sessions, 11 o'clock he thinks it is, and can follow his ramble
with a late leisurely breakfast. Also on the bill today is Hugo
Malarkey, a young Irish-American poet whom he has almost
met twice (but on each occasion Malarkey either mislaid
himself or mistook the day or the time), and a cantankerous
octogenarian called Isabel Trent who would do very nicely
as Lady Bracknell. Matthew wonders, as he walks along
the corridor with its grandly patterned carpet in reds and
purples, as if the ingredients of a summer pudding have been
extruded and rearranged geometrically, who on earth devises
these programmes. But of course he knows. It is the festival
co-ordinator, Lucinda Cosgrave, and she is standing at the
end of the corridor waiting for the lift which, to judge from
the unflinching green light on the panel, is firmly stuck two
floors away.

"Matthew," she says warmly. She has an extremely small
mouth marooned in the midst of an enormous white face, and
she greets him like a friendly blancmange. He realizes with
horror that she is genuinely pleased to see him. "Will you join
me for breakfast?"

He panics. He does this in hotels anyway, but the additional
ingredients of Lucinda, breakfast, and an indefinite wait for
the lift (it has now begun to move, but in the wrong direction)
have him instantly drowning in nervous sweat. "I'm terribly
sorry, I can't, there's something I have to see to. Eleven
o'clock, isn't it? I'll be there." The lift is naturally at an
intersection of corridors, so he hurtles off down one at
random. The blackberry-strawberry pattern in the carpet
repeats over and over, like a musical ground-bass, like a fugue
that's going nowhere. He chants quietly: blackberry-strawberry,
blackberry-strawberry. There's a right-angled bend, then more
of the same, punctuated by glossy white doors with their bright
clickety numbers: 328, 329, 330. And then, as abruptly as it
started, the corridor ends in a landing with circular staircases

sweeping up and down from it. Matthew slams on his anchors, feeling like a creature in a cartoon and wondering whether the entire length of carpet he has covered will roll itself up behind him or with him in the middle. It doesn't, obviously, so he pauses to consider the nature of the space in which he finds himself. There's a musty though valuable-looking chandelier, which may have been here since the building's country-house days, and fine polished mahogany bannisters; the carpet has subtly modulated, with a distinct strand of blueberry insinuating itself. Clearly the reasonable course would be to head downstairs towards the ground floor; but Matthew, working from instinct and fatalism, knows that this will have him somehow colliding with Lucinda Cosgrave as she emerges at last from the lift. He reflects that a hotel – no less than its close relatives the theatre, the funfair, and (for that matter) the ancient, creaking pleasure steamer of fiction – is a contrivance of illusion within which, somewhere, there is the door to disillusion, to the inevitable backstage. He looks around the landing again: it has five impeccably white glossy doors, one of them unnumbered. It seems worth a try.

Demystification is only the mirror-image of mystification, not its opposite: thus the pleasant shock of an illusion broken may be at least as great as the surprised delight of an illusion created. So, at any rate, Matthew feels as he confronts the peeling cream paint of the back staircase with its curtainless window and single bulb in a pale shade like an upturned plastic saucer. He also feels immediately at home, as if this is an index of his former alienation, and knows why: the hotel is trying, not wholly successfully, to present itself as something special and individual, but the back staircase has the generic honesty of all back staircases. There are webs against the window-panes, where spiders doubtless live happily uninterrupted lives.

Like a child suddenly released from an especially loathsome lesson, he hurries downwards, and at the first corner almost collides with someone sprinting upwards, a contingency which he hadn't paused to consider. The upwardly-mobile sprinter is, however, indisputably worth considering. He is about Matthew's height, say five-tennish, perhaps eighteen years old, with cropped blond hair and intense, deep-set blue eyes; compactly, unexaggeratedly muscular, his is a body designed for the beach rather than enslaved to the gym. Matthew takes all this in at once, because the boy is wearing nothing apart from a pair of white shorts and, draped round his neck, an inadequate-looking striped towel whose shortcomings are confirmed by the fact that he's not so much damp as dripping wet. "Oops," he says grinningly at the near collision, "sorry." And skips past up the stairs, leaving Matthew with a tantalizing glimpse of vanishing legs and bare feet, and a light scattering of dew. For a puzzled moment he wonders whether the staircase links staff bedrooms to a subterranean bathroom before realizing that the boy had simply been for a bathe in the sea, which is probably something he does every morning of his life, and that people who live by the sea take the stuff for granted as an ordinary part of their environment with an instinctive ease which is all but unimaginable to his inland self.

The way out proves to be otherwise unimpeded: the stairs lead to a bleak hall, from behind whose closed doors come the smells and clatterings of the kitchen, and whose open door reveals a cobbled yard. He slinks a bit guiltily through this, and finds his way into the terraced gardens of the hotel. He feels foolish – not, as it happens, because he has made a fool of himself, for this is a more or less everyday occurrence – but because he had allowed himself to forget how easily and instantly that particular folly can appear. Just one look, one smile, one glimpse, and it's an obsession for days or weeks, an image that will recur years later in some incongruous dream. And no sooner is the obsession planted than it starts to sprout narratives. He imagines an assignation with George in room 309: surely there was a boy – wasn't there? – who might have looked like that in the bar last night. He tries to give the boy a name – Craig, Gary, Mark, Steve, hunky boy-names which ring false though not quite false enough. He considers dashing back into the hotel, back up to their room on the pretext of having forgotten – what? And, anyway, that at once conjures the possibility of colliding with blancmange-faced Lucinda as she at last emerges from the lift. Lord, he thinks, what fools mortals can be.

The hotel garden seems to have been designed by a creative partnership of Dali and Disney. A steep path with eccentric twists and a creaky balustrade leads towards the beach, but it is edged and overshadowed by monstrous vegetation: gigantic ornamental ferns, fuchsias with huge gaudy blooms like lanterns. An enormous monkey-puzzle tree presides over the whole affair as if it thinks itself the crowning joke, a kind of brilliant botanical punchline. The path ends, however, not at the beach itself but in a gateway onto the lane at right-angles to it; and this in turn emerges onto a genteel, stuccoed Victorian seafront. It's the sort of place, Matthew reflects, which would probably call itself a Marine Parade or an Esplanade; and, sure enough, a little way along, a row of two or three houses knocked together proclaims itself to be the Esplanade Hotel and advertises "Vacancies", as well it might. He buys a paper from a dour newsagent and sits down on a bench to glance at it. High above him, beyond the stupidly exuberant banks of foliage, the windows of his own hotel are bright with sunlight and geraniums.

He arrives back later than he's intended: even Lucinda Cosgrave has breakfasted and gone. The croissants are misshapen, runts of the litter, and his coffee tastes of the pot. Around him waiters are stealthily shifting objects about or more pointedly flapping cloths clear of their tables, like nurses changing sheets in an almost vacant ward. "Gary," calls one, "give us a hand with these." And Gary emerges through the blubbery swing-doors of the kitchen, contained and somehow diminished in his whites, as if he too has been starched and ironed. He grins shyly at Matthew as he passes; or Matthew imagines he does, then imagines he imagined it. There is no end (he thinks) to his folly. From outside and below come distant scrambled shouts, the universal fragmented language of the beach, and in the unblemished blue sky beyond the window there suddenly appears a multi-coloured kite, like an impertinence.

In the lift, which he has to himself, there is just time to recall a recurring dream in which he is travelling helplessly upwards, past his intended floor, past more floors than any building could possibly contain, to find himself alone and stranded on a fenced-in roof without a lift-shaft in sight. (It goes back a long way. It goes back, he realizes, to Marlon Brando on that roof at the start of *On the Waterfront*.) In Room 309, he expects to find George still asleep; at least, having formulated no alternative expectation, he is somewhat surprised to find not George but a note, scrawled on the hotel's hideously crested paper: "GONE TO BEACH," it says, "SEE YOU LATER. LUV G.' Both tone and intent seem out of character, or simply without character. He gathers together the things he'll need for the reading and slides them into a briefcase: published books, work-in-progress, spectacles, pen for autographs. He adds a few copies of his latest collection, just in case the local shop has sold its meagre stock. By now the briefcase is beginning to seem quite bulky, and this in turn makes him feel more substantial. He wonders about scribbling a reply to the note, but really there is nothing to be said.

Only when he has left the room and is padding along on the blackberry-strawberry carpet does the ridiculous "what if?" possibility propose itself. What if those ironic-illiterate capitals were nothing of the sort? What if G were not George but Gary? And, if that were so, to which of them is the note addressed? The fact that Gary, as far as Matthew knows, is at this moment scurrying about in the kitchen or restaurant rather than reclining gorgeously on the sand (well, he corrects himself, shingle, then) ought to demolish the notion yet predictably fails to do so.

In the conference room where this morning's event is to take place, quite a few members of the audience have already assembled. They are the sort who are always well provided with complicated things to do: knitting, or the *Guardian* crossword, for instance. One or two of them actually have copies of Matthew's books, and as he passes he catches a severe-looking woman in the act of surreptitiously comparing him with his jacket photograph. He wonders whether he passes the test or whether the image, like a particularly plausible waxwork, is somehow more convincing than the reality. At the front of the aisle, Lucinda beams sweetly towards him. "Do you mind," she says, "being in the middle? I thought Hugo first, then you, and Isabel finally, in deference to her great age. Will that suit you?"

"Perfectly," he says. "Am I the first to arrive?"

"You are. I've saved seats in the front row for when you're not actually reading. I don't want everyone on stage together, sitting round a table like a committee."

"No, no, that's quite right," he says, wondering what kind of committee four such ill-assorted individuals might conceivably comprise, and then recalls some of the literary awards panels he'd encountered.

Lucinda glances at her watch. "I do hope the others won't be late. They're both famously unpunctual."

But, luckily in a sense, this particular worry turns out to be misplaced, for at that exact moment Isabel and Hugo erupt into the room in the midst of an incoherently blazing argument. Hugo is doing an unconvincing impersonation of a bewildered Irish simpleton, while Isabel is in her most thunderously infuriated Lady Bracknell mood. "I hope, young man," she tells him, "that both your testicles drop off. And the front wheels of your car likewise."

"I'm not staying to listen to this crap, and anyway I don't drive a car. Call me," he says to Lucinda, "when the old lady's calmed down a bit." And he turns to go.

"Don't be such a prima donna, young man."

"Prima donna? Now who's being a prima donna? I'll be in my room. Or the bar, if it's open."

"Oh dear," says Lucinda, helpless and hugely pallid.

"He'll be back," says Matthew, without conviction.

"I do hope so. In the meantime, would you mind *awfully* reading first?"

"Of course not."

The audience – or that part of it which was within earshot of these exchanges - has traded its air of cultural dutifulness for one of high excitement. Matthew wonders how on earth mere poems are going to satisfy their expectations now, but the tension is at least preferable to dozy complacency. Almost at once, perhaps sensing this and wanting to seize the occasion, Lucinda is on the platform making her introductory announcement, even though it's barely eleven o'clock.

He climbs onto the stage, opens his briefcase, arranges books and folders on the table, the literary stallholder setting out his wares. He adjusts his spectacles so that he can peer learnedly over them at the audience, and then he peers. There's a fuller house than he'd anticipated, friendly and attentive faces who after the unscheduled prologue may now be all the more kindly disposed towards him. He looks around anxiously for George and soon locates him, as expected, in the back row. Nearby, having at the last moment squeezed through the door and still in his kitchen whites, is Gary. Matthew feels for a moment appalled and betrayed, before it dawns on him that he has perhaps been the object of their entirely separate pursuits, that after all they've both come to listen to *him*. He smiles gratefully at them, at everyone, and starts to read. Beyond them, the window is edged with salmon-pink geraniums, and a brightly-coloured kite is dancing and diving in the clear blue sky.

THE AMATEUR

Simon Raven

"WHAT ABOUT A trip to the September meeting at Perth?" I said.

"No," said Rollo Rutupium very firmly, "not Perth."

"Why not? It's one of the most attractive courses in the kingdom."

"So I used to think," said Rollo. "I changed my mind."

"Why?"

Rollo thought heavily for half a minute.

"Once upon a time," he said at last, "I had an affair with a very appetizing undergraduate in Trinity Hall."

"What's she got to do with it?"

"He. This was over forty years ago . . . before all these women shoved themselves in where they weren't wanted."

"Oh, come on Rollo," I said. "It must be rather jolly there now, with plenty of girls around."

"There were plenty forty years ago, if you knew where to look. The thing was that they all had their own colleges and had to go back to them for most of the time. A man could get away from them if he wanted to. They weren't in one's room giggling and whining and demanding and wearing out the furniture all day and all night – which is what it's like now, my nephews tell me."

"Well, that's their worry. This catamite of yours in Trinity Hall – what's he got to do with the Perth Racecourse?"

"He wasn't my catamite for a start. A catamite is a boy whom you bugger. Although I have always been in favour of widely varying sexual practice with all the genders, I absolutely drew a line at buggery. Messy, painful and (as it now turns out) potentially lethal."

"All right," I said, "this fancy boy of yours. What's he got to do with Per— "

"He wasn't a fancy boy either. Definitely not mincing or dainty. He was butch and wholesome and just a little bit bandy. Played cricket and rugger for Trinity Hall. Blue eyes and Viking blond hair and a slightly snub nose. Medium height. When he played tennis in white shorts, his bonny bow legs (smooth as silk) used to flash and twinkle all over the court like magic."

"Steady on," I said, "that's enough."

"No, it isn't," said Rollo. "If you want to appreciate this story, you must first know all about Micky. Micky Ruck, he was called. I sat next to him by accident in one of Professor Adcock's lectures on the late Roman Republic. Adders was buzzing away about that crook Clodius, and suddenly there we were, Micky and I, playing footsie and kneesie and thighsie like a pair of demented fourth formers . . . Mind you, I was quite a dish myself in those days. Tall and languid and sinuous . . . hardly a hair anywhere on my body, except a small blob of pert pubes."

"Love at first sight?"

"No love about it. Sheer randiness. Yearning for flesh and skin. But there *was* affection. I enjoyed his sort of accommodating naivety, while he admired my upper class demeanour and cynicism. So in no time at all we were lusty bedfellows – he used to laugh a lot, I remember, just before he came – and excellent occasional companions, playing squash and watching cricket at Fenner's. However, there was just one cloud in the sky."

"Scandal?"

"No. We usually met in my own college, King's, and in King's in those days nobody worried about that kind of carry-on. However, the trouble was that Micky was afraid

that because he liked doing it with other boys he might turn
into a full-time homosexual. The Classics master at his school,
unlike the Classics master at mine, hadn't pointed out to him
that the norm in both Greece and Rome, at any rate among
the best people, was an easy-going bisexuality. So I now made
this plain to him, quoting chapter and verse, and just to set
his mind at rest I arranged for my cousin, Heather Sopworth
of Girton, to give him a go. As I told you just now, you could
always find a girl if you needed one, even then . . . long before
they infested the entire university."

"And how did he get one with Heather Sopworth?"

"Spiffing. Heather was a grand girl, as I knew well enough;
we'd been intimate playmates since we were twelve. She told
Micky that he was the best she'd ever had except me, and
explained that a taste for boys made boys far more attractive
to girls (jealousy and curiosity) and also made girls far more
attractive (by sheer contrast) to boys. He could have the best
of all possible worlds, she told him, but he should remember
that he had only a limited time in which to enjoy them: boys
will be boys, but not for long. When he became a man, she
said, he'd probably be pretty attractive, but by then women
might expect him to be faithful to them, or even to marry
them, and that would be a bore. So gather ye rosebuds while
ye may, Heather urged, on both sides of the garden path."

"I still don't see," I said, "what any of this has to do with
Perth."

"Patience," Rollo said. "So Micky was gathering rosebuds
in all directions, Heather's and mine and God knows who else's,
when it occurred to me one May morning that I should be going
down for good in June, after which I should have National
Service for two years, much of it very likely abroad, and that
there would be an end of Micky Ruck. I therefore decided to
extend my stay in Paradise by arranging a last spree with Micky
the following August and September, before he must go back to
Cambridge and I myself must list for a temporary lancer. Micky
and I would have a Grand Sporting Tour, taking in Festival
Cricket Weeks – there were plenty of those then, before the
game was put in the charge of a money-grubbing inquisition
from the Corporal's Mess – and lots of tennis tournaments,

both real and lawners, and plenty of golf and racing. We could start at Lord's, make our way up through England and then Scotland to Gleneagles, and then on to the goal and crown of the whole expedition, the September Meeting (here we are at last) at Perth."

"Bravo," I said.

"One possible obstacle, however, was Micky's adoring mum, who liked her little boy to be with her during the hols. Luckily she was a howling snob. I hadn't inherited then but she knew who I was, so to speak – Micky never really understood all that, bless his heart – and she was very pleased with our friendship. As for the idea that 'something' might be going on, it didn't bother her. She wasn't fussy. I did have to pay a toll of a night in bed with her – but it was no trouble. Like her son, she roared with laughter when she was coming, and she kept on calling me 'Micky darling' by mistake, which had interesting and rather exciting implications. Anyway, I soon had her imprimatur for our journey.

"And so off we went, Micky and I, in that Lagonda I used to have, playing in the odd match for the Butterflies and IZ – Micky belonged to neither but a few smiles at the right people soon settled that problem – watching the late county games, going to early National Hunt meetings at Hereford and Stratford and Sedgefield (proper country meetings, none of those pimply pimps and lacquered whores that you get at the meetings near London), popping in at Doncaster for a bit of Flat, di-da, di-da, some tennis (Royal) at Chester and some Shakespeare in Edinburgh, until at last we came to Perth, where we put up at a very decent pub in the forest some miles north of the course.

"We had a day spare before the racing started, and so, since Micky was getting into one of his periodical states about being too queer – he'd been laughing like a satyr all the way from London and was afraid he was enjoying himself too much – I took him to see Penny Pertuis, a busy widow whose husband had been in the same regiment as my father. Penny was a versatile lady, who now taught anthropology at the University of St Andrew's; she showed us round the golf course as far as the ninth, where we retired into the bushes for a picnic

followed by a tremendous three ball. I let Micky do most of
the actual fornicating, to restore his confidence, and what with
him laughing and Penny bawling obscenities, which was her way
of showing gratitude, I thought we'd have the entire Committee
of the Royal and Ancient charging down on us like a squadron
of the Greys. But no, we were only spotted by a red-headed
Scots laddie looking for lost balls to sell, who happily made
up a foursome – nothing so rorty as a wee ginger Scot.

"Blissfully tired after a long day in the fresh air, we set out
back towards Perth, taking Penny, who had decided to come
to the races with us the next day. We telephoned the pub to
book her in and order our dinner, and on the way back we
paid a visit to the Palace at Scone. Although the place had
just closed when we reached it, Penny knew a private way in.
In any case the purpose of our call was not to see the Palace
itself but to inspect a remarkable graveyard they have there, in
the woods near the chapel, because Penny the Anthropologist
had some theory about eighteenth-century burials in that part
of the world and she had heard that there might be something
helpful there at Scone.

"Now, Penny's theory had to do with the sepulchral use of
the obelisk. There was, so they said, a particularly fine obelisk
at one end of this very grave ground, an obelisk which had
been put up over the remains of one Purvis Pride the Pride
of Birnam – the Prides, then as now, being great men in the
county and devils for hunting. The Pride under the obelisk had
been killed steeplechasing in 1789, at the age of nineteen . . .
this during a cross-country race, which had started in the hills
up at Belbeggie and ended (so Penny told us) at a tavern
which then stood by a copse in the middle of the meadow
that formed the centre of the modern circuit. Young Purvis,
when well in the lead, had broken his neck at the last obstacle
of all – the stream in which the good woman of the tavern did
her washing. She'd hung a huge nightshirt out on a hedge to
dry, and the wind had got up and blown it straight on to horse
and rider, blinding them both just as they were about to jump
the steeply banked stream. The horse, a stallion called Jupiter
Tonans, had perished with Purvis and was buried with him.

"Penny's theory," Rollo went on, "was that obelisks were

reserved for the remains of gallant men – soldiers and sailors, explorers and adventurers. What she wanted was to read the inscription on the Pride obelisk, which was said to include a phrase which could explain why Purvis Pride, a mere local huntsman and stripling amateur jockey, had been allowed the full funereal apparatus of a proven man of action.

"Having climbed a bolted postern in the wall, which ran parallel to the Perth-Balmoral road, we approached the burial ground through graceful conifers and along a sunken path. This opened out in a delta at the east end of the cemetery, where the trees gave way to the ranked monuments. Although the evening had not yet fallen, the grave ground in front of us (about one hundred yards by fifty) was diffusing its own shade of subfusc illumination from the lolling mounds and crumbling pedestals, the black slabs and sweaty cylinders, which made up the assembly of seventeenth- and eighteenth-century sepulture. We filed through the stones, Penny leading, Micky and I, seeing as little as possible of the spikes and balls and skulking crosses, until we came to the far end, the end nearest the Chapel (which was just visible through high bush and ladybirch) and the Palace itself, about a furlong beyond, on the far side of a broad, trim lawn. But our attention was soon distracted both from Chapel and Palace by the grave, which we had come to see. A marble obelisk, of a tall man's height and topped by what looked like a mortarboard without its tassel, stood on a small grass island, which was surrounded by a moat of dark water about seven foot wide.

"'Apparently it's quite deep,' said Penny, 'not for wading. And anyone that jumped would break his napper on the obelisk. Luckily I can read the inscription from here with my race glasses.'

"She took these from their case . . . the ones her husband had used all through Italy.

"'Take it down,' she told me, and glinted through the glasses at the inscription on the side of the obelisk, which was facing us.

"'Brave rider, Purvis Pride'," she read, "'brave stallion had to ride; *Jupiter Tonans* him did call, who slew them both by cursed fall.' Not a high standard of verse,' observed Penny. 'But there's a bit more – in Latin. "*Nonne quidem stuporum poenitet animum equitis hic sepulti in saecula saeculorum cum nobilitate equi sui?*" Interesting use of the abstract: "the nobleness of his horse" instead of "his noble horse".'

"'In sum,' translated Micky, looking over my shoulder at the transcript, '"surely the soul of the horseman repents of his *stuporum* – debaucheries – buried here as he is for ever with his noble horse?" Informing us that the horse, *Jupiter Tonans*, is in there too.'

"'That we knew,' said Penny, 'though it is useful to have it confirmed. The glowing tribute to *Jupiter Tonans* obviously explains why Purvis Pride's tomb was dignified with an obelisk. Clearly the obelisk is for "the noble horse" rather than his rider. But there remains a slight mystery: it seems that Purvis was guilty of certain *stupra* of which, it is hoped, he will repent at leisure, perhaps influenced by his "noble" companion. Evidently these *stupra* were considered no great matter; otherwise this memorial would have not been allowed an obelisk in the first place however great the fame and nobility of *Jupiter Tonans*. The nice question is, *exactly* what were they, these *stupra*? Micky has translated them as "debaucheries", but what specific debaucheries?'

"'The word is commonly used both in Latin prose and verse,' said Micky the classicist, 'of any sexual misdemeanour and in particular orgies or adulteries. Perhaps Purvis Pride junior went round tumbling the local wives? Not much of a crime for a well-connected young man in the eighteenth century.'

"'A considerable crime in Scotland,' said Penny. 'The Kirk would not have stood for it . . . and would certainly not have permitted him this kind of internment in this kind of place.'

"'No doubt,' I myself put in, 'Father Pride the Pride of Birnam had a liberal palm for greasing other palms. Come to that, the Kirk or the episcopalians – whichever administered this place – might not have been too keen on a bloody great stallion being permitted Christian burial.'

"'Good point,' said Penny. 'A nice fat bribe covers the difficulties all round. No doubt Father Purvis squared it for both of them – for *Jupiter Tonans* and for little Purvis.'

"'It would still be amusing,' said Micky, 'to know precisely what he squared in the way of *stuporum*.' He stooped down and looked into the black moat. 'Purvis Pride, Purvis Pride,' he intoned, 'what naughtiness *did* you get up to?'

"Answer came there none, except for Penny's comment: 'Pretty boys should not go too close to still waters. Remember little Greek Hylas, who was hauled in by the water nymphs.'

"'They don't have water nymphs in Scotland,' Micky said, 'the Kirk would never allow it.'

"The next day," continued Rollo, "we all went to Perth races. The course, as you know, is not far from Scone; indeed, if you stand by the second jump out from Tattersall's you can see a bit of a rampart or whatever through the trees which separate the circuit from the Palace gardens. So here we came and stood for the big race, a very long steeplechase during which the horses and their riders would take this fence three times.

"'You will observe,' said Penny as we walked across the meadow from the enclosure, 'that the Purvis family is well represented. Purvis Pride – surely a descendant – is to ride his gelding, Long John Silver. Black and White halved with Black Cap.'

"'Same colours as the Hall,' Micky said. 'Trinity Hall,' he explained to Penny, 'my college. We call it the Hall for short.'

"'So I surmised,' said Penny.

"'Of course I've backed him,' bubbled Micky. 'The layers gave me a hundred quid to a tenner.'

"'Extravagant boy,'

"'It's well worth a tenner,' Micky said, 'just to be standing here in this lovely place.'

"One quite saw what he meant," Rollo pursued. "In front of us, the other side of the course, were the trees up the gentle slope to the peeping Palace; behind us was the meadow and two hundred yards away the copse near which had stood the vanished tavern, by a stream that had also vanished, where the eighteenth-century Purvis Pride had broken his neck. Beyond the far end of the course the countryside idled away, pine and bracken, to a semi-circle of low hills.

" 'What are those blue remembered hills',' I quoted, " 'what spires, what farms are those?' "

" 'That is the land of lost content",' murmured Micky, continuing Housman's poem, while a single tear ran down the left side of Penny Pertuis's nose.

" 'Pay attention to the racing, boys,' she said huskily.

" 'They're off!'

"It cannot be said that young Purvis Pride's Long John Silver distinguished himself. Nor did his rider. A series of blunders, the first of them at the fence by which we were standing, soon put him a good twenty lengths behind the rest of the small field (seven in all). The second time round he was trailing even further, but he managed to stay upright for a further circuit, and as he went past us for the third and last time he appeared to be rallying slightly and drawing nearer to the pack of six horses in front. When the field emerged from behind the copse, with half a mile to run, Long John Silver had come level with the last horse and seemed to be making good ground. Over the last ditch, with two plain fences still to jump, he was lying fourth . . . but thereafter reverted to his previous form, sagged back to the rear of what was now a forlorn queue. Ye Banks and Braes, the only mare in the race, was going to win by a corridor: Long John Silver passed the post last by thirty lengths.

" 'So much for my tenner,' said Micky; 'boring race.'

" 'I don't know,' said Penny. 'For a time he quickened rather bravely. Then something took the heart out of him.'

" 'I don't think there was ever much heart there.'

" 'He seems to be showing a bit more now,' Penny said.

"And indeed, having barely flopped past the post, Long John Silver with Purvis on his back in his black and white colours had started to gallop again and was coming very fast round the bend and towards the fence at which we were still standing.

" 'He's riding very long,' said Micky. 'I didn't notice that before.'

" 'Perhaps he's lost his stirrups,' I said.

" 'No,' said Penny. 'He's riding long.' She concentrated through her glasses as horse and jockey drew closer. 'And he isn't riding Long John Silver,' Penny squawked, 'he's riding a stallion, dear Jesus – '

"'The stallion veered to its right, jumped the rails between the course and the meadow, set straight at us, came swiftly closer. The rider, a wedge-faced youth with a shapeless black cap and no helmet, lent down and across, seized Micky by the scruff of his jacket and hauled him up like a circus act. He wheeled his horse (Micky now being bunched in front like a parcel), jumped back onto the racecourse, then over the hedge on the far side, and galloped away through the scattered clumps towards Scone.

"'Now we know,' said Penny, shivering and jerking, 'what form Purvis Pride's *stupra* took. The dead Purvis Pride. I told Micky he shouldn't have looked into that moat. You see what's happened?'

"'I think so,' I retched. 'It must have cost the Pride of Birnam a pretty penny in bribes to arrange for that monument – if his son's tastes were known when he was living.'

"'They must have been known. *Stupra*. Abomination. Perhaps they thought he would be . . . safer . . . in consecrated ground. Perhaps they forced his father . . . to add an obelisk to keep him down . . . a moat to keep him in . . . just in case, they thought. Just in case.'

"'What now?' I said. 'Shall we go to the graveyard?'

"'No point,' Penny said. 'We can't compete . . .'

"Nevertheless we did go there. And saw nothing we had not seen the day before. The waters of the moat were dark and still as ever. We went back to the pub – what else could we do? – and ordered dinner."

"Halfway through dinner," said Rollo, "Micky came back. He was shrivelled and yellow and taut. He ate ferociously, and didn't talk till he had finished. Even then he spoke mostly in monosyllables, at once clear, courteous and impersonal, as if he didn't know to whom he was speaking, as if he were the voice of an answering machine. He named neither of us and made no reference to what had occurred, beyond saying, 'I am there. We must go to me there. You must take me to me.'

"'Now?' asked Penny.

"'Tomorrow,' stated what was left of Micky Ruck.

"And so the next morning we took him there to him. We

called his name. Poor shrunken Micky leant over the moat, while Penny and I stood discreetly just behind him. 'Micky, Micky Ruck,' Micky called. His reflection appeared in the dark water, the reflection of a rosy, laughing boy with blond hair and a snub nose, full of jollity and juice.

'Micky, Micky Ruck,' Micky called.

"But the reflection laughed the more, waved happily, and faded.

"'Please take me away,' said Micky to Penny and me, as if he were addressing two complete strangers and asking for a lift.

"And now you know," said Rollo Rutupium, "why I shall not, if you will kindly excuse me, be accompanying you to the September meeting at Perth."

EMBRACING VERDI

Philip Ridley

I REMEMBER THE first time I saw Verdi. It was the day we buried Dad and, as our funeral car pulled away from the kerb, I caught a glimpse of him in the rearview mirror. He was wearing a black leather jacket decorated with studs and splashed with gold. His almost white hair sparkled in the sunlight. Instinctively, I twisted in my seat to stare back at him. As our eyes met, he smiled and waved. Mum tapped my knee and sighed, telling me to sit straight and act properly. It was, after all, a sad occasion and not one for restless fidgeting. But the image of the blond boy haunted me all afternoon. The funeral took second place as my mind created fantasy after fantasy about him. I guessed he was in his late teens, which seemed ancient to me, being only twelve at the time. That night, after the relations had gone and Mum had retired sobbing to bed, I dreamed about him. In this dream I told him all my fears and worries, how I missed my father but was already forgetting him, how I hadn't cried once although I wanted to, and the blond boy embraced, kissed me and told me his secrets.

Two weeks were to pass before I saw him again. This time he was standing opposite the school gates when I rushed out at four o'clock. The sight of him made me stop dead in my tracks.

I felt a strange, tickling sensation in my chest and stomach, like spiders crawling inside. Boys pushed past me, annoyed that I was blocking their way. Since my father's death no one had spoken to me. I think they were afraid of my loss, ashamed almost, as if grief and tragedy could be contagious, spread like the common cold.

The blond boy stared at me for a few minutes. Then he strolled across the street. Panic glued me to the pavement. I wanted to run both away from him and towards him. finally, he stood in front of me, put his hands on my shoulders and smiled.

"You're Cloud, aren't you?" he asked

I nodded.

"Can I walk home with you, Cloud?"

"Yes," I said, breathlessly.

Some boys from my class stared at me as I walked down the street with the blond boy. They nudged each other and whispered things, obviously impressed with my new friend. As we walked along, the blond boy hummed an endless succession of haunting melodies. I recognized one or two of them as being from operas. Finally, when we reached the corner of my street, he stopped and murmured, "This is as far as I can go."

"Oh," I said, fumbling for words. Fear of loss, the desire to be with him, made me brave. "Come home with me. Have something to eat. See my room."

He flicked sweat from his eyes, squinted against the sun and removed his leather jacket. He wore a white T-shirt, ripped across the chest. I saw his brown skin beneath and one dark nipple. The spiders grew frantic inside.

"Please," I begged. "Stay."

"Perhaps another time."

"Meet me tomorrow."

"Don't you want to know who I am?" he asked.

"No," I said. "Just meet me."

"I'm called Verdi," he whispered. Then walked away.

I watched him until he turned the corner. For a few minutes I just stood there, waiting; I felt sure he would come back for me. But he didn't. And I went home with an empty feeling where spiders had crawled.

That night, as we ate dinner, Mum started to cry again. She pushed the plates aside and buried her face in the tablecloth. I tried to comfort her, but didn't know the right words. It was guilt more than grief, I think Mum and Dad had been arguing non-stop for six months before his death. The night he was killed they had been having a particularly violent row Mum had screamed abuse and accusations. Dad stormed out of the house and drove away in the car: that was the last we ever saw of him. A few hours later, on his way back from wherever he had been, he swerved to miss what he though was a child and crashed into a letterbox. Ironically, it wasn't a child at all. Just a walking doll set in motion by a couple of pranksters.

I helped Mum upstairs and put her to bed. She took a few of her tranquillizers, asked me to wash up the dinner things and make her a hot drink. Later, as she lay drowsily sipping cocoa, she clutched at my hands and kissed each finger in turn.

"You love me, don't you, Cloud?" she asked.

"Of course."

"Why didn't he love me, Cloud? Tell me that. Why couldn't your father love me? I loved him, you see. I fell in love with him the first time I met him. And I always loved him. No matter what I said, or did, I always loved him. So why couldn't he love me? Am I that difficult to love? Why did he betray me? He was seeing another woman, Cloud. Oh, I know I shouldn't talk ill of him now he's gone, and you'll probably hate me even more than you already do. But you have to know. Otherwise you won't understand what all those arguments were about and why I said the things I said. Oh, he denied it. But I knew! A woman can always tell."

Every night since my father died I had gone through this ritual with my mother. She would accuse Dad of not loving her, of infidelity, of keeping secrets. I, in turn, would try to convince her that she meant the world to him. Later, she would ask for the photograph album and, laying it across the eiderdown, make me turn the pages as she gave a running commentary on this frozen record of her love for my father. Occasionally she would point to a photograph and say, "Look, look at his eyes. He loved me there, you see." And she would peer intently at the image, squinting hard at the glossy surface, as if trying to see something she had missed before, some clue, some hidden message.

There were photographs of my christening, my first birthday, my first day at school, photographs of me in Dad's arms, kissing him, embracing him, being carried high on his shoulders. Mum would ask me if I remembered it all, and I would answer, "Yes, yes, everything. I remember it all." But I didn't. None of the photographs was real for me. None of them reminded me of the vague feelings – growing steadily vaguer – I'd had for the man called my father. He didn't look the same in any two photographs. And when I peered at them, bringing them close to my nose, searching as my mother searched for clues and secrets, all I detected was the emptiness behind my father's smile.

That night I dreamed of Verdi again. In this dream we sat crosslegged on a kerb and Verdi showed me a clockwork doll. It had a large brass key protruding from its back and it looked like my father. Slowly, Verdi wound the key and the doll's face clicked into a mechanical smile. Verdi explained there was nothing human inside it – no emotion, no joy – just a complex system of cogs and wheels that gave it a kind of reality. Then he put it on the ground and we watched in wonder as it walked across the street. My mother sat on the opposite kerb. She smiled affectionately when she saw the doll and waited for it with open arms. As its plastic hands touched her knees she squealed with pleasure and embraced it. As one of her hands stroked the doll's hair the other instinctively wound the key.

The next morning, at breakfast, I had a to suffer her habitual early morning accusations: I no longer remembered my father; I hated him, I was glad he was gone: I was cold, emotionless, self-centered.

"You haven't cried once, Cloud. Not once. If I were to drop dead this very minute, you wouldn't bat an eyelid. Don't you see? It would be so much easier for me if you were to grieve as well. We could comfort each other instead of blocking each other out. You're making me feel ashamed of missing your father! Why are you doing that? Don't you think I had a right to love him?"

I had learnt not to argue with her, not to be drawn into her world of anger and recrimination. Instead I merely smiled

and nodded and ate my cereal. This, of course, was seen as
further proof of my heartlessness. She began to poke me in the
chest; accusations turned to abuse, and insults until I feared
for my safety. In desperation, I gathered my scattered books
and rushed from the house.

At school that morning, for the first time since my father's
death, boys spoke to me, their curiosity about Verdi overcoming
their embarrassment. Where had I met him? Why did he want to
be friends with me? Was I about to bleach my hair and spike it
up like his? Where did I go with him? Could they meet him?

I told them I had been friends with Verdi for ages, went
with him to wild dangerous places where all the punks go,
that I was accepted by both him and his friends, that I did
things my classmates would never even dream of: I got drunk
with Verdi, took drugs, went to frenzied orgies. Verdi was my
best friend, the one person I trusted. And I, in turn, was the
one person, out of all his many friends, whom he trusted, the
one boy who heard his secrets.

Being seen with Verdi had given me a power and popularity
I had never experienced before. Now, through my association
with him, boys wanted to be my friend. It was their way –
albeit vicariously – of touching him.

That afternoon, at four o'clock, he was waiting for me. I
rushed over and grabbed his arm.

"I want you to come somewhere with me," he said.

"Where?"

"Somewhere special. Somewhere that means a lot to me. A
place that meant a lot to someone I used to know. Will you
come?"

"Yes. Of course."

As we walked along, he hummed his operatic tunes and put
his arm around my shoulder. I could smell him, the leather
and sweat, the lemon-scented aftershave. He walked slowly,
his buckled boots jangling with every step like cowboy spurs.
He seemed so sharp and clean, glittering like a newly polished
diamond. His jeans, bleached almost white, were ripped at the
knees and thighs. The body beneath was hard, unyielding, like
peeled wood.

I followed him blindly, content just to be with him. We

walked down some stone steps and then along the banks of the canal. After a while Verdi stopped by a large grey stone and sat on it. He took off his leather jacket, laid it on the grass and told me to sit down.

"It's nice here," he said. "It's a good place to come and think." He gave me one of his usual smiles. "Do you like it here, Cloud?"

"Yes."

"Good."

I laid my head against his knees. He hummed his melodies and stroked my hair. The touch of his fingers made the now familiar spiders scamper in my stomach.

"What tune is that?"

"It's opera," he answered. "I love opera, you see. It's all I can listen to. The only thing that means anything. That's how I got my nickname. Someone said I should be called Verdi because I was always humming opera. So that's my name now. Just think: I had to wait eighteen years to know my real name!"

"My name's a nickname too," I said. "My father gave it to me. He always said I went round with my head in the clouds, so he called me Cloud."

"He knew a lot then, your father." Verdi cupped my head in his hands and stared into my eyes. "What was he like? Tell me about him."

"Who?"

"Your father."

"Oh, he's dead."

"But tell me about him, Cloud. Just because he's dead doesn't mean there's nothing to say. Was he cheerful? What did he do at home? Tell me things, Cloud. You're his son. You must know things. Did you love him?"

The question took me by surprise. I pulled away from Verdi and stood up. He frowned. I tried to think of something to say, something that would please him and make him desire me. There was a desperate, pleading look in his eyes: so I told him what he wanted to hear.

"Yes," I said. "I loved him. I loved him more than anything. He was my whole world. Sometimes I dream that he's still alive. But when I wake up I realize that he's gone, and I cry. I miss him more and more. He did things for me, you see. Told me stories. Yes. I remember now. He told me stories before I went to sleep." I hadn't thought about this before, but now, carried away by my fluent improvisation, the memory came back, vivid and real, and I stood there, amazed that I had forgotten something that had once meant so much to me. "Yes," I continued, sitting beside Verdi again, clutching his legs, resting my chin on his knees. "He told me lots of wonderful stories. No one tells me stories any more." And suddenly I was crying. All the grief I had buried with my father rose inside me, a bitter distress that left me numb.

Verdi knelt beside me and cradled me in his arms. I felt his breath, hot against my neck. As we embraced each other, our lips met and he kissed me. It was a gentle, comforting kiss that quelled the spiders.

Afterwards, he untucked his T-shirt and dried my eyes. As he pulled me to him, I reached out and laid my hands against his bare stomach. I felt as if my blood flowed through my palms and into his body.

"Cloud," he whispered, "will you do something for me? Even though it seems strange? Will you do something for me without asking why?"

"Of course," I said, "anything."

"I want a photograph of your father. Make it the most recent you can find. Will you do that for me?"

"Yes," I said.

Verdi stood up and said he had to go, but he would meet me the next day. When I asked where, he replied, "Here. The secret place."

After he had gone I sat alone for a while, watching the sunlight sparkle across the surface of the canal and listening to the water trickle. I was filled with a joy I had never experienced before, a warm contentment that made me calm.

That night, as Mum sipped cocoa in bed, I got the photograph album without waiting to be asked, and laid it across her lap. Immediately, I turned to the back of the book where the most recent pictures were. She watched in wonder as I examined each in turn.

"Cloud," she sighed. "You do miss him."

There was only one photo of both me and my Dad. It was important that Verdi have an image of me as well. I took it from the album.

"Can I have this?" I asked. "To keep?"

"Oh, yes," she said, hugging me, kissing me. "Of course, Cloud. See how much he loved you! You can see in his eyes and smile."

"Yes," I said, "I see."

The next afternoon, as planned, I returned to the secret place by the canal. Verdi was waiting for me. He asked me to sit beside him. Putting his arms around my shoulders he kissed the top of my head and asked, "Did you bring it?"

"Yes," I said, handing him the photograph. "It was taken at Easter. Just a month or so before he died. That's me before I had my hair cut. Do you recognize me?"

Verdi nodded. He stared in silence at the photograph: his hands were trembling. I asked him what was wrong. He shook his head and held me tighter, clutching me so hard it hurt, squeezing the air from my lungs. It was as if he wanted to crush me into his body, make me part of him.

"Verdi!" I gasped. "Let me go!"

He was crying – a helpless, desperate sobbing that shook his whole body. Finally, with a yell so loud birds exploded from nearby trees, he fell to the grass. The photo was screwed to a ball in his hands.

"Verdi," I said. "Please don't cry, Verdi."

Gradually, the tears stopped, but it was a slow process, and by the time he had regained composure the sun was setting and the sky was streaked with red. He picked grass from his mouth and smiled.

"I'm so popular now," I said. "All the boys in my class want to be my friend. It's because of you, Verdi. Because of you."

He kissed my cheek, smoothed the photograph against his chest, then slipped it into his jacket pocket and stood up. He looked at me and touched my hair.

"Will you meet me tomorrow?" I asked.

"Perhaps not."

"Oh, no, Verdi!" I stood up and grabbed him round the waist. "Verdi, you mustn't go!"

He held me at arm's length and stared into my eyes.

"Just because you can't see me doesn't mean I'm not around, Cloud," he said. "You're popular now. People like you. That's a rare gift. I'm going now. Don't follow me. Thank you for the photograph."

I watched him walk away. He didn't look back once. I sat alone by the canal for over an hour.

When I got home I went straight to my room and fell on the bed. Before long Mum came up. She sat on the edge of the mattress and ran her hand up and down my spine.

"Come on," she said. "No one is ever gone. He's still with us. You were lucky to know him. Just don't forget what he's taught you and he'll always be with you. Nothing is for nothing."

I hadn't heard her sound so joyous and confident. I sat up and looked at her. Her face was brave.

"Come on," she said again. "It's time we sorted through his clothes. Help me. It's time to move on."

We went to her room and opened Dad's wardrobe. One by one she laid his suits and jackets on the bed. Carefully, sweets, bits of fluff. She made a pile for jumble and a pile of things she thought would be useful for me one day.

There was one jacket left in the wardrobe. I went to get it and sat on the bed, laying it across my lap. In the breast pocket I found a photograph. I looked at it and my heart froze.

"What's that?" Mum asked, putting the jumble into an old suitcase.

"Nothing," I said, slipping it into my pocket. "Nothing at all."

Mum came over and kissed me. "I love you, Cloud," she said. "Really."

"Yes," I said. "I love you."

That night, as I lay in bed, I looked at the photograph of Verdi I had found in my father's jacket pocket. I tried to take in every detail of the image; Verdi sitting on the rock at the secret place, his jacket slung casually over his shoulder, his blond hair glittering in the sunlight. But there was something different about him. Something that, at first, eluded me. Then I realized what it was: he was happy. His smile was so wide and so joyous it made the spiders crawl in my stomach. I had never

seen him happy before. It transformed his whole face, made
him younger, brighter, more real. But there was a shadow at
the bottom of the picture: my father, as he stood with the sun
behind him, taking the photograph. I stared at the shadow.

SUNDOWN

Peter Robins

LATE IN THE afternoon, thick soup prepared and set at the back of the stove, Anna Johnson goes to her porch. She makes for a broken-backed chair but, before settling, drops a creased brown envelope onto the scrubbed boards, well within reach. Next, just as she did yesterday, and the day before, she folds her hands idly in her lap. At last she fixes her gaze beyond the low hedge of copper beech, the tarmaced road and the flat pasture. If it were closer, or her own sight keener, Anna knows she would be able to distinguish clumps of sedge and the low dunes stretching almost to the ocean's edge.

Protected by three whitewashed walls she can observe the effects of a late October breeze on the landscape. Although the wind blows familiar sounds about her, Anna's face is not touched by it. Nor does the breeze expose the white roots of her newly combed hair.

The postboy, freewheeling in a sudden gust, waves as he passes. He no longer expects a nod in recognition so he is not disappointed. Yet he still greets the woman who'd once treated him as an extra son. As a schoolboy, together with Anna's own two, he'd waited for some scones from her oven at five o'clock and, while they'd cooled, he'd drunk from a jug of frothing milk that either George or Eric had brought from the cowshed across the cobbles.

Anna does see the postboy. That is, she registers his passing. It occurs to her that very soon she'll not be able to think of him as a lad just left school. He'll be twenty before the year's out. Five years younger than Eric and six – to the day – younger than George.

She becomes aware of discomfort and looks down. Her thumbs are pressed so firmly against each other that they've grown yellow and bloodless. They remind her of her grandmother's hands, and of one particular afternoon. The old woman had sat, upright and silent at the kitchen table for three hours after Anna's father had been kicked into the soldiers' truck.

With a quick expulsion of breath – more like a gasp than a sigh – Anna forces herself to look up. A graceful web of swallows is banking before it veers south. She follows its progress until individual birds are absorbed in a grey mass. Then she drops her eyes once again to the distant haze. She calculates it will be another forty minutes before the sun falls below the horizon in a scream of lilac and scarlet. Since this is her fifty-fifth October, she needs no evening paper to verify dawn, sunset or lighting-up time.

When it is dark, she knows there will be just the winking beam. It is the only light from the village strong enough to penetrate a windbreak of trees to her left.

She sits, recalling – as she does each afternoon – something her grandparents had told her when she had been a toddler.

- That light over the harbour's an angel's smile to all seafarers.

At night, Anna remembers, her grandfather had set out under it. Every following morning she had run to meet him as his boat chugged easily into the calmer waters. After close-on half a century she can still picture that moment as he levelled with the harbour wall: the old fisherman with both arms aloft, a cod writhing in each fist, and tepid sunlight mellowing his roughened skin.

The image fades, Anna feels instead a stranger's weathered fingers – a neighbour's – leading her slowly from the quayside.

The lighthouse beam had winked just as usual the following evening but the rhythm of the Johnson household had been disrupted. With no grandfather and no income from the fish market it had never been the same again. Anna's grandmother had called it existence rather than living. And the twelve months that had followed brought grimmer hardships. While a herd of Friesians moves steadily across the home pasture towards the milking shed where Eric waits, Anna recounts to herself for the umpteenth time the events of another never-to-be-forgotten October day.

Foreign soldiers had ransacked each smallholding and cottage on the island, demanding in their coarse language those tiny luxuries everyone had stored against the winter. Even the walnuts and eggs that had been pickled, as always, for Christmas, had been taken.

Anna can still hear the indignation in her grandmother's voice.

- Anyone would think the vandals were scared their ration trucks wouldn't make it through the snow we'll be getting soon enough. Damned mainlanders. What about us? Don't they care if we starve?

Although she drops a hand to swat a fly that's about to settle on the envelope by her feet, Anna's thoughts linger on that winter. As always, they focus on the last day of February. The intervening years have done nothing to ease the pain this memory evokes.

Four soldiers. There'd been four, and all of them little more than boys, as her grandmother had said at the time. They'd prised up floorboards and kicked over everything in the cellar. And then they'd left, taking almost nothing with them except Anna's father. He'd waved once. There wasn't time for more as they'd kicked him up into their truck.

And for what? Anna sighs as she murmurs to herself the answer her grandmother had so often given to that question.

- All for a couple of bottles hidden in the loft. Just a drop of something to warm our bones. My son sent to a camp for *that*. Vandals. What had he done? Brewed up a litre from potato peelings, that's what. Used a few scraps that'd have gone to the pigs anyway.

Both of her men gone, Anna's grandmother had concentrated all her energy on the little everyday routines. Whether they'd been put by neighbours or her grandchild, the old woman had countered questions on anything other than household tasks with silence. Each day during the month that followed, she'd stood by the open door at sundown. What she'd said never varied, and to Anna it had seemed her grandmother didn't care whether anyone listened.

- One morning, the ice'll melt on that road.

There'd been the long evenings shared by the old woman and the small girl.

As she sits on her porch with the wind beginning to strengthen and pluck dry leaves from the beach hedge, Anna recalls those evenings as a time when she'd been able to forget her hunger and misery.

Warm in the vast bed made by her grandfather's grandfather, she'd first listened to old stories of their family. Her grandmother had retold them while unpicking fishermen's torn jerseys for the wool. They'd been tales of forebears who'd lived and died before photography had been invented. Yarns about ancestors who'd left from the jetty in autumn when their crops had failed. And there'd been other tales, too, of brave souls who'd groaned and ached for weeks in ships that had set sail for America and other newly-discovered lands.

As she smiles a little at the recollection of those evenings, it occurs to Anna that – if she's one hope for the future – it is to live long enough to pass on the stories to Eric's children. It does depend on Eric having any, she realises that. Not just him, of course, but on the slim, red-haired infants' teacher to whom he takes flowers and chocolates. Even if they marry and, for the sake of the farm, have children . . . even then, Anna has to accept, they might decide the past is best forgotten. They might tell her to be quiet and turn on the television instead.

- Now George wouldn't have seen it that way.

Unaware that no one is listening, Anna speaks aloud.

He'd known them all: every one of the old family anecdotes. Even before he'd been seven he'd corrected Anna if she so much as omitted one detail. He'd remembered little things, like the flute a great-great uncle had packed, or the coat an even more distant aunt had made from blankets for her voyage to Australia. Not just a coat. It had to be bottle green, he'd insisted.

Stroking the dog that ambles out onto the porch, stretches itself at her feet and instantly falls asleep, Anna smiles again. It is not just the dog that causes her to do so: more the memory of another afternoon which the creature's disappearance conjures up.

Old Rex had been a puppy then, bounding away after anything that stirred among the dunes and the sedge. It had been a bright, windless afternoon. George had trotted barefoot by Anna's side, looking up with a sunburned nose, while urging her to relate stories that were older still: of islanders whose real names had been forgotten, although suitable ones had long since been agreed on by the villagers.

She'd done so. George – she'd maintained ever since – had absorbed every detail at first hearing.

Hadn't he been overheard – she reminds herself – repeating to his younger brother, weeks later, the adventures of those men who'd rowed out from the inlet centuries before the harbour had been built? Hadn't he described for Eric the journeys those oarsmen had made – four days and as many nights beyond the horizon – in search of copper and tin and dyed linen? George had told it all in the very words she'd used to describe how some of the voyagers had brought back treasures and, sometimes small, dark-haired women. He'd added, just as she had done, that some had never returned alive.

Staring westward, rotating her thumbs in endless circles, Anna Johnson seems to hear her elder son's voice as distinctly as she had years previously.

- And did those bearded sailors have battles with sea-serpents? ... Did they go hungry? ... Did they get ill from fevers?

She tries to recall her reply. It must have been something, she's sure, about pioneers needing to expect dangers because the world beyond the skyline had always been full of hazards ... always would be.

Something else from that still not forgotten afternoon recurs to her. Another of George's never ending questions.

- And those who never came back, were they being punished for daring to explore so far?

Anna laughs as she remembers this. She laughs as loudly as she had done when George asked her and she doesn't care now, as she sits by herself, if Eric does come trudging round from the milking shed to stare at her, and scratch his beard, and wonder at her sanity.

It had been the phrase *punished for daring* that she'd seized on. No sooner had George said it than she'd guessed where he'd picked up that idea. From that moment she'd decided against letting him go so often to Sunday School. Far better, she'd thought at the time, to let him ramble in the fresh air, out in the fields, and practise his flute. There was no way she'd have the word punishment flung from a pulpit at any child of hers.

Anna's lips tighten. Anyone passing close to the porch would notice an unusual spark of anger in her eyes. Eric, however, is attending to the cows, and the postboy is already in his own room three kilometres away.

She's thinking of the village priest.

- Old hypocrite in a black nightshirt.

Though she still goes to his church each Sunday morning, Anna never listens to one word of the sermon. The line of miniature fishing boats that hangs from cords above the congregation interests her far more. And, after the service, her nod to the old fox – as she also terms him – is barely civil.

- Foxy hypocrite.

The words slip unnoticed from her lips as she thinks of an incident in her own quiet sitting room. She calculates that all of twelve years must have passed since she discovered the priest pawing young George's body. One minute wielding punishment over children like a herder's stick, and the next fiddling about with their jeans. Remembering that afternoon, when she'd walked in merely to ask the creature if he'd like coffee, she decides it had been his brazen manner that had outraged her as much as anything.

She gives a fair imitation of the unctuous priest, though Rex is her only audience, and he barely raises an ear.

- Ah, Mrs Johnson, I was just instructing George about some

matters he'll need to know before being confirmed by the Bishop.

She wishes her reply had been quicker but she'd still not change one syllable.

- Were you, Pastor? Just what is there that farmer's sons like my two, or our neighbour's lad, need to be told about the way the world couples and goes on?

The wind begins to stir Anna's hair and she shuffles her chair deeper into the porch. Rex opens an eye, hoping the evening walk might be earlier than usual. Pulling the creased envelope nearer, so that the wind no longer twitches its flap, she is careful not to dislodge the cassettes.

Although she has never taken them from their wrappings, let alone played the recordings of concerts given by her elder son, Anna does consider how far she might have been responsible, with her tales of their adventuring family, for George's restlessness.

Outlines of the many arguments there'd been when George had left school drift back.

- So what's wrong with the new college they've opened here on the island, eh? Just tell me that.

Anna remembers her husband's impatient question. And she recalls adding that the journey would take no more than twenty minutes on a motorbike.

George's eyes had sparkled at the mere mention of a motorbike but he'd not taken the bribe. In his light tenor voice he'd gone on insisting that the local music professors were no more than provincial fuddy-duddies. And they'd both watched – George and herself – as his father had hobbled to the kitchen door, pulled on his work boots and muttered something about just not knowing who George took after.

It had seemed plain to Anna then – as it does now – that George had taken after her side of the family. Unlike Eric, who never could remember anything except how to repair a tractor or tend a cow in calf, George, like her ancestors, had been ever-ready to explore. He'd never forgotten it had been his great-great-great uncle who'd packed a flute to remind fellow passengers of the island they were leaving. Hadn't George carried that same flute, like an heirloom, with him onto the plane, though maybe for a different reason? In George, Anna knows, there'd been a wish to learn new tunes rather than to repeat those learned in the village schoolroom or the church.

She doesn't need to turn her head and peer through her bedroom window. She can describe for herself – down to each colour and every nameless face – the photographs on her dressing-table. She does so again. There's George receiving his university degree but not looking at all like the foxy priest in his black nightshirt. Then there's George, probably in some bar or at a fancy dress party: a crowd of strangers, all laughing, some of them drinking champagne, and two of George's friends kissing him. And the third photograph. That, George had explained, had been taken outside a concert hall in a city she'd heard mentioned on television. There was George again – in the centre of things, as usual – surrounded by friends who'd been to hear him play. All of them looked smarter than anyone on the island. All in suits and ties though it wasn't for a funeral.

Clouds begin to thicken above her. Scanning them, Anna accepts that the good October weather is breaking up. It'll not be a spectacular sunset after all. Not in any way like the evening when she'd sat so long on the porch with that telephone message clanging and echoing in her head like the passing bell. It still seems to her that she couldn't have been there more than an hour, though Eric and his intended insisted it was past midnight when they'd persuaded her to go with them into the kitchen and drink brandy.

Anna realizes she has come face-to-face with the questions again. At first, they'd recurred hourly. Now (she does a rapid calculation), three hundred and sixty days after the telephone call, some still rise unanswered, but only before sunset when she sits alone in the porch.

She works through them like a litany: Where could George's common sense have gone? Knowing himself to be sick, why hadn't he come home? The island's airport had been open for three years. Hadn't he himself used it to dash back for his father's funeral? Why had there never been a hint of chest trouble in his letters? Why had he distrusted the new hospital in the city?

The last question troubles Anna most. She watches dry beech leaves blowing among the purple daisies and wonders why her son had wished to be nursed by strangers rather than fellow-islanders. She would have reminded him – if there'd ever been the chance – of two of his cousins among the doctors. At least a dozen of the nurses, she would have said – would have been at school with the boys.

Once again aware of pain in her thumbs, Anna releases them and blows her nose on the hem of her apron. She remembers her grandmother had once said that, on the island, everyone was part of a great family, like the swallows. George, she has to accept, seemed to have forgotten that. Even the nameless seafarers, in the stories she'd once told him, had been carried home by those among whom they'd been reared.

It had been strangers who'd carried George in. All of them in smart city clothes and wearing black ties. Even the women had worn them.

Of the hours that had followed, Anna recalls most just how much the visitors had talked. Chattered like rooks, they had, their quick voices rasping against her numbness. Black as rooks, too, they'd seemed to her, in their plastic jerkins and trousers. And all of them had rattled on about George: sometimes to her, more often to Eric's intended, whispering away in their corners.

Reliving those hours, as she does each afternoon, Anna wonders increasingly whether she should not have left all the serving coffee and sandwiches to Eric's girl. Then she, Anna, would have been free to have rapped her knuckles on grandfather's old table and spoken to them all. She knows now what she should have said. There have been enough opportunities since to perfect it, syllable for syllable. She'd have pointed out a few facts, mentioning that the sea had taken George's great-grandfather just as it had taken islanders before the church records had been started. The story of the soldiers who'd taken her own father to a camp wouldn't have been left out. Loss, she would have told them, was nothing new. There'd always been wars and there'd always been sickness, and always would be. She'd have mentioned that George's own great-great-grand uncle had never reached Australia to play his flute. And she knows how she would have ended. Just as she had begun: by asking what all the whispering was about.

Anna vents her impatience – and maybe her annoyance with herself at an opportunity not seized – with a sigh. Almost a year later, she can think of only one sensible thing that any of the visitors had said.

- George put up a magnificent fight, Mrs Johnson.

Although she smiled politely at the time, Anna wondered then – as she still does – what else the feather-brained creature had expected. The will to endure had been in George's blood. Of course he'd fought the unforseen, just like all his forebears who'd ventured beyond the skyline. Sometimes, Anna concludes, those who explored the unknown won. Sometimes they did not.

She stretches her shoulders, picks up the envelope and, before stuffing it in her pocket, checks that the cassettes are in the order that George had packed them. As she gets up and tightens the belt of her raincoat Rex, too, stirs, yawns and looks up. Anna pats his head and then, without another glance to the west, sets off along the road that winds beyond the school and the church-yard to the harbour wall.

THREE FRIENDS

Jerry Rosco

for Glenway Wescott

AT THE BEAUBIEN métro station in East Montréal, Lucien Mason and his wife, Jacquelyn, waited outside without much patience for a train to take them home. Lucien, twenty-eight, was as restless as a child. Dressed in denim, he paced back and forth, his curly hair nearly hiding the green eyes as he looked down. Jacquelyn, dressed casually but well, tried to admire the graceful sloping white walls of the station, but what she really wanted was the comfort of their little flat and some tea. Sunday visits to her mother always ended like this.

Moving swiftly, nearly silently on its rubber wheels, a blue-and-white métro train swept into the station. The couple boarded a half-filled car and sat together. The train doors closed.

Three youngsters sitting next to Lucien and Jacquelyn were whispering and laughing. They were all fifteen or sixteen: two girls dressed like fashionable ladies of the 1920s and a boy with long blond hair and round grey eyes. When the boy looked up, his beautiful face shone radiantly, and, as he pursed his lips to begin a joke, it was easy to see the carefully applied white lipstick.

At the Berri station, the two girls kissed the blond boy with the lipstick and hurried off together. The doors slid closed. The boy removed his jacket and stretched his attractive form, clad in skin-tight clothing. Once he glanced at Lucien, briefly. Then he looked again, longer. Lucien was well aware of the energy he felt only a few feet away, but he avoided meeting the other's eyes. Then he saw the leather belt. It was an old Indian belt, hand painted, with a silver buckle. Years ago it had belonged to him.

The large grey eyes met his look directly. Lucien hesitated, but he knew his station was approaching. "Excuse me," he said, leaning forward. Jacquelyn looked at her husband.

"*Oui*," the boy said, a little surprised but not shy.

"By any chance are you a friend of Philip Perrot?" Lucien asked. The youngster's face brightened. "I live with Philip. We are good friends. You know him?"

"Yes, I gave him that belt long ago."

The boy looked down, and then up, his face filled with surprise. "You are Lucien," he said, extending his hand. "I am Serge Gaudreault. Philip speaks much of you. You are his better friend, eh?"

Lucien smiled, but his eyes dropped to the worn leather belt. "We are old friends but we don't see each other. Do you know Paul Moret?"

"*Oui*, Paul," the boy said. "He is a good friend with Philip."

"Yes," said Lucien, "Philip and Paul and I are good friends."

The métro train came to his stop, and Lucien was struck by the thought that within five or ten minutes this boy would be making himself comfortable at Philip's apartment – a place Lucien would never visit.

"Say hello to Philip for me," he said. The boy nodded and smiled at the couple as they moved out onto the platform. The train doors closed.

The evening had turned cool. Lucien and Jacquelyn walked home in silence.

Something was moving in the air on the quiet April night; some force, like all forces, was rushing to a conclusion and a dissolution. Something – something inevitable – was silently winding its web around the lives of several people and binding them to each other forever.

At Philip's apartment, Paul Moret waited alone in the living room while his friend showered. Paul, a muscular but gentle young man, looked carefully around the small room. As usual, he noticed the many photos, some of them recent, of the boys Philip knew. Paul smiled and shook his head. Although attractive himself, he'd never had Philip's luck in love. At twenty-eight, he felt old in some ways, while Philip, the same age, moved comfortably in a very young crowd.

"Want to go to a party tonight?" Philip asked as he walked into the room. He was wrapped in a long bath towel, his wet hair hanging straight to his shoulders.

Paul looked up at the slim, strong body he knew well and was tempted to pull Philip close to him. But he didn't. "Come on, Philip," he said, "you know I get up early for work."

"Sure," Philip said, bringing a hand to Paul's shoulder. "Whenever I'm on unemployment insurance I forget that other people work. But maybe we can see a movie together later in the week, eh?"

"Oh, for sure," said Paul, smiling now, "we don't see each other enough these days."

Just then the door opened and Serge walked in. "*Allo*, Paul," the boy said, as he walked straight up to Philip and took his lover by the hand. "Philip, just now I see your friend, Lucien, on the métro. You and Paul always speak about him. He was with a nice woman. He remembers the belt I am wearing."

Philip, surprised, looked down at the Indian belt. Serge saw something strange in Philip's eyes.

"Did you like him, Serge?" Paul asked.

"Oh yes. He has such green eyes, like jewels," Serge answered. Then, in a soft voice to Philip, "*Tu vas bien?*"

Philip smiled and gave the boy a gentle push. "Yes, yes, I'm OK. Why don't you get ready for tonight? We're going to a party, remember?"

Serge frowned and remained for a long moment before

turning toward the bedroom door. Over his shoulder he said,
"So. He is well and tells you *allo*."

Philip sat down beside Paul. "He's a funny kid," he said,
"jealous of you, even jealous of Lucien who I haven't seen in
a year."

"Well, maybe he's just curious. He's only known you five
months."

"Six months," Philip corrected, looking toward the bedroom
where Serge was making a little too much noise opening and
closing drawers. "Tell me, Paul, how often do you see Lucien?
What's he like these days?"

"He's the same as ever," Paul said. And he felt a stirring of
the same old emotions that had overwhelmed the three friends
years before. "He's maybe a little quieter these days. He's happy
with Jacquelyn, he still works at that bar on Mount Royal Street,
and I go there every few weeks. Do you want to see him?"

Philip shook his head. "No, I don't want to see him. I
mean . . . I just make him uncomfortable. Now I think I
should get dressed and dry my hair." As he reached for a
pair of jeans, Philip dropped his bath towel to the floor, and
the sight of his body, hard, flawless, broke something deep
in Paul.

Paul stood up. "I'll be going now. Maybe I'll call you
tomorrow night and we can go to a movie?"

"Sure, call me," Philip said. He was busy dressing now,
thinking of the night and the party ahead. Paul was about
to leave the apartment when he noticed a photograph he'd
never seen before. It was hanging in a frame near the
door.

It was a photo of a blond youth of unnerving beauty; he was
leaning against some rocks on a shoreline. In the background,
some people could be seen, seated on the shore and facing the
ocean, but the boy had his back to the others as he looked,
unsmiling, directly into the camera. He wore tight faded
jeans and a T-shirt that revealed his shoulders and arms and
well-developed chest.

"That photo," Paul asked, "who is the boy on the beach?"
Philip laughed and slapped his friend's shoulder. "That one,"
he said, "is a god."

Paul nodded. "I believe it. Goodbye, Philip, I'll see you soon." And they kissed goodbye.

Less than an hour later, Paul was home, lying in bed and thinking of Philip. He thought of Philip's perfect body, and then his hand moved down his own body. Although he exercised as often and was in good shape, Paul could feel just a bit of softness around his stomach. Imperfection.

Paul thought of the boy, the god, in the photograph. And he thought of how Philip's gods had taken his friend away, to a land of permanent youth, of necessary perfection, to a place where loneliness and age and death were not real destinies, but only moments of incomprehensible terror in the night, moments that would dissolve into forgetful sleep or into the warm embrace and lips of a young, firm-bellied, long-haired god.

Thinking of this, Paul fell asleep.

It was near dawn when Lucien Mason woke with a start. He looked around and saw only the dim, still room, and Jacquelyn sleeping beside him. Lucien was tense and uncomfortable and wondered if he were ill. Then he remembered the boy on the métro, and his thoughts turned to Philip.

Soundless pictures, like bits of old film, flashed through his memory. The three friends were seated around a table at La Grange, the all-night disco. A joint passed from Philip to Lucien to Paul. When the joint was finished, another was lit. Beautiful French boys, dressed in their best clothes, danced with young girls. Lucien would watch the dancers, fascinated. The boys were street boys mostly, hard as nails, and with a cool beauty which made their fancy clothes seem very correct. They were like an extraordinary society of regal beings. The girls knew it and were part of it, but gave away nothing with the swift glances of their beautiful eyes. Lucien would always notice the time of night, or early morning, when many of the boys would begin to dance with each other.

Lucien recalled no conversation in particular, but he remembered the eyes of his friends: Paul's eyes, sad, unsure, alone; and Philip's eyes, like iron. And Lucien remembered a certain night alone with Philip, a failure, and Philip's half-smile as he lit a cigarette, his eyes for once showing regret. Philip had gambled with their perfect friendship, and destroyed it. They both knew it. The gamble, Lucien understood, had been worth the risk.

Lucien sat up in bed, wide awake. He looked at Jacquelyn, sleeping silently beside him. If it had worked, he thought, that would be Philip there.

In the shadows of the room, he saw the warm form beside him become Philip's body, the long beautiful hair, Philip's hair; the loosely curled soft hand lightly touching him became Philip's strong hand. He sighed heavily. If it had been that way, it would be OK, but he knew he was happy with Jacquelyn. And he knew he was lucky, because with her he could enjoy his love and never hide it from his family, his boss, his landlord, and all other interested and concerned people. Philip and Paul could not say the same.

Philip had lost several good jobs because he was just not discreet. Paul was more level-headed and kept his print-shop job, but he was being used by his boss. And they're still young, Lucien thought. What would happen when they were older? Paul is isolated now, and lonely. And Philip surrounds himself with teenagers and never thinks of the future. And yet . . .

Lucien stood up and walked to the window. He ignored the rows of old wood-framed houses on St Timothé Street and looked up at the blue-gray sky of dawn. Strangely, the full moon was still visible. He could hear the wind blowing, an occasional car in the distance, and the pleasant first stirrings of the radiators in the flat. He had seen Philip very little in the last five years, and not at all in the last year. And yet, he thought, practically whispering the words aloud, I still love him as much as ever.

Day broke rapidly over the city, but with the usual strange stillness and gentleness of early morning. Some of the cars were already moving east on St Catherine Street and east and west on Dorchester – not the last of the night-time traffic but cars beginning the working day. Buses moved slowly along in the morning chill. Paul Moret waited for a bus to bring him to work. In the east, young people who had danced all night were now crowding into small coffee shops for breakfast. It was almost like any other morning.

It was hours before Paul was fully awake. On the back of his work overalls, the faded word "Chomedy Printery" were labelled. Above the cigarette pocket the word "manager" was stitched in red letters. Paul felt his job at the print shop had reached a dead end and he knew he would quit sooner or later. But through sheer routine the situation dragged on. At the moment he was showing a new boy how to stack and tie newspapers.

The boy, his long hair protected from the machinery by a knotted scarf, stood back and very earnestly watched the instruction. Paul skilfully handled the tabloid papers as they rolled one upon another off the press. Quick-counting them into stacks of approximately fifty, he showed the boy how to tie the papers quickly, before too many accumulated at the end of the run. After Paul tied three stacks, the new boy tried it, did it well, and looked up with a smile. Paul clapped him on the shoulder and walked away looking back once at the agile youngster bending down at his work beneath the pounding iron machinery.

It was late afternoon when Paul's boss called him away from the printing press.

The man – fifty years old, short, heavy, and grim – looked very angry. "There's someone in my office to see you," he said. He looked away from Paul and began to walk off. A cold feeling, cold like an unknown guilt, came over Paul. He walked slowly to the small office at the end of the floor. When he turned into the room, there was Serge, sitting by the cluttered desk. He was dressed in tight garish clothes, discothèque clothes, but when he looked up his face and blond hair were wild, his eyes full of tears.

"Serge," Paul said in complete surprise, "what's happened to you? Do you need help?"

"Paul, it's terrible," the boy cried, "I come to tell you but I can't believe it's true. It's Philip." Paul looked at the boy's distress and heard the words, and felt years of his life, layer upon layer of his soul, collapse like a building turned to sand. "It's Philip," Serge cried, "he's dead, my Philip."

Everything moved away sharply in a rush of emotion, and Paul reached for the desktop to steady himself. Then he felt himself coming back, back to the dirty room where he stood above the frightened boy. Serge looked at him in a strange way, as if he understood what he had just done with his words. Paul sank to his knees and put his arms around the child. They held each other close; it was the only thing to do because they had both loved the same person.

"I will die without him."

Paul heard the words and it took a full moment for him to realize the boy had spoken. "He did it all for me," Serge said softly, "now I can't go back to his apartment, and I want to die. He thought I was a little boy, a crazy boy, and he was right, but to me he was all the world."

Paul sat back on the floor and looked up at Serge. He couldn't speak but he wanted to know what had happened.

"We were at a party last night," the boy whispered. "Very late, near the morning, he took a bad fall in front of the house of the party. Some others found him and would hold me in the house, but I push to the door and see everything." And the boy saw it again and put his hands over his face.

Paul stood up and pulled Serge to his feet. "Go down to the street and wait for me. I'll change my clothes and we'll take a taxi to my place and I'll . . ." He froze for a moment as a deeper level of realization rushed over him like a wave. "I'll take care of everything," he said.

The boy left and Paul went to a nearby room and changed into his street clothes. Before he could leave the room, his boss walked in. The man was showing the same anger as before.

"Paul," he said, looking at him in a temper, "I told you once before, do what you want with your life, I don't judge you, but please keep your little faggot friends away from the job. If a client was here and saw a kid like that, dressed like that, and I think with make-up, and crying about . . . what? A lover's fight!" he said in a fury, and then suddenly fell silent. He saw Paul's look. The young man looked past him and was putting on his coat.

"I'm finished," Paul said in a controlled voice. "Please mail me my paycheck." He tried to walk away but the man grabbed him. He knew his young manager and he knew he was serious.

"Paul, what are you saying? Are you crazy? You've been here five years. Don't quit a good job . . . over nothing."

"It's not that. It's time, it's time to go." Paul looked at his boss and the man looked hurt and surprised.

"Kid," he said, "I won't let you quit. I said 'faggot' but I meant nothing by it. You know me, you know I meant nothing. I'm a crude man, my wife and kids always tell me that. And I was only in a bad mood because we're so busy on Mondays. I'm sorry you're having trouble with your friend, that boy. It's just, you know, business is business."

Paul walked past the man, then stopped and spoke without looking back. "The kid was bringing me very bad news. It's something . . . I don't know what I'll do. But I think I'm finished here and not because of anything you said. You're a good man, I know it better than anyone. I'll call you next week." He left the room and walked down to the street.

Outside, Paul was surprised to find it was raining heavily; Serge, with no protection at all, was standing perfectly still, waiting, and he was totally drenched. "Why didn't you wait inside?" Paul shouted above the noise of the downpour and the Sherbrooke Street traffic. The boy looked at him in confusion, dazed. Paul stood near the curb trying to find a taxi. Within minutes he was as soaking wet as the boy. Finally they got a cab. "St Denis and Duluth," Paul said. The taxi started and stopped short. The ignition gave the driver some trouble, then the car started again, and stopped. Finally they were moving in the heavy traffic, the rain beating down steadily. At the corner of Peel, some teenage boys, shouting in French and laughing crazily, ran zig-zag through the maze of slowly moving cars. Paul looked at Serge and thought the boy needed sleep desperately. As the taxi approached St Denis and was about to make a left turn, a small mail truck stopped short in front of them and they struck it with a violent jolt. Serge hit his head on the front seat but was not hurt. Their driver was out in the rain, shouting at the mail driver.

At last they were in Paul's apartment. Serge sat on the living-room sofa and began to remove his wet clothes. Paul brought him a heavy blanket and a blue-and-white capsule. "Take this," he said, "it's a Tuinal. You must sleep."

"But I'm afraid to sleep, to dream of last night."

"No, you will not dream with that."

Serge took the capsule, finished undressing, and wrapped himself in the blanket. He watched Paul sink onto the bed in the adjoining room. There was a long silence.

"Paul," Serge called.

"Yes?" Paul answered, just barely audible. Both of them were speaking from the great distance of shock and loss.

"You were lovers one time with Philip?"

"Yes." The silence came again, but there was nothing else to say. Serge stretched out full on the sofa, pulling the blanket up to his chin. The drumming rain outside was hypnotic. Only last night the weather had been so different, cool but almost like spring. It had been the most beautiful night of his young life – and the dawn was the most terrible. But before that terror, the party had been beautifully unreal, like poster art.

They had arrived at the house in LaSalle in a taxi, Philip, Serge and another boy Serge's age. The two youngsters walked on either side of Philip as they approached the old house. Music blared from the upstairs rooms, and the sound of voices and laughter. Very high stone slab steps led to the doorway. They climbed the steep stairway. A glass broke somewhere overhead.

When they reached the upper rooms, people were saying hello to Philip from all sides. Serge felt a flush of excitement. He looked at Philip, whose powerful blue eyes and long hair gave him the look of a celebrity . . . his usual look.

Each odd-shaped room revealed another handful of interesting young people. In one room, people were dancing. A tall handsome youth, said to be Hawaiian, danced passionately with a girl, his long black hair flying spectacularly – and his sharp black eyes glancing clearly in the direction of Philip.

It was a party with no formality or centre. Everyone drank wine. Serge and the other boy followed Philip in through the remaining upper rooms, even through a dark room where lean nude bodies were coiled in silent rapture. Finally, a large skylight opened to a blue starlit sky. They climbed up and found half a dozen others scattered along the gently sloping roof. The full moon above was brilliant.

They lay on their backs, passing the wine bottle around. "How is my bébé-Serge tonight?" Philip had asked at one point, leaning forward a little drunk, but gentle, somehow lyrical in his movement and voice. Serge remembered looking up into that strong yet soft face, which at that moment seemed full of love. "I am well with you, Philip," he said, sitting up. His eyes were closed as the warm kiss brushed his lips, soft but intoxicating, short but eternal. Serge lay back on the cool roof, and when he opened his eyes he saw hundreds of stars and a moon that glowed bright and full. All of the unhappiness of his young life had been worth it, he thought, just for the experience of this one perfect moment.

A tall youth moved across the roof and sat near Philip. They laughed and spoke rapidly in English, too fast for Serge to follow. So he looked at the sky, at the clusters of stars, and dreamed of other parties, and hotel terraces, and exotic vacations, all with Philip.

He noticed a silence and when he looked up Philip was sitting alone, holding the wine bottle, staring at something in the emptiness, and his look was sad, beautiful and solitary. From Serge's perspective, there was nothing behind Philip as he sat there alone, nothing but the blue-black sky and a galaxy of stars.

Now, as the Tuinal pulled Serge down to the threshold of a deep sleep, his body relaxing despite everything, he fought off the horror of death, tears streaming down his face, and concentrated only on that one image, that poster art, of his one and only love, fixed forever in that brilliant pose, immortal against the perfect sky.

Paul listened, dry-eyed and emotionless, to the gentle crying of the youngster in the next room. Finally, the tears gave way to soft steady breathing. Only then did Paul begin to sense fully what had happened. If Philip was dead – the conscious thought stabbed him like a knife – then there was no one, no one who truly knew him.

He understood there were things to be done. Philip's parents lived in the suburbs and, though the police had surely informed them and everything was handled, he was sure no friends of Philip had gone to them – and he was considered a friend of the family.

He changed into dry clothing and prepared to leave, pausing for a moment to look down at Serge, who slept in a drug-induced peace, his red swollen eyes closed at last to brutal consciousness. Paul thought: maybe the kid really loved him. I wasn't the only one who loved him.

Looking at the sleeping boy, Paul pulled back the blanket and saw him in all his beauty. The coiled young body, white, velvety, soft and perfect, moved him nearly to tears. For he saw what Philip had seen, much more than physical beauty: tenderness, sweetness, a precious and gentle flower which must at all costs be protected from the world. Paul covered the boy and left, locking the apartment door behind him.

In the twilight, the long ride on a nearly empty bus was not a bad thing for Paul. The soft darkness, the lights in the distance that appeared and disappeared, the simultaneous movement and stillness, all of it seemed so much like the vague reality of life. He did not think this but he felt it.

He rested his head against the window, looking at the ordinary approach of night on a day when time should have stopped, his hands resting uselessly at his sides, and, at last, the tears falling silently. The thought struck him that the best part of his life was over. And he knew Philip, if he were there in ghost and body and knew of that thought, would shout at him in disgust and disappointment until Paul remembered that, indeed, there is always more to life . . . even more than love between two people.

The bus left Paul standing alone on a quiet and dark suburban road. Walking toward the wood-framed house, he remembered many happy visits to his friend's family. Now, Philip's only sister was married and living in Toronto. And Philip's younger brother was living downtown, a musician in a rock band. So the parents were alone and Paul, approaching the well-lit house, was glad he had come. It was Mrs Perrot who answered the door.

"Paul, I thought you would be here," she said, almost to

herself. The small woman, now in her mid-fifties, looked at him with the sad gratitude of all mothers who grow older wishing for many things and asking for nothing. She took both his hands in hers.

They sat together in the living room. The house was completely quiet. "It's impossible," she said. "That's what I keep thinking. But I slowly realize that I have lost him." The look in her eyes pained him more than anything he had experienced that day. He looked down and listened to the words.

"He was the special one of my children," she said. "Always I believed Philip could do anything he wanted to do. His father wanted him to be . . . to be a little more practical, but I never judged him. I always knew that he would make us proud."

Parent's talk; half of it true, half of it wishes and regrets – Paul was familiar with it.

Philip's father was sitting at a desk in his small library when Paul walked in alone. The gentle man nodded sombrely and looked down. "I'm sorry," Paul said, awkwardly, "he was my best friend. I knew how good he was. It was a crazy accident . . ."

"That's what life is, Paul," Mr Perrot said, looking up at him. "It's always crazy accidents that decide everything." There was a long moment of silence. The man obviously wanted to be alone. Finally, he said, "I'm sorry for you, Paul. I saw you boys grow up together. I know it must be very difficult for you. Sometimes love . . ." He stopped himself, then looked up again. "Look after your own health. Try to be happy."

When Paul was saying goodbye to Mrs Perrot, the front door opened and Marc, Philip's younger brother, walked in. He wore a leather jacket and jeans. His long hair was wild and matted. His face, a somewhat coarser duplicate of Philip's face, haunted Paul on the trip back to the city. And the terrible and true words of Mr Perrot's advice: "Try to be happy."

A cold wind was moving through the region and snow, totally unforseen by the weather experts, was falling. It was surely the last snow of the season, but it was falling like a December storm. In less than twenty-four hours there had been a calm night with a full moon, then an overcast day of heavy rain, then a night of sudden cold and snow.

Paul watched the storm through the bus window. The weather did not surprise him, nor could anything surprise him. Despite his emotions, he tried to see things clearly.

If I could wake up from this, he thought, and go back to yesterday, I would be no closer to Philip than I was, He would be with Serge, or whoever he chose, but he would not be close to me. Maybe that isn't important. But today I am more alone than ever.

And the voice of Philip whispered in his ear, "Like everyone else, alone."

And Marc Perrot, with his common manner and hard eyes, was the closest link to the genes that had been Philip. Paul shook his head. It was no worse to think of Philip's body, now dead, cold. The bus moved slowly through the snow, which was now sticking, into the city.

Miles away in LaSalle, snow already covered the concrete landing beneath the stone staircase. The crazy accident was history – vague history because no one saw it. No one watched Philip's last moment as he sat on the thin railing, with one leg hooked over the side, his foot touching the outer edge of the top step. And in the warm glow of the wine, in the safety of others' admiration, there was no place for those annoying thoughts, those glimpses of loneliness and age and death that come at night. There was only Philip, his mind blank, his intoxicated body rocking from side to side as he waited for his friends. With no enemies in the world, with a good conscience and very few regrets, he was boyishly happy. Even when his foot missed the outer edge of the step and his body surged outward, and even when his other leg – reflexes slowed by alcohol – just missed hooking onto the thin railing, even then there was only surprise, not fear. And that unlucky step into darkness ended in a bright flash of final consciousness.

Philip, the vision of male beauty, with lean body and shining black hair and strong blue eyes full of kindness, with a dozen lovers who would never forget him, there all alone in the night, stepping outward, down through the darkness, into light.

Lucien Mason looked up from the bar where he worked, down past the six customers who sat on stools watching television and sipping beer. He looked at the front door opening and saw Jacquelyn coming in from the snow, and he knew something was wrong.

The young woman walked the length of the bar, unconsciously brushing the snow from her coat as she approached her husband. Lucien leaned across the bar and took her hand. Her eyes were sad and he knew it was bad news.

"Can you close the bar early?" she asked. Lucien nodded "yes" and waited for the words. "It's Philip," she said, and from under her coat she took the early edition of the morning *Gazette*. "I read it here. It said 'Philip Perrot, twenty-eight, of Montreal.' It said he died in a fall early this morning at a house in LaSalle. Can we find out if this was your Philip?"

Lucien leaned heavily on the bar. There was a sensation of sudden calm and tranquillity, yet he heard the blood pounding in his ears. His eyes found Jacquelyn, and in her wide, sorrowful eyes he saw his only refuge, his only home, his only companion through the loneliness of his life. And he saw that Philip was dead.

"Can we telephone Paul?" she asked. "Would he know?"

Lucien leaned heavily on his elbows on the bar. "It was Philip," he said. "I woke up at dawn this morning. It must have happened then. I woke up and I was thinking about him. But we could call Paul. I'll close up and we'll go home and call him."

"Oh, Lucien," Jacquelyn said, looking in to his liquid green eyes, "I never knew Philip, I never really knew him, and you and he were best friends, weren't you?"

"Yeah, we were," he whispered. His face blanched. Most of his weight was pressing down on the hard wooden bartop. He realized they were speaking in the past tense, and that a great part of his life had been sliced away and was gone forever.

The web was closing, nearly complete. An inch of snow covered the ground, covered the concrete landing in LaSalle. But the force of Philip's life was drawing other lives together, closing the wounds of neglect and pride, softening the great regret of human carelessness.

The outside lights of the bar were off as Paul walked up to the building through the thick snow. The door was locked and, through the glass, he saw Jacquelyn sitting alone. She saw him and came to the door.

In the silence and warmth of the darkened bar room, Paul saw that the bad news had preceded him.

"I just told Lucien," Jacquelyn said. She looked at Paul for a long moment and saw exactly what he was seeing in her; both terrible sadness and wonderful strength. They'd never had the opportunity to become true friends, but there had always been a silent understanding and affection between them. In the warmth of her understanding now, Paul felt his resolve uncoil, and the greatest wound of his life showed itself in his large brown eyes. "Paul," Jacquelyn whispered, and they held each other close.

"Where is he?" Paul asked.

"He's in the back yard. He'll be here in a minute." Paul walked the length of the narrow bar. Through the back door he could see Lucien out in the yard, carrying a can of trash to the sidewalk. As Lucien walked slowly back across the yard, he slipped in the snow and fell to one knee. Slowly he got up and walked to the door. When he stepped inside and saw Paul, he was struck speechless, as if his friend had appeared there by magic. Finally, he said, "It was him?" Paul nodded, and their eyes could not meet in that moment.

They sat together at the bar with Jacquelyn, sipping drinks and looking at the morning *Gazette*. When Jacquelyn realized the two friends couldn't speak freely, she stood up.

"I'll sweep the place, Lucien. You boys take your time."

Paul smiled as Jacquelyn walked away, and Lucien said, "You see? I haven't been unlucky in everything."

"That's for sure," Paul said, and he thought of his own loneliness. And of the boy sleeping in his flat.

"Look," Lucien said suddenly, "I don't know what I feel. I mean, I hadn't seen him for a whole year. And we stopped being close years ago. I know we still cared about one another, but it was spoiled and we couldn't fix it."

"You would have fixed it some day," Paul said, "because Philip really cared, he really missed you."

"Missed me," Lucien said, in surprise. "But who was he?

What made him influence us, and everyone so much . . . all these years."

"You loved him," Paul said, unemotionally, "and so did I. He had everything. No one knew him better than us. Sometimes, I thought he lived at too fast a pace, but I was just jealous of his energy."

"I should have stayed close with him," Lucien said. "We should have tried to stay close friends. After Jacquelyn . . ."

"Listen," Paul said, "I know how Philip felt. He couldn't have been happy with a polite friendship. Don't you see?"

"Yeah, sure," Lucien said, the green eyes flashing. "Sex. I thought about that a lot. When you're older, maybe then you can afford to be dignified about things. But while you're still young, sex gets in the way of everything. Still, I wish . . ."

"Forget it," Paul said. "Forget what you wish. We can't change anything." They finished their drinks and began to walk to the front of the bar to join Jacquelyn.

Pain stabbed deeper into Lucien, a pain he knew would never completely go away. It was the kind of pain that, over the years, one comes to cherish.

"You're coming with us, aren't you?" Lucien asked his friend. "I borrowed a car tonight. I can get it through this snow."

"Stop at my place first," Paul said. "I want to get that boy, Serge, the one you met yesterday on the métro. This whole thing has left him in bad shape."

As he drove through the snow to Paul's flat, Lucien thought of Serge, and in his heart he felt the meeting on the métro had been a signal to him, part of a movement of forces that could not be stopped. He ached now for his lost friend, Philip, and he felt awed by the power and sweep of life. Serge, the pretty youngster on the métro who had looked deeply into Lucien's eyes even before Lucien had noticed his old belt on the boy . . . Serge had come to him like a messenger from Philip. With a child's eyes and silken blond hair, wearing funereal white lipstick, Serge had brought him a final farewell that otherwise he would have been denied. It was equally fitting, a part of the mystery, that he should see the boy again tonight.

Paul entered his flat alone and saw Serge, still fast asleep, with his blanket kicked to the end of the sofa. He knelt beside the boy and allowed himself the simple physical pleasure of lowering his head to kiss the taut warm stomach of the adolescent, the sweet fragrance of the young body like the ritual incense of an ancient sacrament.

"Philip," the boy whispered, not quite awake, "*J'ai sommeil*." When Serge opened his eyes and saw Paul, he sat up quickly, looked around the room, then looked down, biting his lip, unconcerned with his nakedness, and fell back onto the pillow. "Paul," he said, speaking quietly in the stillness of the dark apartment, "you have the same touch of Philip, very gentle. It is good, a strong man who is gentle."

Paul held Serge close for a moment. "Come now," he said, "we must go with two good friends of Philip, the people you saw on the métro." Serge did not question this and dressed quickly in silence.

Outside, in the car, Jacquelyn and Lucien turned to welcome Serge as he and Paul climbed into the back seat. No one spoke of Philip, but each of the four people knew there was nowhere else to be on this night, nowhere but in this slowly moving car, with these other people, in the middle of an April snowstorm.

It was cool in the small apartment when they arrived, and Lucien began a fire in his coal-burning stove. They sat on the floor pillows near the stove and Jacquelyn brought out a large bottle of Québec red wine and glasses. For several minutes a comfortable silence lingered. Finally, Lucien began to speak quietly with Paul, of many things in their past, and of some things in their future. Jacquelyn noticed Serge trying desperately to follow the rapid English conversation of the young men, as if in their words he would find some important secret he hadn't known. Instinctively, she took Serge by the hand and in French asked him where he'd lived before Montréal. As they talked about northern Québec, the boy's eyes brightened and he spoke freely while holding her hand firmly in his. Seeing this and understanding his wife, Lucien reached out for Jacquelyn's free hand. The comfortable silence returned, accented by the crackling noises of the hot stove. Then Lucien stretched his other hand slowly toward Paul. Embarrassed, Paul took it.

But instantly he realized how badly he'd needed exactly that contact. Feeling a sudden joy, feeling the close presence of the others, Paul looked up into the eyes of his best and truest friend, Lucien. He turned and saw Jacquelyn smiling at him, and saw Serge watching him intently, anxiously. Then, as if afraid to hesitate for even a moment, Serge suddenly leaned forward and slipped his free hand into Paul's hand, the fingers closing tight around it.

HEMO HOMO

Lawrence Schimel

EVER SINCE I can remember, I've woken with a hard-on. I'm sure there must've been a time when I was pubescent and my dick was limp when I awoke. But since puberty, no matter when I wake up or how long I've been asleep, I've got a boner when I come to.

I don't know if it's just the exhilaration of waking, of finding out I'm still alive after the small death of sleep. I figure there might be something about that small death which links to *le petit mort*. At least it makes for a cute joke.

Or it might be that I have kinky dreams the moment I lose consciousness. REM libido. I wish I could remember some of them; it's as if my mind's a complete *tabula rasa* blank when I'm not awake for all the memory I have of them.

I kinda think it's the first reason, though, since I never have wet dreams. I figure that if it were dreams causing my erections, I must sometimes get carried away and spill seed before I wake. But that never happens. And every time I wake up, my dick has gotten up before me. I live in a curious half-terror that one morning I'll wake up without an erection, although I'm not sure why I'm so afraid of it. It was a relief that today at least I didn't have to worry about what I'll do if it happens.

I stroked myself for a while as I lay there, letting my mind wander through these and other topics. It always struck me as a bit odd that I could think about such philosophical issues when I was jerking off, but I kinda liked the perversity of that. It made masturbation seem even more profound than I already believed it to be.

Eventually I stretched, cracking my back, and finally opened my eyes. The alarm clock's glow was the only light in my tiny studio. 8.47 p.m. Still early. I figured I'd head to the gym for a quick workout, and a quickie in the steam room, before starting my shift as a cabbie. I'm such a creature of habit, to the point where I almost fetishize the normalcy of routine. The gym was definitely a part of that fetishized jumble of habits.

Lately the "in" crowd has moved over to American Fitness, that great big subterranean complex of exercise equipment and such, with too much emphasis on the such-stuff like aerobics classes and a "health" bar and far too many heterosexuals cruising one another.

I'm still at the Chelsea Gym, if for no other reason than it's open until midnight, which better fits my schedule. It's also all male, and almost exclusively queer. Until something came along to disrupt my inertia, it's where I planned to stay. There's something unpretentious about the gym, its two small floors of freeweights. It's top heavy in its focus, arms and chest and such, because that's what most gay men want: big pecs and biceps. A decade into the Aids crisis, it seemed so much of our sexuality was focused on looking, since people were so afraid to have sex with each another. I think gay men are getting past that now, in part because we're forgetting about the crisis, having lived with it for so long it's become a constant. Or we're practising safer sex or calculating risks or throwing caution to the wind and ignoring it.

But still the gym mania persists.

I think it's tied to the fact that you can't change the size of the dick – the vacuum pump ads lie – but you *can* change the rest of your body, and insecurities being such a natural part of our psyches, we've become size-queens about those muscles you do see in day to day life.

There's also, of course, vanity and narcissism playing a heavy role, I reflected as I gathered my gym clothes into a knapsack.

I flexed my bicep and thought how this – my looks, my body – helped me get laid. I went to the gym to keep them as best I could. I did also enjoy the endorphin rush of the workout, not to mention the rush from the sex in the steam room (not officially part of the gym, of course, but everyone did it and everyone knew it was there).

And part of me was concerned about putting on or at least maintaining my weight, in case the HIV got the upper hand.

Not that I needed to justify my going to the gym to anyone, myself included. Lately, however, I was reconsidering all of my actions. Which was another reason I went to the gym: it was a good place for me to think. When the body was occupied with some simple repetitive task – like pumping iron or jerking off – the mind was left free to roam, the subconscious liberated as the front brain kept the body in motion.

It was a quick trip from my minuscule fifth floor walk-up (with glorious airshaft view that kept my rent low, which made it doubly fine for me since the less sun I saw and the less rent I paid the happier I was) on West Twenty-Fifth Street down to the gym, but I took my time, strolling lazily along Eighth Avenue and looking at the boys. A crowd of studmuffins on roller blades lingered outside the Big Cup, while the throngs of men sitting in the window ogled at them through the glass as they sipped their cappuccinos and iced teas. A towheaded blond walking a dalmatian caught my eye as he turned the corner at Nineteenth, but I already had a destination I felt committed to and his pooch tugged him on toward home, so we merely locked gazes for a moment and chalked each other up as "the one who got away".

I made small talk with Carlos, who was just leaving the gym as I got there. For someone like me who didn't hold down a normal job – as a cabbie, people came into my life in five-minute intervals – the gym provided some social stability: that group of people I saw regularly, even though they weren't especially important in my life. They were one of my routines, in many ways. I often looked forward to the gossip and interchanges, but when they switched gyms or moved to San Francisco or Los Angeles or (God alone knows why) Salt Lake City, there was always someone new to take their place. Their familiarity was reassuring in a way, like my waking hard-ons. And these days I felt I needed all the comforting and reassurance I could get.

The Chelsea Gym was also the cheapest gym of any of the neighbourhood gyms, I thought, as I gave my ID to Sam and went in, even the Y on Twenty-Third was more expensive. In fact, the only problem I had with the Chelsea Gym were the mirrors. Practically the entire place was mirrored, for the men to preen and pose and cruise while they pump.

I'm always afraid someone will notice I don't have a reflection.

I try hard to make it less obvious, keeping some piece of equipment between me and the mirrors whenever possible, and ignoring their existence when I can't. So many men, it seems, don't actually work out but sit at one of the exercises and ogle the other men in the mirrors. Which is an enjoyable pastime, I must admit, if a bit inconvenient for me. While I can watch them, they can't see me, so it's hard to cruise effectively, at least via the mirrors. So I pretend the mirrors don't exist as much as I can, and look at people directly when I'm cruising or interacting with them.

The locker room was crowded with naked men as the abs workout class (the Chelsea Gym's token semi-aerobic item) had just let out and they were hitting the showers at the same time that a chuck of the post-work lifters were coming upstairs from frolicking in the steam room and sauna. I loved to be in that whirl and press of bodies, but didn't linger long. I was studiously ignoring the scale over by the sunlamps, and then pretending to myself that I wasn't ignoring it and would weigh myself after the workout. The sooner I was out of the locker room, the easier it was to put out of my mind.

I was working shoulders and back today. Generally I like to start with some rowing, vigorous exercise to get everything going, but both machines were occupied. I began with some front pull-downs, instead, grateful that all the machines faced inward, away from the mirrors. I had barely begun my first set when a stunning young boy I'd never seen before wandered into view. I stared at him, lusted at him, thought it was returned. I wondered if we'd run into each other down in the showers later, if he would tarry to wait for me or if I would hurry to join him.

For a moment, I grappled with the existential problem of loneliness: not just as a gay man, but as a vampire. What would it be like if we were to date, move in together, join our lives. I could share immortality with him.

It was a ludicrous fantasy, of course. I didn't even know this boy, had just seen him for the first time in my life, and already I was planning an eternity for ourselves! I didn't even know his serostatus.

It was natural, though, to want to desperately fill my life with someone else at the drop of a hat. "This is no country for old men," Yeats wrote of Byzantium, which must mean that Byzantium is now reborn in the current gay subculture. That sort of loneliness is even more cosmically acute for someone like myself, always destined to be alone, to outlive anyone I might know or love, to be constantly dependent on humans for nourishment.

My head turned to watch the boy as I continued my set. It was an appealing fantasy: the romance we might have, as much as the pleasure our bodies might take in sex.

I was procrastinating, thinking about so much else, and I knew it. I wanted to pretend everything was as it had always been, didn't want to face what was happening to me.

I'd been HIV positive for at least a decade, with no adverse affects. I'm not sure when exactly I was infected, or even whether it was from unsafe sex or from drinking infected blood. Probably both.

There's a taste to infected blood that's different from anything else. It's like drinking low-fat skim milk, in some ways, thin and watery because there's usually few t-cells. But it's got an extra flavor from all that virus, richer in taste the higher the viral load. So infected blood is like drinking skim chocolate milk. I'm partial to the taste of it, but I try not to indulge too much, for a bunch of reasons. I'm less concerned about multiple strains of HIV, although with the changes now happening to me perhaps I should've been more wary. Infected persons often have other diseases and afflictions, which I want to avoid. And perhaps more importantly, one of the ways that the HIV hasn't affected me is that, thanks to my vampirism, I am constantly replenishing my t-cell levels with the blood

I feed on. So I stay healthy by drinking healthy blood. I do also feel guilty, taking the few remaining t-cells from people who're already losing them to the disease.

And thus I've been asymptomatic for at least a decade, maybe more depending when I was first infected. Until now.

I've begun losing my appetite, my first sign of the disease taking its toll on my body.

This terrifies me. I'm not replenishing my immune system with fresh healthy blood and all that it contains.

And what frightens me even more is that I am afraid the virus is now attacking whatever it is that makes me, biologically, a vampire. The cellular changes that happened that night when I was drained completely of blood, and then restored with *his* blood, making me like him, a creature of the night. It wasn't at all scientific, although that's how I'm thinking about it now, since there's such a science surrounding the virus these days, it's how we're trained to think about it, in numbers and chemicals and not at all as its devastating human effects.

I'd been able to ignore much of that techno-stuff, since my vampirism has been operating like an immune system, keeping me healthy from the HIV infection. Until now, when it seems a mutation of the HIV is attacking what makes me a vampire, *my* immune system equivalent.

The HIV might "cure" my vampirism. But the cure itself will kill me, since my vampirism is the only thing keeping me alive right now.

I'm not exactly discontent being a vampire, but I don't know if that's just because I'm used to it now. I'd be happy to give up the bloodletting and the deaths. It's been a long time since I've killed anyone, though at first I didn't know how to stop feeding, how not to gorge myself past satiation, until I was bloated into a torpor – a dangerous state for me to be in since I so frequently had to flee the scenes of my hunger-crimes.

And as I, once immortal, confront my sudden mortality, certain questions from my past begin to recur. Did I have a soul? Was there an afterlife? Was I damned for all the lives I took to feed myself? Even though they were all in self-defense, my body's natural instinct for survival and self-preservation.

Would I again become mortal when I lost my vampirism, or

would I instead die? But I was not alive now, I was undead. A quibble, perhaps, but an important one: I was not alive now, and I had once been dead. If I lost the state I was in, would I not revert to being dead?

And what would be the difference if I did become mortal? I'd sicken and die soon enough. I've never relished the idea of wasting away to this disease and being unable to die, on account of being undead already. I rail against the cruelties of fate, ignoring for the moment the fact that so many others had died before me and would yet die from this disease, men and women who would've killed for the prolonged years my vampirism had given me.

I'd been sitting blankly at the machine, lost in these reflections. That cute young boy wandered through my view again, drawing my mind back into my body as my body began to respond to the sight of him, arousal stirring my cock within my shorts.

I stood, deciding to skip the rest of my workout, and followed him down the stairs to the locker rooms, and the showers waiting below. I had no answers to any of my questions. And I did not know if there was anything I could do to change what was happening. I was hoping the exercise would increase my appetite, which might prolong my un-life some while longer. I did not, could not know what would come.

So I followed this boy, whose gaze met mine and in whose eyes I felt happy to be lost for all eternity, responding to those appetites which still lay within me.

PROSTITUTION

Aiden Shaw

A MAN HAD been calling me for about three months trying to organize a meeting between us. Stressing how big his dick was he hoped that mine was as big as advertised. I didn't care what he thought and would probably enjoy his disappointment. Yes, I very rarely get repeat customers, they don't like my attitude. I used to worry that the source would run dry. Luckily there seems to be a never-ending supply of men who are willing, or like to pay for sex.

This punter wanted to know where to park, what I did in my spare time, if I had a lover and lots more answers. Before he came round the last thing he said to me was that he couldn't walk very far and asked me if there were any stairs to climb.

I opened the door. Because of the wide angle at which he had to hold his crutches to balance, he had trouble making his way in. His legs moved as one, making up the third leg of a tripod.

"I told you, you don't mind?"

I thought: "You didn't tell me. You said you had a big dick, that you worked in television and that you couldn't walk very far. Anyway, it makes no difference to me, a punter's a punter."

He sat down. I helped him off with his trousers, wondering

what I might find beneath. There were two plastic cases in which his real legs rested, shrivelled and without muscle. He turned over to show me his arsehole.

"Lie against me," he said.

I didn't want to, so asked him to turn back over. Rubbing my stomach and legs he pressed his face up against me. I found this endearing and watched the porn playing on the video. Crawling over to the bed without the aid of his crutches he manoeuvred his legs with his hands, sorting out where they should rest.

"I have strong arms . . . look," he said squeezing me tightly. Then up my body he wiggled, until his face came too close to mine.

"Let me lie on top," I said. "I don't like being underneath."

"Do I turn you off? My dick is good isn't it?"

"Of course you turn me off," I thought. Luckily the telephone rang so I answered it instead of his question. Another punter wanted to come over. I wanted this session to end. Thinking quickly . . . "A regular of mine is leaving town and wants to come round now. I can't let him down. We'll have to finish now. I'm sorry. Just give me half the money." Agreeing to this he asked me to help him put his trousers back on.

"I thought we could get to know each other. It's a shame you have no feelings."

"Have no feelings for you," I thought and helped him with his socks, his shoes, then handed him his scarf. The door bell rang. I had to wait just a minute. I couldn't rush this exit too much for practical reasons.

"Goodbye."

I closed the door, answered the intercom, then reopened the door.

"Hello."

I received a call late one night. The money wasn't really enough but I wanted some excitement, or at least a change of scenery. I jumped in a cab and soon arrived at Little Venice where I realized I was visiting a children's home. Someone invited me in and asked me to go first into a dark room. I offered that he go first. The light went on and it became clear that he was younger than me and nice looking. We were in a small office which also had a bed in it. I fucked this boy's arse. I remember that his dick was very big and his skin smooth like a child's. When we had finished I had to sneak to the bathroom, so as not to wake others who were sleeping in rooms along the corridor.

I said: "You're mine." You said: "Yes I am." I said: "What's your name?" You said: "Mine." I said: "That's right."

A businessman on the way home from the office called by my flat. I had told him that I was experienced at SM. After our brief greeting, he handed me a bag which he had taken to work with him that day. I imagined that he must have found this exciting. Being asked to empty the bag I poured the contents, which looked like junk, on to the bed. I hadn't a clue what everything was for. I smiled knowingly and said: "Lie down on your back." I applied tit clamps and pulled on them hard to gauge how serious he was. Screaming he didn't gesture towards taking them off. I guessed he was serious. "Kneel on all-fours." I picked up a string of "love beads", lubed them and started to push them inside him. I wanted him to take all of them whether he liked it or not. He squirmed, so I put some poppers up to his nose. "Take these," I said. Then knowing he was going under the influence, I forcefully pushed the beads in, one at a time, without a break, plop, squelch, plop. I didn't care how much it hurt him, rather I wanted it to hurt him. I pulled them out, without consideration, then after plying him with more poppers, picked up and rammed a but plug straight into him, hovering at its widest point so that there would be no relief, then in for a second, then right out again, before any kind of satisfaction could be acknowledged.

When leaving he asked me to put all the messy, red slimy stuff back in the bag, without washing it. I never saw him again.

On the fifteenth floor of a tower block lived this American man. There were floor-to-ceiling windows in this flat, so all of London could be seen. I was impressed and found it somehow romantic.

"Can I wash my hands?"

"Sure, the bathroom's just through there,"

I felt him follow me and hover just behind me. I thought to close the door.

"Are you using the toilet?"

"Yes," I said, thinking maybe it was broken and possibly shouldn't be used. I realized I was wrong as he changed, turning into something troll-like.

"You're not going to waste that are you?"

"Whatever," I replied and began to piss feeling uncertain that it would come out with him watching. I thought of unrelated things, my mother, dirty nappies, then a friend I didn't really like. Out it came, in a not very confident trickle. In a fraction of a second he was on his knees and had his mouth round my dick. I pissed for a long, long time, it went on forever. Like a lamb at its mother's tit he guzzled hungrily and swallowed every drop. When I had finished I told him I was hungry and asked if he had any fruit.

"I've never done this before," he said to me innocently. I undressed, again I put my dick in his mouth and again thought of unrelated things. And after little stimulation and lots of imagination I came. I came all over his face and into his mouth. I thought it very messy sticking to his beard and moustache. He now had my piss and cum in his belly. He told me he was a photographer on a two-year assignment taking photographs for charities. Bloody Americans coming over here, stealing our culture with their money, stealing our cum and our piss.

I left and started to enjoy the walk back across Tower Bridge thinking how I felt like a tourist. I saw a boy in front of me, as we got closer we began to try to dodge each other, until it became so silly that he burst into a smile. He was perfect. He made me smile. I looked round at him after he had passed, he did not turn around. I did not want sex, just to have his smile squashed up against my face. He was in a different world from mine.

My heart muscle is hard. Push your hand up my arse, pull out my heart, beat it, beat it until it softens. You know the method, most people don't. Be my guest.

He asked if he could cum on my chest. This made my stomach

turn, but I said: "Yes." "The sooner he cums, the sooner he'll go," I thought. I strained my head as best I could to try to look natural whilst preparing to avoid his sperm landing anywhere near my face. I felt something hit my eye. I jumped inside thinking of the possible hideousness of this, sperm in my eye. I did not flinch, nor move a muscle that wasn't contrived. It was only one of his dreadlocks. I sighed within.

I always loved taking baths, first thing in the morning to wake me up and last thing at night to soothe me. This is a part of my job that I like, washing myself. Today I looked at the bath and thought, "I want to stay dry."

I should get in to warm my blood and wet my skin.

Coming from the city after finishing work a punter arrived who had slim fingers. They were very cold, as were the rest of his hands. These did not warm up during the whole of his visit. The skin of his body was also cold. A drop of fluid came from his dick and fell on my knee. I was confused. "Maybe he has cum," I thought, but this couldn't be the case, it was too cold and his dick was so soft. I then realized that it was piss that was dripping slowly onto me. He had a cock-ring on, yet his dick did not get hard, but only dripped cold piss.

I stood and wanked him off for such a long time. He bent down to suck my dick. I could see in his youthful hair, a gap. "It's a wig sewn on. No it's scar tissue. No he's a waxwork dummy or he is the devil, with a shell of a body, evil within, his movements languid, his limbs without life's warmth." Showing no passion, but with a slug-like driving force, he started to stroke my legs as though we were sticky and spineless and mating. Then his body shifted forward somehow without moving his muscles, then closer, sniffing at my shoulder. I pulled my head away and stepped back in amazement, then watched as he crept after me, seemingly unaware that I had moved and adjusting to the situation all the same.

My skin might have boils, warts, KS or bugs living on and underneath it. There was a communication between his passion and my crawling skin.

When he had gone I finally wanked off whilst I took my bath, and then got into my bed. What perfect aloneness I felt, my bedspace empty of crawling, loving, needy, probably deeply good men. I stopped being awake.

I want to miss someone again because they have gone away and will be coming back, not gone forever.

As I wanked him he pushed my hand away. Bored and aggravated I said: "Don't you want to come?"

"Not yet," he sighed.

"I've had enough," I said. So he decides to cum after all and I roll him over so as not to wet my sheets.

He was making love to me whilst I lay there waiting. I was still, inside and out, hoping not to have to really be a part of this. My dragging skin slid smoothly on a bed of bleak soberness which was my inside, my partially protected inner self being affected far too much. He was playing with my body and each saliva soft kiss and tender touch sickened me with his insensitivity. What he gave and did was not innocent. This lack of understanding was sought after, contrived, so that he wouldn't have to care what I thought, not care what his fully paid-up affection was directed towards.

I don't have regular sex with men I do like but have sex on a regular basis with men I don't like.

I went to see a friend on Sunday, two days ago. I can't sleep now. This woman friend of mine said that I was dead, that I had lost whatever I had had, the spark, the magic. This woman also said that people around me must get bored of my hard way and if not they were sycophantic, or were probably using me.

"Cum can land on flowers . . ." she said, cum being neutral, " . . .or it can land on shit." This made me cry. My friend made me cry. Good, not shit made me cry. I admire her and I love her, but being shirked in this way makes me feel so alone. So many people hate what I do, then in turn seem to hate me for doing it.

"Is it really worth it?" my sister said in anger the last time I saw her.

I was with a punter and I was looking at some photographs he had taken which he circulates for others who have similar tastes. They were pictures of young boys. I asked where they had been taken, he told me Budapest.

I don't ever want to forget this man or this experience.

My job was to give him a medical, like at school. I asked him to lie down and to take off his clothes whilst I inspected his arsehole.

"I'm going to have to check inside, you will have to relax, here sniff these." I put some poppers up to his nose. I put on the rubber gloves that were lying on the bedside table, lubed and prodded his arse with my finger. There was no reaction so I put my whole hand in, turned it, then repeated this in and out.

"Do you get a chance to play with them . . . the young boys?" I asked.

"Yes."

I felt he was holding back, surely he wanted to brag about his excited world. I was right, his reserved monosyllabic answers didn't last long. Soon he was listing the things he did, the fun times they had and I was under cover as an accomplice. I had access to all those files, "paedi" stories of his and maybe his friends. What should I do with this information, go to the police and be connected with this, or satiate my own lust for understanding?

I pressed the tit-clamps as hard as I could. This man had no feeling in his nipples it seemed.

"He sometimes wears a butt-plug when we go shopping . . ." my punter revealed, speaking in a somehow believably affectionate tone. Then enthusiastically " . . .he's wearing it in this photo, look here this one." The boy looked happy enough, maybe it wasn't true, maybe it was and he did like wearing it. How could I know? He continued, pointing and smiling. " . . . electric stimulation up there too . . . oh he loves it."

I couldn't get enough. I want to see him again, to know more. He did tell me to call round any time.

"No. Not in London any more, it's too dangerous. Manchester maybe, sometimes they don't even want money. I just buy them things. I would love to see you give it to him with your big cock."

"Yeah, so would I," I said.

* * *

An old Asian man called round with some presents.

"I don't suppose you smoke," he said.

"No," I replied, but he handed me some cigars.

"Well, I brought you some perfume." This he handed to me as he spoke.

"I don't really like perfume, especially on men," I said taking them and putting them on the floor beside my bed and thanking him.

This is a dream.

There is no one in this whole world that I would rather be with, and I can only believe that this is a whole world when I am with you.

You must see with me, or I might as well not see. If you move too far away from me, it makes me invalid.

He saw me for the first time last night and he wanted to see me again tonight. He picked me up at the tube station and within a two-minute drive to his house he told me that he used to be an artist but that now he was a criminal lawyer.

"I do not have a big enough ego to be an artist," he said confidently. Then he added, "I hate people who can't deal with this."

"I hate madness and evil," I said.

This punter played an opera whilst he licked my arse, sucked my arse, wallowed in my cum, using it to lubricate his circumcised wanking.

"Are you bored, do you want to finish?" he asked.

I asked if I could take a shower. The dog belonging to the this man was old and incontinent. There were two lots of shit beside the bathtub. I showered thinking how dog shit smelled different to punter shit. Now I'm with a lover and it's me who's licking, sucking and wallowing. Again I think of shit and how different it smells when fucking with passion.

There was a time when you were not afraid to look, not afraid to hint. Now you're afraid to laugh, scared to kiss.

*   *   *

The Arab sat down and handed me the money straight away, possibly to get it out of the way.

"I like getting fucked," he said, as though he were a king. "I like to be known to get fucked. I like everything about getting fucked."

This liberated man lay down on the bed naked with his arse in the air, he propped his hips with a pillow. I put my dick in his arse. I was met with no resistance, mentally or physically. He hoisted himself up onto one elbow, balancing with his palm flat on the bed. Spitting on two fingers of the now free hand, he then wove it under his chest, then lower under his tummy, then on further through his thighs passing beneath his scrotum covered with thick black hair, up into the join of his legs and to his goal – his arsehole. This was in order to lubricate himself. This wasn't necessary. There had been no friction. I think it was the gesture that he liked, that of lubing his arse with spit, this being animal, masculine and sexy.

The abyss. People say, "Doesn't it fuck you up?" I say: "I can't think of anything more interesting to do."

I got out of the cab after a journey that lasted a long time. The front door had been left ajar. The customer had been waiting, lying on his bed, tied up with a dustbin liner over his head.

"Help yourself to a drink in the kitchen . . ." came a shout from the bedroom, " . . . but close the door after you, so the cat can't get out."

I took a banana from the fruit bowl then headed towards the voice. I walked in to find the punter in the rubbish sack. The boy that had come with me was already naked and was kneeling over him and looking confused and pure. I smiled at the boy and set to work giving him directions in silence.

On the dressing table I spotted several pieces of evenly cut string, folded carefully. After prodding and poking it became clear what the man wanted so I tied one of the pieces of string around his balls, snugly separating each testicle. I pulled tightly. Having a wooden rod put in his arse he began to moan, then breathing deeply on the amyl-nitrate from some tissue that I put under the plastic covering he moaned even more. I wedged the wooden rod in place with my knee so that I had both hands free to pull at the string.

Up until now the other boy had been rubbing his hands around the man's chest, I couldn't bear getting him to do anything else. It seemed a crime that he were here. Such sweet hands should only ever do what they want to, or what I want them to. Possibly he should place them over my mouth to stop these ridiculous orders. Then I would be able to smell his fingers and kiss their softness. But this situation was not ideal. He had chosen to be here and to do this, so I got him to hold the wooden rod.

This boy was perfect as only someone would appreciate if they'd seen so many versions of what lay in the bag. And I did want him to rub those same soft hands on me and it mean something true, again as only someone would appreciate if they've had so much of the other stuff, the mauling, the not minding, the bruising and the not letting myself mind.

I could easily have changed this situation so that I fucked this boy's little bum and left the punter tied up. I thought, "Do I want to manipulate the boy?' This time the answer was "No".

Somebody once asked me. "How much do you love me?"

"This much," I said and stretched out my arms as far as they would go.

"Is that all," they said. So I stretched further, expanding my chest and reaching as far as I could. But still this didn't seem enough. Once again I stretched. This time I reach so far back that my knuckles met behind me. At this point my skin begins to split, my ribs cracked, I opened up, and my heart burst out and fell onto the floor. We both watched it as it became cooler and cooler, beating less often until finally it was cold and still. A crowd appeared and came rushing towards us, but because they didn't recognize it they trampled over my heart. What I've learnt from this is never to show somebody how much I love them.

Yesterday I sat and listened to the problems of a man playing solitaire. I watched. His tragic, burlesque sensitivities were

performed for this prostitute. I could not understand all
of his lazy drawl. I found him funny. The other part of
himself that he gave me was aggressive, tugging at my dick
and mashing my balls. I told him how much it hurt, so he
breathed in some amyl-nitrate to release himself from grace.
Tugging and mashing even more he pushed my head towards
his dick. He was young and his dick pretty but I decided that
I would not give in to him. This was a battle ending in a sigh
of tedium.

"What do you do?"

"I fuck," I said.

I felt this was enough for any whore to offer. With this
information he then began to stab at my arsehole with his
yellow finger, because he now knew that I didn't want this.
I withdrew. The more he demanded the less I gave. So I
just knelt over him looking around the room. He came, so I
stopped even pretending to wank, climbed off his bed. I left
his home after I was paid. We met up four of five times after
that and did whatever it was that we did.

I was asked to come along and play "master". The other
prostitute answered the door naked, he was a man not a boy,
he was hairy, he was from Iraq.

"Hello," he said with a – I could give you every physical
pleasure you could ever want kind of a smile. I began to take
off my clothes and by the time he got back from the kitchen
I was naked. We looked at each other, two men, strangers
standing so close, looking so different.

"I like this," I said, pointing to, then placing my hand on
and stroking the thick black swirls on his chest, stomach and
crotch. He smiled at me and pulled me towards him, then
kissed me. We went into the bedroom where the punter was
lying face down on a pillow. I saw a leather belt so I picked it up
and knelt over his back. I did the tricks that I knew, presumably
the other man had already done the ones he knew because he
looked bored and didn't have a hard on but did have his finger
up the punter's arse with his other hand pushing the punter's
face firmly into the pillow. The punter couldn't see us so we
kissed each other and there was a magic around our heads. We

kissed because we both knew what we wanted and needed, and in response our dicks got hard. The punter heard this silence and must have sensed that there was something wrong, that something was happening that wasn't meant to be happening, something nice, something not good going on above his back so he tried to stop this, he tried to get up.

"Keep still," I said, and my pathetic intimation that he was still involved, that this was all for him, that he owned this scene, seemed to be enough and he did lie still so that we could keep on kissing until our heaven broke into smiles.

Punters can rub, lick and fiddle, but it's not these things that work for me. It's not the act that counts.

NYMPH AND SHEPHERD

Colin Spencer

HE'D ALWAYS BEEN ashamed of his thinness. He was easily horrified, not so much about outside things, but mostly about himself. He thought it was his thinness that made him so spiteful. People laughing at him . . . the bones . . . a sharpness like a knife that could kill . . . it was all so distasteful. In the Army and afterwards, trying to get jobs and nothing going right. He couldn't endure people. They distrusted him so easily. Sometimes at first they believed him, taken in by the superficial charm, the angel face, the kindness he could simulate that could turn so easily into anger. And trying up here in this room to write, write poetry, he had to believe in something – that he could write, that he must write. Then of course they saw through him. "Steven," they'd say, "it's no good, you know, if you don't help yourself what can we do?"

Every time that had happened. At first people were full of hope and kindness, they'd get him a job, say they'd send some work of his to someone, perhaps buy him a meal, even a new winter coat; and then he'd sense their disappointment. It hadn't worked out at all. Somehow, he didn't know how, for if he did he would have tried to undo the harm he'd done, they had become disgusted with him: said he wasted everything, said he had no idea how to behave at all. Then he'd be full of self-pity, he'd cry and weep, "you've destroyed something," he'd sob, "something which was beautiful." But they'd think he was lying again, for their disgust generally hinged upon lies.

Steven, Steven . . . he closed his eyes. It was raining outside. He was twenty-two and looked much younger. He'd been living in this room for just under a year now. He'd painted a picture. It was an abstract. It was red and yellow with a black shape caught in a web reminiscent of a spider. It was raining this evening as he'd planned and Henry would be caught in the web like a fly. Henry had been kind. Stupid, silly Henry with his pink full lips that were always so wet. Henry the social worker, the gentle, compassionate Henry who clung to his soft, joyous, merciful Christ and could so easily be moved to tears. He was stronger than Henry, he felt sure of that, even though Henry appeared to shield and look after him. He was stronger and this evening would prove it.

He got up at eleven. He had woken perhaps an hour before, and lay in the bed in the tumbled blankets and the thin, twisted sheet, staring across the room over the littered objects, out to the window. He could hear the sea and the traffic below going past. He made himself some tea and sat there on the edge of the bed shivering a little, stirring the tea and sipping it. He smoked cigarettes, put a record on, a record somebody had lent or left there. He drifted across the room from one object to another, picking them up, replacing them. The unwashed cups, the cut-glass vase used as an ash tray, the cracked shaving mirror, the empty cigarette packets, the unfinished letters he wrote to people he didn't know and who sometimes didn't exist, the hair nets, the face lotions which had hardened at the base of the bottle, the clothes strewn over chairs and tables, the slim book of Surrealist painting, all touched by thin inattentive fingers, brushed and disturbed, then left alone again.

There was the girl in the next room he was fond of, a half-formed tenuous friendship, with Steven, nervous and agitated saying: "I don't know whether you'll be offended but I do like your hair like that, I think it suits you." The girl laughing. They danced. "Doll," she said, "you're my cosy doll." The mornings always passed the same. They had no money.

Once she gave him two shillings to buy some eggs and bread and he came back with rosewater. Once she found him in her room wearing her clothes from dingy black underwear upwards and they rolled on the bed roaring with helpless laughter. "Let me show meself to me public," he said, and he wriggled at the window saying he was Mata the spy, then he sipped some tea and lowered his eye veil and stared down into the street below. Then the girl started to have a young man, a barman – whom Steven could hear three times a day; they locked themselves in and Steven could hear them moving upon the bed, whispering and laughing together. Then he had anonymous letters, threatening and insulting him, describing acts of violence and sadism that they'd inflict upon him. He couldn't bear them together in her room. He told the landlord. He went down the stairs and told him, and then the girl. He said, "You're glad I've done it, aren't you? You're glad. He was bad for you, wasn't he?" The girl was told to leave. The room remained empty next to him. It was clean now and scrubbed, with the bed stripped, naked.

Now all he had was Henry and this evening he would lose him. Henry all softness and innocence, wrapped up warm in his cashmere pullovers, his thick winter coats and scarves, and his large clumsy hands, white and hairless, protruding from so much comfort and expense seemed to Steven almost improper and obscene. His eyes were a little watery, his hair, quite white, stood up about his head like a halo, and Steven was everything and everything to him. He called him "the little poet", and Steven read his work out loud to an attentive and ever sympathetic listener. They met in a theatre queue and there was something about Steven which immediately went to Henry's heart. For Henry, he seemed like the lamb that is lost, balancing precariously upon some cliff-edge of the soul. At first Steven hadn't wanted to talk to the incongruous stranger – he was embarrassed and afraid of physical ugliness. But Henry had smiled so foolishly and chatted away so amiably and bought him a gin in the interval that Steven found himself luxuriating in all the attention.

Slowly through the following weeks they became friends. Henry insisted upon seeing the boy two or three times a week. Then he listened attentively and with a sense of growing concern to stories of Steven's extraordinary background.

"You know I never really knew my father," Steven said wistfully and with a strange, half-excited smile, "he was always away, sailing across the sea, he was very strong, the men respected him, after his death he became almost a legend, you know . . ."

Henry nods sympathetically.

"In the Navy they still tell stories about him, how he fought six men, bandits who tried to steal the locket that my mother gave him. It was worthless really, you know they couldn't have sold it for much, but he kept it next to his heart and always the last thing at night he'd look at it and then kiss it gently. He was a fine man."

"He must have been," Henry murmured, then he paused, "how did he die?" he asked quietly.

There was a silence. Then Steven looked down at his glass and gently moved the gin about inside it. When he looked up at Henry there were tears in his eyes. "He sacrificed himself," he mumbled.

Henry was spellbound. "How?" he whispered.

"He died in the Spanish Civil War," Steven said, looking straight ahead of him.

"But you said he was a sailor," Henry queried.

"I know," he sighed and stared at Henry with something of a master's impatience with an unusually dense pupil. "I know, but when he knew they needed him, he bought himself out. He had a great, oh a great passion for poetry and he fought side by side with many great poets. After he was killed," Steven shuddered, "after he was killed they wrote letters to my mother, in them they said that he had inspired them all constantly to greater and greater sacrifices. And then . . . and then he was massacred at Guernica."

Henry was deeply moved; smiling down at the boy, he said, "Of course you've inherited some of your father's fineness of spirit, I can see that."

"It was too terrible," Steven muttered, wiping away a tear. "And then of course my mother died soon afterwards from a broken heart . . . I couldn't have been more than five but I remember it so vividly . . . the colour of her hair, her hands, so slim and pale and frightened in a way. And the garden, I can just remember where the old summer house was, overgrown with creepers, its roof fallen in and the lilac and wisteria, I wonder if it's all there now? And then being suddenly taken away from it all, shrieking, for I saw her fall . . ."

"Fall?"

"She fell down the stairs. God, I shall never forget it, distracted she was with grief, terrible grief, she had on . . . a blue dress down to the ground it was . . . to the ground."

The gullible Henry was a great luxury for Steven. He never asked awkward questions, never pestered him over details that didn't seem to fit, never laughed, and always believed him with the generous simplicity of a child. Henry was thirty-eight yet he seemed older; when he fussed he reproduced the mannerisms of an old man. Up to this time his life had been insulated from the world, kept rigidly in a small circle of people who felt and thought and acted as he did, who did their social work thoroughly and well though in the extreme simplicity of their natures. He was still devout, certain that through prayer he could find a place for Steven in the world he knew, but that world suddenly seemed to have grown smaller, things didn't quite fit as they had, and this made him feel uneasy.

Steven grew to be more and more dependent upon him. If Henry was late, then he would quickly grow impatient and irritable, he fidgeted and chain-smoked. He hated Henry to do anything out of character, to smear the respectability that Steven loved and coveted. Once when Steven was talking of his father, his sea adventures, his wonderful heroism, the exploits that were rewarded by so many decorations culminating with his audience with the King, Henry – trying somehow to make a gesture, feeling lightheaded, a little crazy, and perhaps wanting a little of the hero worship that Steven so lavishly bestowed upon his father – walked out, balancing upon a breakwater, calling out to Steven. His tall, thin figure wrapped tightly in his winter coat stood wavering a little on the slippery black wood, his arms out, an umbrella like a pendulum swinging to and fro in his hand, while he talked to the sea, defying it. Steven was humiliated. "How ridiculous he looks," he thought. His dream disintegrated, fell at his feet in all its insubstantial tawdriness. And Henry's figure upon the breakwater, thin and black against a moonlit sea, was a symbol of all Steven's emptiness. He had sent him there? He walked away, refusing to answer Henry's thin and piping voice which called him back, calling to him to the sea's edge to watch.

Out of desperation and as a kind of reprisal, wishing somehow to humiliate Henry as he had just been, that same evening he took Henry to a bar he often went to. As they walked in Steven was greeted by smiles and several heads nodded towards them. "I never realized," Henry murmured, "that you had so many friends." Steven shivered with disgust. "They're not my friends," he hissed in a stage whisper, "I can't bear them."

Steven felt a certain power and sadistic pleasure sitting here with the naïve, uncomprehending Henry seeing him so solidly respectable in a bar so sordidly notorious. He sipped his drink and smiled up at Henry. "What do you think of it here?"

Henry looked about him, peering into the semi-darkness. "Oh . . . oh it seems very nice," he murmured.

Steven smiled a smile of triumph tinged with worldly bitterness. "Very nice, my God," he thought, "little does he know." He leant over towards Henry and whispered, "Terrible, dreadful people come here sometimes."

Henry looked at him blankly.

"Oh," he said. He thought of Steven, so young and innocent, mixing with the wrong kind of person. "You don't . . . you wouldn't come here often, would you?' he asked uneasily.

Steven laughed, with a hint of masculine bravado. "Often? Good God, no, I wouldn't have anything to do with that kind of person." At the back of his mind Henry remembered vaguely the smiles of recognition as they had walked in; then, he thought, they must have mistaken Steven for someone else.

In a loud and important voice, Steven said:

"So you don't think there's anything wrong with these . . . these." He made a gesture of disgust.

"Wrong, Steven?" said Henry, mystified.

"Yes. Wrong."

Henry peered again around the bar. They all seemed

extremely nice, normal people drinking and chatting with each other. "I don't understand, Steven," he said.

"They're . . ." Steven hesitated, as if to give greater weight to the importance of his pronouncement, "they're perverts," he said in a half-anguished whisper.

Henry was slightly taken aback. He looked around the room again, they hadn't changed, they still seemed the same. He laughed, "Oh, I don't think you can say that. How can you possibly know, dear child?"

Steven's trump card had not even been noticed, it had been passed over as if it was a mad assumption with no knowledge behind it at all. He sat back in his chair and felt grimly hateful. How he despised them all. All these creatures for defying him, for not being sordid and bizarre and sexually monstrous as he wanted them; and how he hated Henry for being so simple, so stupidly simple and kind. He sat back in his chair and sulked. When Henry addressed a remark to him, he ignored it completely. He sipped his drink, finished it, went up to the bar, icily ignoring the barmaid who said, archly, "Hello, Stevie dear," and bought himself another drink.

Then after a few minutes he realized with horror that Henry had begun talking to someone else, an enemy of Steven's of some years' standing, and Henry was courteously treating him like a normal human being. He watched them, simmering with rage, and then for a second time that evening he turned abruptly on his heel and walked out of the bar.

Steve had lied and lied, he had told so many stories about himself that now he could no longer recall them all or remember exactly what he said. He was terrified Henry would discover the truth, would find him out in a lie, that the gullible Henry would suddenly, almost unawares, understand what kind of person he was. He could not bear to lose Henry as he had lost everyone else, yet he was bored to tears and irritated to distraction with the untroubled goodness of the older man. He needed his attention and love, yet he hated and was impatient of Henry's obtuseness and stupidity. In this last week he had day-dreamed for hours. Henry was dead. Killed suddenly in some accident. Then he would discover that in his will Henry had left everything to him. He dreamt about the small house in the country filled with rare *objets d'art*. Then Steven could see himself walking about the house, stopping to caress a small statuette, fingering a Ming vase, drinking fragrant wines from delicate glass, sipping the palest tea from thin china, enjoying the garden, reading his poems aloud in the soft warm air of the evening. Then there was the private income, and the clothes he would buy, the endless fashion shows he held in front of mirrors, many sided, gilt ormolu; the new style he'd do his hair, the way he would keep his youth. The car, the chauffeur – ah, life seemed endlessly fascinating, a crystal paradise. If only somehow it could all come true.

Sometimes he hated Henry's goodness, he felt he wanted to damage Henry permanently, to disillusion him, to make him see that life was cruel and terrible, not innocent and simple. He was exhausted with his own deceit and lies. He had come to the end of them. Could he tell Henry the truth? Was he strong enough? He day-dreamed for a time, imagining how he would tell the truth, seeing the scene: his figure grown larger in proportion, his voice loud and clear, like music, the words almost poetry, and Henry would be falling. Henry, the fallen. He had destroyed Henry through this godlike instrument, the truth. He had wielded it and Henry was slain. Yes . . . that was an interesting idea. Would the truth make Henry desperate and ill with shame and horror, so that perhaps he'd drive carelessly? Could he say, clinging to Henry, "Don't go away, you've been the only person who's ever really been kind to me, don't go, don't leave me," knowing he would; knowing he'd run outside into the rain and drive the car desperately anywhere just so that it went away from him. With Henry's moral disgust like sickness in his throat. He lay on the floor, his back to the wall, thinking; he twisted a pyjama cord in his fingers, wound it round his wrist, his hand, his fingers, drew it tight, so that the fingers became startlingly white, then he lessened the tautness and the blood rushed to them, grew pink, scarlet. He was wasting his life. He looked down at the odd papers lying upon the floor, the scribbled words, the sprawling blank verse which talked of fires, of torments, of women strangling their babies; and of flowers and streams, blue skies, peace and the Virgin blue as sky, as water, as peace. He pushed them away with his hand and turned his face to the wall, looking up at the window, at the streaming grey-white sheet of water that ran down the pane. He wanted to change everything, for one evening simply to tell the truth, with no ulterior motive behind it, the truth, in its purity, and then cleansed, a new Steven, perhaps he'd be able to work – with Henry even – to become part of the world that he saw about him.

There was a tap on the door. Steven didn't move. Suddenly he felt out of breath, as if he'd run a great distance. Then he got up and walked slowly to the door, hesitated, then opened it. Henry had bought him some roses, all buds, crimson. Steven held them to him. He looked out at the rain. He could see the car, the door buckled, the roses crushed. Henry's pale, watery eyes which seemed to reflect the endless reproachful rain outside, looking down at him, questioning. How ugly he was. Sometimes he almost frightened Steven with his stupid almost cretinous face. The truth: he clung to the roses. He crossed and recrossed the room The poems on the floor were trodden and kicked aside. "I will destroy my old life," he thought. Henry sat down on the bed, tiny drops of rain fell off his hair and on to his face, the bed sank beneath him with a groan, its bulge touched the floor.

Then Steven thought again, "Perhaps the truth will kill him? Perhaps I shall kill him by telling him the truth?" The rain, the accident he'd dreamt up and obsessively thought of. He sat there at the window looking out. He held the roses, nothing was any good any more, he wanted to crush the roses against the window, they would cry, their redness, the rain, the truth.

"We can't go out," Henry said, quietly, "when it's like this. It's not much fun driving in the rain."

Steven sat there, very still. "I want . . ."

"Yes?" Henry asked, eager and fidgeting.

"I'm not like . . ."

His mouth was dry.

"Shouldn't you put those in water?" Henry suggested, pointing at the roses.

"They're mine," Steven said, and he half got up. "They're mine," he said, crushing them against him, screwing the buds up in his hands, so that the petals spilt over him and onto the floor and he watched with satisfaction the pain and dismay upon Henry's face.

There was silence.

Then Steven cried, "I want to do this, I want to do this," then he let his arms fall and the flowers, broken, damaged, fell to the floor. He looked as if he was going to be sick. Henry was silent.

They stared at each other.

Steven turned back to the window and placed his hands over his face and as if talking to himself, he mumbled, "I'm ill . . . I'm ill, I'm not very well, I'm . . ." He sat on the window sill, the pane next to his cheek was ice cold, he shivered. Then again, "I have too much to bear, too much." Henry remained silent, he put his hand through his wet hair, then still staring up at Steven, he wiped his hand slowly upon his coat.

"I'm ill," Steven moaned, "I'm ill."

Then suddenly angry again, he strode to a drawer and pulled it out; it was full of odds and ends, remnants, papers and used envelopes; he pulled out what seemed to be letters, and now shaking with wrath and nerves, his hands quivering, he thrust them back into Henry's lap. "Look, look what I have to endure, this filth, this muck . . . I can't stand it. I'm terrified."

Nervously, Henry fumbled for his spectacles. He murmured, "My poor child, my poor child." he peered at the letters, adjusted his spectacles. Steven was staring down at him, breathing quickly. He appeared to be almost asthmatic.

The drops of rain from Henry's hair had fallen upon the letters, he brushed them away, the ink ran. He turned the pages over and over, fingering the paper, then he looked up at Steven. He stuttered a little. "I'm ssssorry, I can't rrrread the writing . . . it it goes backwards, the letters are so ill-formed."

Steven stared down at him.

"I can't make out what it says at all." He whispered. "Except here it says something about um . . . 'I want to' . . . see, what is this word Steven?" Henry's finger pointed to the page. He looked up at Steven, wide-eyed, innocent, inquiring.

Steven stamped his foot. "Read it, can't you," he was almost in tears. "Read the word. Can't you see what it means?"

Henry thrust the pages towards Steven. "I can't. I can't," he mumbled.

"You refuse to, is that it?"

"No, I I I . . . the writing, dear boy, read them aloud to me, read them like you do your poetry sometimes." Steven snatched them from him and began to tear them up. "No . . . no, why?"

"They're vile," Steven hissed, "vile, they can't be seen by your pure eyes, after all you might die from the shock of it, it would appal you, appal you, do you hear?"

Henry looked up at him, uncomprehending. "Yes," he said. "Yes. But won't you tell me what's the matter?"

"You don't know?" Steven asked bitterly. "You don't know?"

"Try and tell me, Steven, try."

Somehow then it was so easy just to say, "I'm a liar Henry. I'm a liar, everything I've told you is lies." He looked at him, the gentle, the kind, the unsullied Henry. Somehow he had him in his power, he'll do anything for me Steven thought, anything. It was too great a thing to risk losing. "I'd rather not say," he whispered.

Making an effort, quietly but firmly, Henry said, "Perhaps you'd be happier if you thought of someone else for a change now and again Steven."

"I don't think so," he answered, icily.

"Perhaps you don't realize how you've changed my life, you shouldn't get so upset when you realize how much happiness you bring to other people."

The power, Steven thought, the power, but casually he said, "I wasn't aware of it."

"Yes. Yes." Henry insisted. "I see now what a narrow life I led before I knew you, trying to shepherd my flock through their troubles, without knowing really what they were. I've understood so much more since I've known you. You've enriched my life."

Steven remained very still, listening.

"Oh I know you think I'm a silly old fogey sometimes," Henry giggled a little nervously, "when one lives alone for a long time one grows, well," he frowned, "curious habits. Do you see that you're the sunshine that floods a dusty room? What would I do without that sun now?"

Power comes from the sun, he thought, power.

"You're so free, Steven, compared to me. I often think you know, that you're like some strange spirit moving in a deep deep forest. Don't laugh, it's curious that I love something so untamed and wild."

Steven was quiet now, listening carefully, he sat down next to Henry upon the bed. "Would you care for me? Look after me I mean, really care . . . ?"

"Of course," Henry answered.

"For how long?" Steven said. "For how long? For years maybe?"

Henry laughed. "Perhaps you'd even have to look after me."

He insisted. "Would it be for years?"

"Maybe. I don't know. Perhaps you'd be able to stand on your own feet quite soon, you mustn't think of yourself as helpless you know."

Henry's voice went on and on, patient, reassuring, trying to construct a world for Steven from the fragments of experience that he had cautiously gathered and kept; trying desperately to fit these upon a person and a situation that he could not understand.

Steven despised him more and more, it was all meaningless, without relevance and therefore without hope. Why was that? Didn't Henry love him? Why couldn't he understand him? They were miles apart that was the trouble. But he was real anyway, he was in pain, he felt that he was down next to the earth and sick in the stomach with it, and yet . . . momentarily and vaguely he half-realized that in his lies, in the false glamour of the world he made up, he extinguished the real Steven. The Steven he had just shed bitter tears over never saw the light of day, he destroyed himself in his own desperation to become part of the world he saw about him. That was the irony and he felt he would never have the strength to defy it.

Henry patted him on the shoulders and got up. "Well, I suppose we ought to move if we're going to go anywhere. The rain has stopped."

Steven looked up at the window. Somehow that seemed a portent, but of what he wasn't sure. He began to collect the papers upon the floor, the letters half begun to people he only vaguely remembered, the poems written in wild confusion on scraps of old envelopes.

Henry crossed the room and got his feet entangled in the pyjama cord. "Will you go?" Steven said. "I don't want to go out anywhere."

"Are you sure?" Henry asked, trying to untwist the cord from his ankles.

"Quite sure," Steven piled the papers one upon each other. Henry struggled. "I'm quite sure."

"I shall worry. Couldn't we enjoy the evening together . . . couldn't we?" Henry pleaded.

"Will you go?" Steve cried. "I'm tired, I want to think, I want to do some work . . . writing."

"Very well," Henry said, "very well." He placed the cord in a neatly wound bundle on the top of the dresser and picked up his coat.

Steven got up from the floor and went again to the drawer, "Wait a moment, please, Henry." He took two envelopes placed beneath some clothes, "Will you post these for me – please. And don't worry, I shall be all right. I promise you."

"Of course," Henry murmured, and took the two letters in his gloved hand, "you wouldn't consciously hurt me would you, you wouldn't deceive me would you? I think you're fond of me in your own way, isn't that so, Steven? Isn't that so?"

"Of course, Henry, of course," he murmured. "But please go . . . please." Steven opened the door. Henry went slowly down the narrow stairs. He was mystified and distressed; Steven seemed to touch and disturb the very deepest part of him. He wanted so much to help him and yet he seemed always quite unable to.

It was only when he got to the pillar box that he turned the letters up in his hand and as he slipped them through the opening noticed, with a shock of revulsion and distress, that they were addressed to Steven in that same weird back-sloping hand.

THE GREEK AMBASSADOR

John Stapleton

THE COPS KEPT me waiting for a long time, in various rooms and then in a cell for a while. I kept hearing that metallic door sound in the distance all the time. I had just been questioned over the murder of the Greek ambassador. Denty we used to call him. I denied ever having met him, and said I had been in the bar most of the night before. They probably could have checked that but they didn't. They were just nosing about, seeing what they could dig up. Half a dozen of us had been picked up in one swoop. All I wanted was a drink. After about four hours they let me go and I walked out into the sunshine which looked like prison corridors the way it slanted through the tall buildings.

Monty was waiting for me outside the police station, dear funny old Monty who always liked to look after us kids and who got precious little in return. He grinned at me and I tried to grin back but it didn't work. Two hundred yards from the station was a pub. This was no time for subtlety. I drank and I drank and I saw Monty coughing up at me from his bed in some cheap hotel, I saw rich bodies coming over me and felt their cocks rubbing against me. I wasn't quite sure what I was doing anymore.

We called the Greek ambassador Denty because he had a

funny little bent prick and often enough he would just get one
or two of us to jerk off in front of him while he watched. He
hadn't been so bad, as queers go. He always paid well, that
was something. It was Steve's fault, what happened. Steve was
a mad fucking bugger, madder than me by far. He was crazy
about cars. The old guys'd always go for him 'cause of the way
he looked. He did look pretty cute in a handsome aggressive
sort of way, even I had to admit that. I had fucked him once
when he'd lost a bet over something. We never talked about it
because it went against our unwritten code that friends never
fucked each other.

Steve was always in trouble. Somehow or other he'd get his
hands on a car and go roaring around and always get caught.
All his greatest moments of glory had been in stolen motor
cars. He'd disappear for six months and then he'd be back
on the scene, searching and waiting for just the right moment.
Someone would trust him a little too far and the whole thing
would happen all over again. The world is full of suckers. I liked
Steve 'cause he was one of those salt of the earth substance of
the suburbs types that one could rely on as a mate, even if he
was fucked in the head.

This guy Marve who ran a club called Slats had told me
that Denty was asking after me. Denty liked the way I made
a fuss about splurring all over the place, though God knows
I had to shut my eyes fuckin' tight and think of sexy things,
those pictures which'd make me come, 'cause you understand
I didn't find the sight of this funny old Greek man lying naked in
his bed all that exciting. Trying to look like I was into it. They're
waiting outside for you, diamond boy, little Lil's going to tell on
you if you don't spread your legs; the diamonties, the diamond
skill, lick, lick. I would shiver and wait in moist places, waiting
for the licking to stop.

I didn't find out until afterwards that Denty was the
Greek ambassador, but I don't think it would have made
any difference.

I had been to see him several times before and we got on
pretty well in a funny sort of way. Afterwards he was always
very motherly towards me; and sometimes I would talk to him
about things that I couldn't talk to anyone else about. He was

much kinder than a lot of the freaky creeps I had had to deal with and I didn't mind jerking off in front of him if it gave him that much of a thrill, particularly when I thought about the money involved. He quite liked me to bring a friend along, so we could both jerk off at the same time and he'd lie on his bed doing it too.

Well, this day when Marve at Slats told me Denty had rung up asking after me the first thing I did was go around to the pub and see who was hanging about who might like a couple of quick dollars, and Steve was the first person I ran across. I always felt a bit embarrassed about doing it in front of someone I thought of as a friend, someone my own age, but money was money and we did all these things, no use kidding that we didn't. Besides, maybe I could get it up easier with Steve about.

"Such a cute number, pity he's so hung up dear."

"Don't waste your time sweet, I know for a fact that he robbed old Richard's place, two original Whiteleys. Drink?"

Denty lived in an enormous house. He always insisted that I arrive late and be very discreet. I just figured it was because he was very rich and didn't want anyone to know what he was really like, but when you think about it he must have been pretty important, being an ambassador and everything.

You should have seen Steve's eyes light up when we got there. Denty had three cars you see, an old Daimler, a BMW sports and a Toyota. I think it was the BMW sports that really kindled up Steve. We knocked and waited and all the time he kept looking around at the driveway. "Oh man, oh man," he kept muttering under his breath. "Oh boy, oh boy," I thought to myself.

Denty opened the door and, like them all, his eyes wobbled when he saw Steve. I didn't mind. He didn't know what he was letting himself in for. Steve was trouble, any way you wanted to look at him.

Old Denty invited us in, his hands fluttering all over the place. He offered us a drink. I liked getting out of it on anything so I had a brandy and Coke and Steve drank Southern Comfort. After a couple of drinks and idle chit-chat it was time for the bed scene.

I think Steve's always hated the fact that he goes off with

men, because he doesn't think he's queer at all, which is pretty wishful thinking on his part if you ask me. He was always talking about fucking chicks like he was some big stud, saying he only went off with guys for the money and that he didn't like it at all. Sure man sure, anything you say. I had always been lonely before I took up in the gay scene, not really fitting in with the kids at school. I guess that's why it didn't bother me like it bothered Steve, 'cause even though some of the tricks I went off with weren't exactly smashing, in general I quite liked some of the things they did to me, even if I did get a bit pissed a lot of the time. I couldn't really understand people who didn't drink. For me it was all a bit like joining a secret club, friends, drink, money, maybe even a car someday. And all the time I had little images of white skin which could make me come more or less when I wanted to. Keep them happy, make them think you're enjoying yourself. Pretty simple really.

Well there we were with our pants around our ankles and Denty lyin' on the bed getting all squirmy when suddenly Steve stops playing with himself and just goes berserk, picks up this really expensive lamp and throws it at the wall and then gets this really heavy glass ornament and smashes it down on poor old Denty's head. As if that wasn't enough he picks it up and does it again, which was just about the end of old Denty apart from a moan and a twitch or two.

I only found out he was the Greek ambassador the next day when it was in all the papers.

I was very frightened by the whole thing and had no one to talk to about it. I ran into Monty on a street corner and started to tell him about it, but then I stopped because nice as Monty was he was a drunk and didn't know what he was saying half the time. Not one to tell secrets to. I didn't have any money because naturally enough Denty hadn't paid me and Steve had taken all the money he could find. He had wanted me to come with him in the BMW but I refused. He called me piss-weak and roared off, nearly crashing into a parked car. I had sat in the gutter a bit before running off into the night, not really knowing where I was going.

I tried to console myself by thinking it was all in the game, and I liked being part of the game. It went against everything my parents would have wanted me to be ("the seething nights, those crashing tears, oh babe, how did I get myself, in this whole wretched affair") and yet it was something to be, something to say I had been, at one with the streets, survival of the fittest. Actually I did better than most of them. I had a couple of guys with a bit of money who were pretty keen on me and would take me out places; one of them was even talking about getting me an apartment to stay in. Maybe he wouldn't actually hand me the documents, but it was something. I always wanted a decent place of my own, choose the friends I wanted to have a good time with, shut the door when I wanted to be by myself.

I wished I had that apartment now. I would sit there and wait for the telephone to ring. "Thanks for calling. Sorry, can't make it today." I went down to Elizabeth Bay and got up onto the roof of an old apartment block I knew. It was a great place to go if you were tripping or feeling a bit paranoid or anything, because the view of Sydney was fantastic from up there and yet nobody would ever know you were there. Safest place on earth. I sat and watched the sunrise, the pink tints, the ships right down the harbour to the heads, the bridge on the other side. It really was fantastic, even if I was in a bit of trouble.

After I got picked up for questioning the first time I should have got as far away from the city as possible but I didn't know anyone in the country and besides you need money to get away. I didn't have anywhere to go. Lately I had just been crashing around the place, getting into a bit of dope if I could. I liked getting out of it, it was an interesting thing to do. I thought that if I ever got to be as old as thirty then I'd probably stop, but for now it suited me fine. After I left Monty I had been to see Harry, a sort of guruish old dope fiend with glasses that I quite liked, but he wasn't home. There were a few tricks I could go and see but I couldn't get in touch with any of them and none of them had been stupid enough to give me keys to their apartment.

All I really wanted was a drink. There was only one place to go, the pub. There'd always be some old codger there with a loaded wallet who'd buy you a drink, chat you up. I hardly ever went with any of them, but I never knocked back a drink.

The funny thing was that as fucked up as I felt, it was

really a beautiful day, not a cloud in the sky, cool with all the buildings lit precisely, bright brick colours and figures standing out more than real. I walked to the pub and thought about getting drunk.

As soon as I stepped through the door I knew something was wrong. The barman, who was a kind of friend, gesticulated at me but it was too late. Before I had reached the bar there were two plain-clothes men standing next to me. I shrugged and went outside with them.

There were trees in the park which made me feel very lonely. Doors shutting. They told me that Steve was in hospital, that he had been hurt in a car crash but that he would be all right, that he had told them everything. I've never met a nice policeman. There were lots of rooms and corridors and people asking me questions, and this time there wasn't any Monty waiting outside for me. I could feel things changing around me but inside I didn't change at all. I wanted a drink badly but where I was there was no way of getting one. I curled up in the dark inside and didn't come out for a long time.

THE MAN IN THE DARK

Mansel Stimpson

PAUL KNEW THAT he possessed none of the characteristics of the gay male stereotype. And in all probability that was equally true of Richard. Not that he knew Richard, the man he was about to meet, the man who had placed the gay ad to which he had replied. Their contact to date had been limited to a single, quite short, telephone conversation. Yet Paul felt able already to build up a picture in his mind because the name announced on the telephone had not been unfamiliar. Quite the contrary, in fact, for this stranger was a figure from the past. He had been noted for his involvement in gay liberation a decade ago, long before Paul had started to come to terms with his own sexuality.

The prospect of meeting such a man would be daunting to some. Paul, however, merely regarded it as an intriguing prospect. There was nothing strange in this, for, if he had been late in identifying himself as gay, his eventual acceptance had been without reservations. This made him very positive in outlook and strong in manner. The history of Richard's achievements suggested he might well be Paul's equal in these respects, and this was appealing to Paul who had long ago dismissed the idea that gay lovers had to be respectively active and passive for sex to go well. The challenge of like to like had been part of his experience; but not lately, and the possibility of sparking off a new relationship of this kind could not have been more welcome. As he travelled to Richard's house to keep their appointment, he realized to his pleasure that he felt decidedly randy.

Richard opened the door and within moments had destroyed all of Paul's expectations. Not only the way he looked but even the way he stood seemed to deny the strength, the command, which Paul had ascribed to him. When he started to speak the revision of the portrait was taken even further. Hesitancy and uncertainty emerged at once as the joint keynotes of his character, unless he were displaying instead shyness elevated to power – the power that is to conceal the real person. But to discover the real Richard was no easy task. On other occasions when Paul had found himself confronting reticence, he had been able in time to encourage conversation. The flow might still be lacking, but, after a while, the shyness usually slackened and yielded, allowing some impression of the true personality to emerge.

But not so with Richard. All avenues were quickly blocked, even the most obvious.

"Let's not talk about the Gay Liberation Front; those days are long since past." As for more general topics of conversation, the hesitancy and uncertainty remained, but now transformed into a whole sentence. "I'm never sure what I think. As soon as I express an opinion I want to qualify it. Half of what I say seems untrue the moment I have actually said it." Such remarks might have ben calculated to discourage all further talk and at that moment Paul, disheartened yet decidedly curious about Richard, would have been surprised had he known that he would shortly stumble upon a clue, one which would unexpectedly open up Richard in his mind's eye and lead him to an essential truth about this man.

With nothing to hint at such a possibility, Paul was reduced to searching for some new subject to resuscitate the conversation. On entering the house, he had noticed the extensive presence of photographs on the walls, enlargements which were of a size and character to suggest that they were more than just chance decoration. And so it proved, for when Paul mentioned them Richard became more animated at last.

"I've taken up photography quite recently," he declared. "I am sure it should be regarded as a major art form and I hoped to create photographs which would capture the essence of landscape." Those which Paul had seen were evidence that the photographer had travelled widely in Britain in his attempt to achieve this. Whether or not the results justified the endeavour, it was clear from Richard's comments that he had started out with fuelled enthusiasm. But soon the spirit so suddenly established in the conversation began to fade; the old tone was returning when he added limply: "But I am not sure what more I can do now." He sounded like a traveller who had reached the end of a road only to find it was a cul-de-sac.

Taken on their own, his comments might have been tedious. But Paul was fascinated by the puzzle of trying to relate the man who sat opposite him to the activist of the past who had seemed to possess the aura of a leader. He began to wonder if Richard had ever matched up to this vision, or if the colleague with whom he had been closely associated in those bygone days had been so much the commanding figure that he had swept up Richard and implanted on him by association an image which was all his own and which had never represented any part of the man before him. Or was it possible that there was more humour in Richard than met the eye and that some kind of game was being played? For Paul could not fail to notice that Richard was fond of putting forward views about the arts which, according to one's viewpoint, were either off-beat or eccentric.

"But why take account of what an author says about his book?" he said, dismissing a criticism of Paul's concerning a novel which failed to live up to the writer's declared intentions. "Why should his view of it be more reliable than one's own?"

Nor was there in Richard any wish to earn acceptance by approving ideas put forward by Paul. When his visitor expressed reservations over the harsh judgement passed by some on the gay painter who had remained in the closet all his life, Richard perkily remarked that the contemptuous verdict was one which he thoroughly endorsed.

All told, then, Paul was pleased to be offered the respite which came with Richard's suggestion that the two of them should go out and eat in a nearby Italian restaurant. But it was just before setting out that an incident, as yet of unclear meaning, occurred. Passing again through the hall, custodian of those studied photographs, Paul felt called upon to make some comment upon them.

"They really are striking," he said, and if to his own ears the phrase sounded desperately banal it was probably because he did not mean it. Yet the words were hardly out when his eye was taken by a photograph which did possess quality.

"Are these also your work?" he asked, for what stood out was no landscape but one of three photographs of male nudes. The other two avoided the impression of being a gay artist's private pornography, but they were unexceptional nevertheless. The one which mattered was extraordinary because the man portrayed was deformed, or such was the deduction one was encouraged to make. The man himself, secure behind dark glasses, revealed none of his secrets and what might well be a club-foot was hidden from sight by the photographer's choice of composition. Yet he had also chosen to show the crutch which the man needed in order to walk and, furthermore, to show it boldly and directly, not as an object which could be detected in the margin of the photograph by the seeking eye but as a dominant feature. It drew attention as strongly as the firm, attractive male body which, so far as could be seen, seemed to deny that mutilation or blemish could have anything to do with it. But the crutch told one otherwise.

"Do you find it," Richard asked, "disturbing?"

Paul understood what Richard meant, yet disturbing was not the word he would have used. Thought-provoking was a valid adjective because the picture broke a rule, the requirement that in art of this kind nudes should be beautiful and remote from any uncomfortable reality. Puzzling would have been a valid description too, for one felt that the body, no abstract object after all, ought to give some sign of the deformity implied. Yet that face, partially concealed by the glasses, revealed nothing of suffering and thus contributed to the unacknowledged conspiracy to refute the relevance of the crutch. Surely that link had to be admitted if the photograph was to make sense? Or might that be too obvious, seeing that the contrast heightened the impact made? For the moment, the essence of what was present remained elusive.

In the restaurant over the shared meal the fits and starts of conversation served only to confirm Paul's earlier impressions of his host. But there was one additional piece of evidence; it was not what Richard said but what he did. Watching the unconscious nervous gestures of the hands, Paul put away all thoughts of the surface impression being misleading. Whatever he might be, Richard assuredly was not the strong, forceful, self-reliant figure which Paul had created in his own mind as epitomizing a leader of the Gay Liberation Front. Paul regretfully admitted to himself that, merely as a matter of sexual preference, Richard's manner made him much less appealing physically than if the man had been true to the image. He was aware too that sympathy, which he might have felt, had been put to flight by those statements of Richard's such as the one about the painter, which revealed that the two of them possessed radically different attitudes from one another. Paul, musing to himself, wondered if Richard was having reservations, different but no less strong, about him. Certainly Paul regarded the prospect of sex as fading away; but he wondered if this was not for the best in the circumstances. Then, breaking into these thoughts, came Richard's voice: "Let's go now," he said. "You could come back to my place for a coffee."

It was not that sentence, however, but another one, again spoken by Richard, which strongly suggested that he was not averse to making love with Paul despite their differences. They were back in Richard's house when he said to Paul: "I like your belt; it's very like mine." Paul, comparing the two belts which each helped to hold jeans close in to the genitals, was acutely aware that in actuality the design of the belts was quite different. But this specific reference to the area of the crotch still left him, implications duly considered, in two minds. Paul, who had never taken to cruising and who favoured a personal quality in all of his sexual couplings, believed that to encourage Richard when he felt so distant from him as a person would be to use him as a sex object. Experiencing these doubts, Paul even started to explain to him why it would be better to go no further; ironically, it was his bungling way of saying this – his feeling that Richard might be hurt or insulted by his remarks when he did not mean them to sound critical – which caused him to cancel out any such reaction by offering his body after all.

So, unexpectedly, the sexual involvement which Paul had hoped for on setting out came about; even more surprisingly, the sexual pleasure proved to be what he had imagined. Richard led him into his bedroom and lit candles at some distance from the bed. That was to be their light. In all other respects darkness prevailed and, as they stripped one another of their clothes, they each discovered not by sight but by touch, by hand and then by tongue, the body of the other. Here in the darkness Paul found that his partner was a splendid lover, as positive and as ardent as he was himself, and as vocal in his cries of delight. When Paul left Richard's house it was late, very late, but that did not matter.

Each had been appreciative of the other in bed, but when next day Paul came to look back on their meeting he was doubtful if the relationship could be built into something meaningful. His doubts centred on what he had felt about Richard as a person, Richard being the man who had talked to him and taken him out for a meal. As for the man in the dark, the man who strangely enough answered to the name of Richard, he could not decide who he was. What was self-evident was that the lover he had discovered existed only in that private darkness, for only there did the doubts and fears, the anxieties and tribulations of the person known to the world as Richard disappear. They were shed totally, but only for the time that the room was in darkness. To say that a chrysalis was discarded yielding a butterfly was not quite the right comparison. It was more accurate to say that the man in the dark was the man Richard would have been had he not felt so pressured by society for being gay.

These thoughts developed in Paul's mind the day after the meeting. But it was not until another twenty-four hours had passed that the moment of knowledge came to him. He was not even pondering the puzzle of Richard when the realization occurred: whoever had posed for that one impressive photograph in Richard's collection, it was in truth a self-portrait of the artist.

OUTING

Peter Wells

"WHY IS FATE always so fucking inscrutable?" queried Perrin McDougal as Eric knelt at his feet, guiding his dead toes into his shoes.

"I suspect," said Eric rather too tartly, because he hadn't actually thought he'd be acting as nursemaid, "it means, that way, the old fraud is never quite caught out."

They were in Perrin's exquisitely muted bedroom, with its frosty Viennese chandelier reflected in perpetuity in the floor-to-ceiling mirror. This now returned an image of themselves, ironically, in poses of almost biblical simplicity. Though Eric thought he caught a faint ammoniacal pong from Perrin's socks. "Isn't it time, darling, these putrescent articles were, well," Eric tried to sound noncommittal, "*substituted* for something more savoury?"

They used the telegraphese of old friends, accentuated by the frequently sharp, sometimes hilarious, even acid appendage of "*dear*". Though in the present situation, with Perrin so ill, the *dears* had taken on a warmer, more amber hue.

"Can you find me my walking-stick?"

Perrin had phoned up that afternoon and commanded Eric – the tone was properly regal and brooked no contradiction – to take him to the Remuera Garden Centre. Eric thought ironically – though fondly too, because in the contradiction lay the quintessence of his character – that here was Eric almost certainly going to be absent in the flooding spring yet he, Perrin, was planning a lavish bouquet for his "spring" garden.

"What I see," Perrin had announced over the phone in that way that had the faint edge of the visionary to it, "is a mixture of marigolds, blue violas and delphiniums. Don't you remember . . .?"

Eric didn't, but it didn't matter.

"Don't you remember how Aunt Priscilla down in Te Awamutu always had a daphne bush by her front steps and the way it always used to *invite* you – yes, *invite* is the right word –" Perrin kept his legal precision intact, a careful weapon against the unknown, "so that as you ascended the stairs into her hall, the scent was *incroyable*!"

Perrin now rose to his feet unsteadily. His once fleshy form had been stripped by the disease to a frightening gauntness. His stylish garments – once bought in Melbourne or "inexpensively" run up in distant Bangkok – clothed his skeleton in a simulacrum of "health". To the outside world – that crowd of on-lookers who instantly became extras in the cinema of Perrin's declining life – he probably looked only frail, possibly suffering from cancer.

Eric clung to these illusions as he handed Perrin his elegant malacca cane. He was still getting used to the shock of being seen with Perrin in public.

He had told himself as he drove over to Perrin's Epsom bungalow (a clever pastiche of Frank Lloyd Wright, via his Napier disciple, Louis Hay) that the public gaze simply didn't matter, that it was more important to simply help Perrin, that this accompanying him a little along the road was the very least he could do. But the truth was he had gone into a state of near shock when he thought he'd left his sunglasses behind.

He realized when his fingers touched Bakelite – they connected with the impact of a lodestone – that he was sweating uncomfortably, not even watching the road. His heart was banging away, in a mocking Judas dance.

*   *   *

"Give us your arm, dear." Perrin now stood at the brow of his front steps whose very sweep and height had once signalled power. Now they simply spoke danger: Perrin's grasp of Eric's arm was surprisingly tight. Eric registered Perrin's frailty as he leant into him.

He watched the almost random – yet hesitant, hesitant – fall of Perrin's numbed feet.

Suddenly Perrin lurched to a halt. "This!" he cried in a voice full of emotion.

Shit, thought Eric, stopping back his alarm, *the bugger's going to cry*.

"This is where I want to have a whole *flowery mecca*," Perrin waved his hand towards a dug circle of dirt. Even though he was facing financial ruin he'd hired a student to create a new flowerbed. "When people come to see me, I want them – to – feel *welcomed*." The last in a breathless rush. Then Perrin took off suddenly, as if blown along on the coat-tails of his inspiration. Eric hurriedly shadowed his movement, getting ready to catch, hold, balance. But Perrin had miraculously connected with gravity.

"The scent of marigolds!" he cried out in something like rage.

This is the whole fucking trouble, Eric said to himself in an aggrieved way. You can never tell with Perrin what tangent he's going to hare off on next. He thought of the long somnolent telephone conversations they had had each night while Perrin waited for his sleeping pills to take effect. Eric would sit in his armchair, armed with a glass of gin, half watching the televisual fantasy of reality while Perrin's voice purred away in his ear – sometimes thin as cellophane, occasionally close as a voice in a dream: his needs, emotional, physical, his dreams; his plans for the future. To sell the house and go to Venice. A week later to offer the house to people with the disease. Another week and he is planning to repaint the hall a Polynesian shade of blue. "Sea-blue, just that shade of light at dusk – the moment before the sun sinks."

Shit, and I'm only one of his friends, Eric often said to himself. Not even his oldest. What about his *family*? But Perrin's family in far away Te Awamutu were in disarray.

They were busy tending to their own emotional wounds: they would leave Perrin alone to attend to his actual torment.

Yet, if Eric were honest to himself – and he occasionally was, by dint of necessity rather than pleasure (he was old enough now to realize that honesty, though cruel, was the best policy in the end) – Eric's truth was, silently and subtly, that he himself had come almost to depend on Perrin's presence: his closeness. The fact of the matter was Perrin's reality had become ballast in Eric's somewhat unsteady life.

Ahead of them, as if a testimony, lay Eric's blue, shockingly dented Renault.

Eric's boyfriend was fourteen years younger than him. He was a student of architecture who had never heard, thankfully, of aversion therapy as a "cure" for homosexuality. He could not imagine a city in which there were no bars, saunas or nightclubs. Matthew, handsome, athletic like a basketball player, with an engaging sweep of hair that never quite managed to stay down, had pranged Eric's car in fury one night because, as he yelled out for the whole street to hear, "You care more about Perrin's dying than *loving* me."

It was unfair, it was emotional blackmail: it was true.

Eric needed Matthew, his beautiful boyfriend, for the warmth of his flesh, the passion of his kisses: the way he connected him back to life. In the middle of the night he could reach out and let his hand just roll down Matthew's flank and find that softly sweating crease in his knee. This soothed away the phantoms which hid in the dark: Matthew's body was so tangibly real.

Yet for Eric his experiences with Perrin – Perrin sick, Perrin dying – were almost like a pre-vision of the future, a kind of warding off of evil spells so that he would at least know the path of the disease if it should ever strike near him. This was his private truth. And Perrin, who never for one moment doubted Eric's presence by his side, communicated the full phalanx of his illness to him so that Eric's daily equanimity was conditioned by Perrin's. They moved with uneasy duality, two friends linked like horses on a circus merry-go-round, ceaselessly rising and falling together till that final moment when one horse would rise alone.

★   ★   ★

"Now my funeral," Perrin took up as the car moved along the streets.

This is what is so odd, thought Eric, as he drove along. When he was with Perrin it was as if that became the centre of reality in the world. Even driving along it was as if the streets of Epsom outside, with their casual realities – a father pushing his babycart into the drycleaners, a woman ducking into the wineshop in broad daylight – became like a moving cyclorama which streamed past them: Eric and Perrin were at the storm-centre, stilled.

"For my funeral," Perrin was saying in the matter-of-fact, "now take note of this" voice he used for the important formality of his funeral. He was planning it as he had planned his famous dinner parties, with the exquisite silver, linen and flowers acting as courtiers, nervously anticipating the throwing back of the gilded doors, the regal entrance of the food. Now the unpalatable truth was that Perrin's body would be the main course: and Eric, as a friend who had come forward – and for who came forward and who fell back there were no rules – was to act as courtier, arbiter of Perrin's final feast.

"I only want flowers picked from people's gardens. I don't want *one* – *one*!" Perrin tapped the floor with his stick vehemently, "of those embalmed creations dreamt up by florists! And fruit should be whatever is freshest in the shops. Vegetables of the season – organic. And definitely kai moana. That shop in K Road, you know the one. Only the freshest. Can I rely on you for that?"

"You can rely on me for that."

A slight pause. Eric turned and looked at his old friend. "Your celestial highness," he said.

Perrin smiled but did not laugh.

Going through the Domain, they were suddenly accompanied by a flock of graceful runners. Eric slowed down in appreciation. There was one man, sweating in the silent chiaroscuro of sport which echoes so closely the fury of sex. They both watched him silently.

Suddenly Perrin wound down his window. "You beautiful man!" he yelled out in the voice of a healthy male. "You're the most beautiful flower in the whole fucking Domain today!''

Eric blessed the presence of his sunglasses while inwardly shrieking.

Fortunately the runner turned towards them and, in his endorphin bliss, showered an appreciative smile at them. The other men pulled away. They passed in a blur of sequined sweat on muscular flesh, with frolicsome cocks beating to and fro like agitated metronomes inside their tiny shorts.

Swiftly the runners became manikins in the rear vision mirror.

"Thanks, darling," said Perrin in a small voice of exhaustion. "I really appreciated that."

Eric felt a surge of exhilaration as he moved closely behind Perrin through the gates of the garden centre. Already queues were forming, with well-heeled Aucklanders guarding trundlers full of merchandise. Eric realized he hadn't felt so good – dangerous would be the wrong word to use – since the very early days of Gay Liberation, when to hold hands in public with another man was a consummate, if inevitably provocative act.

Now time had shifted the emphasis somewhat, but Eric felt a shiver of pride at Perrin who, once so socially nuanced and named, could now lurch – almost like a toddler in reverse, Eric thought with a saving sense of hilarity. He was completely oblivious to the reactions of people around him. Indeed, as he stopped to pass a cheery word with the middle-aged housewife acting as a trundler-guard, he was actively engaging everyone in his act of dying.

Behind his shades, Eric was aware of people staring. They looked on silently, hit by the stilled impact of thought.

"Perrin!" Eric called out, because it suddenly seemed imperative to keep up contact, "it's marigolds you're looking for, isn't it?"

He moved over to Perrin and, in a movement he himself had not contemplated, hooked his arm through Perrin's frail, bird-like bones and clung on. That was the mystery: it was he who was clinging to Perrin, not the other way round. But

Perrin was off, putting all his suddenly furious energy into pushing the cart along. He was calling out the names of the plants as he went, voice full of glee: "Pittosporum! Helleborus! Antirrhinum! Cotoneaster!"

Now people *were* staring.

But Perrin was unstoppable. It was as if he were gathering in energy from the presence of so many plant forms which, embedded in the earth, nourished, watered and weeded, would continue the chain of life: just as his dust would one day, soon, oh soon, too soon, be added to the earth, composting.

Eric felt an uneasy yet piercing sense of happiness, a lyrical rapture in which he conceived the reality of how much he loved Perrin: of how Perrin was, at that very moment, leading him on a voyage of discovery so that they were, as in the dream, two circus horses together rising, leaping wonderfully high, almost far enough above the world, so that for one moment it was as if Perrin and he were experiencing in advance that exhilarating blast of freedom as they surged away from the globe on which all of life was contained, and beyond which there lay nothing – at least nothing known.

The plants were loaded into the boot. Eric had, at the last moment, tried to modulate Perrin's buying frenzy but, as if in testimony to his mood-swings, Perrin had impetuously bought too much, ordered Eric to shut up, and had sailed past the cash register issuing a cheque which Eric felt sure, with a lowering degree of certainty, would bounce. But Perrin, like a small child now, exhausted, almost turning nasty, threatened to throw a tantrum in front of the entire queue. "I must have what I want," he had cried. "You don't *understand*. I *must*!"

And now, thankfully safe inside the car, Eric began breathing a little easier. He shook off his sunglasses, which now weighed heavy on his nose. He felt the beginning pincers of a headache. Perrin was saying to him that he wanted – he *needed* – to take Eric's car for a drive. He needed to be on his own. He could drive still. Did Eric doubt him? Why was Eric always doubting him?

"Trust me," said Perrin in a small voice, like a caress.

Eric looked at his old friend. How much longer would he have him with him, to trust, not to trust, to doubt – to be astonished by. He did not know. So, doubting everything, doubting his own instincts to be firm, to say no, Eric allowed himself to be dropped off outside a mutual friend's townhouse, a refugee and, standing on the pavement, about to go in, he watched Perrin drive away in his car, faltering out into the middle of the road, hugging the centre line. And seeing Perrin move off, odd, slow and cumbersome, trying so hard to control his own fate, Eric watched his dear love, his friend, turn the corner, with as much grace as possible, attempting to execute his own exit.

THANKS TO GARETH SOUTHGATE

Graeme Woolaston

I MEAN, I don't even *like* football. Back in Brighton I never had a clue what the Albion were up to – except just the once, in '83 when they got to the Cup Final, against Man United. All my mates at school – I was just eleven then – went crazy with excitement, so naturally I got caught up in it. You'll maybe remember that they drew on the Saturday, so there was a replay Thursday evening. We all sat down in front of the telly full of beans, or at least Coke, and by half-time it was already about a hundred-nil to United so that was that little party well and truly over, except the next evening we turned out in pouring rain to welcome The Boys home and I got soaked to the skin, ended up with a heavy cold, couldn't speak for a week, missed out on a chance to win a Sussex Schools under-12s swimming medal, and generally made up my mind to have nothing more to do with football, ever.

And of course when I got older it just seemed plain common sense. Football's for naffs, if you ask me – any sensible gay guy spends his Saturday afternoons either recovering from the night before, getting ready for the night to come, deciding what to wear, shopping for something to wear, or, if things are going well, not wearing anything at all. He certainly isn't freezing his arse off on some bloody plastic seat cheering on his team by calling them useless wankers every fifteen seconds.

But then I moved to Glasgow. This was last year – 1995 I mean. Me and this boyfriend I had then, Terry (I'm Andy, by the way), came up to Scotland because he got sent here by his work, and I didn't have any work at all and was generally down on my luck in a big way. Things picked up for me here, I got courier work on my motor-bike – they just gave me a map of Glasgow and told me to get on with it! – which was what I'd been doing in my last job in Brighton. Then, better still, I was transferred to the van side of the business, which means I get to drive all round central Scotland, which I really enjoy. Besides, in the Scottish climate there are definite advantages to being on four wheels rather than two, believe me. Jesus, but it rains up here. There's no water shortage in Jockland, I can tell you.

Anyway, I'm afraid that just after the New Year me and Terry split up, and in fact he's living down in Manchester now. Naturally I thought about going back to Brighton, but by then I had this van job, so I decided to stay on, for a little while at least. But I didn't much like the flat we'd been living in, which we shared with two rather snooty girls and a smelly cat, so I went hunting for somewhere new. And that was when the rot set in. The football rot, I mean.

Through Gay Switchboard I found a room in a flat in this very grand terrace which has really come down in the world. We've got huge rooms, with high ceilings, and a gigantic kitchen, and I suppose that at one time it must have been a very des res indeed. Now all the flats in our close are full of students and artists and writers and other no-hopers like that. Sad, a bit. At first there were three other guys in the flat – Tommy and Davy, who'd been together for about a year and who shared the main room in the place, and Gerry, who had a room at the far end of the lobby. I was in the middle.

A couple of months later Gerry and me started to share my room. Well, it made perfect sense, didn't it? I had a double bed, and once his room was free it meant we could get a fifth guy in, and cut the rent for all of us. The fact that Gerry has a bod to kill for and I'd bagged him exactly forty-eight hours after I moved in (I don't believe in hanging about in these situations) was sheer coincidence. A little dark-haired guy called Patrick took the room at the end of the corridor.

Now, after you've lived in Glasgow for a while you learn that the moment you meet someone called "Patrick" you already know something about him. And if I tell you that "Gerry" is short for "Gerard" you'll maybe see the point for yourself, and if I add that Tommy and Davy had met because they were both Rangers supporters, you'll perhaps begin to understand that we were a mixed flat – two Catholics and two Protestants. Well, three actually, if you count me. That was another thing I learnt in Glasgow – that I was a Protestant. This had never occurred to me before. I mean, you don't stroll along Brighton seafront thinking to yourself, "Good Heavens, I'm a Protestant", now do you? It was no use me complaining I don't believe a word of all that stuff – I'd been brought up Church of England, and that was that.

So we had Tommy and Davy up one end, and Gerry and Patrick at the other, and the guys even took to talking about "the Rangers end" and "the Celtic end", as I'm told people do at Hampden. And me like piggy in the middle.

"You can be a Partick Thistle supporter," the others told me.

"But I hate football!"

"Then you're a born Thistle supporter."

By now you'll have gathered what I'd managed to land myself in – the one and only gay flat in Scotland, if not the known universe, full of football supporters. Gerry undertook the education which he reckoned I needed to be able to cope with the situation. He taught me all sorts of Glasgow slang: "Huns" (Rangers supporters), "cream buns" (Rangers supporters), "bluenoses" (Rangers supporters), "teddy bears" (Rangers supporters), "Prods" (Rangers supporters), "those-bastards-who-think-they're-going-to-win-nine-in-a-row-but-they're-very-much-mistaken" (don't ask), and then he filled me in on all the background, and honestly, it was like taking an Open University course in the history of Ireland. Yes, Ireland – all the Old Firm business is tied up with that.

But don't get the idea we're talking about "sectarian tensions" here, or any crap like that. This is Glasgow, not Belfast. The guys (and girls) who're into the Old Firm are always taking the rise out of each other, depending on who's winning or losing, and they love the whole thing. I'd already come across this at work. And in fact Glasgow would be a hell of a lot duller without it.

So we'd have Patrick and Gerry singing "The Fields of Athenry", which is about the Irish famine in the 1840s, and then Tommy and Davy would be whistling "the Sash", which is about the Battle of the Boyne in 1690, and then they'd remember they were Jocks after all and start singing "Flower of Scotland", which is about the Battle of Bannockburn in 1314, and then sound off about "Braveheart", by which time we were back to 1297 and I'd be wishing someone would write a song about Stonehenge so that I could trump the lot of them:

> Oh, stones of Stonehenge, when will we see
> Such rocks again?
> That never fall over,
> Despite the wind and rain . . .

Honestly, the Jocks go on about "Braveheart" as if there were still old guys sitting around in corners of Scottish pubs who actually fought with William Wallace, and at half-eleven on a Saturday night I swear half of them think they did.

Anyway, we were getting on fine in the flat, despite the Emerald Isle, when one afternoon towards the end of May I come home to find a huge Scottish flag fixed to the wall at the Rangers end of the lobby. Now, the Jocks are crazy about their flag (the white X on a blue background), and you see it everywhere, but not normally stuck up next to the bathroom.

"What's that in aid of?" I asked.

"Euro '96," the guys said.

"You what?"

So I was told that the European Championships, which I'd never even heard of, were about to start, and Scotland were in them.

"Are England in it as well?" I asked.

There were four deep sighs.

"Of course they're in it," Gerry said. "They're the host country. And they're playing Scotland, three weeks on Saturday."

"Oh well," I said cheerfully, "at least England are sure of winning one game."

Dirty looks.

Later that evening, when all five of us were sat round the kitchen table finishing off some wine, I remarked: "You know, I'll have to get a Union Jack, and put that in the lobby as well."

Four glasses stopped on the way to four Scottish mouths.

"Why?" Tommy asked, very very quietly.

"For England," I said brightly.

The blood drained from their faces. Four ashen-faced Scots stared at me across the table. Then, Rangers and Celtic alike, they all started at once: "*The Union Jack is not . . .*" – but I couldn't keep it up, I fell about laughing. This was one thing I'd learned some time ago, that the Union Jack is the flag of Britain, not England. But I hadn't been able to resist the chance to get them going. After being here for more than a year I'm becoming good at this, in fact I'm thinking of writing a book about it: *Fifty Ways to Wind Up The Jocks*. ("This William the Bruce guy – was he the one who let the cakes burn while he was watching the spider?").

"So what *should* I put up, then?" I asked.

"The St George's Cross," Tommy said.

"Well, where am I going to get hold of that?"

They shrugged. As it happened, a couple of days later I passed a little shop where I saw they had St Andrew's flags in the window. I went in: "Do you have a St George's flag?" I asked. I swear the guy couldn't have looked more horrified if I'd asked him if he sold a fully illustrated guide to the joys of sheep-shagging.

"We don't get much demand for it," he said.

In the end I had to ring this old school-friend of mine in Brighton called Phil, who I knew was nuts about football.

"Yeah, of course I'll send you one," he said. "Got to help you keep your end up in Haggisland!"

And sure enough, a few days later a little parcel come through the post, and within five minutes I was up the stepladder fixing the flag of St George to the wall next to my room. I looked down at Tommy and Davy, who had very glum faces but couldn't say much.

"Did I get it right this time?" I asked cheekily.

That evening Gerry was late getting back from his office (he works for an insurance firm).

"Have I got to pass that obscene object every day for the next three weeks?' he asked, the moment he walked into the room.

"Yup," I said.

Now, the strange thing is that in Euro '96, as you probably know, the England fans all adopted the St George's Cross as their flag for the first time ever, instead of the Union Jack – you remember how Wembley was full of it, on all sides? And there was me already ahead of the field, despite the fact that, to be honest, if you'd asked me about the St George's Cross a couple of years ago I'd have been hard pressed to say what it even looked like. Which just goes to prove a favourite theory of mine – that gays are the trendsetters and the fashion setters in this world. Even when we haven't a clue what we're doing.

Now that I was getting into the England supporter kick (though I still couldn't have told you the name of a single player – it was news to me that Lineker wasn't in the team any more) I decided I'd better do the job properly. I swotted up the words of their songs:

> *Enge-land, Enge-land, Enge-land*
> *Enge-land, Enge-land, Enge-la-and . . .*

Took me hours.

A couple of evenings after I'd put up the flag I come home later than Gerry and found him playing the most god-awful music on the stereo.

"What the *fuck* is that?" I asked.

"It's a tape of traditional English folk songs and dances."

It was the kind of music Morris dancers dance to, when they turn up outside your pub on a baking summer's day and have you diving indoors begging for mercy, or at least earplugs: "*Will* you turn it off?" I said.

"Certainly not. I'm enjoying it."

You never saw a more evil smile on a man's face in your life. The tape moved on to some ghastly song:

> *Come all ye young ploughmen who plough with a plough,*
> *Singing fol-diddle-dol, fol-diddle-dol,*
> *fol-diddle-dol de-ray . . .*

"WILL YOU SWITCH THAT OFF?" I bellowed at him.

He got up and turned it off, still with the same smile.

"I thought you'd like it," he said. "I thought it would make you feel at home."

"You have a very sick sense of humour."

Gerry's a couple of years older than me – twenty-seven – dark haired, rather craggy looking, not what you would normally call "handsome" at all. But he's tall – the same height as me, just under six foot – and, as I've already said, with a terrific, lean physique. I sat down in one of our armchairs and studied him for a while. He was deep in *The Herald*, still wearing his business suit, which rather oddly I found quite sexy – it made him look smart, and man-about-town. But I didn't know much about his work. I knew he wasn't out at the office, of course, and I thought there were other stresses as well, he wasn't all that happy there. But he wouldn't talk to me about it, he told me he liked to forget the office once he was home. It wasn't the only thing he wouldn't talk about. I knew next to nothing about his family, and when I asked him he gave the distinct impression he didn't expect me to understand what a Scottish Catholic background was like. He might have been right, of course, but I would at least have tried, if he'd have let me.

After a few minutes, and he'd finished with the sports pages – I knew better than to interrupt him when he was reading about Celtic – I said: "Gerry, I've got a problem."

He looked up: "What's that?"

"When the football starts next week – I've got nobody to help me support England."

He roared with laughter: "Are you kidding? There's loads

of English people up here. Away out and recruit some of them."

"Yeah, but they're not my type of English people."

"And what type is that, may I ask?"

"Working class."

This is true, I might say. I come across a lot of other English people as I go about in the van, but they're all snooty Surrey types who make it very clear they regard me as NQOCD – Not Quite Our Class, Dear.

"I know where you could find plenty of working-class Englishmen in Glasgow," Gerry said.

"Where?"

"Barlinnie Prison."

"Oh, very funny. Listen, I was wondering . . ."

"Yes?"

"Would *you* support England for me – I mean, join me so I wasn't alone?"

I thought I'd killed him. It was about ten seconds before he started breathing again: "*Are you serious?*"

"Yes. What's so awful about the idea? I just want some company."

He dropped his paper and stared at me.

"You know not what you ask, my child."

"Does that mean 'no'?"

"It certainly does."

He picked up *The Herald* and went back to reading it.

"That writer guy you know is in the paper again," he remarked.

I wasn't interested. I was quite pissed off with him, I thought he could have been a lot less sarky about my idea. I chose my words deliberately before I next spoke.

"If you really cared for me, you'd help me support England."

He lowered the paper and looked at me over the top of it: "Andy, no one ever cared for *anyone* that much."

And up went the paper again. But I had been serious. I knew there was no question of "love" between us, I wasn't that daft, but I was beginning to wonder what exactly we *did* have going. The sex was good, I enjoyed his company, we went swimming together at weekends and out to the clubs every Friday and

Saturday – and yet, though we were even living in the same room, he always managed somehow to keep me at a distance. I realized this was starting to get on my nerves, I wanted something more from him.

For a moment I felt like tearing the paper out of his hands and asking: "Do you care for me or don't you?". It wasn't that he didn't show me affection in bed, and say the right things, but the problem was, he never said them when he had his clothes on. And I didn't know what to make of this. Was it just something about him, as a person? Or was it because he was Scottish? When I first came up here someone said to me: "The two sentences you'll never hear spoken with a Scottish accent are, 'The English are a fine people' and 'I love you'."

Of course I didn't tear the paper out of his hands, or anything like that. Instead I said: "If you don't help me support England, I'll go on a sex-strike."

His guffaw nearly blew the paper away.

"What's so funny?" I complained.

"You talking about a 'sex-strike'! You sound like Princess Diana when she says she wants to avoid publicity."

"Oh, ha ha."

I'd been joking, of course, but I'd have appreciated it if he hadn't been quite so amused. Once again I wondered how he saw me – just as a live-in shag?

Anyway, the next Saturday the other guys were all in Tommy and Davy's room, just through the wall from mine, watching England play Switzerland, while I sat and watched the same match by myself. And God, was I bored. I swear that ten minutes of watching guys running around chasing a ball is enough for anyone, after that it's the same thing over and over again. I cheered up when England scored, but when Switzerland got an equalizer, and I was nearly deafened by the cheers from the next room, my spirits sunk, and when the game ended with all the commentators agreeing that it had been a terrible England performance, and they hadn't a chance of getting anywhere in the tournament, I knew what I was in for from the Jocks.

Talk about smug. It was bad enough after the England-Switzerland game, but when on the Monday Scotland held Holland to a nil-nil draw they became impossible. They lived and breathed smugness for a week, they had smugness for breakfast, lunch and tea, they drank pints of smugness in the pubs and bought carry-outs of smugness from every off-licence in the land. There was no getting away from it, I had to put up with it at work, from everybody I delivered to in the van the moment they heard my accent, and of course day in, day out in the flat. Only Gerry toned it down a bit, he didn't take the piss like the rest, and in fact one night he ruffled my hair in bed: "Don't worry, my son. I've an awful feeling you'll be able to get your own back with interest after Saturday."

Saturday we sat down as before, four of them in one room and me in mine, to watch England against Scotland, the first time they'd played each other since 1989. And this time there were no cheers from through the wall. Two-nil to England, and a far better game from them altogether, even I could see that.

"I won't say a word," I said when we were all together in the kitchen. "Not a word. Not a syllable. You won't hear a single word from me about it, I promise. Nothing at all. I won't even mention it. I'll keep completely quiet. I won't say a thing. Not—" at this point a wet dishcloth hit me on the back of the head.

The next games were played on the Tuesday, at the same time, which meant I couldn't watch England against Holland, since only the Scotland–Switzerland match was on telly up here. So for once all five of us sat down together in the same room.

Well, no doubt you remember what happened – Scotland went up one, while England were an amazing four up on the Dutch. At this point, in the second half, it meant both England and Scotland were on the way to the quarter-finals, because of goal difference (whatever that may be). By now all the piss-taking between us was over, the Scots were cheering the news of the English goals and I was cheering Scotland – I thought it was going to be the perfect result for me, both teams going through together and a chance for us all to celebrate. But then the Dutch got a goal back, and Scotland had to score again to win through. In the last ten minutes of that match I was as much on the edge of my seat as everyone else, groaning every time the Scots missed a chance and just longing for them to score, I really wanted a Scottish victory. But the extra goal didn't come, and Scotland were out of the competition. Afterwards we all sat around glumly in the kitchen, consoling ourselves with a bottle of whisky.

The next day I said to Gerry: "Now that Scotland are out of it . . ."

"Yes?"

"Well – *now* will you help me support England?"

He looked at me for a long, long time, as if it was the most difficult decision he'd ever had to make in his life. At last he said: "Very well. Very well. For your sake, I will." Then he turned away and said quietly, half to himself: "The things I do because of my dick . . ." I pretended I hadn't heard.

On the Saturday, when we sat down to watch the quarter-final against Spain, he remarked: "If I was still a good Catholic boy I could offer this as a penance." It was the first time he'd ever said anything to me about his religion, and I wasn't entirely sure what he was on about. But I got the gist of it. Once again Tommy, Davy and Patrick were in the other room – supporting Spain. Like, as I knew from work and from the papers ("put Juan past them"), virtually everyone else in Scotland. I was seriously pissed off about this, I felt like pointing out that four days earlier they'd been damned thankful for English goals. And now they were all back on their anti-English kick again. How petty could you get? I wanted us to murder Spain, just to show them, and wasn't entirely happy that the match went all the way to a penalty shoot-out before we won.

Afterward I asked Gerry – who, to give him his due, had cheered us on: "Why do the Scots hate the English so much?"

He looked quite shocked.

"Oh we don't *hate* the English." He smiled. "We just like them to lose at football."

"Yes, but *why?*"

He gazed at me as if he didn't want to answer.

"Andy – imagine what the English would feel like if they were totally dominated by another country. If that country even chose their government for them, despite the fact that they kept voting against it."

"Yeah, yeah," I interrupted. "I've heard all that before, and I understand it, I can see that point of view. But why don't the Scots do something about it?"

His smile was back: "Vote Nationalist, you mean?"

"Why not? Then you could do what you like. You could vote Billy Connolly for President if you wanted to."

He looked away. He sounded sad when he next spoke: "I'm afraid the Scots will never break away, Andy. We're far too fond of sitting on our arses moaning about the English."

I was taken aback: "Well, you said that, not me."

He turned to me again: "Mind you, we've got plenty to moan about sometimes. The English are always doing us down in sly little ways – and you're as bad as any of them."

"*Me?*" I was astounded: "What do you mean?"

"Yes, you. Look at all those little cracks you keep coming out with about 'Jocks' and 'Jockland' – not too subtle, are they?"

"But that's only a joke! It's just – just a way of speaking, that's all."

"Well, it can be very irritating."

I couldn't believe what I was hearing. He'd never said anything like this to me before: "Does it irritate *you?*"

"Yes."

"Well then, why—" I stopped myself in time. "Well, I'm sorry. I didn't realize it was annoying. I only meant it—"

"As a joke. Yes you've said that already."

We didn't carry on with the conversation. We just sat in a slightly chilly silence. But it could have been a lot worse, I was glad I hadn't come out with what had been on the tip of my tongue: "Well, why didn't you say something about it?" Because then he might have answered, "I shouldn't have had to" – and I'd have lost my rag. Don't you just *hate* it when your boyfriend says that to you? "I shouldn't have had to tell you." Which not only puts you in the wrong but makes out you're completely stupid as well – as if you're supposed to be a mind-reader on top of everything else. Oh, I can't stand it when people say that, nothing gets my goat up faster.

We patched up our little row before long, though, and the rest of the evening was fine. And on the Wednesday Gerry joined me again to support England in the semi-final against Germany, with the other guys through the wall as before.

Well, I don't suppose I need to remind you what happened. Shearer goal, all square at full-time, England miss sitters in extra time, German goal disallowed, penalty shoot-out, still all square after five penalties each – and up steps Gareth Southgate.

And didn't you just know he was going to miss? Didn't you just take one look at the man and think, "He's going to miss"? When he did, the blast of cheering from Tommy's room nearly blew the wall down, and when twenty seconds later a German got the winning penalty it was a wonder the house was left standing. Across the road all the roofs were flying about in the wind. God, what a sickener.

Gerry looked as if he was about to have a hernia. He'd backed England through the match, but now he was obviously dying to join the celebration. I glared at him for a moment, then we both fell about laughing.

"Are you coming to the pub?" the others asked, in the lobby.

"No," I said.

"Oh, don't be a sulk. Come along and drown your sorrows!"

I had to be persuaded to agree, I didn't much fancy the idea. And sure enough, when we got there it was wall-to-wall with joyous Jocks – sorry, Scots, I mean. Quite a few of them were in German football tops, which pissed me off even more.

"What do you want?" I asked Gerry. "A pint of twenty-nine? Or forty-two, or seventy-six, or whatever it's called?"

He grinned. "Yes, I'll have a pint of eighty, thank you." This is their weird name for bitter. The other four of us stuck to lager.

The rest of them were soon jabbering away together happily, and I began not paying much attention, because even yet, after a year up here, when the Jocks – sorry, Scots – get talking amongst themselves I find it hard to understand what they're saying. I looked around the pub. We hadn't gone to a gay bar, we were in the Horseshoe, this big glittery old-fashioned pub in the centre of town which always seems to be packed solid, morning, noon and night. Not that Gerry and me go in there very often, he doesn't like it much, because, apparently, it's a Rangers pub. When he first told me this I was mystified.

"How do you *know*?" I asked him quietly. I swear I could have drunk in there for ten years without getting that – I couldn't see a mention of the club anywhere. Then Gerry pointed out two Union Jacks in the glass of the front window. Apparently this means "Protestant". It's things like that which make you realize Scotland really is a different country, and maybe you're never going to understand it, you're always going to be an outsider.

And that night I was feeling this more than ever, surrounded by all those bloody celebrating Jo— – Glaswegians. I must have let it show on my face, because after a few minutes Gerry broke away from the others and turned to me : "Why so glum?" he asked.

I sighed.

"I don't know, Gerry. I'm wondering if maybe I shouldn't start thinking about going back to Brighton."

"Why?" he exclaimed. "Just because of a football match? You don't want to let all this get to you!" He swept his arm to indicate the pub. "Tomorrow it'll all be forgotten, and the only thing they'll be interested in is beating Celtic again."

I shook my head: "It's not the football, Gerry. I just feel – I don't belong here."

"Oh, rubbish." He leaned closer in, so I could hear him over the racket in the pub: "You're not serious, surely?"

"I am. All this is – strange to me." I went on: "I mean, look at them. What am I doing here?"

He leaned in even closer, and spoke more quietly.

"Don't say that, Andy. I couldn't bear it if you left. I don't want you to leave – not ever."

I turned my head and just gawped at him. At last, at long flaming last, he'd managed to say something affectionate to me when he wasn't horizontal. And all because of Gareth Southgate's incompetence at taking penalties.

Trust Gerry to choose not just a straight pub, but a pub full of slavering football fans, to come out with something like that. I wanted to plant a kiss full on his lips, but you can be sure that if I had, it would have been Requiem Mass time for both of us. All I could do was grin at him like an idiot, like a big lumping teenage idiot.

I'm writing this two months later, but I'm told it won't be published for nearly a year, so God knows where I'll be by the time you read it. Gerry's busy making plans now to buy his own place, and the current idea, of course, is that I'll move in with him. But I don't know. I'll maybe go back to England even yet. But maybe not. I might stick with Scotland, even though it means putting up with all the crap about the English. Not to mention the possibility of the Huns winning nine in a row.

JUST ANOTHER NIGHT IN FINSBURY PARK

Ian Young

DARKNESS COMES ON quickly in the autumn evenings, and Finsbury Park – even in daytime the greyest of London districts – succumbs passively to a chilly gloom. Deserted streets become more depressing under the hard, magnesium glare of silver lamps jutting from concrete pillars, too high for vandals to bother with.

London is a conglomeration of villages that have been absorbed over centuries by the spreading city. Each has its own High Street and its own small park. Some of these districts are green and picturesque, but Finsbury Park is not one of them. Tucked into a neglected pocket of North-East London, it's a grey, dusty, ugly district of looming Victorian and Edwardian row houses made over into flats, of oil shops and repair garages struggling to survive, of boarded-up factories and crumbling brickworks, and a few scraggly paradise bushes poking out of the dirt of neglected gardens.

At its centre, gathering rubbish and wind-blown newspapers, a grimy brick and stone tube station of indeterminate age squats under a jumble of rusting bridges, like some enormous, collapsed machine. Twice a day it stirs itself to life, wheezing and clanging in the crush of shuffling rush-hour crowds, and then emptying, leaving its musty passageways and gloomy tunnels as desolate and lifeless as before.

On the side streets off the Holloway Road, at random intervals among the tall stone houses, identical rectangular patches of grass appear, provided by the local council with bench and one – only one – bush apiece. At the edges of these utilitarian parks, the walls of the remaining buildings show the paint and plaster outlines of what once were houses: for the little parks are the last of the war-time bomb-sites, playgrounds now for quiet, Indian children, watched over by their sari-clad grandmothers.

This is the London that Thatcherism passed by – and left even more broken and depressed. It's not the worst London had to offer, by any means: it hasn't sunk to the despair that wafts like a bad smell through the crime-infested filth of Brixton. It's just a grey area, a pocket for dreary weather, with an odd, unsettling quietness about it. Some of the abandoned buildings have been taken over by squatters – young, homeless, unemployed. A few storefront groceries run by Rastamen keep erratic hours selling take-out patties and bags of flour. Sikhs and Chinese stay open a little later than everyone else. By nine o'clock, no one is on the streets, and most of the house-lights are out. Only the sweeping headlights and the swish of cars on their way to other places keep the district from appearing completely deserted.

The boarding house I lived in was the last of a line of crumbling, wedding-cake gothic piles on Turle Road. Before the bombing it had been in the middle of a row called Finsbury Mansions, but a couple of direct hits had demolished the end of the street. Part of the empty space was now a hideous secondary school, sardonically named after George Orwell. The rest served as the local cricket pitch. Some evenings, shadowy figures would linger there for a while after dark, running through the thick shadows (there are no lights) and sometimes calling to one another, determined to finish their game before rain or total darkness sends them home.

That fall the evenings were especially cold and damp, and I would bundle up in my old tweed overcoat and brown wool scarf for my nine o'clock walk down the High Street and through the twisting back roads, with a packet of shrimp chips in my pocket and – if it was a Friday night – (what luxury!) a precious, thinly rolled joint.

It wasn't raining when I set out, but a cool wind was springing up, blowing papers and discarded wrappers through the weeds in the boarding-house garden. Fugitive newspaper pages clung to the rose-bushes by the wall like crude veils. In the autumn cold I hunched against the damp English wind that gives half the population chest complaints by middle age. My friend the black and white cat wasn't at his usual window-sill perch tonight: probably inside, sensible and warm.

I headed for a little row of shops on one of the twisting back streets. The street lamps there are older, and more friendly, than the penitentiary-style lights above the main road. The shops were shut of course, most of their windows dusty and unrevealing, or lit by a single bare, low-watt bulb. Heath's Tools had a front window full of second-hand engines, belt-drives and odd-looking gears. A faded cardboard sign, left over from the Sixties by the look of it, incongruously promised "Fun in the Sun" on Majorca. I cupped my hand, pressed my nose against the glass and peered inside. Metal desks and wooden swivel chairs were piled one on another, and off to one side, a battered-looking garden gnome presided, arms akimbo. At the back a table was piled high with papers and tins. It began to spit rain.

The chemist's shop was the only one of the row, on either side of the street, with a properly illuminated window. Fluorescent lights threw a flickering glow onto tubes of toothpaste and stacked boxes of paper towels. A poster showed a well-groomed young couple, each smiling into the other's face while running along a beach, bizarrely dressed in a selection of trusses, supports and elastic knee and elbow bandages. I thought of collaging it with "Fun in the Sun", perhaps adding a tank or two, and some picturesque beggars.

The raindrops began to get bigger and I smelled the distinctive, musty odour of rain on dusty cement. I ducked into the doorway of an Indian grocery; its windows were piled high with sacks of rice, dented tins of curried okhra and faded sample packets of custard powder and Ovaltine. From a window above the shop across the road, a light revealed a room with beige walls and a painting of a country cottage of the sort used for the tops of biscuit tins. No one seemed to be in the room. I leaned back against the door-jamb of the grocery and took the slightly bent joint out of my pocket. I was about to light it when I heard someone whistling.

The tune was familiar, a haunting, slightly melancholy dance that scurvy, syphilitic old Henry VIII had expropriated along with the monasteries, and passed off as his own. "Greensleeves" – and the metal-cleated footsteps that came with it – told me who it was even before I spotted him from my shadowy doorway.

"Andy."

"Fuck, why'ncha frighten the life out o'me!"

"Sorry. Here, come in out of the rain and smoke a joint with me."

"Yeah, right on man. What a pissy night, i'n' it."

Andy was a fellow boarder in the lodging house we called "the mansion". He was an intriguing fellow, a bit secretive, usually friendly, but moody and unpredictable. He was a skinhead, and I had never seen him go out in anything but regulation skinhead garb: jeans held up by black braces, workshirt or T-shirt, worksocks and one of his half-dozen pairs of Doc Martens, to which he added a trade-mark touch of his own: metal cleats – "the better to kick your fuckin' head in wiv". In fact, Andy was remarkably gentle by nature, until the rare occaions when some real or imagined indignity to himself or another triggered his violent temper and he erupted in a reckless storm of fists, boots, blood and fury. He worked at odd jobs, mostly on building sites and dishing up food in cafeterias. Like most skinheads, he took pride in being scrupulously clean.

Andy was tall, like me. His lean body and strong hands contrasted with luminous, long-lashed green eyes, full lips and prominent cheekbones. He had a sneering smile that seemed cheeky, mischievous and appealing. With those he liked (the rest he preferred to ignore) he adopted a quiet, conspiratorial manner that assumed an immediate intimacy. He was tremendously sexy.

He joined me in the shop doorway and turned down the collar of his leather jacket. "Sid came round today," he said, dragging on the joint. "We went for a ride in his car, out to his place. Ever been out there?"

"I have indeed," I said, as he blew the smoke into the street. "Nice house he has. Epping, isn't it?"

"Yeah, Epping, near the forest."

"I don't know why he keeps it so gloomy though. The dining room and the front room look as though he never goes into them. I don't think he ever opens the curtains either. Bit creepy. He's a funny bloke."

Sid Brown was a fiftyish Jewish stockbroker who'd gone into early retirement so he could write and live an openly gay life. Somehow, he hadn't gotten around to doing much of either and instead had become something of a recluse, puttering about his semi-detached in a housing estate at the edge of the Forest and occasionally venturing into central London with enough money to pick up a rent-boy, which is how he'd met Andy, who was always willing to supplement his wages with the right customer.

Sid had become an occasional, welcome visitor to the mansion – nervous, funny, a little seedy, and alternately miserly or generous, as the mood struck him. He always wore a Gay Is Good badge pinned to his suit-jacket, and smoked constantly, usually letting the ash tumble off his lapels onto his wool cardigan.

"He's got some great old boxes in that place," Andy said. Antique boxes were one of his odd interests. "You know what he said to me?" he asked, unscrewing a roach-clip that looked like a bullet. "I think he's a bit lonely out there all on his own. He asked me if I wanted to move in with him – you know, into the house in Epping like. Asked me a couple of weeks ago."

Andy looked straight into my eyes, nodding slightly, nodding, nodding, as he did whenever he wanted to be sure you were paying attention.

"Permanently?!" I said, stupidly, raising my voice a bit.

"Yeah, of course!" He sounded a bit indignant. "He says I could do a bit of gardening for him and help out around the house like. Says I can type up his manuscripts for him and . . . we might go into business together."

"What sort of business?" I asked, as a picture of Andy with a tea-towel in his hand flitted through my mind. *That* would be a change! We were huddling together against the shop door now, Andy in his jeans and black leather and me in my overcoat, sharing the last of the joint. It was very strong grass and we were both getting a nice buzz.

"This is good grass, man. From the Rastas?"

I nodded.

"Financial Advice," he said with a leer that turned into a grin. I'd forgotten his chipped front tooth. "Or maybe he just wants to pimp me to wealthy gents. Anyway, it'll get me out of the mansion, won't it. Your room's all right but mine's fucking cold. And too bloody noisy right next to the toilet." He turned suddenly toward me and ran his fingers up my lapels, looking me straight in the face. "Here, d'you think I'm too old to do it for money?" I could see his breath, and feel it, warm against my mouth.

"You're in your prime, my darling!"

"Fuck off."

"No seriously. If you want to do it, do it. You're good-looking, you can get all the tricks you want. Just remember though, pal, unless you're planning to do yourself in soon, there *is* a future to be thought of."

"Yeah, well. That's what I mean." He took a sudden look around the street as if he'd heard someone coming. "I'm sick of it round here. There's nuffing for me, nuffing at all. I like old Sid. It'll be all right, moving in with him. I mean, I didn't say I would. Said I'd think about it. He was a bit pissed off I think."

"Well, you don't want to look too eager, do you."

"Well, that's it, i'n' it."

"Did he go down on one knee when he proposed to you?"

"Fuck off or you'll get my knee in your balls. Epping's a bit boring but I expect I'll get used to it. Not that this place is so fuckin' exciting."

"Oh, I don't know," I said. "Look, the rain's eased up. We can walk down to the laundromat and see if Mrs Singh's cleaning the machines. She might favour us with a song. See, always something to do."

"Ha. Ha."

We were both buzzed by this point. I noticed Andy was wearing his tight jeans, ripped in one knee and nicely outlining the bulge at his crotch. He was leaning against the shop window with his head back and his eyes closed, hands in his jacket pockets, one boot-heel hooked on the window ledge. He looked great. I leaned against him with my thighs around his and clasped my hands around the back of his neck; short, sharp hairs pricked my palms.

"Kiss me you fool," he said, his eyes still shut.

His mouth felt warm and his tongue scraped against my teeth. He kept his tongue in my mouth for a long time before he broke away. "Shit," he said, and looked around. "I'm getting cold."

"Let's go home then."

"We'll go home and fuck."

Well, I thought, lucky me.

The mansion always looked odd standing at the end of the street where the row came to a sudden stop, a ragged wall showing the traces of what were once stairways in an adjoining house. As we came near, Andy broke away and ran ahead of me onto the uncut grass, jumping high in the air and swinging his latch-key on a string over his head, not making a sound. On the back of his black leather jacket he'd painted a white A in a circle and SKINS RULE underneath. His small bottom looked good in his tight-fitting jeans. Sid wasn't the only one who wanted to get into that arse. Andy would never let him — or anyone else.

The house looked dark from the outside but the kitchen light was on in the back, as always. "Cup of tea, Andy?"

"Yeah, get warmed up. Be down in a minute."

It was bright in the kitchen. Electric wires and disconnected pipes hung from the ceiling and a roll of new linoleum stood in one corner, ready to replace the cracked Victorian floor tiles that had worn thin, exposing the blackened wood underneath. The window over the table looked out onto a ramshackle porch that had once been a greenhouse. Now it was full of old furniture, rolled-up carpets, broken bicycles and stacks of gritty flower-pots.

I put the kettle on and looked at the clock. Too late for the news. Then I saw the note pinned to the television.

It was from Russell, our landlord.

Lads – Gone over to gay painting show at Pink Triangle. Yes I'm come over all artistic all of a sudden! Frozen meat pies in the fridge, help yourselves.

Did you hear, Sid's decided to go to Australia – Sydney. Sidney in Sydney. To live wit his sister, his Mum's very ill. Says he's sick of living on his own. He's put his house up for sale and all his furniture, silly bugger so I don't suppose he'll be coming back. I'm going to buy that hall-stand. Says he's got to go next week. Shall we give him a party?

Harry owes £5 on the rent from last week. The back toilet is plugged up again. Be good, I know you will!

Russell

The kettle shrieked as I took the cups off the hook. Andy came downstairs, without his coat and shirt now, just in his jeans, braces and boots, but with his glasses on. The round, old-fashioned National Health specs gave him a strangely scholarly look. His bare chest was smooth and white, at odds somehow with his brown neck and big hands. One shoulder had a tattoo I liked, a Robertson's Marmalade golliwog, waving. Andy was whistling to himself, not "Greensleeves" this time, but the Stones' "Just Another Night".

He broke off suddenly. "You'll come and see us – out in Epping – won't you? We'll all have tea in the drawing room. Lah di dah!"

"Of course," I said. "If it all works out." I folded Russell's note and stuck it under the radio, trying not to think too hard.

Would it have been possible? I imagined solitary, neurotic, fifty-year-old Sid, dithering about in a cloud of cigarette ash and suspicion, and horny, twenty-year-old Andy, with his ornamental boxes and violent fits, the two of them settling into domestic bliss together among the suburban families . . . Pretty bloody unlikely. On the other hand, you never know. I looked out the window. The back garden beyond the greenhouse was nothing but blackness. The last cricket players had gone home; the rest of the boarders were asleep, or nowhere in sight. Only the two of us up and about now, just me and Andy, under the kitchen light. Outside, the wind was springing up again, and the greenhouse windows were rattling.

"Yeah. If it works out," Andy answered. "I really like the forest, all the green trees. I like that funny wet smell the earth gets." He carried the cups – no saucers – over to the arborite table. "Yeah, I'm getting too old for it, man. Gotta settle down. Gotta get fuckin' organized." Then, without a pause: "You think old Sid would rent you a room?" And suddenly he was looking right at me again with those clear green eyes of his.

"I don't suppose so."

He was quiet for a moment. He swallowed a mouthful of tea and leaned back to tip the chair on its back legs, hooked his thumbs in his braces and flashed his grin at me. "Let's go to your room," he said. "It's nicer than mine" He took his glasses off and laid them gently on the table. "Is this the new tea?"

"Yes. From Russell's Mum," I reminded him. "Expensive!"

"The best, eh!" he laughed, and I laughed with him. "Right on! Only the fuckin' best!"

And we headed upstairs with our half drunk tea as the damp English wind rattled the loose panes in the greenhouse door.

SKUNK

John-Paul Zaccarini

"CAN I SPEAK to Skunk please?"

"Speaking."

"It's about the ad. Just a few questions."

"Yep."

"You're white?"

"Yep. Mediterranean. Olive."

Lie.

"Body?"

"Slim, swimmer's physique, very defined, pert buns."

Opinion.

"Cock?"

"Yes."

Truth.

"No, I mean—"

"Hard, seven inches, good purple head, nice veins."

Fact.

"What do you do?"

"What do you want me to do?"

Question.

They love all this, gets 'em going, I should be paid extra for my telephone manner.

The agreement is made, our terms are set out, I know exactly what I have to do.

"I'd like to meet you in the toilets at Bethnal Green at around 11.30. I'd like you to wear something sporty looking –" yeeugh – "and after I blow you I'm going to lick your arse and behave like I really want to fuck you. You have to refuse and kick up a fuss and bend me over quite roughly and fuck me stupid. I'll bring all the necessaries. Got all that?"

"Yep."

"Good. Eighty quid's my limit."

"A hundred. It's late and it's an out-call."

"OK. You better not disappoint."

The situation is arranged so that there is absolutely no element of surprise, the buyer knows what he wants and he's going to get exactly what he wants, he is paying for it after all. Everything will go to plan.

I take a taxi, making sure that I get a receipt because if the arsehole I'm going to fuck doesn't want to include it in the expenses, then I can get it back off the tax. It feels good to do legitimate business, to be in an honest, bullshit-free line of work, to have an accountant. I think that pleases my mum, that I'm making a living and don't get into any trouble and at least I'm not on the dole. That pleases her a great deal.

"He was always a hard-working boy. Knew what was right and what was wrong. I think he got it from me."

Yes indeed I did mum.

People have asked me if this sort of work isn't soul-destroying. They look at me odd when I ask them what they mean, as if "soul-destroying" was self-explanatory. Most of them lost their souls as children and those that were lucky enough to escape infanthood soul intact lost it in the Eighties so what the fuck do they know anyway. It's pop psychology. I have no time for that.

"I don't have a soul to be destroyed, just a cock that's earning me a fuck of a lot of money."

People look at me differently. A pretty guy like me would normally be out of their reach, they would only dream about getting it on with me, but when I tell them I'm a prostitute, suddenly there is a possibility. Hope.

Fucking laugh. Hope. I warn my friends about hope, I remind them that it comes in deviously attractive packages like me. And then I remind them about fear.

The guy is making all sorts of wolfing, gobbling, slurping noises, going at it like a hungry, toothless dog at a sausage thrown at him for being obedient. He looks up at me every now and then and I have to wipe the grin off my face and look ecstatic. Sometimes when he's looking ever-so involved I stick my tongue out and make childish faces at him, like we used to do in maths class whenever Mr-can't-remember-his-fucking-name turned his back. It helps take my mind off what's going on, I just have to concentrate every now and then to make sure I don't go floppy on him. Makes me laugh the way I've got to pretend I'm really enjoying it, especially since he must know how I hate him.

Or maybe he doesn't. Maybe he's just too hungry to care and hunger is the one thing that will rob anyone of their dignity. Hunger is a result of poverty, poverty comes from a fucked-up world system based on State corruption and State corruption is this lawyer on his knees who's so used to power that he needs to be degraded by a rent-boy to keep him sane so he can go back to his lie of life, wife and kids, glossy rich lie of success, sparkling spotless sheen of normality, sucking at my cock like a person who's been starved of food and water.

No, maybe he doesn't realize that my cock is a knife stabbing his throat, maybe he would never think that I pray for those little tears that happen on your cock during a particularly rough blow-job. I crave to bleed in his mouth, because he thinks he's safe, exempt, he's just a bit too cocky, pathetic rich bastard that he is.

Now I have no trouble keeping my erection, in fact I'm feeling so spiky it hurts. He's licking my ring and through all his huffling and spluttering all I can think is that the little hypocrite wants me to fuck him, and that thought turns me on, because even though he'll see me put the condom on, when he's face down, his body bent double holding the cistern, he won't know the difference, he won't know that my spunk, along with its little friend who's staying over is nestled deep within his bloodstream.

* * *

I almost killed something tonight. It's not dead yet, but it is being strangled slowly, like me, and will soon be susceptible to any malignant entity and won't have a chance. It'll just give up and die, no defences left. Like me.

There's no looking back now. It's like I've made my decision but I promised myself never again because I want to live even though every day I try and fight the sensation that I'm dying.

Bullshit pop psychology for which I have no time.

"Turn the cab around, I want to go to the West End."

Sometimes, I half wake up in the night and my room is a club or a bar or a party or a café filled with every gorgeous man I've ever seen on the scene and they're all cruising me but my bed is in the middle of it all and I want to sleep but I also want to cruise but then I'm back in my own room again but the hunks and Soho boyz are still there. I writhe, try to attract their attention, they come close but never touch, they watch with desire but never speak and I can't reach them even though I'm so wanting, and then I realize that I'm not awake in reality or asleep in dream but in that nether world which I hate.

The West End is like that for me now, a semi-lucid dream, hyper-real, virtual, an MTV barrage of beautiful, empty images of desire that are interactive only in the pop-techno sense of the word.

Tonight, at this fairy grotto of a club, the guys on the floor are locked into the beat. If only they were there completely and not looking to see who's looking, what he's wearing, who's got pills to sell, who's got the status, how well they're dancing. I watch, cruise, dance, get cruised, dance, drink, smoke. I'm addicted to this, though nothing ever happens. It's like TV, makes me forget. I go to consume, spend, deplete and I get nothing in return and by the same token I give nothing either.

Queens teeter back and forth, dizzy with themselves constantly on the verge of fainting from the vertigo of their success, their high places, their acceptance and popularity in a ghetto where they feel safe, a ghetto built with white, male, capitalist bricks, where they can live out their true political agenda, consumption, being a commodity and above all being a star in the Hollywood travesty that is the gay scene.

"Fierce, sweetheart." Big kiss, squeeze on the arse, a wink and then off to flirt elsewhere. I didn't have time even to see the guy's' face. Attention like that comes easy if you look right. It went to my head once, all this flattery, attention, sleeping with the most gorge guys about. But exactly what is it that gets you noticed, that makes you successful? Pecs, arse, face, sass, style and just enough intelligence not to be a bimbo but not too much brain, let's not get carried away here, this is the gay scene after all.

I turn and see a guy that I'd seen here and there, out and about, in a few mags. The only word I can find to describe him was "perfect" and I spat on the word as I used it. Faraway perfect, billboard perfect, advert perfect.

I turn again, to the mirror and see myself. I, like so many others on the scene, have made myself beautiful, nothing natural about it, I just invested in a body, that's all. If you've got the time and the money and above all the desire it's easy. This beauty that I am, this slim, muscular, torsoed, skinhead, pretty Genet thug is an image I've studied and cultivated meticulously.

I guess I'm pretty spectacular, people look at me, want me, applaud me, even give me star status because I'm beautiful. I'm not beautiful, I'm just another commodity that people want. A spectacular sexual commodity. Judging by the desire that follows me like a bad smell, I must be some sort of fetish object, like so many of these fantasy gay boys here tonight. It must bug them at times but they must be grateful that they're not fat or ugly because judging by their lack of brain cells they may as well slit their wrists straight off if they are ugly and gay too.

Browse through the magazines and you'll see our image everywhere, beautiful boys, fit, hairless, clean and inviting selling you products you have no need for, or else a need created to make money. We are the central concern of a culture overwhelmed by capitalism and body fascism. No fat people, no ugly people, just the smooth muscle boyz we're all supposed to be looking for.

I cast my gaze across to Mr Perfectly Successful. He is a

spectacle because his home is Compton Street, the bar, the park, the gym, he can't bear to be alone, because he's nothing but a performance and without spectators he is nothing. Alone, in front of the mirror not even his vanity can make him feel real. Alone, he has no power, and isn't that what beauty is, power?

Alone in his room there is no one buying, no one reproducing his image, no one bartering for him, no one to compete with. His exchange value, his fluctuating market price, means nothing there. He suddenly wants to feel involved, not merely an exhibitionist before a row of hungry spectators eager for some satisfaction that can never be real. He goes through one commodity boyfriend after another and the more perfectly beautiful boys he consumes the higher his status becomes and yet the only boy he really wants to sleep with is himself.

But no matter how hard he tries, he can't stop, can't stop going to the gym, too far gone, can't stop suddenly being a success. Paranoid, conspicuous, he does everything for other people to see. He doesn't have a private life, because he's no one if there's no one watching.

A guy jiggles up next to me, beaming a gorgeously generous smile, offering me some water. I sip, give it back, make as much small talk as I can handle before he tries to come on.

"I know what you're on, sweetheart, and all this must seem very Eeeeeeasy to you, but you bore me stupid and I wish you people would just grow the fuck up. Thanks for the Evian, enjoy your night."

I amble downstairs, thinking that the club has done the thing required. Distraction, no involvement, no thought or surprise, guaranteed satisfaction and complete, ecstatic abstraction from reality.

I enter the main dance area and work my way into the middle to feed off the mass energy of sweat, poppers, testosterone and male desire working out to the beats and the booms, the drugs and flirtations, the posing-it, losing-it, the camping and the butching-it.

Drag queens cha-cha-cha past me, so well rehearsed that no one can out-bitch or upstage them. Straight girls gawp with envy, disco bunnies covet the spotlight that follows them, butch maries look but won't ever lower themselves to comment, but everywhere people give them the attention they work so hard, but seemingly effortlessly, to get.

It's time to get out, my head is too full of this negative shit, but there's this one fella who's sort of interesting. He dances weird, like he's hearing a music deep within the music that the rest of us can't hear, it's mesmerizing, beautiful to watch and what interests me about him is that, apart from being completely gorge, crazy-colour blue hair and avant-garde attire, he is completely unaware of the riot of attention he is generating. He smiles to whoever manages to catch his eye but mostly just looks at the floor getting into this vibe like he's not got a care in the world.

I find myself staring at him and he looks at me, smiles shyly, which makes me feel all hot inside, and then looks back down to the floor. I really want him, but I can't figure out why I feel so nervous and clumsy, why I look away when he tries to cruise me when no one else has managed to get their attention reciprocated. Why am I doing all those classic things that I've learned not to do? Why am I afraid to catch his eye when I want him really badly?

I don't like feeling scared, so when I spot Mr Star of the Scene I fix my cruising laser on him like some gay Terminator. He is model perfect, dressed like he earns and looks like he could show me a reliably horny time. I'm not scared of him. But I'm scared of the boy with the blue hair who I fancy more because he's different, maybe even possessed of a personality. So I do the predictable, classic gay thing. I don't look back at the boy and I cruise the guy with the pecs, the buns and the Bacardi-blue eyes. Satisfaction guaranteed. Nothing you didn't ask for. No surprises. Safe.

My friends ask me how I can shag so frequently for pleasure when I do it all day for a living.

"If I didn't I'd be on smack. Which would you rather?"

I guess some people just have too much energy for their own good.

I don't know what goes on in the heads of my casual shags. I don't care really, it's none of my concern so long as they have a good time, because I know if I told them what was happening to me, I don't think they'd believe me.

It's a structureless, amoral, undifferentiated place that I go to. Nothing stays the same for very long, one image is replaced by another, one story becomes another, with a different voice and sometimes several, polyvocal and not always harmonious.

No personality required, just enthusiasm. Personality is largely irrelevant, so long as they're not Tories (I'm not that amoral) I don't mind really, because, two animals, naked, sweaty and fucking couldn't give a shit for anything except the job at hand.

I wonder where I will go with "Stephan" tonight. The way he's rubbing my crotch as we snog in the taxi, it feels like I'm in for a trip. But I still try to resist getting caught up in his glimmer, his perfume of happy, normal gay success. I don't want to get too giddy, too seduced by his image, I just want his body, his cock and most of all, his reality. I don't need another virtual experience. And believe me, in bed, is the only place to get to know a gay man. There you'll find some reality.

Sometimes.

Stephan has a boyfriend, Miguel, a journalist on a gay newspaper. Stephan is an art photographer, does black and white arty photos of well-defined men. Middle-class coffee-table porn. He has a coffee table too, and his latest book is on it. Miguel and Stephan live in a fab house in Brixton. Bijou, walls lined with CDs and real art (by real I mean they bought it from galleries and it set them back a fair bit of wonga) and, by the looks of their bathroom, shares in the Body Shop.

I wonder if he wants to fuck me, and will I say yes if he does?

It must be reiterated, this Stephan is fucking beautiful, representing everything I detest but nonetheless I'm really horny for him. I guess there's some conditioning you'll never get over. Makes me wonder, though, whether all this conspiracy theory isn't just a load of crap. Maybe that is what is really beautiful, maybe this is all really the only way it can be.

Snap out of it you flake.

"D'you like the flat?"

"Gorge, babes." Makes me want to nick something.

He kisses me roughly, puts his hand up my sporty tank-top and pinches a nipple hard. He can't wait for it and I love the feeling of power it gives me because I can tell he's going to show me a most excellent time. And I won't disappoint him. I'm a professional.

I enjoy sleeping next to someone after sex. Holding them, kissing them to sleep, thanking them almost. Thanking them for allowing me to feel real for a few hours. In the morning we'll be friends, we'll smile genuinely, be warm with each other, but there won't be that honesty, that humanity of the night before. A night where no rules cluttered the flow of things becoming, where there were no morals or ideas, no pasts or futures, just our hot, human bodies together, sharing simply what it means to have a body.

I sleep well, but have a dream that he's blowing me in the shower and I reach for a loose razor blade in the soap dish and he looks up with his chiselled angelic face, hair wet, flattened, eyes wide and full of love, looking so beautiful sucking my cock and I begin to inscribe a track across his cheek with the razor, a red flower of a wound blossoms violently on his face and he falls back from my cock and all the pleasure, all the love, all the compassion has gone and I strike him, this time across the nose. It falls open, then his lips, his chin, his eyebrow.

I don't want to do it, he's a little boy whose soul was sold, bought, I don't know, it's not his fault he's beautiful, that he lives this life but I have to keep slashing until there is no beauty left. He is so terrified, so frozen with disbelief, I'm not mutilating, I'm operating I tell him, trying to make him understand that I have to do this, I have to try and—

"Coffee's up."

I look at him odd through sleep-glued eyes. He's still smooth, peach-dreamy skinned and sunny healthy eyes, like Pacific coral reef honeymoon. His face is the perfect holiday from reality, I decide.

"Black. No sugs thanks, babes."

He totters off, white towel snug and inadequate round his

pert buns. I start getting horny all over again. So I wank while he's pouring, I've got a job in an hour, don't wanna be here all day.

All day there is one thing going through my head about last night. I've done three jobs already, three more to go. Yesterday I did eight. This week alone I've slept with over thirty-six people for money. I've slept with three for pleasure. If I chose, I needn't work for another six months. But subversion needs money and I'm saving until the day the situation is right and then I'll be ready.

Still, that one man, that capitalist dog on his knees begging and humiliating himself, the rich man who is hungry, the man whom I have no pity for echoes in my thoughts. It haunts me, what I did to him. If he has any sense he's using a condom if/when he fucks his wife. If he isn't then I wish I'd slit his throat right there and then.

I finish my day's work, I didn't want to particularly but I forced myself. Business as usual, I have a duty to something, not sure what it'll be yet, but when the time is right I'm going to make a real stink.

It's hard work but at least you know your work is direct, without lies or unfulfilled promises. At least you know you deliver the goods described in the contract. Knowing that your product is your own, that it doesn't filter down through a bureaucratic network of leeches. You set your terms and you have no boss, only a succession of masters, slaves, doms and subs.

Maybe that's why I don't fall in love for more than a night.

At least I'm real, not an image in a porn mag. I'm real because if you want to, you can fuck me. And I've got more power in the hardness of my buns than any rich filthy daddygodboss. And I'll use it, I'm not frightened. No fear. No hope. Just a cock that makes me a fuck of a lot of money.

And one day that will no longer be enough.

The day scares me and I don't like being scared.

Here I am again in a café, dissecting and filing information. Accumulating my database of gay life. Why, if I hate it all so much, why not just leave them to it? Because it was the last thing I thought had some potential for changing things.

We're supposed to be different, subversive, outsiders. But we're just the same, collaborators, reactionary.

My cock is alerted to young boy-flesh sitting continental and lonely over a cappuccino and gay mag. He looks up to cruise me and I'm not interested any more. I'm gayer than gay it seems.

This ghetto offends me.

I see Stephan and a dishy Soho boy whom I presume is Miguel sauntering down the road hand in hand.

You wouldn't do that in Peckham, so don't look so fucking smug.

This ghetto offends me because it's full of people with the wool pulled over their eyes.

A group of friends all laughing and drinking, animated, stylish and successful, a paradigm of happy middle class politically correct gay scenery. They've bought it, the lie, the peace offering, all they care about is that they have this wonderful playground to romp in where all the normal rules don't apply. Except that when they leave the confines of the ghetto they have to accommodate normality and grovel to its mores. They've bought it.

I have sex with men. Does that make me gay? I don't know. It's natural for me to fuck a bloke, it's not natural for me to exist by gay norms. Gay is culture not nature. Gay is the same not different, and I thought that was the whole point, being different. Gay is money, gloss, beauty, success and I want to be animal, perverted, naked, natural.

It doesn't account for all homosexuals, it's just the homoversion of mainstream culture, the dominant white ideology of greed, of capitalism. Yet that is all that is represented, the image of homosexuality, the norm. We shouldn't be normal in a world where normal is constrictive, paranoid and fascist. Gayness is the sparkling jewel in capitalisms' crown of consumption and we queens do capitalism the best.

Married, mortgaged, monotonous heterowannabes, paranoid like the rest of a society where everyone must be defined. I don't care to be defined, I don't care to be controlled. If I hate, if I verge upon the criminal or the insane then it's because there is no room for freaks in this world, there is no room for difference, no room for that which desires to remain undifferentiated.

I hope I stop hating. I hope I find my compassion again and start hating systems of belief rather than people but they make it hard work sometimes. My hatred is huge, my anger sometimes overpowering and I know that that way fear lies. And fear is the seed that grows into fascism.

Most people have it in them. Fascism. In some way or another. Most people live in fear. Most people live in hope.

ABOUT THE AUTHORS

JAMES ROBERT BAKER is the author of *Adrenaline, Fuel-Injected Dream, Boy Wonder* and *Tim and Pete*. He lives in Los Angeles, USA.

PETER BAKER is a former editor of *Films and Filming*. His books include *Casino, Clinic* and *Cruise*. He lives in Spain.

DIESEL BALAAM has contributed fiction and humorous pieces to a wide variety of gay magazines. He is co-author of *Black Confetti*, "a truly bizarre" collection of short stories. He lives in London, England.

NEIL BARTLETT is a co-founder of the Gloria theatre company and Artistic Director of the Lyric Theatre, Hammersmith, London. His books include *Who Was That Man?, Ready to Catch Him Should He Fall* and *Mr Clive and Mr Page*. He lives in Brighton, England.

SEBASTIAN BEAUMONT is a sometime model and the author of *On the Edge, Heroes Are Hard to Find* and *Two*. He lives in Brighton, England.

DAVID PATRICK BEAVERS is a playwright and screenwriter and the author of *Jackal in the Dark, The Jackal Awakens* and *Thresholds*. He lives in Los Angeles, USA.

PETER BURTON is Literary Editor of *Gay Times* (London). His books include *Rod Stewart: A life on the town, Parallel Lives, Talking to . . . , Amongst the Aliens: Some aspects of a gay life, The Art of Gay Love* and *Gay Portraits*. He lives in Brighton, England.

MATTHEW BUTLER (under a variety of pseudonyms) contributed short stories to the fledgling British gay press in the late 1960s. He gave up writing to concentrate on a career in bookselling and now lives in Spain.

TONI DAVIDSON is Literary Editor of *Gay Scotland*. He edited *And Thus I Will Freely Sing* and *The Psychoactive Sync*. He lives in Glasgow, Scotland.

PAUL DE HAVILLAND's first published story was "Purple Prose in Soho". He lives in Wokingham, England.

GARY DUNNE is an editor and author whose books include *If Blood Should the Lino, As If Overnight* and *Shadows on the Dance Floor*. He lives in Sydney, Australia.

RICHARD K. EDWARDS teaches sociology at Pine College, Massachusetts. He lives in Boston, USA.

DAVID EVANS' books include biographies of Freddie Mercury, Dusty Springfield and Cat Stevens and the novels *Summer Set, A Cat in the Tulips* and (writing as Ned Cresswell) *A Hollywood Conscience*. He lives in London, England.

JAMES FRIEL has published three novels: *Left of North, Taking the Veil* and *Careless Talk*. His first novel won a Betty Trask Award and his third was shortlisted for the *Mail on Sunday* John Llewellyn Rhys Prize. He lives in Chester, England.

PATRICK GALE is the author of *The Aerodynamics of Pork, Ease, Kansas in August, Facing the Tank, Little Bits of Baby, The Cat Sanctuary, The Facts of Life* and *Dangerous Pleasures*. He lives in London and North Cornwall, England.

DAMON GALGUT has been Resident Playwright and Literary Advisor to the Performing Arts Council of the Transvaal.

He is author of *A Sinless Season*, *Small Circle of Beings* and *The Beautiful Screaming of Pigs*. He lives in South Africa.

STEPHEN GRAY is a lecturer and poet and author of *John Ross: The true story*, *Time of Our Darkness* and *Born of Man*. He lives in South Africa.

RUFUS GUNN is an inveterate traveller who spends much of his time in Eastern Europe. He is the author of *Something for Sergio* and is constantly on the move.

JOSEPH HANSEN originally published under the pseudonym James Colton. He found fame with a sequence of thrillers written under his own name and featuring gay insurance claims investigator Dave Brandstetter. His books include *Fadeout*, *Death Claims*, *Skinflick*, *Gravedigger*, *Backtrack* and *Job's Year*. He lives in Los Angeles, USA.

JOHN HAYLOCK has taught English at universities in Baghdad and Tokyo. His novels include *See You Again*, *It's All Your Fault*, *One Hot Summer in Kyoto*, *A Touch of the Orient* and *Uneasy Relations*. He divides his time between the Far East and Brighton, England.

TIM HERBERT's stories have been published in a number of magazines and anthologies and he is the author of *Angel Tails*. He lives in Sydney, Australia.

ANDREW HOLLERAN is the author of *Dancer From the Dance*, *Nights in Aruba*, *Ground Zero* (a collection of essays) and *The Beauty of Men*. He lives in Florida, USA.

WITI IHIMAERA is an editor, short storyist and novelist whose books include *Tangi Whanau*, *The Matriarch*, *The Whale Rider*, *Bulibasha*, *The King of the Gypsies* and *Nights in The Garden of Spain*. He lives in New Zealand.

FRANCIS KING published his first three novels whilst he was still an undergraduate at Oxford and since then has written another forty books. His novels include *The Waves Behind the Boat*, *A Domestic Animal*, *Flights*, *The Needle*, *Acts of Darkness*, *The Ant Colony* and *Ash on an Old Man's Sleeve*. He lives in London, England.

MICHAEL LEECH is a dance and theatre critic and travel writer whose work appears on both sides of the Atlantic. He lives in London.

ROBERT LEEK was born in The Netherlands but emigrated to New Zealand in the mid-fifties. Trained as a graphic and fashion designer, he has worked in the theatre as actor, administrator, critic and designer. His books include *Passion* and *Sweet and Sour Cocktails*. He lives in New Zealand.

SIMON LOVAT is a sometime actor and playwright and the author of *Disorder and Chaos*. He lives in Brighton, England.

JOSEPH MILLS has contributed to several Scottish or gay anthologies and is the author of *Towards the End*. He lives in Glasgow, Scotland.

JOHN MITZEL's books include *Some Short Stories About Nasty People I Don't Like*, *The Boston Sex Scandal* and a study of John Horne Burns. He lives in Boston, USA.

JOHN PATRICK is an editor and publisher and is the author of a vast range of both factual and fictional erotica including *Barely Legal*, *The Best of Superstars* (which appears annually), *Boys of the Night*, *Mad About the Boys* and *Angel*. He lives in Florida, USA.

ROBERT PATRICK is the author of many gay plays, including *The Haunted Host*, *Kennedy's Children*, *Untold Decades* and *Blue is for the Boys*. He has published short stories and a novel, *Temple Slave*, and lives in Los Angeles, USA.

TONY PEAKE was born in South Africa but is now based in London. He is a literary agent and the author of the novels *A Summer Tide* and *Son to the Father*. He lives in London, England.

FELICE PICANO, novelist, poet and publisher, is the author of fifteen books, including *The Lure*, *Like People in History* and *The New Joy of Gay Sex* (with Charles Silverstein). He lives in Los Angeles, USA.

NEIL POWELL has been a teacher and a bookseller; he is a poet, critic and biographer of Roy Fuller. His first novel is *Unreal City*. He lives in Aldeburgh, England.

SIMON RAVEN has been a television scriptwriter (*Edward and Mrs Simpson*), essayist (*Boys Will Be Boys*) and novelist whose major work – two interrelated sequences: *Alms for Oblivion* and *The First Born of Egypt* – offer a scabrous portrait of England since World War II. He lives in London, England.

PHILIP RIDLEY is a painter, screenwriter (*The Krays*, *The Reflecting Skin*), playwright (*The Pitchfork Disney*, *The Fastest Clock in the Universe*) author of novels for children (*Mercedes Ice*, *Dakota of the White Flats*, *Krindlekrax*, *Meteorite Spoon*), short stories (*Flamingoes in Orbit*) and novelist (*Crocodilia*, *In the Eyes of Mr Fury*). He lives in London, England.

PETER ROBINS has been a BBC radio broadcaster and producer and co-founder of publishing companies Third House and Trouser Press. His novels include *Easy Stages*, *Survivors*, *Touching Harry* and *Ruined Boys*. He lives in London, England.

JERRY ROSCO is co-editor with Robert Phelps of *Continual Lessons: The journals of Glenway Wescott 1937-1955*. He lives in New York City, USA.

LAWRENCE SCHIMEL has been published in more than eighty anthologies besides editing several, including *Yankee Vampires*, *Dixie Vampires*, *The Fortune Teller*, *Hard at Work* and *Stocking Stuffers*. He lives in New York City, USA.

AIDEN SHAW is a porn movie star and prostitute, poet and performer and author of the novel *Brutal*. He lives in London, England.

COLIN SPENCER is a painter, dramatist, writer of more than a dozen books on food, author of *Homosexuality: A history* and several novels which include *Poppy, Mandragora and the New Sex*, *What the Greeks Did to Mrs Nixon* and the quartet *Generations*. He lives in Winchelsea, England.

JOHN STAPLETON is a journalist and critic. He lives in Sydney, Australia.

MANSEL STIMPSON is a film and book critic who occasionally writes short stories. He reviews regularly for *What's On In London* and *Gay Times* and contributes to the *London Magazine* as well as presenting films at London's National Film Theatre.

PETER WELLS is a highly regarded screenwriter and director (*A Death in the Family* and *Desperate Remedies*). He made his fiction debut with the collection *Dangerous Desires*. He lives in New Zealand.

GRAEME WOOLASTON is administrator of a sculpture studio and the author of *Stranger Than Love*, *The Learning of Paul O'Neill* and *The Biker Below the Downs*. He lives in Glasgow, Scotland.

IAN YOUNG is a bibliographer: *The Male Homosexual in Literature*; an editor: *On the Line: New gay fiction*, *The Male Muse: A gay anthology*, *The Aids Cult: Essays on the gay health crisis* (with John Lauritsen); and a poet: *Double Exposure*, *Invisible Words*, *Some Green Moths*. He is also author of *The Stonewall Experiment*. He lives in Ontario, Canada.

JOHN-PAUL ZACCARINI is founder of the Angels of Disorder company which produces physical, polemical performances aiming at a poetic fusion of theatre, circus, mime and dance. He has performed extensively in Britain and Europe. He lives in London, England.

FURTHER READING

Adlard, John. *Stenbock, Yeats and the Nineties*. (Cecil and Amelia Woolf, London; 1969).

Anonymous. (John Saul). *Sins of the Cities of the Plain*. (Masquerade Books, New York; 1992).

Bloxam, John Francis. "The Priest and the Acolyte". (Reprints include *Jeremy*, Vol 1, number 10, London, 1970; Reade, Brian, *Sexual Heretics*, Routledge & Kegan Paul, London, 1970; Wright, Stephen, *Different: An anthology of homosexual short stories*, Bantam, New York, 1974).

Burton, Peter (Edited, with an Introduction by). *The Art of Gay Love*. (Hamlyn, London; 1995).

Carpenter, Edward, (Edited by). *Ioläus: Anthology of friendship*. (George Allen & Unwin, London; 1902).

Connon, Bryan. *Somerset Maugham and the Maugham Dynasty*. (Sinclair Stevenson, London; 1997).

Crisp, Quentin. *The Naked Civil Servant*. (Jonathan Cape, London; 1968).

Gardiner, James. *Who's a Pretty Boy Then? A hundred and fifty years of gay life in pictures*. (Serpent's Tail, London; 1997).

Hyde, H. Montgomery (Edited, with an Introduction by). *The Trials of Oscar Wilde*. (William Hodge, London; 1948).

Maugham, Robin, *Escape From the Shadows*. (Hodder & Stoughton, London; 1972).

Reade, Brian (An anthology selected and with an Introduction by). *Sexual Heretics: Male homosexuality in English Literature from 1850 to 1900*. (Routledge & Kegan Paul, London; 1970).

Sandars, N. K. (An English version with an Introduction by). *The Epic of Gilgamesh*. (Penguin Books, Harmondsworth; 1972).

Smith, Timothy d'Arch. *Love in Earnest: Some notes on the lives and writings of English "Uranian" poets from 1889-1930*. (Routledge & Kegan Paul, London; 1970).

Spencer, Colin. *Homosexuality: A history*. (4th Estate, London; 1995).

Stenbock, Eric, Count. "The True Story of a Vampire". (Reprinted *Jeremy*, Vol 1, Number 8, London, 1970; quoted Burton, Peter, *The Art of Gay Love*, Hamlyn, London, 1995).

Sutherland, Alistair & Anderson, Patrick (Edited by). *Eros: An Anthology of Friendship*. (Anthony Blond, London; 1961).